THE JUDAS TESTAMENT

Daniel Easterman was born in Belfast in 1949. He studied English, Persian, Arabic, and Islamic Studies at the universities of Dublin, Edinburgh, and Cambridge, and lectured at the universities of Fez in Morocco and Newcastle upon Tyne. The author of eight bestselling novels, he lives in the north of England with his wife, homoeopath and health writer, Beth MacEoin. He also writes as Jonathan Aycliffe, under which name he has penned several successful full-length ghost stories.

THE JUDAS TESTAMENT

DANIEL EASTERMAN

HarperCollins*Publishers*

HarperCollins*Publishers*
77–85 Fulham Palace Road,
Hammersmith, London W6 8JB

This paperback edition 1995
1 2 3 4 5 6 7 8 9

First published in Great Britain by
HarperCollins*Publishers* 1994

Copyright © Daniel Easterman 1994

The Author asserts the moral right to
be identified as the author of this work

ISBN 0 586 21089 X

Set in Linotron Meridien by
Rowland Phototypesetting Ltd,
Bury St Edmunds, Suffolk

Printed in Great Britain by
HarperCollinsManufacturing Glasgow

For Beth

O soave fanciulla, o dolce viso
Di mite circonfuso alba lunar;
In te ravviso il sogno
Ch'io vorrei sempre sognar.

ACKNOWLEDGEMENTS

These things are never easy, but at least the burden is lightened by the many people who contribute to the task of turning an idea into a finished book. Top of the list for all-round help, support, and advice is, as always, my gorgeous wife, Beth. My editors – Patricia Parkin in London and Katie Tso and Karen Solem in New York – applied their usual light and miraculous touch to an ailing first draft and brought it – I hope – to life. Mary-Rose Doherty smoothed many a rough path. Jeffrey Simmons, my agent, proved the power behind the scenes as usual (and a special word of thanks here to his mother, Jane, for her kind remarks on the text).

Many thanks also to Colleen Cairns, who did the bulk of the research, and who successfully followed up so many apparently mad requests; to Roderick Richards of Tracking Line for information on police matters; to Igor Kisenov and Katya Wik in Moscow for their attention to detail, and to Barry Martin of Russia House Ltd for arranging things there; to Alan Robinson for his invaluable help with security matters; to Clare Robertson-McIsaac for putting together such a delightful concert programme; to Reg Gill, Wembley's helpful cemetery superintendent; and to my mother-in-law, Nancy, for keeping things running smoothly.

I should also put on record my debt of gratitude to the various authors whose works I have plundered for background material and sundry facts. Notable among these are Mark Aarons and John Loftus, whose informed study of Vatican assistance to Nazi fugitives, *Ratlines*, is an impressive and depressing indictment of a most sorry episode in modern European history. If nothing else, I hope this exercise in fiction may help alert a few more readers to the betrayal of trust committed after the war by political and religious leaders here and in the United States, and now brought to light by their efforts and those of other writers. There is, sadly, less fiction in these pages than any of us might like.

PART ONE

PROLOGUE

June 1945
Russian Occupied Berlin

Overhead lights flickered and went out. The next instant a projector at the back of the room came to life. Numbers flickered on a vast screen, then a burst of music filled the room as the image of a swastika took their place. The swastika was replaced by the figure of a German eagle and the single word *Wochenschau*.

Then, abruptly, standards bearing the same eagle, bearing a garlanded swastika between its claws and, underneath, a square flag bearing a second swastika and the words *Deutschland Erwache*. The sound of marching feet. The face of Adolf Hitler, his mouth set and unsmiling, then a full-length shot, showing him atop a high tribune, beneath the outspread wings of a giant eagle. He was reviewing a march-past of stormtroopers. The camera angle shifted to show fighters in the air overhead, the unmistakable silhouettes of Messerschmitt Me 262 jets, followed by Me 163s with back-swept wings. Most of the men in the audience had never seen either plane in action, although many of them had seen drawings of prototypes.

Then down again to the Führer's face. A victorious look now, rapt with unspoken delight. Back slowly, back slowly, the arm outstretched in the *Hitlergrüss*, further back now, cutting away to show the tribune and the building in front of which it had been erected.

A shout went up from the audience, silenced immediately by an order snapped in German. The building on the screen was unmistakable: Buckingham Palace. Surely it was not possible. But the film clearly showed German troops and German tanks and German amoured personnel carriers parading along the Mall and turning past the tribune down Constitution Hill.

Unhappy onlookers lined both sides of the Mall, their arms raised dispiritedly in the Hitler salute. They were silent and cowed, their faces stamped with defeat, their heads bent.

The music stopped abruptly and a voice blared out. Not in German, as the audience had expected, but in English. They recognized the voice from broadcasts they had heard and laughed at back home: it belonged to William Joyce, the plummy-voiced traitor whom the *Daily Express* had once nicknamed 'Lord Haw-Haw'.

Yesterday morning at 0900 hours the British Prime Minister Winston Churchill signed a formal declaration of surrender to the victorious forces of the German Reich, thereby bringing the protracted war in Europe to a close. Defeated on all fronts, the wretched armies of the former British Empire were today laying down their arms at the end of a long and futile struggle against superior might and brainpower, a struggle which the stubbornness and egomania of their leaders had needlessly prolonged, and which had cost the lives of millions of young men. In the end, inferior troops, inferior equipment, and inferior morale could not resist the onslaught of German skill and endurance, nor could the civilian population of Britain endure attack by the new terror weapons launched against them from the shores of France.

As he spoke, the scene shifted to an interior. At a long table covered in green baize, men in formal dress and military uniforms were signing papers.

Our beloved Führer, Adolf Hitler, was in London to receive the British surrender from the Prime Minister and his Chiefs of Staff. We see him here in Downing Street, the undefeated conqueror of Europe, the Führer of a thousand-year Reich.

Hitler's face, smiling. The face of Churchill, grim and joyless. His hand, signing a paper, shaking slightly. Hitler again, receiving the paper, signing it in his turn with a careless flourish. And Churchill's face once more, frowning.

He looks worried. And so he should. Because he knows the game's up. It won't be long now before General Guderian, Britain's new military commander, gives instructions to convene the first in a long series of war crimes trials in Coventry. They all know they'll be for the high jump. Churchill, Bomber Harris, Montgomery, Portal – the whole miserable pack of them. These are the men who bragged and bullied for six long years until they brought England to its knees, and most of Europe with it. They'll go to the gallows, you can be sure of that.

But there won't be any lynching parties. For once in their history, the British are going to have a taste of justice. German justice. All the old perks and privileges, all the favouritism and toadying, all the doffing of hats, that's going to be swept away. A new wind is sweeping across Europe, and its name is Fair Play for All. That's what the war was about.

The system of justice and order that is the pride of the German Reich will now be brought to the shores of England. The Reich will appoint its judges, good men and true, fearless men who won't be in the pocket of a milord with an ancient title or a Jew with a bag of silver.

The screen now filled with scenes from German trials, all taking place in elaborate courtrooms where swastikas and eagles loomed darkly over the heads of the judges. The audience sat without moving, shocked into silence.

After installing General Guderian in Downing Street, the Führer proceeded to Buckingham Palace, where he was formally received by King Edward and his consort Queen Wallis, who had been flown in from the Bahamas the day before, ready to take up their new duties. The royal couple, looking radiant, welcomed their country's conqueror, greeting him as an old friend and as the liberator of their people.

Film of the Duke and Duchess of Windsor together on

a balcony, waving. Then a pan to the right to show Hitler standing beside them, not waving, but watching.

The Jews won't like it, of course. They'll do anything to save their miserable skins. They were behind the Baldwin conspiracy in 1936, which resulted in the king's forced abdication, and they were responsible for pushing little England into a war it never had a chance of winning. Germany extended the hand of friendship, but the Zionists and the Rothschilds made sure it was not grasped. Instead of joining forces with each other to defeat their common enemy, the massed forces of Stalinist Russia and the cells of red conspirators in their own towns and cities, Britain and Germany lost the flower of their young manhood in a senseless war. Well, we know how to deal with the Jews in Germany. It won't be long before the long-suffering British have seen the back of them. And this time they won't be coming back.

During this last section, there were shots of synagogues being burned, Jews being herded into the streets by SS troops. In one scene, a Union Jack was ripped unceremoniously from a synagogue door.

After taking lunch at the palace, our beloved Führer drove to Shipton in Oxfordshire, where he was made welcome by Sir Oswald and Lady Diana Mosley. Since his release from internment in 1943, Sir Oswald has been under constant surveillance by the British security services. The Führer has invited him to serve as a caretaker Prime Minister until it is possible to hold elections, when it is confidently expected that Sir Oswald's party, the British Union of Fascists, will be swept to victory on a tide of popular acclaim.

Film during this section of Sir Oswald and Hitler shaking hands and smiling at the camera.

Then, abruptly, film of the Capitol in Washington, under a cloudy sky.

Meanwhile, in Washington yesterday afternoon, the former German chargé, Hans Thomsen, was recalled for talks with Secretary of State Edward Stettinius. It is believed that he will go to the White House in the morning for a meeting with President Truman, in order to open negotiations for a formal end to hostilities between the United States and Germany. Diplomatic sources are of the opinion that the president intends to make a state visit to Berlin sometime in the autumn.

Two flags appeared on the screen, a German flag beside the Stars and Stripes. The scene shifted again. This time there was a clear sky. The camera dropped until a large dome came into view. And dropped again until the whole of St Peter's Square could be seen, packed with pilgrims.

And in Rome, His Holiness Pope Pius XII congratulated the Führer on his latest victory.

The scene shifted to the interior of the Vatican. Pius XII could be seen smiling and shaking hands with Hitler.

This follows last week's meeting between the Pontiff and Europe's new master, when a fresh Concordat was signed, replacing the outdated agreement of 1933. At that meeting, the Pope declared his readiness to recognize those political changes of territory which have taken place since the beginning of the war. In return, the re-established fascist government of Marshal Pietro Badoglio has declared its readiness to recognize the terms of the Lateran Treaty and to preserve its special relationship with the Vatican State.

Joyce paused for a few moments, then resumed in a triumphant voice.

People of Britain! Your long night is over. Hand in hand with your German brothers and sisters, you stand at the threshold of a new and wondrous era. Peace, justice, and freedom shall take the place of the tyranny you have known. Beneath the shadow of the swastika, a united Europe shall stand firm against the subhuman hordes that have been unleashed against it from the steppes of communist Russia. Together, we shall forge on the anvil of common suffering a glorious destiny for the Aryan race.

The music crashed again, accompanying yet more scenes of goose-stepping soldiers, of enormous swastika-emblazoned flags, of SS standards glistening in the sun. The last shot was a view of the Houses of Parliament. Over Victoria Tower, the red, white and black flag of the Third Reich fluttered majestically in a stiffening breeze.

'Lichter!'

The screen went blank. Above, lights flickered back to life. A deep silence filled the room. There were about a hundred men there, seated on folding metal chairs that had been laid out with military precision in nine rows. No one moved. No one spoke. One man struggled vainly to suppress a cough.

The men's heads had been shaved. Their faces were pinched, and bore traces of fatigue and pain. Beneath the loose grey uniforms of prisoners-of-war, it was possible to make out thin, exhausted bodies.

The room in which they sat was deep underground. It was twenty metres long and eight wide, with a low ceiling. The hum of an electricity generator could be heard from behind one wall. Behind that was another sound, the pumping of a carefully-constructed system of air-ducts which ensured that the complex to which the room belonged remained invisible from the surface and that there was a constant supply of reasonably fresh air inside.

The walls had been draped in black cloth, and in their centres four long blood-red banners hung from the ceiling to the floor. Each one bore a white circle in which a swastika was set. In the world outside, fifty metres above the complex, banners like these would have been ripped from their moorings and burned by Russian soldiers. Down here, there were no Russian soldiers. Down here, the only soldiers wore the black uniform of the Waffen-SS.

SS guards were posted all round the room. They stood with their backs to the wall, cradling loaded guns in their arms.

At the front stood a German officer. He wore on his shoulder tabs the plaited silver threads of an SS-Standartenführer. On his right forearm was a small diamond enclosing the letters 'SD', standing for Sicherheitsdienst, the Reich secret service. He was a young man for his rank, a graduate of the Vogelsang *Ordensburg*, who had been promoted towards the end of the war on the deaths of his own senior officers. Nothing about him gave any hint that he might be nervous. His highly-polished boots and SS dagger, his black cap with its death's-head badge were all adjusted to parade standard.

The film had had the effect he had anticipated, which the men who had made it had planned. The prisoners in front of him were not just stunned. They were devastated. Everything they believed in, everything that had kept them going, some for as much as three or four years, in Gestapo prisons and SD interrogation centres, everything that had given them hope of release and return had been destroyed in a matter of minutes.

'Gentlemen,' the officer began, speaking in lightly-accented English, 'I hope you have found this week's newsreel more interesting than usual. You will be returned to your cells in a few moments. Each one of you will be provided with a copy of today's edition of the London *Times*. You will be able to read the terms of the British surrender, along with articles giving you full details of recent events. You may peruse them at your leisure.

'Before that, however, I think it will be only proper if you allow me to introduce myself. My name is SS-Standartenführer Klietmann. I am the new commandant of this prison, and you must now consider yourselves to be under my jurisdiction. It is my understanding that conditions here have been allowed to become lax in recent months, under the command of SS-Obersturmbannführer Grossmann. That situation is now at an end. SS-Obersturmbannführer Grossmann has been relieved of his duties. From now on you will have to reckon with me.

'I intend to run things here according to the book. Breaches of discipline will be severely punished. Any attempt to escape will be paid for by the death of each would-be escaper and one other inmate. There will be no successful escapes. You will find that security here is now the tightest in the Reich.

'When you have finished your reading, you may wish

to give some careful thought to your personal situation. Please do not think that the German people intend to let the guilty go unpunished. The war crimes tribunals which are already being set up will not be restricted to those who led the British war of aggression against Germany. Naturally, the spotlight will fall on Churchill and his henchmen. But we shall not rest until even the most petty criminal is brought to justice. There is much to answer for. The full extent of British crimes has yet to be brought to light. But you may rest assured that no efforts will be spared to discover those crimes and their perpetrators.

'In your own case, there can be no question of guilt. You were all arrested on German soil or on the soil of nations administered by the German Reich. Later today, you will be visited in turn by a team of lawyers appointed to prepare your cases. You will in due course be assigned defence counsel. In a few days you will receive written instructions from the appropriate authorities in Britain, asking you to make a clean breast of things.

'Your refusal to divulge the facts concerning your missions has so far been commendable. You are all brave men, and under different circumstances I do not doubt that you would have been highly decorated for your courage. But the war is over. Your country has been defeated fairly and in open combat. It is now your duty to assist the forces of law and order to assign guilt where it is due and to exonerate the innocent wherever possible.'

The commandant paused and stood to attention.

'You are dismissed. I hope you will all prove co-operative. I assure you that it is very much in your own interests to be so.'

The doors were opened at the back of the hall. At a signal, the first row stood. As they filed out, they avoided the eyes of their fellow-prisoners. More than one man was weeping openly.

'God help us all,' said someone very quietly.

CHAPTER ONE

Paris
July 1979

It was the worst time of year in Paris, when the tourists were in bloom. The cafés along the Boulevard St Germain were packed with gauche young Americans and globe-trotting Australians. You could see them everywhere, posing for the world, forcing on passers-by the illusion that they were Parisians born and bred, that they were bored with Ricard and Amer Picon, and that they sat in those same cafés, at those same tables, in those same wicker chairs, day in, day out, the length and breadth of the Paris year.

They were lounging at Aux Deux Magots and the Café de Flore, Gitanes dangling from their lips and Gucci loafers caressing their well-travelled feet. They feigned indifference while inwardly they remembered Des Moines and Warrnambool and wondered at all this sudden, fleeting inheritance. Paris was theirs for a season, to have as they had never had a city, to sashay through by day and cruise by night, to inhabit in all its brightness and greyness and long summer loneliness.

Jack Gould in his innocence would never have guessed, unless he had overheard one or other of them speaking English. He did not sashay. He did not come to his neighbourhood café to be seen or to watch others. To be honest, he hardly noticed what was going on around him. While he sipped the small coffee in front of him, his eyes were glued to a book held on his lap, the first volume of Neusner's *History of the Jews in Babylonia*.

At twenty-two, he had already become a 'type'. He wore a tweed jacket with leather elbow patches, quite inappropriate for the fine weather, a grubby white shirt, and dark green corduroy trousers with a worn seat. When he could afford tobacco, he smoked a stubby pipe. His hair was a mess, and he wore wire-rimmed glasses clumsily repaired with insulating tape. It was easy to miss the fact that, underneath it all, he was as good-looking as any of the leather-jacketed poseurs lounging on the terrace outside.

The café was a small establishment in the rue Chabanais, half a block from the Bibliothèque Nationale. Jack went there once in the morning and once in the afternoon, to take a break from his researches in the library. Since he could not afford a proper lunch, he usually took some bread and goat's cheese and washed them down with a bottle of Badoit in the nearby Jardin du Palais Royal. His morning and afternoon coffees, very black and heavily sugared, gave him the kick he needed to see him through day after day of ancient texts.

The dissertation on which he was working, 'Star and Sceptre Prophecies in the Damascus Document, the Qumran War Scroll, and the Florilegia', had driven him to Paris much against his will. He was in the second year of a doctorate in Hebrew Studies at Trinity College, Dublin, and he was perfectly happy working there or in the Chester Beatty Library in Ballsbridge. He disliked the Bibliothèque Nationale and its antiquated bureaucracy, he hated having to speak French (a language he knew imperfectly), and, if he was honest, he was ill at ease in a city where so many other people seemed to be having a good time. Jack Gould's accomplishments were those of a master linguist. He could make sense of the most fragmentary Hebrew document or reassemble the pieces of a first-century Aramaic scroll as easily as some people stick crosses in their football pools once a week. His teachers adored him.

No one doubted that his doctoral thesis would be the first of many major contributions to his field. But as a human being he was an unmitigated disaster. A disaster and – though he never admitted it – a twenty-two-year-old virgin.

He scarcely noticed when someone sat down at his table. It was a small café, and often crowded. He did not look up from the book he was reading.

'Jack Gould? It is, isn't it?'

A young woman was sitting across from him. Blonde hair, a startling face, a light blue tee-shirt. Smiling like an old friend, though he did not recognize her. Or, perhaps . . .

'Je m'excuse, mais . . .'

'Oh, there's no need for all that. We can get on well enough without speaking French.'

The Irish accent was not strong, but there was enough of it to declare where the woman came from. He trawled his memory in an effort to find her face somewhere in his past.

'I'm sorry, Miss . . .'

'You don't know me, but I know you by sight. My name's Caitlin. Caitlin Nualan. I'm a junior sophister in Semitic Studies at Trinity. You gave a seminar on Ezekiel last year: I was in the back row. You probably don't remember me.'

'Yes, of course . . .' He halted, shaking his head. 'No. No, I'm sorry, I don't remember.'

'You were very preoccupied.' She paused. 'I didn't know you were in Paris.'

At that moment, a waiter came up. Caitlin turned and spoke easily in what seemed to Jack like perfectly-accented French.

'Un café crème, s'il vous plaît.'

She glanced at Jack's half-empty cup.

'You'll have another one?'

He shook his head, looking at his watch.

'I'm sorry,' he said. 'I . . . I have to go. I'm doing research at the Bibliothèque.'

He got up, tossing some money on the table.

'It's been nice meeting you,' he said. 'I hope you enjoy Paris.'

She was waiting for him the next morning when he entered the café just after eleven. At the same table, as though she had not moved. Her hair was tied back, and she wore a light denim jacket over a fresh tee-shirt. Today's was pink. As he approached, she lifted something from the table and waved it at him.

'You left this behind yesterday,' she said.

It was his copy of Neusner, the 'light reading' with which he passed his time in the café.

'Thanks,' he mumbled, reaching out a hand for the book. But she did not pass it to him.

'I had a look at it last night,' she said. 'It's summer and this is Paris, and you're reading a book like this?'

He did not answer.

'Would you like a coffee?' she asked.

He shook his head. He could hardly remember when a woman had last spoken to him like this. Entering, he had noticed that she was, after all, quite lovely. Beauty troubled him. It did not scan like Hebrew poetry, it had no conjugations, no declensions, it could not be reduced to paradigms. He felt threatened by it, as by all things out of control.

'Don't tell me you start on the hard stuff before lunch,' she said.

'I . . . No, that is . . .' He hesitated, bowing to the inevitable. 'I'll have a coffee.'

She gestured and a waiter appeared as if from nowhere. Jack was impressed by the confidence of her manner, by her self-assurance. She asked for coffee and brioches, then turned back to him.

'Sit down, for God's sake. And tell me about yourself.'

He sat, and it began.

*　　*　　*

He was hard work. She told him that afterwards, the first time they went to bed. Had she known, the hardest work lay ahead. Paris helped, of course. Not even the most staid academic could wholly resist the city's charms. She took him everywhere, above all to places no guidebook mentioned. The copy of Neusner stayed under lock and key in her room. By the third day, he had stopped asking for it back. By the end of their first week together, he had forgotten it entirely. She turned him inside out.

That he was in love dawned on him only slowly. It was not an emotion he had known before, not one in which he had ever felt much interest. Like beauty, it was beyond his control. He was like someone who, having been asleep for a long time, comes awake bit by bit, hearing as though from far away a loved voice whispering his name. And who, on waking, finds that the voice was not far away at all, and that the one he loves has been there all along, watching him anxiously.

She became his eyes and ears for a time, until he relearned how to use his own. She belonged to his world only partly and somewhat in jest, and at all times she refused to talk about it with him. He tried at first, only to find that her ignoring him was more painful than not talking about what he found familiar. Thus, gradually, she drew him into her own world.

In the first week, she forced him to become a tourist. He would come to the café each morning just after nine to find her waiting for him with hot coffee and rolls. After breakfast they would make their way to the different sights the city had to offer: Notre Dame, the Arc de Triomphe, the Eiffel Tower, the Sainte-Chapelle, the Louvre. He was like a child to whom it is suddenly revealed that the world is more than the four walls of his bedroom. He stumbled often, but she picked him up and dusted him off, and took him on to the next landmark.

The main thing, she found, was to keep him as far away from the Bibliothèque as possible. Deprived of his papyri and concordances, he was a blank page. In the second week, they stopped the sightseeing. She took him to small bars and cafés where there were no tourists, and they would sit for hours at a time, talking. It was the first time he had ever found anyone genuinely interested in him, not for what he knew, but for what he was. He found himself telling her all about the Jack Gould his teachers never knew.

'My father's a Jew,' he said, 'my mother's a Catholic.'

'What does that make you?'

He shrugged.

'Nothing,' he answered. 'Just myself. Whoever that is.'

She tried to find out. Of herself, she said little. She told him that her parents had died ten years earlier, within eight months of one another, her father of cancer, her mother of grief. They were buried in London, in Paddington Cemetery, near where she had been brought up. He asked if she still had relatives alive, but she said there was no one to whom she was close. Some aunts and uncles, that was all – people she had not seen in years, with whom she had nothing in common. He respected her reticence and did not probe further.

There had been men in her life before, she made no secret of it. He and Caitlin were not yet lovers, yet Jack felt real agonies of jealousy to hear that others had gone before him, however briefly.

One evening they went to see Louis Malle's *Lacombe Lucien*, in a small cinema off the Boulevard St Germain. He found it hard to follow the dialogue, but from time to time she leaned across and whispered what was happening in his ear. The story concerned a young French labourer who becomes a collaborator during the Nazi occupation. Jack hardly noticed what happened. It was enough that Caitlin leaned close and whispered to him every so often.

When they came out of the cinema, she was withdrawn.

He had not seen her like that before, and he wondered why the film had so affected her.

'What is it?' he asked.

She did not answer. For a long time she was silent. People passed by them, talking animatedly, but she paid no attention. She leaned back against a wall.

'What's wrong?' he asked.

'Come here,' she said.

He did not know what to do.

'Come here.'

And he stepped close to her, very close, closer than he had ever been to a woman. She reached out for him and drew him to her. Then she kissed him. Her face was wet with tears; they rasped his tongue with salt. That night they became lovers. But she never told him why she had been crying, or for whom, and he never asked her.

Within a few days they knew there could be no going back. At the beginning of September they decided to marry. A short ceremony at the Irish Consulate was followed by dinner at a small restaurant on the Left Bank. He wrote to his parents, telling them of the marriage. His mother wrote back to say she was upset that they had not been invited to the wedding, but Jack sent her a long letter, enclosing a photograph of Caitlin and explaining how happy he was. So much happiness: not even his mother had thought him capable of that. And he sent a second photograph, one of himself in the new clothes he and Caitlin had bought together. None of his old friends would have recognized him.

He did a little work each day in the Bibliothèque, but the obsessiveness had left him for good. He had learned to look forward to mid-afternoon, when it was time to close his files and step out into the sunshine. Caitlin would be waiting for him in the little café on the rue Chabanais, at their regular table, two cups of coffee in front of her, and two plates of tarte tatin. They would drink and talk for a while, then return to their apartment in the Marais and, as often as not, make love. All that summer, passion did not betray them once.

About a fortnight after the wedding, they returned to find the apartment ransacked. The intruders had concentrated on his study, going through his papers systematically. Strangely enough, when everything was accounted for, nothing seemed to be missing, not even the jewellery Caitlin had left in an unlocked box in the bedroom. All that evening, she seemed thoughtful, and more than once he thought she was about to tell him something. Something made him think she knew who had been responsible for the break-in.

The following day, while they were walking at lunchtime in the Jardin du Palais Royal, a man approached them. The stranger came up to Caitlin, greeting her and kissing her on both cheeks, as though they were old friends. He was middle-aged, well-dressed, and, to Jack's eyes, a sophisticate. Caitlin and he spoke for about a minute in rapid French which Jack could not follow. He could pick out only a few words at random:

'*Malheureux . . . peut-être dangereux . . . ce n'est pas terminé . . . pas impossible de rentrer . . . nous avons pris nos renseignements . . .*'

Looking at his wife, Jack saw that she had gone pale. She did not raise her voice, but he sensed the tension in it.

'*Je dois m'en aller,*' she said at last, taking Jack's arm. The stranger did not once so much as look at Jack.

'Who was that?' Jack asked as they walked quickly away.

'No one. An old friend. Look, it doesn't matter. Forget it.' It was the first time she had ever snapped at him. Later, she apologized, saying the man was someone she had met years before; he had been a friend of her father's when he was alive, and had once tried to interfere with her when she was just a teenager.

That night in bed, she told Jack she wanted to go back to Dublin.

'I haven't finished my work here yet.'

'It'll have to keep,' she said. 'I need to be in Dublin, to catch up on my own work before term begins. You can have microfilms sent over. I'll pay for them. And . . .' She hesitated, taking his hand. 'There's another thing. I'm going to have a baby.'

CHAPTER TWO

Dublin
18 June 1988

The letter arrived by first post on Monday morning. It was the third in a pile of seven, taking its turn behind a request for microfilm and an invitation to what promised to be a dull reception at Trinity College. From the envelope in, it was redolent of wealth: the heavy paper, the discreet, expensive letterhead, even the casualness of the signature alerted him to something a little out of the ordinary. He did not recognize the name of the house at the top of the page: Summerlawn.

The postmark had been unfamiliar too: Dún na Séad. He had to look it up on a map. It turned out to be Baltimore, a little fishing village south-west of Cork. But who in Baltimore could possibly have an interest in the library here or in his own work? And who in a fishing village could afford such writing paper?

The answer was a man called Rosewicz, Stefan Rosewicz. The name meant nothing to Jack. What was it? Polish? Czech? He could not say with any certainty. Certainly, he had never heard it mentioned as that of the owner of a collection of priceless Hebrew and Aramaic manuscripts located in the Irish Republic. And yet Rosewicz's letter was simple and to the point: he owned a small but valuable manuscript collection that needed expert attention, both for recataloguing and preservation. Was Dr Gould interested in taking the position? The work would not be arduous, there was no pressing deadline, and he would be paid well. Very well.

Slowly, Jack raised his hand, holding the letter. On one finger he wore a plain gold ring without encrustation. He clenched and unclenched the fingers of his other hand to form a fist. It formed and unformed, curled and uncurled. As though he clutched something and released it once more. He caressed the paper as though it were skin, absent-mindedly.

He did not move for a while. He let the letter sit in his hand, heavy as silk. He knew without knowing that he was on the verge of the extraordinary, that it was trickling into his life, there into the mouse-brown, book-lined world of his office on a Monday morning at the beginning of summer. He had been waiting for this for a long time, perhaps a lifetime – he really did not know how long or why. But he knew without knowing that his life was about to change.

He was now assistant curator of biblical manuscripts in Dublin's prestigious Chester Beatty Library on Shrewsbury Road. He had joint responsibility for one of the world's finest collections of Old and New Testament papyri, a collection that ranked alongside those of the Vatican Library or the British Museum, but was little known outside specialist circles. Where London possessed the *Codex Sinaiticus* and the *Codex Alexandrinus*, and Rome the early *Codex Vaticanus*, Dublin could boast of the manuscripts generally known as the 'Chester Beatty Papyri'. These were a collection of biblical fragments discovered at the ancient site of Aphroditopolis in Egypt between 1928 and 1930, and bought a year later by Chester Beatty himself. Around them, a major library had been built.

He picked up the telephone and keyed the short number at the top of the letter. It rang five or six times. An Irish voice answered, a middle-aged woman's voice.

'Summerlawn. Can I be of any help?'

The housekeeper, he supposed. In the background he could hear music. A cello and harpsichord. He recognized the piece straight away: the adagio section from Bach's sonata in G minor. A recording? Or were there musicians at Summerlawn?

'I'm looking for Mr Rosewicz. Is he at home?'

'If you'll give me your name, sir.'

'Please tell him it's Dr Gould from the Chester Beatty Library.'

He heard the phone being put down on a table, then the sound of footsteps. A few moments later, the music stopped in mid-passage. More footsteps, a man's this time, firm and unhurried, on stone first, then muffled by carpet.

'Here is Rosewicz. How may I help you?'

Here is Rosewicz. Like a legend set by a medieval cartographer on unexplored territory. The accent was distinctly East European.

'You wrote me a letter, Mr Rosewicz. My name is Gould, from the Chester Beatty.'

'Good heavens. That stupid woman. She said you were a doctor from Westmeath. It is too much. She will have to buy a hearing aid.' The voice paused. 'Forgive me, Dr Gould. You have been extremely kind to telephone so soon. You have read my letter?'

'Yes. It arrived this morning.'

'And what is your decision?'

'My decision? I haven't had time to think about that yet. I was only ringing to ask a few questions.'

'Questions? Yes, of course. What questions do you have?'

The music had started again, only this time the cello was unaccompanied. In between, there had been another sound. Had it been the sea, or was that merely his imagination? Where exactly was Summerlawn?

He asked his questions one by one, dutifully, as though by so doing he might eliminate Rosewicz and the temptation he offered. To be presented with such a mystery down there in the heart of the country seemed too good to be true. And yet, he supposed, the collection so vaunted by its owner would in all likelihood turn out to be of very little merit. A dull thing, devoid of grace or beauty, a few fragments scrabbled together at public sales, nothing to set the pulses racing.

But Rosewicz was serious and informed. His own knowledge had reached its outer limits, he explained; he needed an expert, someone who could set his house in order. He had over three hundred manuscripts, some medieval, a handful much earlier, including, he said, Cairo Geniza fragments and material from Nag Hammadi. Jack's interest was whetted. It began to sound as if Rosewicz was no mere dabbler.

There was the problem of getting leave from the library. But the job could be justified as research.

'There is only one thing,' said Rosewicz. 'I do not publicize the existence of my library. I do not give interviews or allow outsiders to have free access to my materials. You will have to agree to silence, if you come. Is that acceptable to you?'

'I'll have to think about that.'

'It is most important. You cannot work here otherwise.'

Rosewicz suggested that Jack should come down at the weekend for a preliminary visit. He would show him the library and explain the problems he was facing. Jack agreed. As he put down the receiver, he could hear voices in the background, a woman laughing, and a dog barking far away.

Later that morning, Jack had coffee with Moira Kennedy, the Curator of Western Manuscripts and his immediate superior. Her office was cooler than his, shaded by green plants. Outside, the first tourists of the day had arrived and were making their way to an exhibition of Persian miniatures.

31

'Have you ever heard of a man called Rosewicz?' he asked. 'He lives near Baltimore, in County Cork. In a big house from the sound of it.'

She frowned, then nodded.

'Yes, I've heard his name mentioned. Why?'

'He wants me to catalogue his manuscripts. How come I've never heard about him?'

She shrugged, but he saw her look away momentarily, as though embarrassed or ill at ease.

'His name comes up from time to time. You'd have heard him mentioned in the end.'

'You talk as if there were some sort of secret . . .'

'A secret? No, not that. But Rosewicz keeps to himself. You're privileged if he means to show you his collection.'

'You know about it, then? This collection.'

'That he has one, yes. That's about all anyone knows. About all he'll say. We know of a few things he has, through information that's leaked out of sales. He has a couple of items from Qumran, for instance. But mostly he buys on the underground circuits. People in the know say he has things we'd all like to see.'

'Then why . . . ?'

'Why bring in somebody like yourself?' She shrugged again. 'I don't know. He must need help badly. Someone he can trust.'

'Have you ever met him?'

He thought she almost laughed. She smiled instead, not pleasantly. She was forty-five, forty-six, he guessed. They had worked together for seven years now, ever since he obtained his doctorate, and still he knew next to nothing about her. Nor she about him.

'No one I know has ever met Rosewicz. You'll be the first. Make the most of it.'

'How come? You said he went to sales.'

She shook her head. Her hair was grey, brushed back in a hard bun. She had thick-rimmed spectacles. Did someone love her? Was there someone for whom she let her hair fall silently loose? With a shock he realized that he neither knew nor wished to know.

'Not in person,' she said. 'He uses middlemen. I told you, he keeps himself to himself. He's a man of mystery, I suppose.'

'Does he have a family?'

'How should I know?'

'I heard someone. A woman, in the background.'

'A wife, a mistress, who knows?'

'What about the house? How long has he lived there?'

'A long time, I think. He was born in Eastern Europe, Poland or Czechoslovakia. He came here in the forties or fifties. A refugee.'

'How does a Polish refugee have so much money?'

'Aristocracy, I suppose. But you can find out for yourself when you go down. I suppose you're going to ask for leave.'

'If you don't mind.'

'Well, as a matter of fact, I do. We have the *Diatessaron* Exhibition coming up in October. And I need someone to help me go through the collection of papyri that arrived last month from East Berlin. There's a lot of work to be done.'

'This would count as research.'

She hesitated. It would not be hard to find someone at Trinity to handle the routine work for the exhibition. It was too good an opportunity to miss, getting someone in to see Rosewicz's collection. Gould could be her spy.

'Will it help?' she asked.

He knew what she meant, though it was something he and she had never talked about.

He nodded once.

'I think so,' he said. 'I've not been away since . . .'

'Very well, but I'll want to know everything. Just between ourselves. Do you understand?'

* * *

That evening the sun shone across the whole of Ireland. For the first time in well over a year, Jack Gould left his flat in Ballsbridge and walked into town. He was already impatient for the weekend, like a child before a long-anticipated holiday. He tried to reason with himself, arguing that nothing would change, that he would spend the summer cooped up in a library as usual, and in the autumn return to Dublin unchanged. But deep inside him a small voice asked for more.

He walked distractedly through the dwindling sunshine, through St Stephen's Green, down Grafton Street, as far as Trinity College. It astonished him to find everything as he had left it, as though it had been waiting for him. There were flowers in the Green, white flowers the colour of a communion dress. He had to hold back the tears, had to pass quickly by the playing families, the young mothers with their prams. And he thought of a cello playing in a house he had never seen, and he imagined cliffs, and the steep sea deep beneath them, and his own breath dim on a window-pane in the height of summer.

CHAPTER THREE

He looked up Summerlawn in the Irish volume of *Burke's Guide to Country Houses*. It had been built by a Cork branch of the Fitzgeralds in the mid-eighteenth century, next to a tower-house of the O'Driscolls, and had been subject to all manner of calamities and restorations since then. A detachment of Black and Tans had burned down part of it in 1919, and it had been attacked three years later by both sides in the civil war; but unlike so many others, it had survived. The Fitzgeralds had stayed on after the Republic, but in the end their money and their patience had run out. Scions of an Ascendancy whose day had passed, they had become strangers in their own country. The house was sold, first to an American called Kelly, pretentious of his Irish origins but impatient of Ireland as she really was; and, a few years later, to Rosewicz. That had been 1947. Ten years before Jack was born.

As he replaced the volume of Burke on the shelf, he dislodged a second book. He picked it up carefully from the floor. *Where the Wild Things Are* by Maurice Sendak. Siobhan's copy, the one from which he had read to her night after night for what now seemed a lifetime. Or a fleeting moment.

He sat down, opening the book without thinking, forgetting how dangerous memories could be. Something fluttered from it: a loose sheet of paper, a drawing in crayons, barely recognizable as a tabby cat. The cat's name had been Brian. Beneath the cat, someone had written in a childish hand: *For my daddy, with love, Siobhan.* She had been four years old then. He clutched the sheet, hardly seeing it for tears.

'The past is past.' That was what he told himself every morning. But it was not true. The past is always with us: in our waking hours it rushes in without warning, in the shape of a child's drawing or a forgotten photograph. And in sleep it never leaves us, our dreams are made of it.

The past was a café in Paris, an open window looking out on steep rooftops, crumbs on a tossed sheet, a woman's naked body turning in a mirror. And it was an open sea on the edge of autumn, gulls, and a woman's hand in his, Dublin as he had never seen it before, sunlight in places he had thought merely shadow, the daily walk through the Green, weekends in the Wicklow Mountains, sunshine and grass, snow in the winter, Caitlin's voice calling from another room, a child's laugh, a door slamming in the distance.

He sat with his head in his hands, motionless, so long it seemed he would never move again.

One scene recurs with disturbing regularity. Once it ran through his head constantly, like a recording that cannot be wiped out. Now it is like a dull ache that flares up from time to time into something more painful. He is in a meadow full of flowers. There is a light breeze. He can feel warm sunlight on his face. The sky is full of wheeling birds. He is sitting on a rug, surrounded by the remains of a picnic. He can see Siobhan playing with a red ball. She is throwing it to Caitlin, who catches it and throws it back. Siobhan is six and growing dexterous. When she misses the ball, she laughs and runs after it. He sits and watches. There are birds everywhere, white birds. He feels the sun on his face and arms. The ball bounces, is caught, thrown, and returned. He lies back, watching the sky. There is not a cloud in sight. A little distance away, he can hear the sea. And the cries of white birds. Suddenly, there is a shout, Caitlin's voice. He lifts himself and sees Siobhan running after the ball. Caitlin is running after her. The little girl does not hear or does not listen. Caitlin has thrown the ball hard. It is rolling down a slope. A slope that leads to a steep cliff. And, as if in slow motion, he sees Siobhan reach the edge. There is a whirl of white as the birds swoop. And Caitlin reaches her, and the birds swoop, crying. He stands and sees them topple. There is a flash of colour, then nothing but the birds.

It did not happen like that, he knew. But it is that series of images that recurs.

Returning from Paris, they had found a flat in Ballsbridge, near the Chester Beatty, where he was already giving a hand with some catalogue work. They had very little money, but from time to time Caitlin drew out a small sum from an inheritance of ten thousand pounds or so. She took a year out from her course, returning to finish her senior sophister year when Siobhan, their daughter, was a year and a few months. That year also Jack finished his doctorate and was taken on full time by the library. Somehow they managed to look after Siobhan, with his mother's help.

He never tired of Caitlin's face or body, never resented the time Siobhan demanded of him, never regretted the changes that had taken place in him since that summer in Paris. And now he was sitting alone, holding a child's book on his lap, fighting with his past.

The doorbell rang. He felt himself go tense. Laying the book aside, he got to his feet reluctantly. The bell rang a second time, but he did not hurry.

When he opened the door, a policeman was standing outside.

'Dr Gould?'

He felt himself swaying.

'Dr Gould, I have some bad news. May I come in?'

The man's voice was soft, but it seemed to echo, hurting Jack's ears. He reached for the jamb, collapsing against it.

'Are you all right, sir?' the garda asked.

He nodded and tried to stand up straight. He felt sick and dizzy and he wanted someone to hold him until the sickness went away.

'I'm all right,' he murmured, looking round. 'I'm all right.' The hallway was empty. There was no one there. No one but himself and his memories.

The past is always with us.

CHAPTER FOUR

Jack had more or less made up his mind to go to Summer-lawn, but there were still things he wanted to know. All Tuesday morning he thought about Rosewicz: who exactly was he, what did he really want? Jack had an old friend from his Trinity days, Denis Boylan, who had gone on to work for the *Irish Times*. He rang him that afternoon.

'What did you say your man's name was?'

'Rosewicz. Stefan Rosewicz. He's a Pole.'

'I don't care if he's a bloody chimpanzee. Could you spell that, for Christ's sake?'

Jack spelled it out.

'It'll be tomorrow or the day after, Jack. I'm up to here in deadlines. Honest, I am.'

But he rang back on Wednesday morning.

'Will you meet me for a spot of lunch, Jack? Be in Bewley's Westmoreland Street at one.'

The café was crowded. Boylan took him to sit in the smoking section. His plate carried a generous helping of pie and chips. He showed no signs of putting on weight, in spite of the fodder. Loud voices danced all around them. A priest at the next table discoursed on the Irish Derby and Oaks to be run that month and the next. He had two outstanding horses in mind.

'You're wasting your time, Jacko. There's nothing but some old cuttings from the time he bought this house of his down in Cork, what's it called?'

'Summerlawn.'

'Jesus, a nice Anglish sort of name. Well, it wasn't a

popular purchase. They could tolerate an American with dollars called Kelly, but a Polack . . .'

'"They"?'

'The locals, Jack. The Skibbereen Seamuses. There was a parish priest at that time, a man called O'Mara: Gaelic League, wee *fáine* on the lapel. *Dia's Muire dhuit* and *conas taoi?*, you know the sort. He tried to get up a petition, to get the state to buy the house. That was before the days of An Taisce. It all came to nothing. Your man got his house, and things went quiet after that.'

'That's it? That's all there is?'

Boylan nodded. He scooped up peas on the curve of his fork and heaved them into his open mouth.

'But that's impossible. The man's a millionaire. The house is an architectural treasure. One of the few this country has left. There must be more than that.'

Boylan shook his head again. He put down his fork and picked up a cigarette from the ashtray beside his plate. Next to them, the priest was calculating the odds on a horse called Cruachain Aigle.

'Your darling man keeps himself well out of the public eye. He's kept his head down for over forty years now. I'm sorry that's all there is, Jack. You could try the Georgian Society or the Tourist Houses and Gardens people. They'll be sure to have something on this Summerlawn.'

'It's not the house I'm interested in. It's Rosewicz.'

'Then you'll just have to take him as you find him.'

Boylan pulled hard on his cigarette and set it down again.

'It's good to see you again, Jack. We should get together for a few jars sometime. Get some of the lads together in Mulligan's.'

'I don't go out much these days, Denis.'

Boylan looked at him anxiously.

'Isn't it long enough now, man? Is it not time . . . ?'

Jack pushed back his chair abruptly and stood.

'Thanks for all your help, Denis. I'll be in touch.'

Without another word, he turned and headed for the door and the safety of the street.

The night before he left, he had a dream. It was not a recurring dream, nor any species of nightmare; and yet it left him afraid – or uneasy, rather – waking to a world he had thought sad and lonely yet sound at heart, to find it inwardly corrupt. It came with him into wakefulness, as though he had become a carrier for an infection: a long and continuous whispering, moist lips against his ear, breath like cold mist trickling through, words mixed and incoherent, broken, at times barely audible yet suggestive, spoken in a child's voice, a voice that trembled slightly, not Siobhan's voice, but a cold and penetrating, damaged voice, all night without cease, or so it seemed.

He woke and brushed his teeth and drank two cups of hot black coffee, and still the whispering persisted, like a cruel itch deep in the recesses of his brain, where it was darker still.

The darkness of the dream surrounded him from that moment of first waking until he came clear of the city beyond Dolphin's Barn, when, in a sudden access of exhilaration, he saw the road open suddenly in front of him, naked of traffic, and the sun on it, tilting off the glossy surface like a kind of rain. It was with him the whole way then, the sunlight and his gladness in it, as though exposure to its rays had opened up something in him that had been shut.

He took the Naas road, with the Wicklow Mountains blue on his left hand, heading south and steadily west, into the Curragh, in the constant green shadow of open fields. There were hills and barrows, and once, near a copse of yews, a ring of standing stones, ageless. And when he looked to the roadside, he would see the ruins of English castles, their blank windows, fallen, ivy-cluttered walls.

He wound through villages without names, silent pubs

as ubiquitous as churches, the traceries of old bunting barren above dry streets, children without names standing alone to play, an old man with a dog, the beating of a drum in a high place without windows. He felt the child in him, tugging at his sleeve. Walsh, Tobin, Lalor, Byrne, the names of old shops full of quiet Sunday merchandise.

People had come out from Dublin to be alive, to go to the country for a Saturday drive or a weekend holiday, he saw their number-plates ahead of him or behind, in his mirror, dwindling as he went deeper into green country-side. He passed a coach of tourists headed west, and another on the narrow road into Monasterevin. Their faces were pressed against long, slanted European windows, their eyes were as empty and as restless as their travelling, paid-up hearts. He longed to be rid of them. They would stop at grand hotels in the fold of hills and dine on salmon and listen to a tune played on a penny whistle, all bought and paid for by an agent in Dusseldorf or Miami Beach. And they would resent the televisions, and the aircraft overhead, and any boat that was not a coracle, and the coaches they travelled in, and themselves.

He shook himself free of them at last, heading down into the hill country after Caher. Mountain and forest now to Cork, and the lush dairy lands around Mitchelstown stretched out between. He passed a gaudy horse-drawn caravan by the side of the road, tourists playing gypsies for a week; and two miles further on, a family of real travellers, playing at nothing but how to stay alive. He took a brief lunch in Cork, then headed on to the coast, a long drive on bad roads.

In Baltimore he stopped at the pub and asked the way to Summerlawn. The man behind the bar eyed him oddly but gave him directions. It was not far.

'Will you have a drink before you go?'

He nearly refused, impatient as he was to get his journey over, to see Rosewicz at last; but on second thoughts he paused and asked for a draught of Guinness. He stood at the small, scrubbed bar, drinking his pint in silence. There were only two other drinkers in the little faded room, old men with slow pipes and halfs of porter.

The barman wiped some glasses, putting them aside for the evening trade.

'Have you come far today?' he asked.

Jack nodded.

'Dublin,' he said.

'A long drive. And the roads in the state they're in.'

Jack sipped the sour black liquid. Froth clung to his upper lip, and he wiped it away with a quick movement of his hand.

'You're a friend of himself up there, are you?'

'Mr Rosewicz?'

'That's him. Do you know him well?'

Behind the bar, a row of fading photographs looked down: the Pope flanked by John and Robert Kennedy, the Kerry Gaelic football team, and above them Christ displaying his bleeding heart. Jack could sense the hostility in the man's voice.

'I've never met him,' he said.

The man looked at him narrowly across the bar, wiping a pool of beer from it with his cloth.

'Is that so?' he said.

Jack nodded slowly. In the corner, the two ancients filled the room with tarry smoke.

'Do you see a lot of him in the village?'

'See him?' The barman turned away to straighten a row of whiskey bottles. He paused for a moment, then turned back. 'He never sets foot in Baltimore, and that's the truth of it. Not from one year's end to the next. And him here forty years and more. His daughter will be here from time to time, but himself does like to keep to his own company.'

'What sort of man is he?' asked Jack.

The man straightened and drew back a little, as though pulling away from an edge of some sort.

'That'll be one pound twenty. You'd best drink up now

and be on your way. No doubt they'll be expecting you for afternoon tea.'

All the way to the house he thought of the barman and his unexplained hostility. Or had it been nervousness? They were queer folk out here in the country, but they were well enough used to Dubliners, and he had never run into wariness like this before.

A thin, winding road led up out of Baltimore on to the headland, where it began the long thrust into the Atlantic. As he turned a bend, he saw a clear expanse of unbroken water and the dipping and soaring of white birds, kittiwakes and albatrosses from Clear Island. And then, turning again, a bright scattering of islands across to Roaringwater Bay, and boats with coloured sails off Spanish Island, tacking and turning into a light wind.

Here, rising, the weather was clear and sweet and steep. He could climb into it for ever and at any point step off, like a man who discovers happiness for the first time. The sun was moving deep into the west, out to the roaring Atlantic. He came through a tunnel of tall trees and wild purple fuchsia growing in mossy banks on either side, and the road dark and dappled with lozenges of light.

As he emerged, he was blinded for a moment by the suddenness of the full light. He closed his eyes, slowing the car involuntarily. When he opened them again, Summerlawn lay in front of him, unexpected and dazzling, a white house on a high place facing the sea. It was a three-storey building with seven bays of windows. The breakfront was divided into three bays. In its centre was set a tall, pedimented doorcase flanked by Doric columns above which Jack could make out a large Venetian window.

He felt his heart tighten within him. All along the wide front of the house, the windows sparkled as if welcoming him. A flock of seabirds bent low about a chimney stack before rising and lifting out to sea. He drew up outside a tall iron gate set between stone pillars. At the end of a long, tree-lined avenue, someone was watching.

He switched off his engine and got out. Up here, a sea breeze tugged at his hair, loosening it. There was a bell-push beside a small speaker in the right-hand pillar, and above them a hooded security camera. He pressed the bell, and when a voice answered, announced himself. Moments later, a buzzer sounded and the gates swung open. He looked up the long drive at the house. It stood there patiently, with its back to the loud sea, as though it had been waiting for him.

CHAPTER FIVE

The housekeeper led him through a series of spacious, mirrored rooms to a long terrace at the rear of the house where Stefan Rosewicz was waiting for him, an old man at a marble-topped table staring at the sea. Hearing Jack approach, he turned. He had white hair cut very short, a high forehead almost free of wrinkles, gaunt cheeks, very large, intelligent eyes. His dress was elegant and suited to the season, a white open-necked shirt beneath a linen jacket, casual trousers, canvas shoes.

As Jack stepped forward, Rosewicz stood and stretched out a hand in greeting. Jack noticed that the tip of the little finger was missing.

'Dr Gould. I trust you have had a pleasant drive. I find the weather very beautiful today.'

'Thank you, it's been lovely all the way. And it's very lovely here.'

'Naturally; that is why I live here.' He turned to the housekeeper, who was standing by the french windows. 'Mrs Nagle, will you bring our guest a glass of something cold? What will you have, Dr Gould?'

'I'll have whatever you're having.'

'You have the Irish will to self-denial, I see. Well, let us have two glasses of lemonade.'

The housekeeper nodded and slipped away.

'It is real lemonade, not that revolting concoction they sell by that name in bottles here. Please, take a chair.'

When Jack had seated himself, Rosewicz looked at him with a frank, penetrating gaze.

'You inherit the Irish diffidence from your mother, I think. Your father was Jewish, was he not?'

'Yes,' answered Jack. 'He was a German refugee. How did you know?'

Rosewicz shrugged.

'You don't think I asked you to come all the way here to see my little treasures without having made some enquiries about you?'

Jack said nothing in reply. Just what sort of enquiries had Rosewicz made, and how extensive had they been?

'Don't worry, my young friend. I know nothing about you that you would not want me to know. A little of your background, that is all. I had to satisfy myself that you might be the man for the job.'

'And just what is the job?'

Rosewicz waved a hand impatiently.

'Later, Dr Gould, later. You have only just arrived. You are tired. You shall have a cool drink now, and a little tea if you wish, then Mrs Nagle shall show you to your room. There will be time to relax before dinner. We can talk properly then. I will show you a little of the house. And the library, of course. I expect my daughter Maria to join us for our meal. She had to travel to Cork today on urgent business, otherwise she would have been here to entertain you.'

The housekeeper reappeared with a tray on which were two tall glasses and a tall glass jug. Jack noticed that both the jug and the glasses were Lalique. He had seen similar pieces in shops in Paris, all of them well out of his price range. The lemonade, when he tasted it, was delicious, a perfect balance between sweet and tart.

Rosewicz raised his glass.

'To our collaboration.'

'I haven't agreed to work for you yet.'

The Pole observed him carefully.

'You will,' he said. 'I have not the slightest doubt of it.'

'You are very confident.'

'I have reason to be. When you see my library, you will understand. Now, drink and enjoy the sunshine. The view from this terrace is unparalleled anywhere in Ireland.' He paused. 'You must excuse me, I have matters to attend to. When you are ready to go to your room, ring the bell over there and Mrs Nagle will attend to you.'

Rosewicz stood and bowed from the waist in a half-formal manner. Jack wondered how old he was. He had the bearing of a much younger man. Very erect, almost military. But he seemed to Jack like a man under some strain, or holding himself hard awake from a stupor that threatens him.

Jack sipped his lemonade and gazed out to sea. The house had left him stunned, in its compassionate, unguessed-at beauty, its grand isolation, the perfection of its position. The dry account in Burke had not prepared him for it. Not even in his dreams had he set foot in so magical a place. It would be filled with enchantments, he was certain of it. Far below, the sea beat against a sheer cliff. And there was sunlight everywhere. Yet he did not feel afraid. And he did not think of a child playing with a red ball by the cliff's high edge.

Two things happened before dinner, while he was in his room, resting and getting ready for the evening he knew lay ahead. His elation, inspired by the sunshine and the freedom he had felt in driving, had largely waned. The habitual depression was back again, marching round the little chintz-lined bedroom with its band of stale memories in tow. He had curled up on the bed, passing in and out of light passages of sleep with the skill of a swimmer moving in familiar waters.

Around six o'clock, he heard the sound of a car engine making its way along the head towards the house. Then silence and, minutes later, footsteps somewhere, and voices, very muffled. Maria must have returned. He imagined her a middle-aged spinster, or a widow. There would be neither a husband nor a family, for all that Summerlawn was large enough for several broods; gregariousness would not, Jack had already divined, figure high in the list of Stefan Rosewicz's virtues.

Later he heard music. It was faint at first, and then rose in volume, as though a door had been opened somewhere. A piano played softly and without strain, halting from time to time, then picking up again at the same bar, or further on. Several of the pieces were poignantly familiar, almost as though they had been selected for him: the andantino from Schubert's Piano Sonata in A, several pieces from Bach's Two- and Three-Part Inventions, which he had last heard on the harpsichord. They were almost too painful to listen to.

Then, at the very end, as the last notes of the Bach faded away, the pianist played a dozen bars from something much more recent, a jazz piece he did not recognize but which sounded like something by Jelly Roll Morton. So someone round here had a sense of humour. But he could not imagine it was the middle-aged Maria.

They did not dine until eight-thirty, when the sun was already tired and falling, reddened and alone, out beyond the islands where they stumbled one at a time into the Atlantic. Rosewicz had not returned to talk to him, and the nagging sensation of abandonment this had engendered in him had worked further on his mood. He began to wonder what had ever possessed him to respond with such alacrity to the whim of an old fraud eager for someone to admire a few trifles in his private library.

Mrs Nagle had been up a little while before to remind him to dress informally but smartly. He had decided on a light summer suit with a pale blue shirt and striped tie. Even in his best clothes, he felt a little shabby here, in surroundings of such opulence. He had not experienced such a keen sense of inadequacy since his first commons in Hall at Trinity.

There was a small balcony outside his window. Stepping

49

on to it, he looked out at the darkening sea, trying to recapture the happiness he had felt earlier. It is never quiet here, he thought. The sea beats against the cliffs all day and all night. In the winter, the whole house is battered by storms.

He looked down, his attention drawn by a sharp sound below, like a footstep. Part of the terrace was visible from where he stood. He heard a man's voice, not Rosewicz's, then a woman's answering. A moment later, he caught sight of a blue silk dress, flashing into view and out of sight again.

At that moment, a gong sounded from the hallway. He closed the little french window on to the balcony and prepared to go down.

Rosewicz was waiting for him at the bottom of the stairs. He was dressed in a casual silk suit with a tie that Jack recognized as one of a range designed by Giorgio Armani. Jack had seen some once in Switzers and flinched at the price.

'Mrs Nagle is busy in the kitchen, so I said I would accompany you to the dining-room. I must apologize for having left you so long. But I had urgent matters to attend to. I promise you will not be so neglected in future.'

'Well, I'll be leaving tomorrow anyway.'

Rosewicz said nothing. He led Jack down a long corridor lined with paintings. They were mostly old family portraits that Jack supposed had come with the house. Or had Rosewicz rescued them from some ancestral home in Poland, before the Communist takeover? Jack had already guessed from Rosewicz's bearing and suavity that he must be a refugee aristocrat. But he still could not guess where his money had come from. He supposed some people had found ways to smuggle funds out of the country.

The door to the dining-room stood open, revealing darkness and a mellow glow of candlelight. Rosewicz ushered his guest inside.

The table had been laid for three. Warm, polished wood,

the glow of candles, silver and glass, the whiteness of pure linen, china like crisp new paper, white flecked with gold. But he noticed none of that.

'This is my daughter, Maria,' Rosewicz said. 'Her Polish name is Marja; but we spell it in the Irish fashion here.'

Jack was not listening. He could not take his eyes off the woman who was pushing back her chair and stepping towards him, smiling, with her hand outstretched.

Whatever little space had been left in his heart by grief was abruptly and wholly filled. He could hardly breathe. It was as if she had taken the air, leaving nothing but herself in the room. He had not thought that, after Caitlin, a woman's beauty could take him so off guard, could render him dumb and blind. Maria Rosewicz was utterly unlike Caitlin in looks, and yet he felt for the second time in his life that terrible leaping of the heart he had felt before only in her presence.

The next moment, she was shaking hands with him. He was speechless, his mouth was dry, his head was whirling; it was as if he was falling into a dark pit that had no bottom.

'Dr Gould, it's lovely to meet you. We seldom get to see a new face at Summerlawn. Daddy frightens off visitors. Don't you?'

Rosewicz had come up behind her, smiling.

'I can see you are dazzled, Dr Gould. Maria dazzles everyone she meets. Is she not beautiful? She is one of the last remaining pleasures in my life. I married her mother over thirty years ago. Before she died she left me a child.'

Jack had begun to recover himself. He stammered, forcing a smile.

'I'm very pleased . . . pleased to meet you. Do you . . . Was that you I heard playing the piano earlier?'

She reddened and nodded.

'I'm not very good,' she said. 'But I practise every day. When I can, that is.'

'I thought it was very beautiful,' he said. He hoped she could see that he meant it. 'You played the Bach very well.

You have the right touch. It reminded me . . .' He broke off, confused.

'Yes?'

'Nothing,' he lied. 'Just that I've heard those same pieces played very well before.'

She smiled, nodding. But for a moment he thought he had surprised an unguarded look in her eye, as though she knew what he had really meant to say.

Then the door opened and Mrs Nagle came in with a tray bearing three bowls of chilled soup.

'I think we should seat ourselves,' said Rosewicz, drawing back Jack's chair for him. 'Mrs Nagle hates her soup to go cold. Even when it's chilled.'

CHAPTER SIX

Dinner passed half in a dream, half in waking. They talked of nothing personal or intimate, yet Jack sensed that, in everything he said, in his slightest gesture, his host and hostess found significance.

Maria, it transpired, had studied music at the Accademia di Santa Cecilia in Rome, the world's oldest musical academy. She played several instruments, but preferred the keyboard. Tomorrow, she said, she would show him the small collection of early harpsichords, spinets, and clavichords that she kept in the old Tower House. They included two examples of the work of the Ruckers family and several by leading Italian craftsmen. He knew almost nothing of such things, but he listened to her talk of them with fascination, and as he did so his mood began to change again. She talked about wood and metal as though they were living things. The musician's touch brought them to life, she said, just as a magician can bring speech to trees or movement to stones.

Several times during the meal, he caught her out of the corner of his eye, observing him closely, almost as if he were an old friend she had not seen in years and about whom she wanted to reassure herself. She was very beautiful, and he found it hard not to return her gaze each time. She had dark Pre-Raphaelite hair that fell to her shoulders in waves, green eyes that could move in seconds from amusement to distress, a long neck and smooth white shoulders whose nakedness was painful to him.

Rosewicz seemed restless. Several times he brought the

conversation back to the house, eager with details about its history and architecture. His enthusiasm invested the place with life.

'Look up,' he said.

Jack raised his head, straining to see through the shadows.

'You won't see another ceiling in Ireland like it. The plasterwork is by Stapleton. It's one of his finest pieces.'

'I'm sorry,' Jack said. 'I know so little about architecture.'

'You don't have to know,' Rosewicz insisted. 'You have to feel. I knew nothing about architecture when I came here, when I bought Summerlawn. I fell in love, that's all.'

'I think you chose well. The house is very beautiful.'

'Summerlawn is almost the last of its kind,' Rosewicz said. 'I have not given it to the state because the state does not deserve it. They have presided over the ruin of so many houses like this. Does that seem selfish to you?'

Jack shook his head.

'Not if you can preserve it yourself. But it does seem a little selfish that you let nobody but a few friends inside.'

'I have my reasons, Dr Gould. Leave it at that.'

'It is a beautiful house, Mr Rosewicz. I'm not blaming you.'

'It will belong to Maria after I die. And after her to her children, for as long as there is someone to live here. It will not become a museum. A place for tourists to walk round, gawping, with their cheap cameras and their chatter. I would sooner see it burned to the ground.'

Jack said nothing. The vehemence in Rosewicz's voice was like a wind.

'They're all gone or in ruins now, all the great houses: Powerscourt, Desart Court, Castle Morres, St Anne's at Clontarf, Santry Court, Killester House, Shanbally Castle, Loughcrew. Burned down or left to rot, or stripped for their wood and stone. And hundreds upon hundreds of houses like them or smaller. I can think of over seventy here in County Cork alone. The death of the great Irish houses is the greatest architectural tragedy of the century.'

'Father, I think that's an exaggeration. And you are being a little harsh. You should remember that our guest is Irish himself.'

Rosewicz grunted. It was evident they had had similar tussles before.

As the evening passed, Jack felt a growing sense of unreality. He liked Maria and felt himself at ease in her company; but Rosewicz himself made him nervous.

After a dessert of strawberries came coffee and brandy. Maria excused herself before they were served.

'I have to be up early,' she said. 'I attend morning mass in Skibbereen.' She paused and smiled at Jack. 'You're welcome to come as well, if you'd like.'

'I'm not very regular at mass, I'm afraid. Another time, perhaps.'

It was an unintended admission that he might, after all, stay.

'Father?'

Rosewicz nodded.

'I'll come with you, of course. But after that I want to spend the day with Dr Gould. He and I will have a lot to talk about.'

Maria shook Jack's hand again and wished him goodnight. Her father kissed her gently on the cheek. Jack sensed that they were very close. But that there was something else, something less tender, a tension almost, or a gap; as though one of them was putting on an act.

When she had gone, Rosewicz turned to him.

'Why don't you bring your brandy with you, Dr Gould? It's getting late, and I'd like you to see the library before you retire.'

'Of course. And please call me Jack.'

'That's very kind of you. I hope it means we shall become friends. And you, of course, must call me Stefan. Please, follow me. The library is not far.'

*   *   *

He could not mistake the smell. Old books in leather bindings leave such a heavy stain imprinted on the air. The library was a vast, circular room with a high domed ceiling in which glass panes had been placed to let in light. On every wall, shelves heavy with books ran from the polished floor to the border of the ceiling. In the centre, a circular table of highly polished mahogany held stacks of volumes. Five or six leather chairs, a dozen classical busts in white marble lifted on pedestals, and a tall set of library steps completed the furnishings.

'What a very lovely room,' whispered Jack.

'Yes,' said Rosewicz, behind him. 'The loveliest in the house, I think. It was designed by Davis Duckart when he built the house in 1768. People used to come from Dublin to see this room. You'll find part of the original collection in the National Library now.'

Rosewicz crossed the room to a broad shelf holding encyclopaedias in several languages. He drew out a volume of the *Encyclopaedia Judaica*, then reached inside the space left by it and pulled some sort of lever. He stood back and moments later a whole section of the wall began to roll out into the room. When it had extended about a foot, Rosewicz pushed it to the left and it slid effortlessly across the wall beside it, fitting the curve perfectly. In the space behind a small white door was revealed.

Rosewicz turned and smiled at his guest.

'You are very privileged, Jack. Very few people other than myself have ever set foot in the room behind this door. I had it built specially to house my collection. But before we go inside, I wish to have your solemn word that you will not speak or write to anyone else about what you see.'

'You are being very trusting. You scarcely know me. How do you know I will keep my word?'

'I don't know that you will. That is why it is important.' Jack hesitated. He disliked committing himself to something without knowing exactly what it entailed. But he was burning with curiosity by now. And what, after all, had he to lose?

'Very well,' he said. 'You have my word.'

The door was fitted with an expensive digital lock. Rosewicz punched in a number and pressed down on a heavy metal handle. The door swung open without a sound.

The room they stepped into was quite unlike the library from which they had come. Low-ceilinged, white-walled, lit by fluorescent tubes, air-conditioned, it was more like an operating theatre than a place of study.

'This is where you will work,' said Rosewicz.

The walls were lined with steel cabinets, each fitted with a lock. Jack could not understand his host's evident concern with security. He remembered the camera at the gate earlier in the day. And he had noticed that the house itself had what looked like an elaborate alarm system and that all the outside windows he had seen had been fitted with strong security bolts. No doubt Rosewicz's collection was valuable, but surely such a high level of protection was excessive.

Rosewicz opened the first of the cabinets and took from it a stack of papyrus fragments, each protected in its own acetate shell. Carrying them to the long metal table that stood along a side wall, Rosewicz switched on a Berenice lamp and an illuminated magnifying glass on a stand.

'Here,' he said, 'you can start with these.'

It was early morning by the time Jack left. Late though it was, he could not sleep. He could not tolerate the thought of bed. For over an hour he sat in an armchair, cold and preoccupied, and, in spite of the meal he had eaten a few hours earlier, still hungry. He had, he thought, taken steps he would not be able to retrace. Or which, retraced, would only lead him further astray.

Rosewicz, he now knew, was not the dilettante he had taken him for. The hours Jack had spent with him in the library had been profoundly disorienting. His host had shown himself a capable if limited scholar, well versed in the secondary sources of Biblical archaeology and the latest theories of scriptural origins. A gifted amateur with the money to indulge his passion. Jack already regretted his promise to say nothing about what he had been shown, a promise he felt morally compelled to keep. He knew scholars who would lie or steal, one or two who might even kill, to spend just a month or two with the materials he had seen that night.

From his drawers and cabinets, Rosewicz had taken the most astonishing collection of early Jewish and Christian papyri Jack had ever seen outside a major institution. At least fifteen codices of books from the Septuagint Bible, none later than the second century; three separate Aramaic chapters of the *Book of Enoch*, together with a Greek translation of the ninety-first chapter and seven Ethiopic manuscripts of the complete text; vellum manuscripts of the Acts of the Apostles in Coptic; part of the rare Syriac text of Tatian's *Diatessaron*; early copies of the Samaritan Pentateuch; apocryphal Gospels; rare Mishnahs, Babylonian and Palestinian Talmuds; and numerous fragments of what appeared to be Essene texts.

Jack knew that the next few months would be a period of intense activity. There would not be time to read and analyse any of the documents properly: Rosewicz was not employing him for that. And even if he had been able to read them, his vow of silence would have prohibited him from ever publishing even a short article, let alone the major study he knew they merited.

Not even Rosewicz knew exactly what he owned. His knowledge of Hebrew, Aramaic and other ancient languages was too rudimentary to permit anything but the most cursory acquaintance with the contents of his treasures. But he was learned enough to appreciate the significance of most of his collection and astute enough to want to guard against the academic and religious storm that would rage around it once its existence was revealed and the nature of its contents made public.

Jack went out on to the balcony. Beneath him, in the darkness, the sea shivered against rocks, unseen. As his eyes grew accustomed to the dark, he saw that the heavens were full of stars. They lay stretched above him, Jupiter, Venus, Mars, Orion, Cassiopeia, familiar to him from long hours spent bent to a telescope as a child.

What was Rosewicz trying to do? What did he really want, and why? Jack was suspicious of him. Not of his supposed dilettantism, he had satisfied himself on that score. But there was something deeper, something graver and less tangible. The beauty of the house and its setting, the soft and lambent light of the dinner table, even these stars, had all seduced him. Or, perhaps – he admitted it now to himself – it had been less those things than the feelings Maria had reawakened in him, feelings he was as yet loath to acknowledge. Everything here had tied him foolishly to Rosewicz and whatever it was that Rosewicz intended.

And there had been Rosewicz's question, so seemingly casual, yet so evidently rehearsed. From a locked drawer, the old man had removed a plain brown envelope. Inside it was an old photostat, a reproduction of part of the first few lines of an Aramaic scroll.

'Can you read it?' Rosewicz had asked.

Jack had bent down, squinting. The quality of the reproduction was poor.

'It isn't easy,' he had said. 'Something like this, I think: *"Neither the roaring of loud waters nor the burning of bright fires shall deflect me from my Covenant with Thee, O Lord, nor shall the Sons of Light find me faithless."*'

'Yes. That's exactly right.' Rosewicz had paused, as though on the verge of saying something more. In the end, he had put the photostat back in its envelope and returned it to the drawer, locking it.

'Have you ever seen a scroll beginning with those words?'

'No, never.'

'Or heard of such a scroll?'

'No. What's this about? Surely you have access to the copy from which this photostat was made?'

Rosewicz frowned, making up his mind about something. He shook his head.

'This is not the time. But we shall talk of it again. I promise.'

That had been all. Jack stood beneath the stars, torn between his curiosity and a sense that all might still be well if he fled in the morning. He could see white water flickering out there now, pleated by rocks. Apart from a few small islands, there was nothing between here and North America, nothing but a great gulf of blackness, and water so deep a drowning man could go down in it until it crushed him.

Suddenly, on the terrace, he heard voices. Two men, talking softly. One was Rosewicz, the other the man Jack had heard earlier. He could not make out what they were saying, but he was sure they spoke a language other than English. It sounded a little like German. A few minutes passed, then silence returned. Silence and the sea.

CHAPTER SEVEN

The sea moved against the rocks all summer long, an unchanging diapason behind his life at Summerlawn. It was there in the mornings when he woke and first went to his window, and again at night when he lay in bed at last, his mind spinning, sometimes out of control. The sound of it he would carry with him afterwards, as some of us carry loving words or a snatch of music long after the speaker is dead or the instrument cracked. But he knew that, even in his absence, the voice he heard inwardly had not fallen silent.

The sun and the sea on it, and white birds; and a house set above them; and Maria: the constituents of the happiest summer he had known, and the saddest.

The work was not arduous. He would rise at eight and have breakfast with Rosewicz and Maria, if she was there. After that, in spite of his own eagerness to get down to work, his employer would as often as not engage him in conversation, full of earnest questions about rival theories in Biblical scholarship or the disputed attribution of important finds. Like many keen amateurs, the Pole often knew more about small details than the best general scholar, and Jack frequently had to palm him off with approximations until he had a chance to get back to Dublin for a few days to check his facts at the library.

After a few of these conversations, Jack became aware that his host was not a man to have the wool pulled over his eyes. Once or twice Jack tried to fob him off with long words and jargon, only to receive a stern rebuke. Rosewicz knew when you were jerking him about, and he told you so in a few well-chosen words. For some reason, more instinct than calculation, Jack decided that Rosewicz could be dangerous. It was usually late morning before Jack finally got into the library and was able to shut himself into the little manuscript room where he did most of his work. Rosewicz was not interested in a simple labelling and cross-referencing job. He wanted each of his manuscripts, whether complete papyri or fragments, provided with a serial number, photographed, and entered into a *catalogue raisonné*, with details of first and last lines, dimensions, condition, place of origin, and, where appropriate, a summary of the contents.

The trips to Dublin were falls from grace. Each time he returned to Summerlawn, it was as though he were again entering Eden after a time of banishment. He lived in dread of the summer's end and his final expulsion. The thought of autumn and winter in Ballsbridge lay on him like a succubus.

After lunch he would work for several hours, until late in the afternoon. Then, as often as not, Maria would come for him, telling him to put down his books and come with her for a walk. Did she know he was falling helplessly in love with her? Would it have mattered to her? It was impossible to guess.

At times he sensed her drawing close to him. They found much to talk about, and he realized that she was lonely here and in need of a friend. And at times too he would catch her unawares, looking at him, and he felt bewildered, not knowing what he would do if she reciprocated his feelings.

And yet, at other times, she seemed to pull away, as though frightened that she had gone too far. He wondered if she already had a lover. It was hard to believe she had not, hard to believe that there were not dozens of men competing for her. And what had he to offer? He had almost become again the desiccated creature he had been all those years ago in Paris. Nothing had been added to him since then but tiredness and grief. What use were those to a woman like Maria?

He quickly learned that, if she was not in love with him, she was in love with Summerlawn. They explored it together, he walking dazzled, as though in sunshine, in and out of rooms of unimagined splendour. He had walked round stately homes before, in Ireland a little, many times in England and in France; but always in the company of others, the tourist pack with cameras and luncheon boxes, ghouls battening on a long-dead prey, the rooms and furniture and paintings cordoned off with yards of red rope and elegantly-lettered signs.

Here, he could reach out and touch it all at will. Or stand and gaze with almost a proprietorial eye, in silence, while Maria looked on. He would ask questions, and she would answer precisely and with affection. Affection for the house and, he thought at times, for him. Throughout that long, indolent summer, she taught him about painting, about glass and ceramics, about styles and periods of furnishing, displaying a remarkable knowledge of matters whose surface he had only skimmed.

There were gardens all about the house, lawns and terraces and wooded glades full of summer flowers, where they walked together or sat to talk. It was here that the boundaries of his paradise were most sharply demarcated. Not by stinging nettles or gorse or tourist caravans, but by the snaking wires of a concealed, high-tech perimeter fence. It was Maria who warned him off it on several occasions, when he was about to stray across its path. There were, she said, electronic eyes positioned at regular intervals along the borders of the estate. And trip wires were set, like the eyes, to register the bulk of a human intruder while ignoring foxes or badgers. Her father, she said, had a mortal fear of burglars and had, in her opinion, turned mere precaution into obsession. But Jack sensed she was lying and that, behind the fiction of keeping his treasures safe, there lurked a mystery of some kind. He imagined that Rosewicz must at some time have been involved with anti-communist subversion, possibly in one of the organizations supplied and funded by the World Anti-Communist League, and even mixed up with Western intelligence operations in Eastern Europe. But surely the days for excessive precaution on that score were gone.

A short drive took them by a winding road down to a beach in a wild, secluded cove. They would go swimming there, in bright water full of slanting sunlight. Sometimes they would pass a shoal of translucent jellyfish. Maria told him they were Aurelias: they could sting, but they were not fatal; he trusted her and swam almost absentmindedly among them. Afterwards, they would go back to the house to find Rosewicz waiting for them. He was usually on the terrace. Jack wondered if he spied on them from there.

Not that there was anything to spy on. As time passed, Jack found himself bewildered by the innocence of his relations with Maria. He sought for the reason in himself, and found it in his own diffidence, his fear of involvement. Of re-involvement, rather, after all that had happened. And he found himself, even in their most relaxed times together, shying away from the things that really mattered, his own feelings, his past. While she, Maria, seeming to sense or even know what troubled him, bypassed the most obvious questions and concentrated on what lay closest to the surface. He suspected that Rosewicz knew all there was to know about him, and that he had passed his information on to his daughter.

But as time passed, it all changed, almost without his realizing. During that period, Maria made several unexplained trips away from the house, remaining absent for days at a time, once for an entire week. She never said where she went, but he suspected it was to the Continent, probably to Italy, for he once caught sight of a Rome airport label on the handle of a case as she was carrying it in. He missed her when she was gone. Much of the magic of the house she took away with her.

On her return, she would be taciturn and withdrawn at first, and there would be no walks or swims for a day or two, and only stilted conversation at the dinner table. During her absences or her periods of withdrawal, he worked harder than ever, staying up late with mounds of papyri and index cards. And then whatever it was that troubled her seemed to pass, and she would be herself again, enticing him away from his duties, or finding excuses to be escorted to Skibbereen.

When she came back from her long trip, she was unusually introverted, keeping out of his way for two days, as though he had offended her without knowing. On the third day, she came to him after dinner, when he was sitting on the terrace, watching the sky darken. Rosewicz had made his excuses and gone to bed early. There was only the sound of the waves far below. He heard her approach him quietly.

'You have to put up with me when I'm like this,' she said.

He turned. Suddenly he felt very angry.

'Put up with you? I don't have to put up with anything. You're not my wife or my lover, even if that makes a difference. I'm not even sure you're my friend.'

He saw the hurt in her face and at once relented.

'I'm sorry,' he said. 'That was cruel.'

'No,' she answered, shaking her head. 'You were right. You have no reason to put up with any of this.' She hesitated, as though making up her mind about something.

'Come upstairs,' she said. 'There's something I want to show you.'

'Not your etchings, by any chance?'

She did not respond to the weak joke. Without another word, she turned, expecting him to follow.

They had not gone far before he guessed where she was leading him. Approaching the house on that very first day, he had seen, above the east wing, a low dome sleeved in copper. Some time after, asking Rosewicz its purpose, he had received in reply a noncommittal shrug. 'An old observatory,' his host had said. 'Built in the nineteenth century. I keep it locked up. I have no use for it.'

The door to the observatory lay at the end of a long corridor down which Jack had never previously ventured; it was dimly lit and hung with gloomy tapestries. Maria took a key from her pocket, as though she always carried it. Seeing his glance, she nodded.

'I come up here sometimes to be alone. Father doesn't know.'

'What if he finds us up here?'

'He trusts me,' was all she said. She slipped the key into the lock and opened the door. Behind it lay a winding staircase lit only by a weak electric bulb. It felt surprisingly chilly.

'I should have warned you to bring a pullover,' she said. 'We can go back if you like.'

He shook his head. She led the way upwards, into the dome. There were more and brighter lights here, worked by a chain near the door. He saw four armchairs, a low table, shelves packed with books. In the centre of the room stood a huge brass telescope, polished and shining, a thing of mirrors and levers, wheels and ratchets and pulleys. Light glinted off its barrel in tiny, earthbound stars.

She sat him down on a stool, pointing out the eyepiece.

'Have you ever used one of these before?'

'Not one like this.'

'Here, let me show you.'

She showed him how to adjust the lens. As he turned the handle, there was at first nothing but blackness, then, quite abruptly, there were more stars than he had ever seen. They made him feel dizzy. And then, slowly, carefully, she turned them into planets and moons for him.

For over an hour, they sat together. She showed him galaxies, but all he cared about was the moment when he would next see her face, the closest thing in his universe. He turned the wheel as she instructed, and the telescope swung and lifted, focused and refocused, reaching into blackness to tear from it entire worlds made of nothing else but light. But in the end he tired of it, so much blackness, so much light, without gradation. When he took his eyes away finally, she was weeping quietly beside him, he did not know why.

'I used to come up here with my sister,' she said. 'During the summer holidays. We came to watch the stars, and we wound up talking.'

'I didn't know you had a sister. The way you both talk, I thought there was no one but your father and yourself.'

She nodded, brushing a hand across one cheek.

'That's right,' she said. 'My sister left us. Then she died.'

He understood, or thought he did.

'I'm sorry.'

'Of course you are. Everyone is. But it doesn't do much good.'

She shivered.

'I haven't been up here since I heard of her death. It hasn't changed. None of . . . that . . . has changed.' With a half-mocking sweep of the hand, she indicated the telescope, the night sky, the stars. The realm of immutability.

'What was her name? Your sister's name.'

Maria hesitated, as though she had to rack her memory for what should have come as second nature. He wondered what it was she wanted to hide about her sister.

'Katerina,' she said. The name sounded flat and insincere on her tongue.

'What happened to her? How did she die?'

She moved involuntarily away from him. He felt the cold in the room like a warning. She sat down, shaking her head slowly. He could scarcely see her in the muted light.

'She left home, got married, had a child. There was an accident. She died. That's all.'

He left the telescope and sat down in the chair next to hers. Her face was swollen with tears. She turned to him.

'And you,' she said. 'You must tell me about your wife.'

'My wife?'

'My father says you were married. That your wife died, like Katerina. Is that true?'

He took his time in answering.

'Yes,' he said at last. And he felt crushed in that tiny, half-lit dome, crushed between stars and the sea rolling out beyond. For a long moment, he was breathless, as though affirmation of the truth had sucked the air from his lungs. He had never spoken about Caitlin's death before, not to anyone, not properly. But he spoke to Maria, as though compelled. Once started, he could not stop. He told her everything, and she listened as though her life depended on it, he could not imagine why. The years they had spent together, the home they had started to make in Ballsbridge, Siobhan's birth, their plans.

'It was a red ball,' he said. 'A big red ball. I bought it that morning, just before they left. I had to stay behind, I had work to do in the library, work that couldn't wait. They went with my parents, to Howth Head. We had a favourite spot where we often had picnics.'

He paused. He saw her watching him, felt her concern. He described the game, the bouncing ball, how his wife and child had fallen together to their deaths.

'I always see it happening as if I was there. My father told me the details, I made him tell me. There are always birds. White birds. The sky is full of them. And when Caitlin and Siobhan fall, they come swooping down. Like angels.'

When he finished talking, she held him with her eyes, carefully, in a silence he thought nothing could break. The observatory had grown intensely cold. Their breath hung entangled in thin, ordinary air. He felt as though there was no weight in anything, as though gravity had passed from the world as easily as light seeps through space. He had not understood before how heavy an individual death could be.

Maria's voice touched the silence like a tiny stone skimming the surface of still water.

'And now,' she said, 'everything's falling apart again, isn't it?'

He was not surprised that she understood. Only that she had not said so sooner. He could hear his heart beating.

'You've fallen in love with me,' she said, 'and you don't know what to do.'

He looked at her as though to deny it, but words would not stop his heart beating. They were very close. He had only to reach for her. She did not move, did not speak. Silently, he reached across and took her hand. She let him take it, returned the pressure, said nothing as he moved closer and finally put his lips against hers. Just touching her had carried him in a moment from grief to the keenest arousal. He wanted her desperately now. And she closed her eyes, and he pressed hard against her lips, feeling her mouth open, his tongue wet against her tongue, reaching one hand behind her head to draw her to him, slipping from his chair to come closer, needing her now, willing her to his embrace.

Suddenly, inexplicably, she pulled away and put a hand hard against his chest, shaking her head.

'No, Jack, please. We can't. Please don't make me. Don't ask why. But it's impossible.'

He had been so certain. Her touch and kiss had made her feelings clear, or so he had thought. He pulled back, dismayed.

'I don't understand . . .'

She was looking at him as though through a haze of pain.

'What is it?' he pleaded. 'Is there someone else? What's wrong?'

She shook her head, standing and making for the door.

'It's late, Jack. I'm cold. We have to go.'

He stood and made to grab her, but she opened the door and hurried out. Stumbling, he followed her down the narrow, twisting staircase. At the bottom, he caught up with her, snatching at her wrist, but the look she turned on him made him drop his hand as though he had set it on a hot plate.

'Please, Jack, let's not talk of this again. I'm sorry if you got the wrong idea. I can't explain now. In the morning, perhaps. Wait until then.'

He saw her to her room. Opening the door, she hesitated and turned to him. For a moment, he thought she had relented and was about to tell him the reason for his rejection.

'Jack, I'm sorry about what happened tonight. I should never have taken you up there. It's just . . .' She stood very still, watching him. Her eyes were clouded. 'Jack, I want you to promise me something. If you do care for me. Please watch out for my father. Don't trust him. I don't think he means you harm, but you could be harmed in spite of that.'

'Harmed? I don't understand. Why . . . ?'

But she said nothing further. Her door closed and he was alone in the corridor.

CHAPTER EIGHT

She left the next day, without her promised explanation and without saying goodbye, leaving no word as to when she would be back. Across the fields, the sun shone through whirling flocks of white birds. He went back to the observatory to switch off the lights and found it bleak, full of dust. All that day and the next he remained disconsolate in his air-conditioned library room, reading and cataloguing. From time to time he wondered what Maria had meant about being careful of her father.

On the afternoon of the third day, he went for a walk in the woods. Even the sound of the breakers was muffled here. There were birds. The sunlight dropped to the ground in patches, rare among shade. Flowers clustered together at the bottom of tall trees, or lay scattered in little glades. Three days and he still could not understand.

Wrapped up in his thoughts, he strayed a little distance beyond the point at which he and Maria had normally turned back. The path went on uninterrupted, climbing between high oaks to a low escarpment. The trees thinned out suddenly, and he found himself looking out across open country, parched fields of furze and bracken. Nothing stirred. The ground seemed to drink up the thick sunlight like soup.

It was not until he saw the gate that he understood the unconscious prompting that had taken him this far from the house. Once, quite casually, Maria had mentioned the existence of a small family graveyard dating back to the eighteenth century. Her mother had been buried there, she said. It was her father's intention that the Rosewiczes should inherit, not only the property, but the traditions of their predecessors.

The gate was rusted now, but had in its day been finely worked. It incorporated convoluted ironwork in which the letter 'F' was doubled and reversed. Jack pushed his way through and started down an overgrown path that led in a matter of half a minute to a tumbling of graves. The stones were, for the most part, much decayed, covered in lichen, and darkly beaten by the coastal weather. Grass and weeds grew uninhibited around the tilted memorials, and here and there a grave slab had cracked and sunk. It was a dismal place, suited to his mood.

A new plot had been laid out to one side of the Fitzgerald graves, less savage, its grasses firmly cut back. A solitary headstone of Irish marble marked the resting-place of Sinéad Rosewicz, wife of Stefan. There were fresh flowers on the grave, lilies and blue irises, not locally grown.

He looked in vain for a second grave. Had Katerina been laid to rest elsewhere? Had the violence of her estrangement from her family been strong enough to make Rosewicz deny her burial here? Or had it been her own wish?

Puzzled, he started back, resolving to ask Maria about it all when she got back. He plunged back into the woods in search of shade. There was a sudden sound behind him. He wheeled round, startled, and saw a man standing a few paces away, watching him. The first thing Jack noticed was that the stranger carried a gun. Not a shotgun, but a compact submachine gun. Hardly typical weaponry for a farmer or poacher. And where the hell had he come from? It was as though he had popped up out of nowhere.

The man's dress was out of place and unsuited to the weather. Black trousers with tightly-strapped leather leggings, stout boots, a black leather jerkin. He was blond and clean-shaven, aged between twenty-five and thirty. He held the gun like someone who had been trained to use it. When he spoke, it was with a touch of a foreign accent. He was certainly not a local.

'I'm sorry,' he said, 'but you're trespassing on private property. I shall have to ask you to leave.'

The words were polite enough, but the tone was peremptory, announcing clearly that he was not going to stand for aggravation.

Jack looked at him coolly. He was in no mood to be scared off by a jumped-up gamekeeper.

'I'm fully aware that it's private property,' he said. 'I happen to be employed by the owner. Just like yourself. My name's Gould. Speak to Rosewicz.'

Some sort of wary recognition flickered across the man's face. He carried a two-way radio clipped to his belt. Without taking his eyes off Jack, he raised the handset to his lips and spoke quickly into it. There was a pause of about half a minute, then a muffled voice answered. A short conversation followed. The man nodded a couple of times, accompanying the gesture with an indistinct murmur of assent. Finally, he replaced the handset on its clip.

'Mr Rosewicz vouches for you, Dr Gould. He says you should return to the house at once. I'm sorry if I startled you.'

There was no smile to go with the apology. Jack said nothing. Turning, he set off back down the path along which he had come. The man in black stood still behind him, watching him go.

Rosewicz was waiting for him on the terrace. Tea things for two had been placed on the table. Mrs Nagle was in the kitchen, preparing dinner. A seagull stood on the balustrade, staring at them.

'What the hell was that about?' stormed Jack, coming on to the terrace. The pent-up feelings of the past few days could no longer be held back.

Rosewicz cast him a pained look.

'Please, Dr Gould, there is no need to swear.'

'I'm sorry. But I don't very much like being set on by men with submachine guns.'

'I am sure you were not set upon. Please, sit down. I would like to talk.'

Jack was on the verge of refusing, but he saw there was nothing else for it. This was Rosewicz's home, he was still his guest and employee.

'May I offer you tea? This is Gui Hua. The postman brought a new packet this morning. I have it sent over from Mariage Frères in Paris. You may know the shop: it is in the Marais. Surely you will do me the honour . . .'

Jack nodded. He would not be easily mollified, but he could not be rude, not least on Maria's account. He sat down.

'Now,' continued Rosewicz, pouring gently from a fine Cantonese pot into matching cups, 'we can talk like civilized people.' He paused, sipping from the little porcelain cup. 'You will have to excuse Henryk. It is one of his less appealing traits to be rough with people he takes for trespassers. I have had to speak with him about it before. He is like a well-trained guard-dog: extremely loyal, but lacking in discrimination. I am sorry if you thought he was about to savage you. I assure you, he would not have harmed you.'

Jack could sense a false note in the old man's explanation, an unnecessary eagerness to explain away his servant's behaviour.

'Normally we have so few visitors here,' Rosewicz went on. 'If you had only told me that you planned to visit that corner of the woods, I would, of course, have notified him.'

'I'm sorry,' Jack said, 'but you're not making sense. This place is covered with sensors and trip-wires. Maria pointed some of them out to me. You employ a man to patrol the grounds carrying an automatic weapon. I don't understand. Why so much security?'

For a moment, Jack thought Rosewicz's hand shook, but

in the next instant he regained control and there was not even a tremor. He lifted the pot carefully to refill their empty cups. Small Chinese figures caught the light.

'Regard it as an old man's whim. I love this house and its contents very much. I lost a great deal after the war, more than you can imagine, and I now cling fiercely to what I have. You yourself know how valuable my library is. I do my best to keep its contents secret, but it is impossible to stop information leaking out. There are rumours. I know men who would not hesitate to have Summerlawn burgled merely in the hope of enhancing their own meagre collections. And it would be unwise to forget that the wealthy are always at risk in Ireland. I would not be the first target for a kidnap attempt.' He paused and looked directly at Jack. 'Or Maria.'

Jack reddened slightly. He wondered how much the old man knew or guessed about his feelings for his daughter.

It was growing a little cold. Something of the perfection had gone out of the weather in the past few days. Jack shivered. For the first time since coming to Summerlawn he felt trapped. By what he could not say.

'Dr Gould, there is something else that we must talk about. I think you know what I mean.'

For the first time since they had met, Rosewicz seemed to Jack ill at ease.

'You want to talk about Maria. Is that it?'

Rosewicz nodded.

'I had not wanted to raise the subject. We are both adults, you are a widower; I have no right to interfere in your private life. But I have noticed . . . Let us say that I have observed how you have conceived an affection for my daughter. It did not come as a surprise to me. Maria is a beautiful woman and charming company. It would be more difficult to understand how someone could fail to be captivated. But . . .'

He paused, avoiding Jack's gaze.

'I have to tell you that Maria is not free. There is some-one else, someone she is engaged to marry. I am sorry that I did not tell you this before. It might have saved you some heartache.'

Jack sat stunned and only half believing.

'Why didn't she tell me this herself? Why did she just disappear like that?'

'I think she was afraid of hurting you. Her earlier absences . . . She has gone to visit her fiancé. Business affairs keep him too busy to visit her here at present.'

'Did she ask you to tell me?'

Rosewicz shook his head.

'No. And if she had done, I should have told her it was her own responsibility. But since she is not here . . .'

'Is she coming back?'

Rosewicz shook his head.

'Not this summer. It is better you do not see her again. I think your presence here only confused her. I think . . .' He broke off, looking at Jack directly again. 'I think it would be best if you were to bring your work to a close. Say, by the end of the week?'

There was nothing to say. In a way, Jack had been expecting his dismissal. He had known for days that some-thing was drawing to its end.

'It is for the best, I think.'

'Yes,' Jack murmured. 'Perhaps it is.' He hesitated. 'May I ask when Maria is to be married?'

'It will not be long,' Rosewicz said. 'She is with her fiancé now. They are making the final plans. If things had been otherwise, you would have been invited. But I am sure you understand.'

There was, for some reason Jack could not discern, more than a touch of sadness in Rosewicz's voice. Sadness or pain, he could not be quite sure which.

'Have dinner with me as usual tonight,' the Pole said. He was like a man grasping at friendship. 'We shall talk of other things. I would not want you to think I have been displeased with you or with your work. It is the world intruding, that is all.'

The day he left for Dublin, it rained torrentially. He carried summer with him on the road home, awkwardly, as a memory of sunshine.

CHAPTER NINE

Dublin

With the coming of rain the tourists packed their bags and left. In a matter of days Dublin was returned to itself. Americans with tam o' shanters and heavy bags of golf clubs took flight for Tampa and Orlando. Italian and Spanish students made excuses to their summer sweethearts and boarded brightly-painted coaches on the first leg of the long journey home. The city put on the first of its autumn colours. There were wild swans in Herbert Park and Irish voices on the forecourts of Trinity College. Jack Gould fed the fish in the long, lily-covered Chester Beatty pond and thought of the past.

Most days he was content. He had almost forgotten the uproar of sunshine on his windscreen, the opening out of the world. Summer was gone, and he was back in Ballsbridge, dividing his time between an empty flat and a room full of decaying manuscripts. He did not talk much about his time at Summerlawn. Moira Kennedy returned to the subject again and again, nervously eager to extract what information she could about Rosewicz and his library. He told her as little as possible.

'Rosewicz is a key figure in the black market,' she told him. 'I've been asking questions. A lot of people know about him, about the way he spends money to get what he wants. But nobody's ever been as close as you. You've got to tell me what you know, Jack. You owe it to scholarship.'

'Come off it, Moira. I owe scholarship nothing. It's a game, and if Rosewicz plays it better than most, good luck to him. He looks after his collection properly, better than some libraries. He has plans to allow limited access to bona fide scholars. That's more than the group working on the Dead Sea Scrolls have ever done. What makes Rosewicz so different?'

He did not know why he was defending his former employer so energetically. They had not parted on the best of terms. And yet he wanted – or part of him wanted – to retain some sort of identification with the man and his collection. There was, Jack thought, a possibility that, once Maria was out of the way, Rosewicz might want him back to complete his work. Jack envisaged major publications to his credit. He had started to think in terms of compensation. He too thought he could play the game.

Denis Boylan rang several times after he got back. Each time Jack fobbed him off with an excuse or had the secretary say that he was in a meeting. It was not that he did not want to see Denis; the man was an old friend, a drinking companion, someone he admired. It was just that Denis wanted him to come back to the world, and that was the one place Jack could not bear to go.

One day, returning from lunch, he found Denis waiting for him at the library, watching the little silver fish swim round and round.

'You're not an easy man to get hold of these days, Jacko.'

'I'm sorry, Denis; I've been busy.'

'The hell you have. Come on, I've got the car outside. We're off to Nesbitt's for a jar and a talk.'

'I'm just back from lunch. I've a pile of work . . .'

'It'll wait. I've been speaking with your boss, the lovely Miss Kennedy. A fine woman, and very understanding. You're excused classes till four o'clock.'

Jack capitulated. He sensed collusion between Boylan and La Kennedy. No doubt information had passed in both directions. Was it friendship that had brought Denis out here, or something else?

It was a short drive to Lower Baggot Street, where Doheny & Nesbitt's was situated. The pub was still full of regulars lingering over lunch. It was a popular haunt for journalists and government officials. Jack recognized several members of parliament arguing heatedly in a corner. Denis ordered two Guinnesses and carried them into one of the snugs. The room was thick with smoke and voices.

'I'm told you're worse than ever after the summer,' Boylan began.

'Worse? What are you talking about? Who says I'm worse?'

'Your delightful boss. Have you never noticed her, Jack? She's got terrific legs. You could do worse than take her to the Eblana some evening. I think you'll find her willing enough.'

'Have you been talking with Moira Kennedy about me?'

'Sure I have. You're a cause for mutual concern.'

'I didn't know you knew one another.'

Boylan took a swig from his glass. White froth attached itself to his upper lip.

'Oh, we've met from time to time.'

'Well, perhaps you should take her out yourself. If you're so fascinated by her legs. You'd be well suited. Now, what did you want to talk with me about?'

Boylan wiped his lip.

'Do you remember when we last met, I told you about a man called O'Mara? A priest.'

'The Gaelic League man?'

'That's him. Well, I found out a queer thing. It seems I was misled. Your boy O'Mara was getting somewhere with his protests after all. He managed to get the local member of parliament on his side, a man called O Murchú – you may have heard of him, he made some daft speeches in

80

the Dáil back in 1951. The time Noel Browne was bringing in the mother and baby scheme. O Murchú was on the church's side. He was in the Archbishop's pocket, so they say. Politically, he had the ear of De Valéra, who was still Taoiseach, and friends in all the right ministries. There was talk of having your man Rosewicz's house taken from him and handed over to the state. There would have been compensation, though far from adequate. A meeting was planned in Cork city. Some bigwigs from Dublin had been sent rail tickets. There was talk of fine speeches to be made. In Irish, Jack. There were to be great speeches in Irish.'

He paused. A bus went past outside, full of passengers.

'But there was no meeting. Father O'Mara was found dead in a field not far from Skibbereen. His back was broken. An accident, by all accounts. They think he fell from a horse. He was a great rider.'

Somewhere a door opened and closed. The hatch to the snug swung back and a hand passed a tray of drinks through the narrow opening.

'You think Rosewicz had him killed?' Jack had barely touched his Guinness.

'Did I say that? Christ, man, I think no such thing. Still, O'Mara's death was peculiar. And, true enough, it was very convenient for Rosewicz. With the priest out of the way, no more was said about the house. O Murchú had other fish to fry. Only . . .'

Boylan frowned. He seemed troubled by something.

'There was one peculiar thing. It happened a few years later. O Murchú seems to have been getting interested in Rosewicz again. The house was in his constituency, and he had friends in the Senate looking for a property in the country, a wee place where they could entertain ambassadors and foreign gentry in style. This is before the days of the EEC, you understand. Foreign trade was hard to come by. There was fresh talk of making your friend Rosewicz an offer he could not well refuse.'

'Rosewicz is not my friend, Denis. I'll beg you to remember that.' The Guinness tasted sour in Jack's mouth, his eyes stung with the rich smoke of a briar pipe nearby.

'As you like. But you do know the man. You have lived with him.' Boylan paused. He had been about to digress. 'Well, not long after Mr O Murchú paid a visit to Summerlawn to lay his cards on the table, as it were, what do you think happens to him?'

'Another broken back, I suppose.'

Denis tutted.

'Now, you do have a suspicious mind, Jack. But you lack the poetic spirit. A broken back would have been all too likely. There was none this time. This time it was a sex scandal. Not the sort they go in for nowadays, the gory details spread all over some tabloid in lurid Technicolor. This was 1952. Sex had not yet been invented in Ireland then. The scandal was restricted to privileged parties. But enough leaked out to finish O Murchú's career. The English newspapers were not so prudish as our own.'

'What was it, an actress?'

Denis shook his head. His hair was thinning at the temples, Jack noticed. He had almost finished his black pint. He had always been a fast drinker, a man who could hold them down well.

'No, a priest. From Maynooth, or so it was rumoured. They were found naked together in a bedsit off Clanbrassil Street. In a bed that had been bought in Clery's bargain basement for ten pounds. Photographs were taken. There was no way out for O Murchú. I am told the young priest committed suicide. There'd be no record of that, of course.'

'A professional job.'

'So it would seem. Well, it finished O Murchú.'

'And you think Stefan Rosewicz was responsible.'

'I reserve judgement, Jack my old son. But I would dearly like to have the goods on the man. I'm planning to call on him tonight. I'm driving down this afternoon.'

Jack stared at him.

'He'll never let you in.'

'Oh, don't worry about that. I know a trick or two.'

Jack explained about the security. About the trip-wires. And the man called Henryk. The information dampened Denis's spirits for a while, but in the space of another Guinness and a bag of bacon-flavoured crisps he was bullish again. He was a journalist, he was trained to overcome obstacles. Jack told him what little he knew of Rosewicz and the life the old man led at Summerlawn. He made no mention of Maria. And he said nothing about the marvellous library and the priceless collection it held. He owed that much to his former employer.

That evening Jack spent with his parents at their house in Terenure. It was four months since he had last been there. For some reason, his visits had been growing less and less frequent since the deaths of Caitlin and Siobhan. He regretted not having known Caitlin's mother and father. Once, on a visit to London, she had taken him to Paddington Cemetery and shown him their graves, side by side, matching marble headstones. He had left flowers, blue delphiniums and a white lily on each grave. Caitlin had seemed strangely cold and inert that day.

In part, he stayed away from his parents for fear that they would intrude on his grief, as though their innocent remarks were fingers plucking at the corners of an unhealed wound. They had loved their granddaughter devotedly and well, and grief for their loss of her was implicit in all they did and said. He could not bear to hear them speak of her, to look at the photographs they kept in an album by the television.

One unexpected result of their unhappiness had been a drifting apart from one another as they entered old age. His mother had become a devout Catholic, his father a regular worshipper at the Machzikei Hadass on Terenure Road. Their rediscovered religiosity only served to increase Jack's own uncertainties. As the only child of a mixed marriage, he had adopted agnosticism at an early age. Now each of his parents separately pressed him to return to an ancestral faith that was as alien to him as that of each was to the other.

He tried to keep the conversation neutral, to talk about his work, about the beauty of a place called Summerlawn, but his mother insisted on bringing out her photographs, on probing for memories, memories he denied. It was not an affectation with him to pretend to such a loss of anchorage. Caitlin had remembered people and places, had recalled events in such precise detail that he had allowed his own memory to wither, unneeded in its shadow. With her death, he found that much of his own past had gone, that whole months and years were little more than jumbled snatches whose sum total was not even days. His mother could not understand and thought he was feigning.

'You'll have to face it sometime, Jack. You can't go on for ever pretending nothing has happened.'

As though he would, as though any of this was a pretence.

They watched television for some sort of comfort: Gay Byrne interviewed a priest from Limerick about celibacy. The telephone lines were crowded by outraged callers for whom permanent virginity was the sole remaining bulwark against the final degeneration of the human race. Jack found them sad, their voices remote and somehow timeless.

'Maureen Lalor called last week,' his mother said. 'She was asking about you.'

An unmarried neighbour, a childhood friend, a sweetheart at sixteen, almost forgotten. One of his mother's weapons in the campaign for his rehabilitation.

He left at eleven, irritated with himself, he did not quite know why. In one pocket he carried a piece of cake his mother had baked that afternoon, soft sponge in a paper napkin. He had promised to visit on Sunday for lunch. Maureen would be there.

The next morning at work he heard on the radio that

Denis Boylan was dead. The details came out later: he had been found at the foot of a cliff not far from Carrigatrough, south of Baltimore. His neck had been broken. They said he had fallen more than a hundred feet. He had slipped on a narrow path.

CHAPTER TEN

It was, perhaps, his familiarity with death, or his too great respect for it, that at first kept him from running to the Gardaí with a story that, on reflection, he knew would not hold water. For one thing, he had no idea how Denis had come by his information about O'Mara and O Murchú. It would, moreover, be shown that he himself had, until recently, been in Rosewicz's employ, and that, for reasons the latter would no doubt leave ambiguous, he had been dismissed from that position. Denis Boylan had been a college chum, little more. If there had been a murder, the Gardaí could, no doubt, find their way to a motive and a suspect without his help. And the cliff paths in that region were, he knew, treacherous even on days without rain.

Moira was not in her office when he reached the library. He had intended to broach with her the subject of her discussions with Boylan, but with the latter's death it seemed, for the time being at least, a little inappropriate.

It was late September, the city skies were white with cloud. Autumnal visitors made their way in pairs through the library, gaping at exotic manuscripts they could not understand. The fish swam in circles in the open pond. Jack stayed in his room translating part of an Essene text, a passage from the Community Rule. He worked from a photograph of the original Qumran scroll that had been slipped to him by Rosewicz. Photographs of the scrolls held by the international team in Jerusalem were virtually impossible to come by. Jack already regretted his breach with Rosewicz: he would have been an invaluable source of information and materials. Perhaps it would still be possible to repair the damage. What, after all, had really happened?

The secretary interrupted him shortly after eleven. Moira Kennedy still had not come in to work.

'I've tried ringing her on and off all morning, Jack, but there's no answer. I hope nothing's wrong.'

'She didn't say anything yesterday about having to go somewhere?'

Mary shook her head.

'When she left yesterday she said she'd see me in the morning.'

'She didn't seem ill?'

'No, she was on top form. She was planning to go to the Gaiety last night with some friends.'

'Do you know who?'

Mary bit her lip.

'A couple of Trustees, I think.'

'Could it have been the Fallons? They're great theatre-goers.'

'I think it was.'

'Could you give Meg Fallon a ring and see if Moira turned up?'

Mary was back in under a minute, shaking her head.

'They waited till the curtain went up, but there was no sign of her. Mrs Fallon says they rang during the interval. There was no answer.'

'I'd better go round. She may have been taken ill.'

'Hang on, Jack – I'll get you a key to her door. She keeps one in her office for fear she'll lock herself out.'

Moira lived in Donnybrook, in one of the tall houses set far back on the left-hand side of Morehampton Road as you go into town. Jack drew up on the wide pavement outside. The air held a smell of rain.

He had never visited Moira at home. She was an experienced spinster who kept her domestic life strictly private.

He knew the house had been left her by her parents, and from a few remarks she had let drop, she had done very little to alter it.

An overgrown garden barricaded the house from the road, a jungle of weeds and grass and unclipped, unloved bushes. The front door badly needed a coat of paint. He rang the bell and waited. No one came. He rang three more times, but there was still no answer. Stepping to a ground-floor window, he tried to look inside, but the glass was thick with dust and grime. It couldn't have been cleaned in years. He could hear the rumble of traffic on the road behind him, but it seemed oddly remote, as though it had no connection to this place. On either side, the houses were quiet.

With the trepidation natural to anyone entering another's house without permission, Jack slipped the key in the lock and twisted it. He pushed the door open nervously, afraid to make a noise, yet trying not to seem like a burglar. If Moira was lying in the house ill, he did not want to startle her.

Even for a dull day, the hallway was surprisingly dark. The fanlight, like the window, was small and grubby, and let in very little light. Jack fumbled and found a switch. A 40-watt bulb went on somewhere overhead.

He was in a narrow hallway made even narrower by bookshelves that ran from floor to ceiling along either side. It came back to him that Moira had once mentioned that her parents had owned a secondhand bookshop on Aston Quay. She had told him that the stock had come to her with the house, that the place was coming down with books, but that she could not bear to part with them. Or did not have the energy.

Silence. The house could not have been touched since her parents' death. He did not think anyone had set a hand to the shelves, whether to take down a book or to dust them, since then. Both books and shelves were thick with dust and cobwebs. Jack found himself instinctively keeping to the centre of the hall, as far as possible from the long, shadowy rows and their accumulated filth. He noticed that a stale odour hung over everything, an odour compounded of food smells, damp, and old books.

Squalor and books were everywhere. Had it not been that the key had fitted the lock, he would readily have believed himself in the wrong house. He had known Moira for years, though not well, and never had it crossed his mind that she might live in such a place, under such dark conditions.

'Moira,' he called, his voice ridiculously muted. 'It's me, Moira, Jack Gould. Can you hear me?' There was no reply. He tried again, louder this time, the words disappearing in the stale air, deadened by mounds of paper. He stood in the silence, awaiting a reply, feeling foolish and frightened at the same time. The house did not feel welcoming. On the whole, he hoped she was not here after all. He had come into her sanctum, seen her dirty little secret; her embarrassment would make relations between them almost impossible. There was a faint smell of gas somewhere.

He let himself into each of the downstairs rooms in turn. There was no sign of Moira. He wondered how she had endured to live here, with her long legs and her well-groomed hair. Dark, untended rooms stuffed with piles of rotting books, the carcases of magazines, old, dingy furniture that seemed to date back to the forties or fifties, horse-hair sofas, worn leather armchairs, tables unsteady with the bric-à-brac of decades, curtains drawn, no light anywhere. Spiders crouched everywhere, there was evidence of mice. Damp patches on the walls and ceilings. Cobwebs thick with old dust. Corners full of shadows.

The kitchen was a mess. The sink and draining-board were cluttered with unwashed plates. A mousetrap in one corner still had an occupant. The contents of a kitchen drawer had been emptied on to the table and left there, spoons, forks, knives, a whisk, a cheese grater, a broken bread-knife. The calendar on one wall was for 1967. The smell of gas came from the cooker, which seemed to date from even farther back, and had sprung a leak.

The stairs were almost impassable, cluttered as they were with books and copies of *National Geographic*. As he climbed, he noticed how cold the house was. There was a bathroom on the first floor. Moira had made a little effort here. The bathroom shelves held jars of cream, there was a brand-new toothbrush in a china mug. But the bath itself was old and grimy, the shower-curtain round it stained and greasy. The toilet seat had come half adrift from the screws that held it.

There were three bedrooms on the next floor. Moira was in none of them. He saw his own face dimly reflected in dust-robed mirrors. One bed was unmade, white with crumpled sheets, on the others bare mattresses gathered dust and damp. In the room he took for Moira's, a smell of stale perfume hung on the air. He opened the curtains and saw specks of dust hanging in pale sunlight. The room was strangely cold. Books lined the wall. The sun ran curious patterns across the faded, peeling wallpaper. He felt uneasy, full of fears he could not explain.

Something drew him back to the bathroom. A tap dripped monotonously into the bath; it had long ago left a long rust stain down the side. High up, a skylight filtered light. He drew the shower curtain aside. There was an old fitting, much rusted and pulling away from the wall. Water seeped from the join. The tiles were stained and cracked, the grouting dirty and missing in places. Some of the stains looked like blood.

He felt nauseated. As though this room, this house were vermin-infested. His bladder felt queer, suddenly and acutely full. He lifted the toilet seat and urinated. A stream of yellow urine filled the bowl. Something in the air made his head light. Beneath the perfume of bathroom creams and soft oils, another scent lurked, sickly and disturbing. He rested his hand on the edge of the bath. There was something resting near the plughole. He bent down and picked it up. It was a small tooth with blood on the root. He dropped it, and it fell back with a dull click.

Moira was not here. He would have to go back to the library and start ringing round. He zipped up his trousers and pulled the chain. Nothing happened. It was as though the cistern had dried up. He felt embarrassed to leave evidence of his visit in the bowl. Reaching up, he pulled harder this time.

This time the cistern responded, but grudgingly. Water seeped into the bowl and, as it did so, the waste water began to sink, then backed up, as though there were a blockage further back. Old plumbing, badly looked after; how could she live with it? he thought.

The water began to change colour. The yellow took on a tinge of pink that slowly darkened. There was a gurgle and something forced its way back through the pipe and into the bowl. He looked at it in fascination. It was a clump of hair, human hair, long and frondlike. There were ugly clumps at the ends, like skin.

CHAPTER ELEVEN

There followed days like ice, days when everything seemed frozen and unmoving, yet volatile at heart. The image of the sodden hair stayed with him, he could not wash it out of his brain. Even from between the lines of dry manuscripts it rose up to him, tangled and bloody. He could not work for fear of it. In the small hours, it woke him, naked in a sweat-cold bed, a silent thing coated in darkness. He had to wash his hands and sit in the harsh light of his bathroom, shivering until the horror passed away.

They had found her in small parcels behind various rows of books. He had not been there to watch, but in his dreams he relived it all the same, just as he relived that other death he had never seen. Forensic evidence suggested that the butchery had been carried out in the bath, behind the shower curtain.

The Gardaí had questioned Jack intensively, but in the end there had been very little he could tell them. The link between Moira and Denis Boylan had been insubstantial, and though they took a note of it, he could see that they allowed it little weight. He mentioned Rosewicz's name and Boylan's suspicions; but their minds were fixed on finding a psychopath, and he knew they would waste no time on anything so tenuous. Nor did he much believe it himself.

It was three weeks before he noticed that Moira's papers had been tampered with. And very cleverly tampered with too. Jack had taken over her duties for the time being, and had spent some time every day going through her files. It was not a difficult task, for Moira, in stark contrast to her domestic life, had been almost fanatically tidy at work. It was that that alerted him, a marked discrepancy between the perfect catalogue she kept of new acquisitions and borrowings and the jumbled state of the materials themselves, that and the careless way some of the papyri had been handled.

He noticed that the focus of the intruder's attention had been a large collection of early Christian manuscripts sent to the Chester Beatty for examination a few months earlier from Humboldt University in East Berlin. Moira had been working on them before her murder. Jack spent several days going through the files, and in the end was able to reassure himself that nothing was missing, although several items had been replaced in the wrong cabinet. The only other person with normal access to this part of the collection was himself, and he knew he had not caused such disarray.

Had Moira been killed in pursuit of a valuable manuscript? His thoughts ran to Rosewicz again, and for a while he thought seriously of approaching the Gardaí with what seemed like further evidence linking the Pole to Moira's death. But it was too flimsy. And he did not think that Rosewicz would have had Moira killed merely to acquire a papyrus, however valuable.

For one thing, a manuscript from the Chester Beatty would be much too easy to identify. And Jack knew that, in the world Stefan Rosewicz inhabited, there were easier ways of getting what you wanted. He spent a week going through the collection carefully. Nothing was missing. Could someone have been looking for an item that was not there? Or simply failed to recognize it? Had Moira's death and the search of her papers been unconnected? He remembered the time someone had rifled through his study in Paris.

In early November the Board of Trustees approached him with an offer of Moira's job. He spent a week thinking about it and had almost decided to accept when something came out of the blue that made him change his mind.

It was a letter from Yigael Goren in Jerusalem, offering him a job. Jack had spent over a year at Yigael's Biblical Institute at the Hebrew University as part of his post-graduate work. Now, he wrote, a vacancy had come up which needed to be filled by someone with precisely Jack's qualifications. There would be a two-year contract in the first instance, renewable. The salary would match or better whatever he was now being paid in Dublin.

Jack's first impulse was to turn Yigael down. However come by, his imminent promotion meant something to him. But not enough. He thought of winter in Dublin, of summer memories, of next year and the year after, of how his life was stuck fast in something very like glue. That evening, bewildered by this new possibility, he went for a long walk by the shore, watching gulls rise from the water's edge on Sandymount Strand. There was gold somewhere, very far away, on the edge of mountains at the sea's extremity. He stayed until it faded and grew dark.

On his way back, passing the rugby grounds on Lansdowne Road, he thought he saw a man standing watching him from the shadows. When he looked again, there was no one there. He could not be certain, but something had made him think the man was Stefan Rosewicz's guard, Henryk.

When he returned to his flat, there was an edge of winter in the air. Lights had gone on behind the windows opposite. He picked up his pen.

'Dear Yigael,' he wrote, 'your letter reached me just in time . . .'

Two days before his flight, he drove south again. There was no sunlight this time, no sense of liberation as he drove out of the city. He came to Summerlawn on a bleak day in a bleak month, with no real aim in view. To see the house, that was all. So he told himself.

He drew up near the gate and sat watching from a distance, though he did not know exactly what he was watching for. Once or twice, he thought he saw a face at an upper window, but he could not be sure, could not even tell if anyone was still living there. What if she were there, what if she were to drive past him in her car? He had not thought what he might do. Evening fell. Behind the house, he could hear the sea moving in its deep bed.

PART TWO

CHAPTER TWELVE

Catholic Institute for Biblical Studies
The Old City
Jerusalem

Father Raymond Benveniste took a handkerchief from his pocket, coughed into it, and replaced it. He was finding it hard to throw off the cold he had caught at the coast two weeks earlier. He slipped on a pair of spectacles and adjusted them behind his ears.

On the desk in front of him lay a papyrus fragment sixteen centimetres by twenty-one. It contained thirty lines of Aramaic writing, marred here and there by holes or smudges, but generally legible. It had been reliably dated to the early first century, almost certainly before the destruction of the Temple. Jacques de Sacy had found it about six months earlier, among a heap of other papers, in an excavation below the Temple wall.

It was not of much importance in itself. Just a letter to a Temple functionary from an unknown correspondent. Most of it seemed to be about taxes of some kind. Ordinarily, Benveniste would have passed it on for further study and eventual publication in an issue of the Institute's quarterly journal. But for one thing.

The fragment contained a reference, admittedly brief, to 'the followers of Jesus', a group seemingly attached to the Temple in some way and 'zealous for the Law of Moses'. There were, of course, several possible interpretations of the passage. On its own, it would send out few ripples. The director was half minded to let it go on its way.

But there were people in Rome who preferred caution above

all things. On his last visit, Della Gherardesca of the Biblical Commission had spoken frankly with him. A number of books had been published recently, suggesting that Jesus Christ had been little more than a Hasid, a Jewish holy man, and that his father had been a scholar, a naggar – the Aramaic word for 'carpenter' used metaphorically. The early church too, it was suggested more and more frequently, and not only in scholarly circles, had been less radical than the supporters of Saint Paul would have had the world believe. The first Christians had considered themselves Jews and been steadfast in their observance of Jewish law. Such ideas were heresy and liable to lead to greater heresy. Everything possible should be done to resist them.

Benveniste looked at the scrap of papyrus again. It was hardly important. But it could be considered yet another piece of confirmation for such scandalous theories. In the wrong hands it could be put to wicked use.

He took a box of matches from his pocket. As a scholar, he was ashamed of what he was about to do. As a priest, he had been trained in obedience. His hand did not even shake as he struck the match.

CHAPTER THIRTEEN

Dublin
4 November 1992

The sun had been shining when he left Jerusalem. In Dublin it seemed as though the same rain was falling that had been falling when he left four years earlier. Stepping from the plane was, inevitably, one of those moments when you have to ask yourself whether you have changed or stood still. He did not yet know the answer. First, he had things to do. He had come to Dublin to bury his mother. A long journey, he thought, for such a small ceremony.

His own flat had been rented out, so he stayed with his father in Terenure. Jack's parents had had no other children; he and his father were alone, with very different griefs. It would be a desolate burial, Jack thought, and he was not proved wrong. Himself excepted, all the people there were old. Their white hair sang out in the graveside wind. They watched the polished coffin slip to its place like children who hear voices others can not. They were docile and attentive, careful as they walked away in pairs or singly. He held his father's thin arm throughout, as though he feared the old man's weakness. He could not summon tears.

Caitlin and Siobhan were buried in the same cemetery, a little to the east. Their grave was cared for, fresh with winter flowers. Jack sent his father money regularly to make sure that flowers grew there in all seasons. When the funeral was over and the old man had said his farewells, he and Jack went across to Caitlin and Siobhan's grave. Jack had brought roses. Their redness was like a miracle against the white marble. He read the names in the stone, as though he still did not believe them. Above his head a bird flew across the graves. And he thought of a falling of sea-gulls against Howth Head, and his life tumbling to the rocks beneath.

They went home together, and in private they said Jewish prayers. Jack recited the Kaddish elegantly, for his father's comfort, not his own. His Hebrew had become fluent in the past two years.

'What will you do now?' he asked when they were alone and struggling for conversation.

'Do? What is there to do, Jack? Your mother's dead, I'll follow her soon. I don't have to do anything.'

'This isn't like you, Father. I don't remember you speaking like this before.'

'Your mother wasn't dead before. I wasn't old.'

'You're not so old. Seventy isn't old nowadays. You're still healthy. You told me that when you left the camp you were like an old man. You were probably less healthy then.'

'I was twenty-three. The war had ended and I was free, really free for the first time in my life. I felt I could go anywhere, become anything.'

All around them, the room shimmered with Jack's past. Walls crammed with photographs, familiar objects that should have been thrown out long ago, the first books he had ever read. In an unnatural reversal of roles, Jack attempted to instruct his father in the nature of grief.

'Come back to Israel with me,' he said. 'It's not too late to make *aliya*. Perhaps you can find some old friends.'

'All my friends are dead. I was the only survivor.'

Old wounds. Jack should have known better than to touch them, now above all, when a new one had just been opened.

'Think about it,' he said. 'You could live with me in Jerusalem.'

'No, Jack. I feel tired. Very tired. Not even Jerusalem could change that.'

'It will pass.'

His father raised an eyebrow. Jack remembered the gesture from his childhood. He had first learnt about irony from his father. He had been a schoolteacher at Stratford College, a mathematician.

'Will it?' asked the old man.

Jack did not answer. He was tired too.

On the following day he visited the library. A lot had changed. There was a new Head Curator, a new Curator of Western Manuscripts, and a new man in Jack's old post, Carmody by name. But Mary was still there. And the fish still swam in the pond.

There was a pleasant lunch followed by a walk through quiet streets, then an afternoon spent in professional conversation with Carmody. When they had finished, they went into the grounds together for a smoke. There had been no further leads in the search for Moira's killer, Carmody said. He was a young, red-haired man from Meath, fresh out of college, eager to please. A Gaelic footballer by the look of him, Jack thought. The product of a Christian Brothers education, drawn to Oriental Languages through a much-praised felicity in Irish and Latin.

'Tell me,' Jack said as he was on the verge of leaving, 'do you ever hear tell of a man called Rosewicz?'

Carmody looked at him blankly.

'Should I?' he asked.

'I thought you might have done. No letters from a place called Summerlawn? Down in County Cork.'

Carmody shook his head.

'Not Cork,' he said. 'Is he a friend of yours?'

'No,' said Jack, 'not a friend. Just someone I used to know.'

* * *

That evening he tried ringing Summerlawn. Something seemed to be wrong with the line. After several attempts, he rang the operator. The number had been disconnected. No, they could not tell him when.

He dreamed of Maria that night, vividly, and in the morning decided to drive down. He did not know why. Someone in Baltimore might know something. His father seemed less withdrawn. Friends would be calling for lunch. Jack promised he would be back by the next day at the latest.

The journey down was uneventful. Grey light on green hills, a cold wind testing the ground for the coming winter, birds rising out of bare trees. After the dryness of Israel, it came as a shock to be back here. His rented car handled badly, making him tense. He did not intend to wait outside this time.

At Baltimore he was tempted to stop in Noonan's for a drink; but having come this far he was impatient to finish his journey. He headed on down to the coast. The sun slipped out from behind a bank of cloud in the west. It had all been a misunderstanding, he thought, nothing that could not be resolved. Perhaps Maria would be there. Returning to Summerlawn, he indulged himself in make-believe.

Something was not as it should be. He knew it from the moment he entered the little road that led to the house. Superficially, everything seemed as he remembered it. Nothing had changed. And yet, somehow, he knew that everything had changed. Before reaching the gates, he stopped the car and turned off the engine.

He stepped out. In the distance, he could hear the familiar sea-wash. Otherwise, everything was silent. Rounding the bend, he saw the gates a little ahead. They were, unpredictably, wide open. It was not until he was almost within them that he saw it. Even then he could not quite believe what he saw.

Where Summerlawn had stood, there was now a

blackened ruin. As he stood there shaking, he saw a flock of black birds rise up from the cracked and broken shell. They circled it twice, then abruptly wheeled about and headed east.

No one in Baltimore was able to give him very much sense. The house had burned down about a year earlier. The flames had been visible for miles. By the time the firemen from Skibbereen had reached it, there had been nothing for them to do but watch the spectacle. They had neither the equipment nor the training to attempt to save the mansion. Now it was just one more big house waiting for the ivy to cover it.

He asked clumsily if anyone had died in the fire, and was assured that no one had.

'Where's Mr Rosewicz now?' he asked.

No one knew. Or, if they knew, they were not telling. He had gone back to Europe, someone thought. Another man was of the opinion that the Pole had bought a small place in London.

'And his library. Was that destroyed?'

No one knew anything about a library. If it had been in the house, it must have gone up in smoke like everything else. Nothing had been salvaged.

Only as he was driving back did he realize that he had not asked how the fire had been started. Had it been accidental or the work of an arsonist?

It was after nine o'clock when he arrived in Dublin. All the way back his torment at the loss of Summerlawn had been growing, and with it the pain he felt every time he thought back to that last night with Maria. In Israel, the night sky was sometimes filled with stars so huge and so rich that he had at times thought they would in time cure him of the hunger with which he had left Ireland. But tonight he believed he would go crazy if he did not see her again.

The light was on, but his father was not downstairs. Jack

105

went into the kitchen. The remains of a casual meal lay on the table and the draining-board.

He called upstairs, but there was no answer. Sometimes his father fell asleep early. He must have gone to bed, assuming that Jack would not return until the next day.

Later, going to bed after a supper for which he had had little appetite, Jack noticed that the door to his father's bedroom was lying open, and that the light had been left burning. He wondered if his father was reading. The old man sometimes woke in the early hours and read a crime novel.

Putting his head round the door, Jack noticed that his father was, after all, asleep. He had left the light on the bedside table burning. Jack slipped inside and crossed on tiptoe to the other side of the large bed. He had not been in here since he was a small boy. His father seemed peaceful, and he took care not to wake him.

As he bent down to switch off the light, he noticed the letter. And then he saw the empty medicine bottle. Frightened, he looked more closely at his father. What he had taken for peacefulness was something else. Eli Gould had made his own *aliya*; he had gone home in his own time, to his own Jerusalem.

CHAPTER FOURTEEN

He stayed in Dublin only long enough to put his parents' affairs in order. More than that he could not face. He had inherited a house and a little money, enough to give him a modicum of financial security. There would be enough cash from the house sale alone to let him live in Dublin for a time until he decided what he really wanted to do. But he could not make such a decision, at least not yet.

Of one thing he was certain: he could not bear to return to Dublin again, not to live there. Everyone he had loved was either dead or gone. His wife and child lay with his mother in one graveyard, his father, separated by his faith, in another. Maria was married and unreachable. Ireland held nothing for him but grief and disappointment.

On the flight back to Israel he discovered that it was not his parents' deaths that preoccupied him so much as the loss of Summerlawn and all it represented. The house and his memories of it, the memories of an entire summer, returned to his thoughts constantly, unbidden and unwanted. He had been cast out of paradise, or so at times it seemed; and now there was no way back. Over the droning of the jet engines he could hear the murmur of waves and the sound of nimble feet on sand. Once, when he closed his eyes, he thought he saw Maria running away from him across a green field. As she ran, she threw a red ball in the air, catching it and throwing it high again. He tried to call out, to warn her of the cliff ahead. Suddenly, she turned and smiled at him, and it was Caitlin's face that he saw.

There was a letter waiting for him when he got back. It bore a Moscow postmark. It was the first time Jack had seen one of the new Russian Republic stamps. He guessed the identity of the writer before opening the envelope.

Iosif Sharanskii was Professor of Middle Eastern Languages at Moscow University. He and Jack had met at several international conferences, and over the years their acquaintance had ripened into a close friendship that endured in spite of very little contact. Under Communist rule, it had been impossible for Iosif, who was Jewish, to get permission to visit Israel, for fear he might not come back. In consequence, all his work on biblical history had been done at one remove, as it were. In spite of that, the quality of his writing had won him great respect, mainly outside Russia. Apart from articles in his own language, he had contributed numerous English pieces to international publications such as the *Journal of Semitic Studies* and the *Zeitschrift für neutestamentliche Wissenschaft*. All were penned in a fluent if idiosyncratic style that gave even the driest study a lightness of touch and frequent, unintended humour.

The letter had been typed on an old Olivetti portable that Jack had given to Iosif years ago, on his fortieth birthday. The 'v' key had been broken and never replaced, so Iosif used the 'u' instead. It gave his letters a curious, medieval appearance. The thin paper and uneven letterhead were even shabbier than their Soviet predecessors. It looked as though nothing had changed for the better.

Dear Jack,
It is now a long time that you haue not written. I think perhaps you do not remember your old friend so much. I think of you uery often, sometimes with tears. And now I think of you liuing and working in Jerusalem,

and I am sure I will be with you soon. I may euen make *aliya*, but not yet. Now that I am free to go, the need is not so great.

Here, things are not so good. The people suffer uery much, but what can we do? Haue another reuolution? No, we just keep waiting, like always. Like your Mr Micawber, we wait for something to turn up. Perhaps it is worse than before, I do not know. Some people say so, but I think they are wrong. Before, I could not make *aliya*, now euen that is possible. What are potatoes when you can breathe?

You must come to Moscow as soon as you receiue this letter. It is most urgent, you must not delay. I cannot explain. Euen now, letters are opened. All is not as it seems here. Please do not wait for the next holiday, not euen for the weekend. Euen if your employers do not giue you permission, you must still come. You will understand why when you are here. Forgiue me that I do not explain. I haue my reasons.

If you are writing to your father and mother, greet them for me. I so well remember them from the time I stayed in Dublin. What a louely city, and how sad that you haue left it. And all those charming fish in that little pond. But I think I understand. And I will say no more of that. Leah sends her loue. And little Sima, that you haue not seen. You will stay with us this time. No more Hotel Akademicheskaya, no more *dezhurnaya* to bribe with stockings and lipstick.

Your friend,
Iosif

He stepped out on to his balcony. From here on Mount Scopus, he could see the city spread beneath him like a model village, and, far beyond it to the east, the Dead Sea. The afternoon sun flickered on the Dome of the Rock. A city of domes and pinnacles, layer upon layer, like a gigantic cake without iciñg.

109

And behind it all, behind the sunlight and the stones and the centuries of rancour, he saw the burned city, the city of ashes and ruins, Jerusalem fallen. And there, in its midst, surrounded by waters, stood the blackened ruin of Summerlawn, mocking him.

CHAPTER FIFTEEN

Moscow
November 1992

Iosif had changed. Not so much aged as altered, indefinably. Jack was reminded of a fine reproduction of a much-loved painting, in every detail perfect, yet remote in texture from the original. As though the flesh, like paint, had been substituted by something less firm.

'Jack,' said Iosif, embracing his old friend, then holding him at arm's length. They were in the airport concourse, while a crowd of heavily-dressed travellers roared and jabbered all round them with no apparent purpose. 'Why do you look at me so strangely?'

Jack smiled. He found it hard. So much had happened since their last meeting.

'You've changed, Iosif.'

The little professor laughed. He was a short man with a round face and darting, impatient eyes. His cheeks and forehead had the labile grace of clay in the process of being worked. He had once said it was his father's face, but that he was refashioning it. It was still unfinished. There was no image to which he aspired. He wore a fur hat and overcoat, both past their best; Jack had been with him on the day he bought them, in a little *odezhda* on Frunzensky Embankment. Inside the coat Iosif had tucked a bright yellow scarf, the only touch of colour he allowed himself.

'We've all changed, Jack. Look around you. You see? Nothing is the same.'

'It looks much the same to me. Fewer *militsia*, that's all.'

'You aren't looking properly. Later, I'll teach you how. But now, you must come. My family are growing restless. They are asking, where is the famous Jack? So, give me your bags. My car is in the parking lot.'

He pronounced the last sentence casually, but with detectable pride.

'Your car? Then things really have changed, Iosif.'

The Russian snorted, but he was pleased by Jack's reaction.

'You see? What I said. You don't see nothing.'

'How often do I have to tell you, Iosif? English doesn't have a double negative.'

Iosif laughed again and led the way out to the car. It was waiting in the car park nearest the terminal: a little green Moskovich that had seen better days. But it ran, and on special occasions like this Iosif could spare enough 93-octane petrol to use it.

As he loaded Jack's bag into the back of the car, Iosif turned to him. The smile had left his face.

'Jack, I am so sorry to hear about your parents.'

Jack had told Iosif the bad news when he wrote to confirm that he was going to Moscow.

'My father couldn't live without her, you know. I understand. I felt like that when . . .'

He stopped. He had resolved not to talk about the past. Iosif took his arm.

'I am so sorry, Jack. It is too much tragedy for you.'

They got into the car in silence.

They came into the city from the north-west, along the St Petersburg Highway, that had, not so long ago, been the Leningrad Highway. Iosif was probably the worst driver Jack had ever shared a vehicle with. He was grateful that the car's top speed seemed to be around thirty-five miles an hour. Everywhere, the names of streets and buildings had changed.

'Nobody can to find their way now, Jack. Gorky Street is Tverskaya, Chkalova has become Zemlyanoy, Marx Prospekt is Makhovaya Street. We change the names, but they are the same streets.'

They passed the three 'hedgehogs', the rust-coloured anti-tank barriers that marked the furthest extent of the German advance in World War II. There was very little traffic. Some of Moscow's tiny band of car owners had already started putting their treasures away for the winter. Others could not afford to keep theirs on the road. The price of petrol was astronomical.

'How did you manage to get a car, Iosif? I thought they were like gold dust.'

'They are. But more useful I think. I am very lucky, because a friend has been forced to sell it. My cousin Yitzhak, who is now in Israel, sends me a little money, so I can buy it. It is for Sima, for taking her out of Moscow, from the pollution that is getting so bad. I drive her and Leah to the countryside. One day, perhaps, we can have a dacha.'

A sprinkling of frozen snow covered the ground, sparkling in bright sunshine. They crossed the river. On both sides, sombre buildings of neo-classical design lined the road.

'It will not be long before real snow is coming,' said Iosif. 'They say it is to be a hard winter. Of course, every year it is the same, but . . .'

He broke off, glancing with embarrassment at his friend, a half-smile on his lips.

'But . . . ?'

Iosif sighed.

'This year it will be harder than most. I do not mean so much the weather. There is not enough food for so many people. What there is, no one can afford. The fuel for heating is scarce. People who spend on food that they do not to starve will freeze to death. There will be a lot of deaths in Russia this winter.'

Bumping over a rash of potholes, they turned left at the glass and concrete tower of the Gidroproiekt Institute. A tiny red Zaporozhet overtook them on the inside and swung back into the lane in front.

'Youngsters,' muttered Iosif. 'They take risks.'

Jack nodded. He wished he were in the Zaporozhet.

The city was swelling around them now. Tall grey buildings with unwashed windows, trolley-buses carrying silent, grey-faced passengers up and down almost empty roads, a handful of roadside vendors trying to scrape a living in the open market economy of the new Russia.

'Why did you ask me here, Iosif?'

'It needs to be a reason? You don't think is enough to see an old friend?'

'In your letter you said it was urgent. You haven't asked me here to talk about the old days.'

Iosif changed gear clumsily and tried to overtake a bus. But the other driver was more than a match for him. He fell back behind it again.

'I do have reason, Jack. But, please, I prefer we don't talk about it now. You are tired, you should rest. Leah is preparing a meal for you, a special meal in your honour. Sima, she thinks it is a long-lost uncle she is going to meet. She is very excited for meeting you.' He paused. The snow flashed back on either side. The city swallowed them.

'It's important, isn't it?'

Iosif glanced round. A tinge of grey showed behind his cheeks.

'Yes,' he said. 'Very important.'

The Sharanskiis lived in Stavokokyuskenii Pereulek, an alley in the New Arbat, just off what had been Kalinin Prospekt and was now Arbat Street. They were a few hundred yards from the Kalinin Bridge that led across the river to the towering mass of the Ukraina Hotel. Jack had visited them there before, but in the old days it had been illegal for Soviet citizens to provide accommodation for

114

foreign visitors. Their four-room apartment was located in a dark block centred on a courtyard. Built during the Khrushchev era, in the early sixties, it looked a lot more than thirty years old. No sunlight penetrated the yard. In summer it was desolate, in winter a prison. As Iosif led his friend in from the street, where he had left the car, it was starting to grow dark.

'You see, Jack?' Iosif waved an arm, indicating the crumbling façade, the dark, foul-smelling stairs. 'We are free people now. Our homes are our castles.'

But stepping into the apartment was like entering a different world. The little rooms were warm and softly lit. The flames of candles glinted on glass and the brightly polished belly of a samovar. Every available corner had been stuffed with books and papers. Not as Moira's house had been stuffed, full of worms and cobweb curtains, but dusted and ready for use.

Leah stepped forward. There was a brief hush, as though to announce her. Her eyes caught the light. She smiled timidly. *How lovely she is*, Jack thought. She had long, loose hair the colour of jet, pale skin, a tiny waist. Round her neck she wore a silk scarf, a Tree of Life design, which Jack had bought for her at Liberty's.

There had scarcely been time for them to exchange greetings when Jack's attention was drawn by a movement behind Leah. Peering out from behind her mother was the most beautiful child he had ever seen.

'Good-day, Seraphima Iosifovna,' he said, in his best formal Russian.

She did not react self-consciously, did not giggle or simper, but kept her huge black eyes fixed on his as though making up her mind about him. Sima was one of those children who refuse to earn a living by being cute for the entertainment of the adults who come in and out of their lives. She was, at the age of six, already her own person. Adults she judged, not according to the quantity of chocolate bars she thought they might harbour in a coat pocket, but by whatever of their inner qualities made its way to the sunlight. Her eyes were serious. She did not smile gratuitously. But when she did, nobody forgot it.

Jack qualified for a smile. It hit him unawares. In her innocence, Sima tore open wounds. He returned her smile, all the time fearing he would burst into tears. He realized that Leah had noticed.

'I'm pleased to meet you, Uncle Jack,' Sima said in English. 'You're very welcome.'

What little ice there had been was broken. Jack was ushered to a table laid for dinner. On a white cloth a mixture of plates and bowls glittered in candlelight. Iosif and Leah had borrowed pieces from friends in order to have enough for a proper setting. The cutlery was pre-revolutionary, the property of a scientist colleague who could afford to shop for antiques.

The food was delicious. As he ate, Jack realized that the meal must have cost at least a week's wages. Academics had been prized by the Soviet state, but not to the point of being paid well. Now, there was no money to pay anyone. A Russian friend in Jerusalem had told him that a senior academic like Iosif would earn around twenty thousand roubles a month. It sounded a lot, but a boy selling papers on the street could make a thousand a day. Leah, Jack guessed, would have spent a week or more just shopping for the items that had gone into the various dishes, getting what she could on the black market.

Afterwards, they sat in comfortable chairs drinking coffee and peppered vodka from tiny clouded glasses. Jack had brought the coffee. From one of his bags he took other presents. For Leah, stockings, an Hermès scarf, and a pendant engraved with her name in Hebrew letters; for Sima, a similar pendant, together with an enormous box of paints and a thick pad of art paper; and for Iosif computer software and a new edition of the collected poems of Bialik. When thanks for these had subsided, Jack took another box from his bag.

'Here,' he said, passing it to Iosif, 'it's for all of you.'

Iosif unwrapped a slimline video recorder.

'Jack, you should not do this. So much money . . .'

'I suppose you can get these without much trouble now in Moscow?'

'Of course not, but . . .'

'Here, this is to go with it. I'll try to send you more when I can.'

He handed Leah a video cassette of Paradjanov's masterpiece *Nran Gouyne*, or *The Colour of Pomegranates*.

'How . . . ?' She stared at him in astonishment. 'How did you remember?'

She had told him on his previous visit of how she had seen *The Colour of Pomegranates* once at the Oktyabr Cinema and never since.

'Now you can watch it as often as you want,' he said.

'Have you seen it?'

He shook his head.

'Then we watch it tonight. If you are not too tired.'

Iosif interrupted.

'I told Jack he must to get some rest. We have important things to do tomorrow.'

'It's all right,' said Jack. 'I'd like to watch the film.'

But it was not the film he wanted to see. It was their faces as they attached the video to their old Padoga television, nervous that it would not work. Jack had had a friend in Dublin, an acquaintance really, a wealthy man who bought a new television and a new VCR every year, to be sure he had the latest model and the latest attachments, buttons he never used or needed to use. Here, people were still deprived of bare necessities, and something like a video recorder was a luxury to be treasured. In the space of a day, Jack had travelled further than the miles of his journey.

The Colour of Pomegranates was based on the life of Sayat Nova, an 18th-century Armenian poet and monk. There was no dialogue, just readings from his poetry and music.

117

The words were Armenian, which none of them understood unless they followed the English subtitles. But the words really did not matter.

Scene followed scene, not as a story is told, but as though painted miniatures had come to life. Water and blood and the juice of pomegranates ran from frame to frame, tying the poet's life together. A man poured ashes on cloth. A shell lay against a woman's breast. A horse pranced.

It was the most beautiful film Jack had ever seen. Sima sat captivated, though she was too young to understand. For over an hour, they sat together in the tiny, damp-walled room, transported to a magical realm.

Jack fell asleep before it ended. That night he had no dreams.

CHAPTER SIXTEEN

He woke early the next morning in Iosif and Leah's bedroom. They had given up their bed to him, making do with thin mattresses on the floor of their living-cum-dining-room. A little light came through the grimy bedroom window. Through the thin walls, he could hear the sound of voices, a toilet flushing in the flat upstairs, a radio playing Russian pop music. Still only half awake, Jack dressed and made his way to the little bathroom.

When he made his appearance in the living-room, shaved and combed, his hosts were having breakfast. At the small table that served as Iosif's desk, Sima, who had already eaten, was busy painting. She smiled when Jack came in. Her hair had been done in pigtails.

'Thank you,' Leah said. 'The film is very beautiful. Now, when my friends come, I won't have to try explaining what it is like. They can see for themselves.'

'Just make sure your daughter doesn't bring any Ninja Turtles home.'

Leah shook her head in puzzlement.

'Turtles? I'm sorry, I . . .'

'It's not important. Better you never find out.'

Over breakfast, Iosif seemed preoccupied. Leah cast concerned glances in his direction more than once. He made a phone call, speaking quickly in Russian Jack could not follow.

'I have made an appointment for us at the State Library,' he said, putting down the receiver. 'You will remember it as the Lenin Library. They are expecting us at ten o'clock. There's no need to hurry: it isn't far.'

Breakfast was *blinchiki*, buckwheat pancakes stuffed with cheese, washed down with sweet black tea from the samovar. Jack had his with soured cream. The tastes were familiar to him from Israel, but the quality was better. Or perhaps it was just the pleasure of eating breakfast in company for once. In spite of his happiness at being with old friends, he felt impossible sadnesses wash over him at times.

Before she left for school, Sima gave him the painting on which she had been working. It was still wet.

'This is you,' she said in her halting English, 'and this is Mummy, Daddy, and Sima. So you will remember us and come back again.'

Her eyes reminded him of Siobhan's. Grey, serious, full of life. He bent and kissed her. Leah watched in silence.

'*Otvezitie menya, pazhalista, v zoosad?*'

Jack looked round to Leah for help.

'She's asking if you'll take her to the zoo. You must tell her you're much too busy.'

'Of course not. Tell her it would be an honour.'

Leah smiled and translated for him. Sima clapped her hands, picked up her satchel and ran to the door. Leah followed her, telling her to slow down.

Jack watched them go. He had, he thought, quite fallen in love with Sima.

The State Library was situated at the other end of Arbat Street, five enormous grey buildings that took up the whole of a city block. From the high roof, stone figures looked down on the crowds passing below. On higher ground behind the main buildings stood the annexe, a neo-classical mansion known as the Pashkov House, incorporated into what had then been the Lenin Library in 1940. Iosif led the way to the main entrance. At the door, a surly porter informed them that the library was closed. He shook his head, muttering '*Sanitarny den*'.

'What's up?' asked Jack.

'He says it's the cleaning day. They close the library once a month for cleaning. An excuse for a day off, really. And a chance to save on heat and lighting. There have been a lot of cutbacks.'

Iosif turned back to the porter and spoke to him sharply. The man seemed ready to burst into a tirade, then, thinking better of it, stomped off to a telephone in the hallway behind.

A couple of minutes later a man dressed in tweeds appeared, hurrying towards them.

'Iosif! I'm sorry you were kept waiting. Damn these sanitary days. We waste enough time as it is.' He paused, glancing at Jack. 'This must be Dr Gould,' he said, changing to English. He reached out a long hand. On one finger there was a small silver ring. A married man, perhaps. Jack took the hand in his. Iosif introduced them.

'Jack, this is Yuri Volnukhin. Yuri is the new director, appointed after the coup in 1991. He speaks very excellent English.'

Volnukhin wore a bow tie with his tweeds, in self-conscious imitation, Jack surmised, of a professor on a middle-American campus, a teacher of Hemingway and Emily Dickinson. Nabokov's Pnin or Kinbote in his home environment. He would have a briar pipe tucked away in an inside pocket. But unlike his role model, Yuri would have to stretch out his meagre allowance of tobacco for weeks at a time.

'Good to meet you, Mr Volnukhin.'

'Dr Volnukhin, Jack. Yuri has a doctorate in librarianship. He is most eminent.'

Volnukhin waved a hand in disavowal. Jack smiled.

'Dr Volnukhin.'

'I'm pleased to meet you, Dr Gould. My friend Iosif has told me much about you.'

'Not too much, I hope.'

Volnukhin smiled. Jack noticed that his shoes had been freshly stained with blue-black ink that did not quite pass for polish.

'Yes, everything. We Russians keep back nothing now, you know. We are stern adherents of the truth. Isn't that so, Iosif?'

Iosif made a wry grimace, but said nothing.

'Well,' Volnukhin went on, 'I suppose Iosif has told you what we are up to.'

Jack shook his head.

'On the contrary, he's told me nothing.'

The librarian shot a quick glance at Iosif.

'Well, on reflection, perhaps that is just as well. A certain amount of − I will not say secrecy, that is no longer a decent word here, but let me say discretion − a certain amount of discretion is required in this matter. You have been asked here on the recommendation of Dr Sharanskii. He assures me that you can be depended on.'

'Well, I don't know what this is all about, but . . .' Jack hesitated. 'I'm sure I can be trusted to keep a confidence, if that's what's troubling you.'

'No, no, I have no doubt of that.'

The hallway was cold. Far away, a door closed, sending echoes down finely-proportioned passages to their feet. Ahead of them a grand marble staircase led upstairs to the main reading-rooms. Half the light-bulbs had been removed, plunging the interior into a state of permanent twilight. A cleaning woman dragged a mop across a marble floor, leaving a trail of dirty water in her wake.

'Why don't you follow me, Dr Gould? Then I can show you at first hand. It will save time in explanations. The storage vaults are downstairs.'

A metal stairway took them down two floors to a basement. Volnukhin led them through low corridors whose ceilings bulged with thick pipes.

'Please stay close to me, Dr Gould. Some of these passages are unsafe. When they opened the Borovitskaya metro station in 1985, certain basic precautions were not taken. Parts of the building were undermined. We lost over 40,000 books. Masonry still falls from time to time in some of the rooms. It can be most dangerous. But we have no money now to repair the damage.'

They came at last to a heavy metal door. Volnukhin took a key from his pocket and slipped it in the lock. It opened reluctantly, and he pushed the door open.

'Until a few years ago,' the director said, 'this room and the others beyond it were part of the *spetskhran*, the special depository. They were off limits to anyone not on a very select list.'

He flicked a switch and a battery of fluorescent lights began to flicker on overhead.

'Even now,' he continued, 'entry is restricted.'

The room was large, filled with metal cabinets and shelves. The temperature was more balanced here than in the cold rooms upstairs.

'Please, Dr Gould, take a chair. We may as well be comfortable. Would you like some tea or coffee?'

Jack shook his head. He wanted to know what all this was about.

Volnukhin looked at him for a moment, then sat down facing him.

'Very well,' he said, 'let me tell you. What you see around you is booty. Plunder from libraries in eastern Europe and Germany, treasures from Italy. At the end of what we used to call the Great Patriotic War, Russian armies took vast territories from the Third Reich. In the course of the initial occupation, before things had a chance to settle down, a great quantity of artistic and other treasures fell into crates and was accidentally shipped to the Soviet Union.

'Our victorious armies, as I am sure you understand, were not motivated by anything as common as cupidity or a love for plunder. They had marched into Europe to bring freedom and peace to its downtrodden peoples, as is well known. When our leaders discovered so many fine things that had been appropriated by the fascist state, naturally they wished to retrieve them and see them restored to their true owners.

'So convoys were arranged and the fascist loot was brought to safety here, to Mother Russia. Paintings by Rubens and Rembrandt that had been stolen from the Dutch, Leonardos and Caravaggios from Italy, entire galleries of French masterpieces. We liberated the private collections of Hitler and Goebbels. They are still here in Moscow. Priam's treasure, which Schliemann brought to Berlin from Troy is here as well. You would scarcely believe the extent of the wealth they brought here to hide away.

'And books. Thousands of books. From Dresden, Leipzig, Berlin, Magdeburg — all the great libraries of the Reich. Manuscripts, incunabula, lithographs, parchments, books and papers of every description. Most of the written and printed material ended up here. Having liberated them from fascist hands, we made sure they were well protected, by locking them up in these rooms.'

Jack looked at Volnukhin thoughtfully.

'May I?' he asked.

'Yes, of course. Be my guest.'

Jack went to the shelf opposite, filled with oversized leather-bound volumes. He took down a heavy tome and opened it. The title-page described it as the *Libro d'Oro* of Aldus Manutius, printed in Venice in 1497.

'That is the only copy of Manuzio still surviving,' said Volnukhin. 'It is almost priceless.'

From a shelf nearby, Jack lifted down a small-folio book bound in calf.

'What is that?' asked Volnukhin.

'It's by someone called Postellus. The title is in Latin. *De orbis terrae concordia libri quatuor, multijuga eruditione ac pietate referti . . .*'

'Yes, yes, a very rare volume. Guillaume Postel had this edition printed by his friend Oporinus in Basel after the theologians at the Sorbonne refused him permission to publish. It was one of the first books to call for a universal religion and a universal state. In the middle of the sixteenth century.'

Jack returned the book to its place.

'You're very knowledgeable, Dr Volnukhin. I can't see why you want me here. These are fascinating books, but incunabula and rare editions are not my field.'

'I am aware of that. Please, come and sit down.'

Jack settled himself again. Why had Iosif brought him all this way to look at books whose authors and titles Volnukhin could reel off like the alphabet?

'Dr Gould, we face certain problems with regard to these, shall we say, inadvertently acquired treasures. They are part of our Stalinist heritage, and, as you know, that is something we wish to disencumber ourselves of. The books do not belong to us, any more than the Goyas or the Raphaels. They are stolen property. Our problem is this: in many instances, we do not know their provenance. There is no record of their original locations nor of the libraries in which they were found. It is likely to prove a great headache. We wish to restitute them, but we also wish to be scrupulous and restore them only to their legitimate owners. There have already been arguments over some of the paintings and sculptures.'

'What do you hope to get from giving them back?'

Volnukhin looked at him as though he had said something faintly obscene.

'Get? I do not understand.'

'Surely you seek some recompense. If only for the trouble you are taking. Even the finder of stolen property may hope for some reward.'

'We want only goodwill. That is as important to us as money at the moment.'

'Very well. I understand. But I still don't see why you've brought me here.'

Volnukhin glanced at Iosif.

'Dr Sharanskii, perhaps you had better explain.'

CHAPTER SEVENTEEN

Iosif shifted uneasily in his chair.

'Yes, of course. I shall do my best.' He coughed lightly. The book-lined walls absorbed the affectation effortlessly.

'There are,' he began, 'certain categories of material which we are able to trace to an original source, but which still make for us a problem. I refer to a large collection of books and papers taken from the library of the Reichsinstitut for the History of the New Germany. You are familiar with this name?'

Jack shook his head slowly.

'Well, it is a forgotten organization now,' Iosif continued. 'It is deserved to be forgotten. It was set up by the Nazis in the 1930s. Among the subjects that is interesting to them is the question of Jews and Jewish history. This is important for purposes of racial understanding. The director of research into the Jewish problem was a man called Wilhelm Grau. He had an assistant called Karl Georg Kuhn. For a time, they are working with von Mildenstein in the Jewish affairs department of the SD, the Sicherheitsdienst. You know of him?'

Again Jack shook his head.

'Well, he is better known since the trial of Eichmann. Later he is working with the Organization Todt, so he does not much concern us. More interesting is his assistant, Eichmann, who thinks he has become such an expert on the Jews.

'During the war there are many organizations competing to build anti-Jewish libraries and museums. It is a kind of craziness, like everything else that happen then. Everywhere, there are people who say they are researching the Jews. Of course, the purpose of this so-called research was not academic, it was not such work, Jack, as you and I are accustomed to do. These people, they wanted to find what they call evidence for their racial theories. What is the English for such evidence?'

'Bunkum,' Jack said.

They both looked at him blankly.

'Or baloney,' he said. 'They are words you should know.'

Iosif smiled. He thought he knew what Jack meant. In the past seventy years, the Russian language had invented more words for bunkum than English had trademarks.

'So,' Iosif continued, 'in the course of this bunkum, they built up a huge library of Judaica, as well as collections of religious objects. Torah scrolls, *tefillin*, Chanuka menorahs, plates for *seder*, challah cloths. It is . . .' he paused, searching for the right word, 'it is ironic that, even after they have exterminated most of the Jews of Europe, the Nazis themselves were responsible to make survive so much of our heritage.'

He halted, self-conscious at his use of the word 'our'. A few years ago, such an admission would have been unwise. And now? He was not quite sure.

'A great deal of this material was confiscated in Eastern Europe, mostly in the *Generalgouvernement* area of occupied Poland. Also in the Reichsgau Wartheland, in the *Regierungsbezirke*. Some they took also from the rabbinical libraries of Vilna in Lithuania. Also the Yidisher Visenshaftlikher Institut, a most important institute for Jewish research in Vilna. They raided synagogues and yeshivas, Tarbut and Yavneh schools, the homes of rabbis and *tzaddikim*, Jewish clubs and religious libraries. Sometimes they are even disturbing documents that had been placed in *genizas*.'

Catching a look of incomprehension on Volnukhin's face, Jack explained.

'*Genizas* were storehouses where worn-out documents were kept. Sometimes also books that had been removed from circulation. If there was no more room in the cupboards, these pages would be buried in the cemetery. They couldn't be destroyed because they contained God's name.'

Iosif went on.

'So, most of this plunder they send back to Germany and keep in the Institute's own central library or in provincial anti-Jewish libraries. Very little of it is ever read. To them, these books and manuscripts are nothing more than curiosities, the bizarre products of Jewish *Untermenschen*. But, Jack my friend, they were not such bizarres. Not bunkums. Many of them were manuscripts of the first importance. And now they are here.'

'Manuscripts? Jewish manuscripts?'

'Not in the sense I think you mean, Jack. Of course, there are copies of standard sacred texts. Torahs, *megillot*, *midrashim*, different editions of the Talmud, a lot of *siddurs* and *machzor* books. There are important copies of the *Pirke de Rabbi Eliezer* and the *Yalkut Shimeon*. Most of these date from the Middle Ages and later. But there are others. These are not in such good condition. Mostly, I think these rabbis who were keeping them did not know what they were. But they kept them because they had been passed down from their fathers. I will show you soon. You will see them for yourself.'

Iosif took a deep breath. He had come to the crunch now, or as near to it as he dared go in Volnukhin's presence.

'Jack, there are texts here which no trained scholar has ever seen. I cannot be certain, I have not had time for examine even a fraction of them as I should; but I think we have here papyri that date back to the first Christian century, and many earlier. Here are copies of texts that have before been found only at Qumran. Also many from a similar period that are not known from anywhere else.'

'That's crazy,' burst out Jack. 'How could archaeological

finds like that get to ~~Poland or~~ Lithuania? Anything that old has only been found in Egypt or Israel.'

Iosif shook his head.

'You are not using your imagination, Jack my friend. These documents did not get to such places as archaeological finds. Of course, you are right, they are from Israel originally. Or they belong to the Jews of Alexandria or Baghdad. Who knows? But bit by bit they come through the Diaspora to such places as Vilna. Think carefully. The Jews who are arriving first in Europe come to France and Spain and Italy. The Spanish Jews are expelled and become Sephardim. Those who remain in northern France and Germany are Ashkenazim. Many of them, their ancestors have come from such places as Baghdad or Antioch. Years later, they are beginning to move east, and soon they settle in Poland or beyond. Also, others have travelled up the Danube valley. These are coming from Byzantium.

'Now, Jack, it is obvious that any of these Ashkenazim could have such papyri as these, scrolls that fathers have given to their sons, precious relics of the Holy Land from which they have been banished.'

The room filled with silence. It had begun to dawn on Jack just what his friend was saying. If this was true, if these papyri were indeed as authentic as Iosif claimed they were, they could be sitting on top of the most important discovery since the Dead Sea Scrolls. Perhaps even more important. When he spoke again his throat was dry.

'I . . .' He paused, then resumed. 'Iosif, just what is it you want me to do? Why did you ask me to come?'

'I told you these manuscripts they are a problem, Jack. With other books, as you see, there are already tensions. We must be most careful how we return them, who we return them to. But these papyri, they are of a different category. They are not merely valuable, they are without price. We have much to be careful, Jack. The Jewish community of Poland was almost entirely wiped out. What is the proper word?'

'Exterminated?'

Iosif nodded.

'Yes, that is the word. Like vermins, no? So, to find to whom these scrolls belong now would be difficult, maybe impossible. Their owners died in Treblinka and such terrible places. And the children of their owners. So I think it is impossible. We could offer them to the government of Israel, but you must know that for us to do so even now would be sensitive. And there is an added complication. If these manuscripts had remained in the hands of their first owners, of those sad people who died, you know that they would still be buried in those little libraries, those *geniza* storehouses. It is a great irony of history that they have come out of that darkness.'

He looked at the director, then back at Jack.

'Dr Volnukhin believes that we are entitled to some form of compensation if we hand them over. Not for himself, I know this, and I assure you, Jack. You have seen what problems we have here. Even to pay for light-bulbs. Some days there is no light, no heat. Scholars cannot work without those things. And there is much need of research. Even a little compensation it would be great help.'

Volnukhin said nothing, but he nodded at Jack, as though embarrassed to admit that what Iosif said was true, that he was, in a sense, a beggar for other men's crumbs.

'Do you understand some of what I am saying, Jack? What I am trying so hard to say? We need someone to be for us a go-between, someone we can trust. Absolutely trust. It is essential. It must be done.'

Jack sat without moving. He felt as though Iosif had hit him over the head with a heavy object. He still could not take it in properly.

'I . . . I don't know what to say.'

'You do not have to say. You have only to look. Later, you can think and say. But first, first you must see.'

At this point Volnukhin broke in.

'Dr Gould, you do understand what it is we are asking

you to do? I would like you to examine these papyri most carefully in the company of Dr Sharanskii. You may spend as long as you wish on them. I realize that it may take some days, even weeks, to do so properly. You will be welcome to come here as often as you wish, provided, of course, that you are willing to keep what you see to yourself. Dr Sharanskii tells me that you can be trusted, and I believe him.

'I would like you to form a rough estimate of the market value of these materials, and also, if you will, to draw up a list of libraries and other institutions you think are likely to have the funds to purchase them, or to be in a position to raise such funds. We make no conditions, other than that everything sold must be made available to bona fide scholars in the normal manner. There is to be no hoarding. And no sales to private collectors.

'When you have done that, you may, if you agree, begin to make tentative enquiries on our behalf. Needless to say, you will be well recompensed for your labours. I take it you have no immediate objection?'

Jack looked at Volnukhin for a long time without saying anything. Had it not been that Iosif was there, that it was Iosif who had brought him here, he would have walked out. He did not entirely like the sound of what Volnukhin was trying to get him into. If these papyri were half as important as Iosif claimed, the rush to possess them would not be orderly or free of disputes on an international scale.

'I will look at them,' he said. 'That is all I can promise at the moment. To look at them and discuss them with my colleague. Will that be sufficient?'

'Of course. That is all I can expect at this stage. These other matters we can discuss later. And I take it I have your word that you will keep all this to yourself?'

'I have already given it.'

'Yes, of course. Very well, I shall leave you and Dr Sharanskii with your treasures. If you should need anything, I will be in my office. There is a telephone here. The library is at your disposal. All its facilities. Whatever you need, you have only to ask.'

They shook hands lightly and Volnukhin left. For a while neither man spoke. It was Iosif who broke the silence.

'He's a good man, Jack. An honest man. He never belonged to the *nomenklatura*. Two years he is spent in gaol for anti-Soviet behaviour. Six months also in Belye Stolbi.'

Jack had not heard of it.

'It was a *psikhbol'nitsa*. What is the English? A psychiatric hospital. They gave him drugs.'

'He had a breakdown?'

'No, you misunderstand. He said he wants to leave the Soviet Union. A doctor decides he has "misinterpreted the surrounding reality". In such a system, if you are opposed, you can be only two things: a criminal or an insane person.'

'Bad or mad.'

Iosif smiled at the felicity of the phrase.

'Yes,' he said. 'But Yuri Volnukhin is neither. I have known him for a long time.'

'He can smell money, Iosif. Lots of it.'

A pained look crossed Iosif's face.

'Is that so bad? He is director of one of the world's top libraries, yet he is penniless. His budget for next year has been – what is the word? – slashed. I told you: it is not for himself he wants money. It is for scholarship.'

Jack nodded.

'Yes. I'm sorry. You're right. He is doing the right thing. Well, where do we start?'

CHAPTER EIGHTEEN

Iosif guided him to an adjoining room lit by weak fluorescent tubes. A long wooden table had been created out of several smaller ones, and on it a heap of disorganized papers had been laid in a line stretching from one end to the other. Scrolls, codices, papyrus and parchment fragments lay together in no apparent sequence. It was a daunting sight to anyone who knew just how much work would eventually have to go into the task of organizing, preserving and transcribing it all. And that was before the jobs of editing, translating and writing learned commentaries could even begin.

'Do you ever wish you'd gone in for an easy profession, Iosif? Something like nuclear physics?'

'Many times, Jack. Many times. Come, I'll show you what I have been able to identify so far.'

They started at the near end and began to work their way down. Iosif had a small notebook in which he kept details of all the main items. He led Jack through them, singling out some texts for special attention, passing over others with only a few words. As they moved along the table, Jack made fewer and fewer remarks. The scale and apparent quality of the collection was driving him into silence. There were no words adequate to what he saw and touched. He knew with the absolute certainty of long experience that, if scholars were given access to this material, biblical scholarship would advance in the next ten years as far as it might have done in fifty or more.

'It's access, isn't it? That's what you're worrying about. You think this could end up another Dead Sea Scrolls fiasco, with one little group of scholars appointing themselves guardians of the texts, keeping it all to themselves and letting information out as and when they see fit. That's what you're afraid of, isn't it?'

Iosif nodded.

'Yes, Jack, you are quite right. That's something we must to talk about.' He hesitated. Jack noticed that it was not as warm as he had at first thought. Somewhere, water dripped.

'But that is not why I brought you here,' Iosif continued. 'It is not why I am so worried.'

'I don't understand.' There was something in Iosif's manner that made Jack's skin crawl.

'There is something else, Jack; something I did not want to say in front of Volnukhin. He does not know, and I think he should not be told.'

'Told? Told what?'

'You have seen a little of this collection now, Jack. I assure you it is all like this, all high quality, all of the most great antiquity. Myself, I am convinced all is authentic. Even without provenance, I am convinced. I think you too are convinced.'

Jack nodded.

'Yes. If these are forgeries, they're remarkably clever.'

'They are not any forgeries, Jack. Believe me. There are German records, *Aufzeichnungen*. These you can see. Dates, places, very systematic. Unfortunately incomplete. But they tell us that these documents came from places where no one would forge or dream to forge. And such people would not have forged. Not such things like these. It would have been for them a blasphemy.'

He paused.

'What is it, Iosif?'

Iosif shook himself, as though trying to cast off an incubus.

'No matter, Jack. No matter. There is one scroll you have not yet seen. It is over here.'

On a separate table near the side wall, a small collection of scrolls had been laid in a row. Iosif bent down and singled one out. He took it to an empty space and very carefully unrolled one end.

'It is not hard to read,' he said. 'The handwriting is legible.'

Jack swung a lamp over the scroll. It was written on parchment, sturdy Aramaic writing of – when? – the first century, he thought, dark black ink, stained and smudged in places but otherwise legible, as Iosif had said. He began to read.

Neither the roaring of loud waters nor the burning of bright fires shall deflect me from my Covenant with Thee, O Lord, nor shall the Sons of Light find me faithless.

'This sounds familiar,' Jack said. 'As if I've read it before.'

'You cannot have,' Iosif replied without hesitation. 'Believe me, I have looked for parallels. The reference to Sons of Light, that is perhaps familiar.'

'Qumran.'

'Yes, Qumran. There is more like that. Much more.'

'You're saying this is a Qumran scroll? Well, an Essene text at least.'

'Just read. Not so many questions. Keep the questions for later.'

Jack read.

I am in the midst of mine enemies, yet it is as though I dwell in a fortified city, for Thou, O Lord, art a wall unto me and a fortress. I am come unto the wilderness for my habitation, yet it is as though I have a garden of running waters for my abode, for Thou, O Lord, art a river unto me and a plantation of cypresses, pines, and cedars.

'There's a line, then what looks like a letter.'

*To his excellency the High Priest, the Nasri, Lord of the
Sanhedrin, Joseph, may the Lord guide him and cause
him to be brought close to the Law.*

'"Joseph"? I can't think . . .'

'Joseph Caiaphas. He was High Priest for a very long
time, between 18 and 36 AD.'

'Which gives us a period for this letter.'

'You will see.'

Jack caught Iosif's eye. What was it? What was troubling
him?

*What the prophet has said: 'The priest and the prophet
have erred with strong drink'. Your letter came to me today
by the hand of your cousin Simon, my wife's brother, who
is welcome in my house. A righteous man who dwells this
night with the Perfect of the Way and tomorrow departs
once more for Jerusalem, in accordance with the instructions of the procurator . . .*

Jack hesitated.

'I'm not sure of the name. Would it be Valerius?'

Iosif nodded.

'Valerius Gratus.'

'Do we know his dates?'

'From 16 AD to 26 AD, when Pontius Pilatus was
appointed in his place.'

'That narrows this down considerably. Iosif, if this is an
Essene text, it's quite unique. None of the Qumran
material has so much as a date or a name.'

'No, Jack. But, as you see, this is not an internal document. It is a letter addressed to Joseph Caiaphas, to be
given by the hand of his cousin Simon. The writer wants
very much to be understood. It is very important for him.
You will understand.'

Jack went on.

We prayed together above an hour, asking the Lord for His guidance in this affair. For these days are dread days, when the coming of the Messiah is at hand, wherefore the Holy City and its people are in sore need of wisdom and truth. Many stray from the Law, and it is to be feared that the hand of the Lord will lie heavy upon them and that He will bring them to destruction, as He brought the generations before them to dust. Be not afraid, cousin Caiaphas, for the Lord shall be with thee, if you should walk in His ways and honour His Covenant as it is honoured by the Nozrim.

'The Nozrim?'

'He means *Nozrim ha-Brit*, the Keepers of the Covenant. You should know that is a name for the Essenes. As was the Perfect of the Way.'

'Yes. Yes, of course.'

In your gracious letter you ask me to explain all that is fit to be known about myself. Who I consider myself to be and how I came to be known here as the Teacher of Righteousness.

Jack stopped reading.

'Good God, Iosif. I can understand why you were excited. This is from the Moreh ha-Zedek, the Essene leader in person. A letter to the High Priest in Jerusalem.'

Iosif did not say anything. Jack thought he looked pale. What was troubling him so much about the letter? It was an extraordinary find, probably worth all the rest of the collection put together, but Iosif looked as if something nasty had crept up and bitten him.

*Of my family you are well informed. You knew my uncle
Judas, who led the* kanna'im *against the Romans when
I was still a boy.*

'Does he mean Judas of Galilee?'
   'I think so. That was the name they gave his followers.
Kanna'im.'
   'He led a revolt against the Romans in — what?'
   '6 AD.'
   'And the Teacher of Righteousness was his nephew?'
   'It appears that way.'

*And your wife's cousin was my father the rabbi, Joseph
the son of Jacob. My mother, Miryam, was also related to
you by marriage.*

Jack looked up.
   'That's odd, isn't it? I . . .'
   He saw Iosif's face. And, seeing it, he felt his heart go
cold, very cold, and he was gripped by a sudden, impossible
fear.
   'No, Iosif, you don't think . . . ?'
   'Just read, Jack. That is all. You will see.'

*You yourself sent presents at my birth, in congratulation,
for I was my father's first-born, and precious to him. And
it was you yourself who instructed him to name me Yashu',
in honour of your brother of that name.*

He almost let the scroll drop from his fingers. It felt so
heavy, so very heavy. His fingers had gone numb, he could
feel nothing.
   'Yashu',' he whispered. 'Jesus.'
   'It is his life story, Jack. Written by himself. I have read it,
and I know there can be no doubt. In your hand, old friend,
you are holding the first Gospel. The true Gospel. The only
true account of Christ's life. In his own handwriting.'

CHAPTER NINETEEN

Afterwards, in the cold light of day and the even colder light of reason, Jack told himself that the frisson, almost he had said the kick, of realizing what the scroll was had been unnatural, unworthy of a scholar, almost a betrayal. But, he thought, what the hell? How many times do you hold something like that in your hand, how many lifetimes would you have to endure before you touched something like it again? Before you came that close? He knew all that and, as he laid the scroll down, he knew he was frightened. It was just that. Quite honestly, he did not know why. Not yet.

'It can't be genuine,' he said. It seemed the only honest response. Otherwise, he saw ahead of him a descent, a steep slope into superstition and unreason, a land of miracles. He was generations of scholars rolled into one, a Ptolemaic stargazer scoffing at Copernicus, a Victorian churchman railing at Darwin, an allopath from Leipzig deriding Hahnemann.

'It can't be genuine, Iosif. It has "fake" written all over it.'

Iosif shook his large Russian head slowly.

'No, my friend, it has not. You would like it to be so, but I assure you you are mistaken. You do not think, surely, that I would give such a thing to you without reading, without testing? I have devoted months to this letter, I have neglected everything else. It was not the first scroll I found, it had been buried in a heap of papers that looked that they are synagogue accounts. You think it is a forgery? Who would be such a fool as to put his clever forgery in such a place? In some *geniza* in the *shtetl*, first of all, where it is to be forgotten? Then, perhaps he has put it in an SS archive. A very sensible place. Or here, in the locked vaults of the Lenin Library, where no one is admitted.

'There are still caves at Qumran that have not been fully explored. Caves where scrolls were found, but which were only carelessly investigated by Bedouin. There are caves in the wadis near 'Ayn al-Ghuwair, where there are also Essene graves; still these are unexplored. I am sure you know of many excellent places where someone might think he is able to hide a forgery.'

Jack said nothing. Iosif had a point. Why go to such infinite pains to create a document like this and then bury it somewhere it was likely to remain undiscovered?

'I have read it,' Iosif continued, 'until I know it by heart. I have removed a very small portion and had it radiocarbon dated. Its fibres have been analysed, the ink has been subjected to spectrographic analysis. I have not been idle, Jack. The scroll is genuine. The material, the ink, the style of handwriting. Above all, there are numerous passages which correspond exactly to phrases in the Dead Sea Scrolls. The vocabulary is the same. The scroll author talks of "Knowledge", "Faithfulness", "the Glory of the Holy Ones", "the Lords of Evil", "the Eternal Fountain", "the Eternal Secrets", "Mighty Wonders". There is much stress on "Lying" and "the Servants of Darkness". He is writing more than once of *hesed* and *zedek*, loving God and loving your neighbour. You will see when you read. But you know that such phrases are typical of what has been found at Qumran. And you know that the first scrolls from the Dead Sea have not been found until 1947. This is too late for a forger in Poland to know anything of them. Believe me, this scroll, it is the real MacDuff.'

Jack did not correct him. The truth was only beginning to sink in. The frisson was turning into a shudder.

'I can't read it now,' he said. 'It's too much all at once. What else does it say?'

141

'He tells his life. He is born in Galilee, in Capernaum, the son of a rabbi. His family are related to leading members of the priesthood in Jerusalem. That you have read. He is destined himself to be a rabbi, but chooses instead to join the Sect of the New Covenant. In time he becomes their leader, along with his brother James. All this you can read, there are many details.

'But the letter I cannot describe. You must to read it yourself. It is a plea for reconciliation. Joseph Caiaphas, he is a representative of the establishment in Jerusalem, orthodox priests who have accepted to be ruled by Rome. But Jesus and his followers, they are opposed to such a compromise. In his letter, he explains to Caiaphas what has led him to this position. He is what we would today call a Jewish fundamentalist. The Law of Moses, he says, is to be obeyed in all things. Those who infringe it and those who desecrate God's Holy Temple, they must be driven from Israel or put to the sword. It is a call to arms. If the priesthood and the Essenes will join forces, he says, not even the Romans will be able to defeat them.'

Jack listened in silence. If the letter was indeed genuine – and he had great faith in Iosif's scholarly abilities – it would confirm the theories of many historians and explain much that was otherwise inexplicable in the Gospels. How, other than by the use of force, could the meek and mild Jesus and a mere handful of followers have entered the Temple, expelled the moneychangers (whose operations amounted to that of a national bank), remained in the building for several days, and then left unharmed? The Temple had been a vast complex with a staff of 20,000, protected by its own police guard and the nearby Roman garrison of Jerusalem of 500 to 600 men. Why had Jesus numbered at least one Zealot – Simon – among his close followers; why had he told them to sell their cloaks in order to buy swords, and declared that he had come, not to bring peace, but a sword; why had Peter and, it appeared, the rest of the disciples gathered in the Garden of Gethsemane been armed; and, above all, why had Jesus been put to death, not on a charge of blasphemy, but for sedition against the imperial power of Rome?

'It will cause a lot of trouble when it's published,' said Jack.

'That is an understatement, my friend. But it is why I bring you here.'

'I don't understand.'

'Jack, this letter must not to fall into the wrong hands. The team responsible for the study of the Dead Sea Scrolls was made up mostly of Catholic priests and laymen. Other institutes are run by Christian churches or they are staffed by believers, some Catholics, some Protestants. Such people, reading such a letter, they would bury it or destroy it or say it had never existed. Of this I am sure.'

'Yes, I see your point. You want me to ensure that this scroll is placed in safe hands. In reliable hands. But in that case, why not keep it here?'

'I have thought of that, but I am afraid to do so.'

'Afraid?'

It was the first time fear had been mentioned openly between them.

'You do not understand, Jack. You do not live today in Russia, you do not see what is happening. Every day the power of the churches is again growing. And side by side, the power of the Jew-haters. What is your word for them?'

'Anti-Semites.'

'Just so. Neo-fascists. Pamyat' and other groups, they have many members, they have much support among the people. They blame much that is wrong on the Jews. It is what we have seen before in Germany or in Arab countries. Always the Jews, always the conspiracy, always the stupid lies. *The Protocols of the Elders of Zion*, did you know, they were first published in Russia? They were written in France, but it is in St Petersburg they first make their appearance, in an anti-Jewish paper called *Znamya*. They believe so much in this thing here, in this *Zhidmasonstvo*, this conspiracy of Jews and Masons.

'And so, you must think, you must ask, what will happen if such a letter as this is published and it is said that it was found here by a Jew? That the Germans found it in a Jewish library? Do you know what they will say, these marchers for Pamyat', these lovers of Russia? That the Jews hate Jesus Christ, that they are not content to kill him, now they must slander his name and make him one of themselves.'

'But, Iosif, surely that is what will happen no matter where the scroll is published.'

'I understand that. But it must not be Russia. And I think it must not be Israel. In America, perhaps. Or Ireland. Your Chester Beatty Library is very famous, very important. There is very little hatred for Jews in Ireland.'

Jack shook his head.

'Do you know how powerful the Catholic Church still is in Ireland, Iosif? They would have the library shut down. Or they'd burn it down themselves.'

'Well, we must think about this. But, Jack, I want you to take the scroll now. That is why I brought you here. It must leave Russia as soon as possible. I think someone knows it is here. I think they are looking for it.'

As he spoke, Iosif's agitation was visibly growing.

'How is that possible?' Jack asked. 'I thought you were the only person who knew of its existence.'

Iosif bit his lower lip hard. The lines of tension on his face were sharp, as though incised there.

'I did something very stupid, Jack. When I find this scroll, when I realize what it is, I want to tell someone, I am not thinking carefully, I cannot help myself. I think of you, of other colleagues in the West, but you are all far away. And I already sense there is a need to be secret. Volnukhin is no good, he is not a Semiticist, there is so much he will not understand. So I speak to Grigorevitch. Grigorevitch you have not heard of, he is head of my department in the university, he is an Arabist. But he knows also much Hebrew and Aramaic, he can understand.

'At this point, I have read only a little, but I know this is the life of Christ by his own hand, I know what it is we have. So I tell him. He is very pleased, he makes no criticism. After all, he is an atheist, he was a faithful Communist, for him it does not matter if Jesus Christ is the son of God or a Jewish rabbi, what is the difference? So he agrees to keep silent, to tell no one. I am very insistent, and he says he understands, he will be like a cell in the Lubyanka, no one will hear a sound from him. But already I am unhappy, Jack, already I am regretting. I am sure Grigorevitch has told someone.

'And now it is some weeks that I am seeing strangers near my apartment. In the street, sometimes in the *kafemorozhenoe* where I take Sima for ice-cream. When I come here, they follow me. I am very careful, I have been a Jew in Russia all my life, I have a feeling for such things. They watch me, Jack. They cannot come in here, you have seen how this place is locked. Volnukhin I asked to allow no one else to enter. And I think they know that to find the scroll among these papers is not one hour's work or even one day's.

'But they will find a way, I am sure of it. They are already thinking how they can find it. Grigorevitch has much influence, he can have me dismissed, I know he is able. So I wrote to you, I asked you here. You must take the letter, Jack, you must take the scroll out of Russia. Before it is too late.'

They were in a deep, silent place, a room behind thick, silence-mortared walls, with the memory of long-kept secrets printed on every surface. There was a chill on everything, a chill of winter and of something else too: the coming darkness, when a short-lived liberty would crack and give way to sudden, panic-engendered fear. Jack had taken so little account of where he was. He was a bird who had flown a little too far, a little too fast. His wings were tired. He had gone out of sunshine into rain, then, returning through sunshine briefly, to a land where the first snows had started to fall. But that was not it, of course. The weather was only good for metaphor, and he needed something else.

'Who are they, Iosif?' he asked. 'These people who follow you. Do you know?'

Iosif shook his head.

Jack looked down at the table, at the cracked and delicate parchment with its fine handwriting.

Neither the roaring of loud waters nor the burning of bright fires shall deflect me from my Covenant with Thee, O Lord, nor shall the Sons of Light find me faithless.

Why did it feel so familiar?

'Let's go, Iosif,' he said. 'Let's get out of here. I feel in need of a warm fire and a glass of something strong.'

When they left, Iosif switched off the lights, one by one, like windows extinguished in a sinking ship as it plummeted. Outside, the first signs of coming winter were evident everywhere.

CHAPTER TWENTY

They started walking back along Kalinin Prospekt, two men without conversation, wrapped in thought. A few sharp eyes singled Jack out, staring at him unabashedly, curious at his presence. Foreigners were still an unusual sight on a Moscow street, above all in winter. For his own part, Jack could not rid himself of the sensation of being watched, but though he looked round from time to time, he could not identify anyone who called attention to himself. He thought that Iosif, made anxious by his discovery, had been imagining things.

Iosif wanted to call in at Dom Knigi, the huge bookshop at the other end of the Prospekt. He had ordered a copy of the new edition of Sperber's Aramaic Bible several months earlier, and still called in every week or so to enquire if it had yet arrived.

They reached Arbatskaya Ploshchad, the square from which the Arbat branched off to the south-west. A group of young people were sitting at the foot of the Gogol monument, drinking vodka. Iosif pulled Jack away from them. As they neared the Praga Restaurant on one corner, Jack noticed that a disturbance of some sort was taking place nearby. A large crowd had gathered at the top of the Arbat, which had been pedestrianized five years earlier. They went a little closer.

A tall man was standing on a makeshift platform in the centre of the street, between the double row of lamps that lined it, one on either side. The crowd had gathered round him, to listen to what he was saying. Here and there, young helpers were handing out leaflets or selling papers. In spite of the cold, there was a sprinkling of black shirts, some embroidered with what seemed to be a bell. And among the black shirts and the young, bright faces, huddled knots of old men holding themselves painfully erect, their breasts thick with rows of sharply-coloured medals, veterans of the Great Patriotic War, still seeking in patriotism some sort of answer for a lifetime's ills. Jack noticed that several of the bystanders were drunk. One of the helpers came over to them.

'A copy of *Molodaya Gvardia*?'

Iosif pulled on his arm, dragging him away.

'What's wrong, Iosif? Who are they?'

'Pamyat'. *Molodaya Gvardia* is a journal for young nationalists. These are the Jew-haters I am telling you about.'

Iosif's face had grown flushed. He was having difficulty suppressing his anger. Jack looked round. Many of the passers-by seemed indifferent, but none was overtly hostile. Others seemed riveted by the speaker. His amplified voice blared out above the sound of traffic on Kalinin and Gogol Boulevard. Jack noticed that several *militsia* were standing on the edges of the crowd, just watching.

Suddenly, there was a commotion at the back. Someone lifted a banner, then another appeared. There were loud shouts.

'What's going on?'

'They are protesting. Not everyone supports these fascists.'

But at that moment, the *militsia* sprang into action. It was like a replay of the old days, when the KGB would move in on demonstrators in Red Square, tearing down placards, bundling shouting men and women into unmarked vans. The previously idle policemen suddenly moved in on the protesters, using small truncheons to beat them. Within minutes, the Pamyat' meeting was free to continue.

'Let us get away from here,' said Iosif, once more pulling

on Jack's arm. As they re-entered Kalinin Prospekt, they could hear the sound of the speaker's voice, strident and hard, like an echo of other voices, identical hatreds.

'Why don't you leave?' asked Jack. 'You're free to go now. The Hebrew University would welcome you with open arms.'

His friend turned on him, furious.

'Leave?! I cannot leave! Every day, two thousand Jews make request for exit visas. We are already very few, but every year more are leaving. They are running like the rats from a ship. Pamyat' attack us in the street, they burn down Jewish apartments, and the authorities do very little. Even they are afraid. It is so much easier to let Pamyat' make us scaping-goats. Everything that is wrong in Russia now, they say it is the Jews' fault. There is still such a great conspiracy, the imperialists, and the Freemasons, and the Zionists. So everybody applauds and thinks, fine, let the so-terrible Jews leave, let them take their dirty tricks away.

'Jack, this is what was happening in Germany under the Nazis. They want the Jews to leave. They help them go. Eichmann, the one we have just been speaking of, he considers himself a great expert on the Jewish affairs, he calls himself a Zionist, he makes friends with Zionists, he collaborates with Aliyah Beth, because these people want Jews to emigrate. But before long, it is not enough. If not all Jews will go, they will exterminate them. You know what happens then.

'But if we go, we weaken those who stay behind. And we create atmosphere where these people will find more scaping-goats, more trouble-makers. We must resist them. So I stay.'

'What about Leah and Sima? Aren't you worried for them?'

A dark cloud crossed Iosif's face.

'Never say such a thing to me!' he shouted. 'Every day I am worried for them. I am worried for Sima to grow up

149

here, where there is such hatred. But I do not want her to think that the answer to such hatred is to run.'

Panting, he leaned against a wall to collect himself.

'I am sorry, Jack,' he said at last. 'I shout at you, and you are only saying the sensible thing, you are only saying what so many friends say. And maybe you are right. Maybe I have not the right to force Leah and Seraphima to remain where there is such risk. But my whole life I have hoped for better than this, and I weep to throw it away. The Communists have gone, there is religious freedom. Here in Moscow Jews are allowed to study Hebrew for the first time in many years. There is now a Jewish Museum being built, there is a Jewish theatre, which we have called Shalom. You are not a proper Jew, I think you do not understand what this means.'

Jack shook his head. When he was younger, his father had spoken like this. 'All the gentle Jews are dead,' he had once told Jack. 'We will not let them do it to us again, we will fight this time.'

'No,' he said. 'I understand. I'm pleased someone has the courage to stand up to them.'

'It is not courage. It is foolishness. But sometimes foolishness is all we have.'

Iosif's anger faded as soon as he got home. Jack marvelled at the calming effect Leah had on him, how her mere presence soothed and softened his old friend. They did not talk about the Pamyat' rally or the discussion that had followed.

Leah had spent the day hunting for food. Jack could not have guessed what sacrifices his friends were making just to feed him. His suggestion of a contribution to the household budget had been rejected emphatically. Leah had shown enormous ingenuity in obtaining the ingredients for that evening's main meal. Now it was winter, prices had started to go sky-high again. She had started early on the other side of town in the *kolkhoz* market on Baumanskaya Ulitsa, from which she had come away triumphantly with two plump chickens. Her friend Katya at the little fruit and vegetable shop on Kuznetsky Most had supplied her with Georgian courgettes, Ukrainian cucumbers, and a bag of apples in return for a bottle of perfume that had been sent as a present from Israel last Rosh ha-Shanah. In other ways, she had obtained cheese, bread, even a bottle of Tsinandali wine.

Jack felt such contentment that evening. It was something he had not experienced in a long time. He told little Sima that he loved her and would marry her one day, and she blushed and asked when he was going to take her to the zoo.

'Would Sunday do?'

She thought for a moment, then nodded vigorously.

'I like the elephants most of all,' she said, using Hebrew, which they had discovered was their best common language. 'My favourite is called Pasha. Do you have elephants in Israel?'

'Yes,' he said, 'in the zoo at Tel Aviv.'

'Do they speak Hebrew?'

'Who?'

'The elephants.'

'Oh, no. They're Indian elephants. They speak Hindi, I think, or Gujarati.'

'That's no good. Even I speak Hebrew, and I don't have an elephant's memory.'

Leah broke in.

'Kiss Uncle Jack goodnight. You'll see him again in the morning.'

She kissed him on the cheek and went off with Leah to her tiny bedroom.

'I meant it,' Jack said to Iosif. 'I'm going to marry her the moment she's sixteen.'

Iosif laughed.

'Is it better now, Jack? The last time, when you were here before, you were a little crazy, I think.'

'I still am. I just don't show it as much.'

'Is that true?'

'You learn to live with it, that's all.'

Iosif opened a fresh bottle of Pertsovka and poured two glasses. Leah returned. Jack noticed that she was tired. She worked three days a week in an art gallery on Kutosovsky Prospekt. Tomorrow was a working day.

'I am asking Jack how he is feeling now. About his sadness.'

'Why do you have to ask?' she said. 'He feels the same way. It is just that he is better at hiding it.'

'I fell in love,' said Jack. And in a rush he told them all about Maria and Summerlawn. Outside, it had started to snow. The room's single stove glowed redly, throwing out a little heat. It was hard to believe that summer had once existed, just as it was difficult to imagine love in any time other than the present. But he had been in love that summer, and, for a little while, he had believed himself loved in return.

Afterwards, Iosif was pensive. When Jack went to bed, vodka-sodden and maudlin, his friend followed him, shutting the door.

'This man Rosewicz,' he said. 'You do not tell me what he is like.'

'Like?'

'What he looks like.'

'Why do you want to know?'

'I think maybe I have heard of him. Maybe I meet him sometime.'

So Jack described the old man as best he could.

'And you don't know what happens to him after this house, this Summerlawns, is burned?'

Jack shook his head.

'I see. Okay, Jack. It is late. I think today has been very hard for you.'

'I've known worse.'

'We will talk more tomorrow. About the scroll. What we must to do.'

*   *   *

Next morning, Iosif's car was gone. He had parked it in the street with neither an alarm nor an immobilizing device. Such things had not been deemed suitable for the great socialist republic in which the car had been built.

'We are truly capitalists now, Jack. We have car thieves. And already we have muggers.'

'Was it parked illegally? Would the police have had it towed away for any reason?'

Iosif shook his head.

'No, is stolen. Only, do not tell Sima, please. It was her pride and joy. I shall tell her it is to storage for the winter, that I have put it there early because of last night's snow. Maybe by spring it is possible to find another.'

But Jack could tell from his friend's long face just how unlikely that was. They were in low spirits as they walked to town.

The morning was wasted in a frustrating visit to Otde-lenie Militsii No. 5 on Arbat Street. It was a three-storey building of dark red stone. The duty officer sat behind a small glass window at the end of a long corridor. A little further, the corridor opened on to a tiny hall. From where they stood, Jack and Iosif could just make out one end of a thick-barred cage in which the previous night's quota of drunks were just becoming conscious.

The duty officer dragged himself away from the riveting business of supervising the cage through a second window and listened to Iosif's story. He passed Iosif a *zajavlenie* on which he was to report the theft and asked him to leave various documents relating to the car. He held out little hope that it might be recovered. Jack noticed that, from the moment his friend gave his Jewish name to the desk officer, the temperature dropped several degrees.

That afternoon, they had a long meeting with Volnukhin.

'Dr Gould has been called back unexpectedly to Israel,' Iosif said. 'He must to leave on Monday. I want him to take one of the documents with him. For sample.'

Volnukhin raised his eyebrows.

'Impossible. I cannot allow materials of such importance to leave the library, much less the country. To leave Russia will require permits from several ministries. It will take a long time.'

'No, Yuri, it must be done by Monday. You have good contacts. You know who to ask.'

'When he returns, it will be ready for him, together with all the papers.'

'No, he cannot return for several months. It is a change of plans, and there is no way to avoid. Please, you must make urgent telephone calls. It is possible if you insist.'

'How can I know the document he takes will be safe? It is a terrible risk.'

'You have my word he can be trusted. It is not of any sense for him to steal one item, when there are so many he can have by being honest.'

'And you think he needs to have such a document?'

'Of course, is essential. Otherwise, no one in Israel will believe such things exist in Russia.'

'Why not just a facsimile?'

Iosif shook his head.

'It is no good. They must examine an original. They must to see that it is genuine. Run tests, examine parchment, handwriting. What I have done. You know all this, you are a librarian.'

Volnukhin hesitated. He looked intently at Jack, as though trying to measure him against some inner standard of probity or greed.

'Very well,' he said. 'You may have whichever piece you want. Provided it is back here by the start of the new year.'

CHAPTER TWENTY-ONE

On Saturday they visited the synagogue on Arkhipov Street. Jack was made welcome, as though his very presence was a token of long-deferred hope. He did not mention, nor did Iosif, that his mother had been a Christian and that he was not even circumcised. The service was brief. Afterwards, Iosif introduced Jack to a tall, thin man in a long overcoat.

'Jack, this is Isaak Moiseyevich Berchik. Isaak is old friend to me. He flies to Eretz Israel tonight. I have asked him to come back with us for lunch.'

All through the meal, they spoke in Hebrew. Berchik was a writer, the author, so he said, of ten unpublished novels. He had never succeeded in becoming a member of the official Writers' Union, had only ever published stories and articles in *samizdat* journals, and had earned his living until now as a bookbinder. A life binding anodyne novels by inferior writers had embittered him. He had hoped that there might be a place for him in the new Russia, but publisher after publisher rejected his manuscripts or made excuses about paper shortages.

He was a nervous man, very intense, and disturbingly humourless. Jack gathered that he spent a lot of time with the Sharanskiis, that they tried to make up for the many deficiencies in his life. He lived alone in a damp, one-room flat, sharing a bathroom and toilet with seven families.

When he spoke, he moved his hands awkwardly, in unsteady gestures. Jack could see that he was eaten up by what he considered to be the unfairness of his treatment at the hands of the authorities.

'The *Goskomizdat* used to say my writing was infantile and repressed, that it showed no understanding of socialist reality. Now the publishers are independent, there are no *Goskomizdats* to look over their shoulders, and they say my work is too gloomy, too rooted in the past, a product of the *Zastoi*.'

He looked round at Iosif.

'I don't know how to explain that to your friend.'

Leah leaned towards Jack.

'It was the period of stagnation under Brezhnev. A bad time for writers, for artists.'

Berchik continued. '"We are putting all that behind us now," they say. "Who wants to be reminded of such times? Take your stories to *Sovietish Heymland*, they will publish them." I say I write in Russian, not Yiddish, and they look surprised.

'And then, of course, there is a new objection. "Russia needs unity above all else," they say. "Everything has broken up, the republics have gone their separate ways, we cannot afford to let things disintegrate further. Jewish separatism represents a threat to Russian unity. Your novels are too cosmopolitan in tone." I tell them I have written nothing about separatism, that I am a Russian like them, a patriot, and they shake their heads and point out the number of Jews leaving Russia for Israel.'

He paused. Jack noticed that his grey eyes flickered, that a nerve in his right cheek pulled the skin back in a small, tight tic.

'So now I shall confirm their prejudices. I shall go to Israel and bind Hebrew books. Maybe someone there will publish my novels. If necessary, I will translate them into Hebrew myself.'

Leah poured wine into Berchik's glass.

'Jack, how about you? Some more?' Her face was solemn. As she poured the wine, she spoke in English to Jack.

'His books are very good, Jack. I have read them all. All he says about publishers here is true. He will never be published in Russia, what he has to say is too uncomfortable, both for the old guard and the new. I am afraid for him. Perhaps you can help him when you get back to Jerusalem. Introduce him to some people who can take care of him.'

Jack nodded.

'Yes, of course. I know some academic presses. One of them also publishes Hebrew prose. They may be interested. And there must be plenty of translators nowadays.'

Leah smiled and poured wine into her own glass.

After lunch, Leah took Sima to play in Gorky Park. The Sharanskiis were not strictly observant and did not spend *shabbat* with any special rigour. And besides, Sima had seen through the story about the car and was badly in need of cheering up.

Jack and Iosif stayed indoors, drinking tea with Berchik. They talked about Israel, and Jack promised he would introduce the writer to various of his friends. He seemed grateful, but even the offer of help did not seem to lift whatever weight it was he carried on his back. It was dark when he left, and very cold. His plane left at nine o'clock.

When he had gone, Jack and Iosif took the opportunity to go through Iosif's transcript of the Jesus scroll in detail. Iosif would read a passage from the Aramaic text, then he and Jack would translate it together, first into Hebrew, then into English. Jack kept a rough copy of the English version.

Caiaphas, Caiaphas, why do you let them desecrate the Temple built by Solomon? Do you not know that the Lord will accept no sacrifice made upon that altar, nor will the smell of burnt offerings be sweet in His nostrils until the abomination that is desolation be taken away from it? I say unto you that this Temple shall be destroyed, and destroyed shall be all who dwell in it.

'He was angry, Jack. If he could have seen what they do to him, all these Christians, how they use him to persecute his own people, how they are killing each other, he would have been even angrier. How unhappy they would be if to meet him, all these true believers with their black Bibles, and their television shows, and their tickets for heaven. No blond hair, Jack, no blue eyes. No, a terrible Jewish fanatic, the thing they have made their nightmares from. How they would crucify him.'

On Sunday, Jack kept his promise to Sima. After the snow it was a clear, sunshine-filled day. They left Iosif and Leah behind and walked to the zoo, not very far away on Bolshaya Gruzinskaya. The loss of the car was forgotten for the moment. Sima ran Jack off his feet, pulling him from the penguins to the lions, from the monkeys to the elephants. Jack generally found zoos depressing places, where miserable creatures paced out asthmatic lives between the bars of stinking cages or in the depths of stone enclosures. Moscow zoo was worse than most. It had been allowed to run down badly. Many of the cages were empty, there was dirt and a foul smell everywhere. But the sunshine and Sima turned even this place into a magical realm in which he could, for a brief moment, forget another child and other elephants.

She would accept only a single ice-cream and turned down the offer of chocolate, tempting as it must have been. Spoilt children had always saddened him, their discontented faces and whining voices, and he prayed that prosperity, if it ever came to Russia, might not create a generation of such unhappy creatures. He was grateful for Sima and her unforced happiness in the simple act of existing.

Once he thought he caught sight of someone watching them. He was reminded of the time in Dublin, when he had fancied he saw Henryk spying on him from a dark corner.

After the zoo, they made their way to the Kalitnikovskii Market. It was a long journey there and back. They took the metro to Taganskaya, then a number 16 trolleybus. Jack had asked permission from the Sharanskiis, who had told him how to get there and what to look for.

The Kalitnikovskii was Moscow's pet market, open only on Saturdays and Sundays. People travelled there in their hundreds to buy birds and fish, dogs and kittens. For people with so little domestic space, it was astonishing how ready they were to share it with animals.

Sima was out of her mind with happiness. She had wanted to come here as long as she could remember, but had always been told to wait for 'another day', that impossibly remote future date to which all children's hopes are relegated. For over an hour she walked entranced among the little cages, stroking gerbils and hamsters, whistling to birds. She fell in love with a small black-and-white kitten, and when Jack asked the stallholder to give it to her she was speechless with delight. She jumped up and down, then ran to him, throwing her arms as far as she could round his waist.

'She's the most wonderful cat in the world,' she declared. 'I shall call her Annushka. And when she's big, we'll come and visit you and Isaak in Jerusalem.'

For a moment he felt like a father with a child again. As he paid, he thought of another child and another kitten. But, miraculously, he found that he was not weeping, but smiling and holding Sima's hand.

On Monday morning Iosif and Jack set out together to visit the various government departments whose permission was necessary for Jack to take a scroll out of Russia legally. They were kept waiting for two hours at the Ministry of

Culture and three at the Central Customs offices. There were forms to complete in triplicate, quadruplicate, and quintuplicate. Old habits die hard, and bureaucratic habits hardest of all. In spite of Iosif's insistence that his guest had to be on a seven o'clock flight that evening, no one showed the least sign of haste.

The last stamp was pressed against Jack's *deklaratsia* at three in the afternoon. They found an empty taxi – Iosif had warned Jack against getting into cabs which already had an occupant – and drove back to the apartment.

'We must celebrate,' Iosif declared. Sima had come home from school and it was one of Leah's free days, so they all trooped off together to the Arbat for coffee and cakes at the Rosa café. Jack remembered the café: it was next door to the passage that led to the police station.

On the way there, Iosif allowed his wife and daughter to get a little ahead, then turned to Jack.

'Jack, I must speak with you.'

He seemed serious. Jack wondered what was wrong.

'What about?'

'It is about Rosewicz. There is something I must ask you.'

'Go ahead.'

'This man you say is called Rosewicz. Tell me, has he any injury you have noticed?'

'Injury?'

'Something that you would see.'

Jack nodded.

'The tip of the little finger of his right hand is missing. But that's all, I think.'

Iosif nodded thoughtfully.

'You are sure?'

'Yes, of course.'

'Then it is as I thought. He is the same Rosewicz. Jack, there is something you must to know about this man. It is most important.'

160

At that moment Sima left Leah and ran back to her father and Jack.

'Look,' she said, 'look! Puppets!'

Someone had put up a little puppet theatre and people were standing around, laughing.

Sima grabbed Iosif's hand, pulling him towards the show. As Jack followed, Iosif turned to him.

'Later, Jack. I will tell you later. At the apartment, before we leave. But it is important. You must know this before you return to Israel.'

There were no black-shirted louts on the street that day, no raucous voices to drown the chatter of pedestrians, no *militsia* with truncheons. The sun was still shining, and Jack regretted having to leave so soon.

They went on to the café. Iosif ordered Jever beer for himself and Jack; Leah and Sima had Coke. They all ate fish sandwiches.

'I shall miss you all,' he said.

'You will be back soon,' said Iosif. 'When this is finished, there are still many more scrolls to be sent abroad. Not so important, perhaps, but of much interest.'

'You will come back and we will find a wife for you,' warned Leah. 'A fat Russian wife to cook *blinis* and darn your socks. A little *khozyaika* from a good Jewish family. You will find what we call a beloved work, a *liubimaya rabota*, and you will have a dozen children.'

Jack laughed.

'No, thank you. I'm content to wait ten years for Sima here. It's all planned, isn't it, Sima?'

'Can Annushka live with us?'

'I expect so.'

'And her kittens?'

Iosif groaned.

'What have you done to us poor innocent people? My daughter is now cat-obsessed. Soon, she is breeding them and our apartment it becomes a cat hotel.'

Jack looked at his watch.

'We'll have to go if I'm to catch that plane.'

'Can I come to the airport too?' asked Sima.

'I'd love you all to come,' said Jack. 'If there's room in the taxi.'

CHAPTER TWENTY-TWO

A taxi was not, after all, necessary. As though by a miracle, when they got back the little green Moskovitch was waiting in the street, almost in exactly the same place Iosif had last left it. There was a man in the grey overcoat and peaked cap of a *militsia* officer standing outside the entrance to their apartment block.

'Dr Sharanskii?' he asked as Iosif approached him. 'Dr Iosif Sharanskii?'

Iosif nodded.

'You reported the theft of a car two days ago. We have now found a vehicle which corresponds to your description. If you will please confirm that this is your car, there will just be a few papers to sign.'

Jack came up behind Iosif. He glanced at the policeman. His face seemed familiar, and Jack guessed he must have seen him on Friday, when they visited the station.

'Is something wrong, Iosif?' he asked.

Iosif shook his head.

'No, it's all right, Jack. He's just bringing back the car.'

The policeman took some papers from his pocket, saying something Jack could not begin to grasp. Iosif turned.

'He says the car has been found earlier this afternoon in Vladikino. There are papers to sign, but to save me trouble, he is now bringing them with him. This way, I do not have to go to the station. Such changes we have had since *perestroika*, Jack. Maybe now I believe what I am reading.'

The bundle of papers seemed formidable all the same.

Iosif fished a bundle of keys out of his pocket, singled one out, and handed them to Jack.

'We do not have so much time to lose, Jack. Here is my key. Do you mind to get your bags yourself?'

'Of course not. There's no need for everyone to go up.'

Jack had packed everything that morning, ready to go. The scroll was in his briefcase, carefully packed in its own cylindrical carrying case.

As he prepared to go up, Sima came towards him.

'I'm coming up to see if Annushka's all right.'

Jack smiled.

'You stay here with your mummy and daddy. I don't have much to carry. I'll bring her down in her basket, and she can come with us to the airport. There'll be room to carry her on your lap.'

Sima's eyes widened with pleasure. Clapping her hands, she rejoined her mother, talking animatedly.

The apartment was on the seventh floor, from which it overlooked the street. The lift, as usual, was out of order, and Jack had to use the stairs. He let himself in and slipped the keys into his pocket. Through the thin walls, he could hear the sounds of neighbouring families, their voices, their televisions, and, from one apartment, a violin playing Telemann hesitantly.

Annushka began to miaow piteously the moment he opened the door of the living-room. He went across to soothe her, but she backed away, hissing. She had not been like that yesterday, or this morning. He wondered what had unsettled her. Then he noticed a puddle on the floor. The stallholder had told Sima she was fully toilet-trained, but Jack thought the animal had seemed a little young for that. He found some tissues in his flight bag and wiped the spot as dry as he could.

'Come along, madam,' he said. 'You're off to the airport to wave goodbye.'

She spat while he lifted her, and tried to claw him; but he was too quick, and the next moment she was safely inside the little wicker basket he had bought for her at the market.

He was about to pick up his bags when it suddenly occurred to him that he was on the verge of leaving without something essential, his English version of the scroll. He wanted to work on it during the flight, so it would be ready for typing as soon as he got back to Jerusalem. He already had a photocopy of Iosif's Aramaic transcription in his briefcase.

The English version would be on Iosif's desk, along with the original Aramaic transcription and a photograph sequence of the scroll itself. They had done a little hurried work together that morning before leaving, and he had forgotten to slip his translation into his briefcase when Iosif said it was time to go.

The top of the desk was virtually bare. No translation, no transcription, no photographs. Surely Leah would not have tidied them away. She had lived with Iosif long enough to know better than to disturb material he had been working on. But Iosif could not have moved them, for he had been with Jack all day, and there had been no time to go near the desk when they came back to pick up Leah and Sima.

Jack felt himself go very cold. He dashed across the room and picked up his briefcase. His fingers fumbled clumsily at the lock. He snapped it open at last, breaking a nail. He looked inside.

The scroll was gone. Panic-stricken, he tipped the contents of the case on to the floor. Files, pads, his laptop all fell out in a heap, but the metal cylinder in which the scroll had been kept was no longer there.

He opened his carry-on bag, the main compartment, then the side pockets, pulling everything in it on to the floor. There was no sign of the scroll.

In his panic, he dashed to the window, looking for Iosif, thinking, perhaps, to attract his attention. He could make them out, Iosif, Leah and Sima, tiny creatures on the pavement far below, just visible in the dim light of a street-lamp. They were making their way to the car. The *militsia* officer seemed to have gone.

As though discovery of the theft had sharpened his thoughts, he realized that something had been troubling him about the militiaman. He remembered the cool reception Iosif had had at the police station the moment he gave a Jewish name. The way the police had stepped in to break up the anti-Pamyat' disturbance. Today's long waits in different government departments.

Such changes we have had since perestroika, Jack. Maybe now I believe what I am reading.

But surely Iosif knew that was nonsense. Surely *militsia* officers did not bring papers by hand to save a Jew a little trouble. Surely they had not started delivering stolen cars to their owners' doors.

He felt his heart stagger to a cold halt. The officer. He remembered where he had seen his face before. Not in the police station. The day before, in the zoo. The face he had thought was watching him.

But why bother with such a charade? Why bother to steal Iosif's car, then bring it back? Why dress as a militia-man? Surely . . . ?

He looked down. They were getting into the little green car, Sima in the back, Leah in front with Iosif. And as he watched them, Jack understood. It was not enough to steal the scroll. They would have to kill Sharanskii and himself in order to keep the whole thing quiet. Someone would have tampered with the car's brakes. Or . . .

The thought was not slow to come. Jack was Irish, after all. A car bomb would be the most efficient way.

He hammered on the glass, shouting, screaming, trying desperately to grab their attention, but he might as well have been on top of the Ukraina Hotel. He tried to open the window, but it was shut fast.

He turned and ran out of the apartment, tearing for the stairs like a man in a nightmare, pursued by demons. No matter how fast he ran and jumped and tumbled down the stairs, he felt as though his feet were encased in lead. He knocked an old lady over, scattering her and her bags. He took the stairs five and six at a time, falling painfully and picking himself up, shouting Iosif's name, Sima's name.

The explosion came as he reached the final flight. The building seemed to rock. There was a cracking in his ears the moment after it, followed by a strict, uncompromising silence. And then a falling of stone and metal. And another silence. A silence that went on for ever and ever, a silence that never stopped.

Outside, a voice cried out in Russian. He was standing still, and his heart inside him. Another voice cried out, and suddenly the world was made of voices. And he came out into the darkness, into the extreme darkness where nothing moved, and the voices washed around him, and a ball bounced and was still, and white birds rushed down from the sky and were suddenly still, and inside his heart was motionless, and inside the silence sank like a stone or a little girl down into water.

PART THREE

CHAPTER TWENTY-THREE

Hard-labour camp 296/14
Nizhnaya Tavda
Tyumen Oblast
Eastern Siberia

It was a long, high room devoid of warmth. Beds stretched down either side, twenty against one wall, twenty facing them, with military precision. It looked like a hospital ward or a barracks, but it was neither. Not quite. The walls were lanced by elongated windows, the glass of which was thick and opaque with frost. The heavy shutters that folded across the windows were kept open during the short hours of daylight and closed when it grew dark. It was growing dark now. Any minute now, Grey Nurse would come along with her long pole, the one with a double hook at one end, to close the shutters for the night. They looked forward to her arrival, for it meant the room would grow a little warmer and they might be able to sleep. And how they loved to sleep. It was the only time, the only time . . .

Grey Nurse didn't speak a word of English, silly cow that she was, but they forgave her that in the moments when she was closing the shutters. Clack, clack, clack, she closed them one at a time. Sometimes a faint chant would go up: 'Shut the shutters, shut the shutters', but she did not understand.

There were three nurses during the day: Grey Nurse, Black Nurse, and White Nurse, so named on account of their uniforms. No one could remember who had first called them that. In fact, there had been a succession of them over the years. Grey Nurse was the tenth or eleventh of that name, Black Nurse the fourteenth, White Nurse the twelfth. Not that anybody remembered exactly. The faces had become blurs in all their memories. And the sound of the shutters at night and morning a blur of sound. Clack, clack, clack.

There she was now, Grey Nurse in her slate-grey uniform, with that funny little hat whose design had not changed in forty years. They used to play games, guessing her real name. But in the end, she stayed Grey Nurse. She always had the same shift, two to ten, and two weeks' holiday every year. White Nurse started the day for them, opening the shutters at 6.00 AM. Black Nurse they only saw at night, sitting at her desk at the end of the room, reading in a tiny pool of light. She'd been there when Seymour was taken away. And Bowers. And Stevenson. There were only twenty-nine of them left now, but no one else was brought in to fill the empty beds.

Always, they talked about the past. About their wives or girlfriends, about their children (those who had any), about old friends. Much of their conversation concerned the war. They were like any group of old soldiers sharing reminiscences. No, not quite. For they had never gone home; not in victory, and not in defeat. It had been almost fifty years.

They really did not know who had won the war. There had been the dreadful film in Friedrichshain, then the war crimes trials. But after that the Russians had come along, and they realized that Jerry had had his come-uppance after all. They thought Stalin must have gone on to take Hitler's place, that Britain and Russia must have gone to war in the end. But surely no war could have lasted that long. Almost fifty years.

It was amazing what they did not know. They had never heard of nuclear weapons, or Jack Kennedy, or moonshots, or the Beatles, or AIDS, or CDs, or Elvis, or

Charles and Diana, or . . . The list of what they did not know was fifty years long. They remembered codewords and passnames and intelligence jargon from a forgotten war. And songs so out of date no one sang them any more.

The last shutter went clack. The only light now was from the low-wattage bulbs that hung from the ceiling. Supper was in an hour. Then a game of cribbage or poker. Then back to bed and the long night.

Down in the corner, Donaldson started to sing. He often did at this time. One of the old songs.

> We'll meet again, don't know where, don't know
>   when,
> But I know we'll meet again some sunny day.

He wavered on for a few bars, then faltered. Lewis picked it up and kept him going, then Dixon joined in.

> And will you please say hello to the folks that I know,
> Tell them I won't be long . . .

CHAPTER TWENTY-FOUR

He was alone. More alone, he thought, than he had ever been. He could not remember how he had been brought here, who had brought him, where he was, where he was to go next. It didn't really matter. He did not want to do anything. All his energies were devoted to one thing only: the act of forgetting.

But he could not forget. Oh yes, he could forget all those incidentals, all those little things that had been washed from his memory like clay through a miner's sieve. But that was only because they had been driven out by those other things, the things he wanted to forget and could not.

As though a tape was running through his brain, he found himself every few minutes standing at the window, watching them get into the car, he heard his voice shouting hoarsely and uselessly into the night, he felt his heart pounding as he ran and stumbled down flight after flight of naked concrete stairs, he heard the world change in a roar. Sometimes he saw Sima running with a ball towards a high cliff, sometimes it was Siobhan getting into the little green car. And when he thought of the cliff, it had changed: it was no longer Howth Head but the clifftop at Summerlawn. And it was not Caitlin who ran after Sima, but Maria.

The room in which he sat was cold and bare, a cell with a low bunk and a single sheet. There was a steel bucket with a lid in one corner. High up, a window let a little light inside. He did not know how long he had been here. They had taken his shoes and tie and watch and belt.

Sometimes they brought him food in a plastic bowl, revolting food that he left until they took it away again. Sometimes there were sounds in the corridor outside, voices speaking in a language he did not understand, footsteps whose purposes he could not even guess.

He fell asleep and woke and fell asleep again. Each time, his dreams were more than he could bear, and each time he awoke he found himself sweating and afraid. He was finding it difficult to keep things apart. Caitlin's face, Maria's face, Leah's face. He was in a zoo, chasing Siobhan, and then he was a tiger in a cage, hungering for blood, and there was a little girl at his feet, her body torn and bleeding. More than once he woke in floods of tears, choking and full of guilt.

'Dr Gould? My name is Shcherbitskii. I have been put in charge of the investigation into your case. How are you feeling?'

'Feeling? I don't know.'

'You have been unwell. We have had to give you drugs. For your own good. Do you understand?'

Jack looked at him blankly. Who was he? What did he want with him?

'You are being kept in a cell at the headquarters of the Moscow Militsia in Petrovka Street. Do you understand that? Do you know where that is?'

He nodded dully. He had never heard of Petrovka Street, but what did it matter where they kept him?

'As I said, you have been unwell. But the doctor who has been looking after you says you are now recovered enough to face interrogation. It is my job to question you. If there is anything you do not understand, you must tell me.'

Jack said nothing. Why didn't they leave him alone? Just let him sleep.

'What drugs?' he asked.

'I'm sorry?'

'What drugs have I been given?'

'Oh, I'm not sure. Andaxin, I think. Aminodin. Do those names mean anything to you?'

He shook his head. Nothing meant anything to him.

'What can you tell me about the deaths of the Sharanskii family? I need to know everything you can tell me. What happened that day, the day before.'

'I don't know anything. I don't remember.'

'You had a shock. I understand that. But if I am to help you, you must give me information.'

'Help me? Why? Why should I need help?'

Shcherbitskii looked at him evenly. Behind his head, an oval hole was set in the door, at eye level. Someone was observing them through it.

'It is possible that you will be charged with complicity in their murder. Do you understand me? Perhaps with the murder itself.'

'Murder? I don't . . . remember. Please, I don't want to talk about this any more. Please leave me alone.'

Shcherbitskii seemed on the point of pressing Jack further, but, sensing the imminence of a despair he was not equipped to handle, he relented.

'Very well,' he said, rising. 'I will come back tomorrow. Think about what I have said. Try hard to remember. Even if it is painful. It is most important for you that you do.'

As he was about to step through the door, Jack called to him.

'Please,' he said, 'ask them to stop the drugs.'

Shcherbitskii frowned.

'They are for your good. You were very depressed. A little crazy.'

'They're making me muddled. Please. If you want to help me, no drugs.'

Shcherbitskii chewed his lip.

'I will see what I can do. I shall return tomorrow.'

They stopped the cocktail of drugs that night. By the next day, he was already beginning to feel more clear-headed.

But as his thoughts sharpened, so did the pain. All that morning, he was racked with grief. And from bitter experience he knew that this was just the beginning.

'How are you today, Dr Gould?' Shcherbitskii was in a benign mood.

'A little better, thank you.'

'The doctor has agreed to stop the drugs on a trial basis. But if you show signs of slipping back, I regret that there will be no choice but to resume treatment.'

'Tell me where I am again. Tell me why I'm here.'

Shcherbitskii repeated what he had said the day before. The policeman was close to retirement. An old hand in a young hand's world. A survivor after the deluge.

He moved his leg slightly to conceal a darn in his worn grey suit.

'And why do they think I had anything to do with the killings?' Jack's voice was tense, barely under control.

Shcherbitskii told him. Jack was an agent of the Zionist state. With Sharanskii out of the way, he hoped to steal a priceless manuscript collection from the State Library and smuggle it to Israel.

'I thought I was in the new Russia,' said Jack. 'Not the Soviet Union. I thought that was all finished with, all that nonsense about the "Zionist State", an international conspiracy. We're all friends now, all that crap is finished.'

Shcherbitskii shook his head ruefully.

'Not to everyone. There are people here who think the Zionists are still the great enemy.'

Jack remembered men in black shirts, a strident voice, an old man in a Cossack uniform.

'So I've heard. Are you one of them? Is that what you believe?'

Shcherbitskii shook his head sadly.

'I'm here to help you. Please remember that, if nothing else. Now, you must try to answer my questions. Why did you help to kill the Sharanskiis?'

The brutality of the question, coming so unexpectedly

behind sympathy, touched a nerve. Jack looked at his interrogator. His eyes had filled with tears. He felt himself close to anger or collapse, he did not know which.

'Kill them? Oh God, you don't understand, do you? How much I loved them.'

And suddenly he found himself shouting. He could not stop himself. He did not know whom he meant, only that whomever he had loved was dead. When the shouting ended, he slumped back on to the bed, weeping openly. Shcherbitskii did not say a word. He did not bend to touch him. Silently, he went to the door. The guard unbolted it, and Shcherbitskii went out.

On the following day, they sat in the same positions, facing one another warily. Jack had been left undrugged for another night. The depression was building in him like a storm. But so was memory.

Shcherbitskii watched him carefully. He was crafting him so finely, he had to be sure his every touch was right.

'Well, doctor, how are you today?'

'Down. Very down. But I'm surviving. I'm sorry I shouted at you yesterday.'

'No, that's all right. You were upset. I upset you. I should not have asked that question. Not in that way. I should have known better. Grief is something I understand.'

'I'm sorry.'

Shcherbitskii smiled weakly and shook his head.

'Not like you,' he said. He looked round the cell. Outside, the grip of winter was tightening on the city. Here, inside, it was cold and damp.

'It's strange,' he said. 'In a way you are all I have left in my life. My wife left me three years ago, my children never visit, my old friends have retired or been kicked out. A bit pathetic, isn't it? You should see my flat. Two rooms in Chimki-Chovrino. I go back there as seldom as I can. I retire myself in a few months. There'll be a state pension, but it's worth next to nothing now. But for the moment,

I have you. You have to believe me, Dr Gould: this is why I want to help you.'

He looked round again, at the unlovely walls.

'Would you like a better room than this?'

Jack shrugged. What difference would that make to anything?

'I do not think you should have been put in such a dismal room. I shall arrange for you to be given better accommodation today. But in return, I seek your co-operation. What can you tell me about the day your friends were killed?'

'Do you still think I killed them?'

Shcherbitskii shook his head.

'I have never thought that. But there are those who do. When they are ready, they will make their move. I would like us to be prepared for them.'

Jack struggled to remember, and bit by bit the details of that fateful day were reconstructed. He told Shcherbitskii all he could, holding back nothing except the identity of the Jesus scroll.

'What was so important about this scroll that you were to take to Israel, the one you say was stolen?'

'It was just part of the collection I told you about. You can ask Volnukhin. He knows all about it.'

'He is being interviewed. And you say this scroll had no special significance?'

Jack shook his head.

'Not as far as I know.'

'Very well. But I have to say that I have a problem about this scroll. It is like this. If it had not been stolen, the matter of the bombing would be very simple, I think. Attacks on Jews have become very common. Some have been killed. The explosion that murdered the Sharanskiis would merely have been an escalation of that. But the theft suggests something else, a tie-in of some kind. Do you not think so? Either that, or the two things are entirely uncon-nected.'

Shcherbitskii looked at his watch.

'I have to go. Look after yourself. Try not to think too much. If you did not kill them, then you are not to blame. And I do not think you killed them.'

At the door, he paused and turned.

'I will speak to the appropriate people about a new room.'

The new room had a proper bed with a warm quilt, an armchair, and a table. They had brought him reading matter, old, tattered copies of *Reader's Digest*. Wanting nothing more demanding, he devoured them avidly and asked for more. A batch of Mills and Boon romances arrived instead. He read them too, and found that he was crying at the sad parts.

'How is Annushka?' he asked when Shcherbitskii turned up again.

'Annushka?'

'The kitten. Si . . . Sima's kitten. She was in the apartment when . . .'

The Russian shook his head. With his cropped hair and stiff little moustache, he might have been a soldier. Or a surgeon. Something hard and uncompromising, a job requiring talent but not emotion.

'I am not sure,' he said. 'But I will ask.'

'I bought her for her. For the child. They shouldn't harm her.'

For a while after that he was racked with tears. They were the first he had shed without the prompting of a maudlin storyline. Shcherbitskii watched and waited. It was how he had spent his life, it was how he would spend the years until he died and was shoved back downwards into a hole in the ground in Tushino cemetery.

'How do you feel now, Jack? May I call you Jack?'

'Jack the Lad, Jack Sprat, the Jack of Hearts. Call me whatever you please. I'm feeling bloody awful.'

'Good. Perhaps you are making progress. Tears are

better than a loss of memory. But now we have to talk again.'

'I don't want to answer any more of your questions. I've told you all I know. You'll just have to find out the rest for yourselves.'

'No, I have no questions today, Jack. Instead, I want you to listen to me. Very carefully. You were lucky I was put on your case. It was an accident, I just happened to be at the station when you were brought in, I just happen to speak fluent English.'

'Very good English. Beautiful English.'

'Thank you. Anyway, that is how it came about that I was given your case. At that time, you were not a suspect, just a foreigner on the loose and a friend of the victims. And a witness, of course. The suspicions came later, they took even me by surprise. And, believe me, I have been in this business a long time. I thought there were no more surprises.'

'Why? Who suspected me? Suspects me?'

'I will come to that later. Or another time. For the moment, you must just listen to me.'

Shcherbitskii paused. Jack noticed that he had a partial denture which fitted him badly. Back home, he thought, he could have that replaced. And, thinking of home, he wondered if he would ever see it again. And then, wondering, he asked himself where home was, and he found he had no answer.

'Jack, I think your life may be in danger. I think that someone, some group of people, wants you killed. Don't ask me how I know this, it is hard to explain. But I have worked inside the system here all my life, and I have an instinct. I am seldom wrong.'

'I thought the system here had changed. I thought all the hardliners had been rooted out.'

Shcherbitskii looked at him almost with disbelief.

'Is that what they tell you there? That there was a coup and a reaction, and suddenly Russia was paradise? Do you think those KGB types just shrugged their shoulders and went home to their wives? There are many dangerous people in Russia still. They have changed their names and the badges they wear, but they are the same people, believe me.'

'Have you spoken to the consul, the Irish consul?'

'There is no consul. There was a diplomatic rift with Ireland two days after you came to this prison. The consul was forced to leave.'

'But . . . that's absurd. Only the English ever have diplomatic rifts with Ireland.'

'Nevertheless, it did happen. And, if I am to be frank, I think it may have been contrived in order to isolate you.'

'But surely . . . Surely Irish nationals are represented by another embassy now.'

'Yes, Italy. And strangely enough, the Italian consul has suddenly gone on leave for a month.'

Jack felt himself go cold. Until now, he had known that he was alone. But until that moment, he had not guessed just how alone and how vulnerable he really was.

'What do you want me to do?'

'I'm going to get you out of here,' Shcherbitskii said. 'Unfortunately, there's nothing I can do until tomorrow morning. At ten o'clock a new sergeant comes on duty. He owes me a favour or two. I've altered your papers to have you transferred to a detention centre on the north of the city. Only I will know you are there. When the Irish consulate is functioning again, I will arrange for a letter to be taken there on your behalf. It will then be up to your own people.'

'Why are you doing this?'

Shcherbitskii shrugged.

'I told you, I'm an unhappy man. You're all there is between me and that flat in Chimki-Chovrino. I want to do something useful before I pack my things. I did unpleasant things under the old system. Now we've got a new system, and the same bastards are still trying to pull strings. I didn't like it then, and I don't like it now. Don't worry. I'll get you out.'

CHAPTER TWENTY-FIVE

He woke to find the room flooded with light and two men standing by his bed, one dressed in a white coat.

'Please to sit up, Dr Gould. Dr Belov would like to examine you.'

'What . . . ?' Jack shook his head. 'What's going on? What time is it?'

'It is three o'clock in the morning. Dr Belov he has been looking after you. He wishes to examine you now. You are to be moved from here.'

Bewildered, Jack sat up. The light made his eyeballs sting. He could not focus on the stranger's face. All he could make out was that the man was wearing a thick grey suit.

'Who are you? Where is Shcherbitskii?'

'Shcherbitskii he has gone home. He is no longer involved with your case. Please to sit up.'

Without waiting for Jack to comply, the man bent down suddenly and took hold of his arm, pulling him up forcibly to a sitting position. The doctor, who had been standing to one side, watched, but did not interfere. Once Jack was upright, however, he moved forward. As he came close, Jack noticed a stain on the lapel of his coat, a little stain that might have been blood.

'I want to see Shcherbitskii. I demand to see him. I won't go anywhere without speaking to him first.'

'Please, Dr Gould, do not make more difficult for yourself.' This from Belov, a stooped and narrow-shouldered man with heavy eyebrows. Jack noticed that he had slender hands, like a woman's, except that the backs of them were matted with thick curls of hair.

The man in the suit nodded at Belov. He was a muscular, well-built man, a compact creature, modest in stature. His hands were clammy as they touched Jack's skin. His face was smooth, as though it had been oiled from birth.

Belov bent down and took something from a little leather bag on the floor. Jack followed the movement.

'I told Shcherbitskii I didn't want any more drugs,' he protested. 'I'm better without them. Don't you understand? I don't want your fucking drugs.'

The doctor raised a syringe and popped the needle through the rubber top of a thick glass vial. Jack struggled, trying to pull away, but the man in the suit held him firmly, without visible effort. His face displayed neither strain nor emotion.

'This will hurt less if you do not struggle,' muttered Belov. Jack's distress seemed to cause him no qualms of conscience.

Jack felt the needle prick his arm, felt it slide painfully beneath his skin. The last thing he remembered was the sound of his own foot kicking the metal leg of the bed in almost perfect time.

'Dr Gould? Dr Gould? Can you hear me?'

The voice was somewhere far, too remote to be of any importance. He kept on dreaming. The dream was not pleasant, but something made him think that coming out of it might be worse.

'Wake up, doctor. I wish to speak with you.'

He dreamed he was in a white room. The room was in a sanatorium. Everything was white: the walls, the ceiling, the curtains, the sheets on the bed. His father was in the bed. For some reason, his father had become a little girl. Her name was on a label at the foot of the bed: Siobhan. But she was whispering another name, a name he could not understand, in a foreign language. Laughter was coming from somewhere. He could hear a ball bouncing as it fell down a long flight of stairs.

'You must wake up now. You have slept long enough.'

He could feel a hand on his shoulder, shaking him. The room vanished abruptly, the bed, his father, Siobhan, all that cruel impersonation.

His eyes opened on another room. It was not unlike the one in his dreams, but less bright, less sharply etched. And it was not his father, but he himself who lay in the bed.

'Good. Very good. Can you hear me now? Can you speak to me?'

'Where am I?'

'Later. Now you must wake up properly.'

It was a woman's voice. Not a kind voice. He turned his head a fraction. She was there, staring down at him, a woman with a thin face and large spectacles.

'Who are you?'

'It is not important. Now you must concentrate on waking up.'

'I am awake.'

He tried to sit up and found that he could not.

'You are strapped down. It is for your own good. It is necessary for you to be immobilized.'

'Where have I been taken?'

The shock of finding himself so helpless had acted like a slap of cold water, bringing him sharply to his senses. He seemed to be in a hospital room of some sort, on a hard bed dressed with starched white sheets.

'It is not important. I wish you to listen carefully to what I say.'

'How can I pay attention when I'm strapped down like this? You don't have to tie me down.'

'We have been advised that it is preferable for you to remain like this. Please do not try to struggle. You will only alarm yourself and make it necessary for you to be forcibly sedated. Now, please pay attention. I wish to ask

186

you about a document. You know which document I mean. It is a scroll which you told Major Shcherbitskii had been stolen from the house of the Jew Sharanskii.'

'Where is Shcherbitskii? I want to see him.'

'He has been taken ill. Put him out of your mind. He can be of no further help to you. Please answer my questions. If you help me, I shall enquire about having you unstrapped. Now, I wish you to tell me all you remember about this scroll. Its origin, its authorship, its content. All that you know.'

He shook his head. How dizzy he felt, how unattached to everything around him. His stomach was simultaneously empty and nauseated.

'I can't remember anything,' he said.

'Yes, if you try, you can remember. If not, you can be helped.'

The vague threat was left hanging in the air.

'It was just what you said, a scroll. First or second century, hard to calculate.'

'Sharanskii had carried out tests. You must have had a more precise dating.'

'These things are not as clear-cut as you imagine.'

'You do not know what I imagine. What I know about "these things". Just answer my questions honestly and all will be well. Lie to me, and it will be less pleasant than this.'

'I'm telling you what I can. What more can I do? The scroll was good-quality parchment. A letter.'

'By whom written?'

'There was no name. The author was an Essene. Does that mean anything to you?'

'You must assume that it does. If I need explanations, I will ask for them. You say this man was an Essene. Go on.'

'That's all. Essenes did not use personal names in their writings. You will know that if you know much about them.'

'Yet you know that this was a letter. To whom addressed?'

'I've told you, no names. They didn't use names. This one was addressed to "my brother", or something like that.'

'Precisely how was it addressed? What words were used? You must remember. The opening lines must have lodged themselves in your mind.'

'It began with a prayer,' he said. He made some lines up, fragments of Aramaic from the store he kept in his head.

And, speaking them, he remembered the real lines that opened the Jesus scroll. He recited them inwardly: *Neither the roaring of loud waters nor the burning of bright fires shall deflect me from my Covenant with Thee, O Lord, nor shall the Sons of Light find me faithless.*

As he did so something jerked to life in his memory. He remembered where he had heard them before. They were not a quotation, not a parallel. They were the opening lines of a scroll that Rosewicz had once asked him about.

Have you ever seen a scroll beginning with those words? . . . Or heard of such a scroll?

No, he thought. Rosewicz had not just asked him about it. Jack remembered the photostat the old man had shown him. His heart went cold as he realized that its opening words had been identical to those of the Jesus scroll itself.

'I do not believe you,' the woman snapped. 'You are holding something back. This scroll was important enough to force someone's hand, to make them steal it and kill anyone who knew of it. Why? What was so important about it?'

Have you ever seen a scroll beginning with those words? . . . Or heard of such a scroll?

What the hell was going on?

'Very well. If you do not tell me voluntarily, then we must help you in your search after truth.'

The woman leaned forward and pressed a small button

set into the wall behind the bed. Jack noticed that she had small, jutting breasts and narrow hips.

Less than a minute passed before the door opened. From where he lay, pinned to the bed, Jack could not see who entered the room. There was a rapid discussion in Russian between the woman and a man. Jack recognized the man's voice as Belov's. He seemed to be arguing with the woman, as though reluctant to carry out instructions she was giving him, but Jack sensed that he was losing the argument.

The woman reappeared at the side of the bed. On the other side was Belov.

'Dr Gould, I am going to give you another injection. It will make you a little drowsy, but will not interfere with your ability to hear and speak. Do you understand? The substance I intend to administer is nothing sinister: a solution of thiopentone sodium, an anaesthetic. It will help you relax and answer the questions being put to you. Please do not try to fight against it, that will not be good for you.'

A needle was inserted into Jack's arm. He could feel the pressure as Belov injected the thiopentone sodium. Within moments, he began to feel relaxed.

'You can open your eyes, Dr Gould.'

The woman was standing over him again.

'How do you feel?'

'Fine. I feel fine.'

'Good. Then I think we can begin again. Who was the author of the scroll that was stolen from Iosif Sharanskii's apartment? The one that begins with the words: *Neither the roaring of loud waters nor the burning of bright fires shall deflect me from my Covenant with Thee, O Lord, nor shall the Sons of Light find me faithless.*'

CHAPTER TWENTY-SIX

'What did Belov say?' Her voice rasped unpleasantly.

The woman who had been interrogating Jack was now in an empty room at the end of the corridor. With her was the man who had taken Jack from his cell at *militsia* headquarters. They were in a wing of Psikhbol'nitsa 3, the psychiatric hospital on Matrosskaya Tishina, next door to the prison.

Notorious for its confinement of political prisoners during the Communist regime, when the KGB had maintained a separate ward there for its own use, the hospital had undergone a radical restructuring of late. Radical, that is, with respect to its former political inmates, rather less so in the case of those consigned there for 'genuine' mental disturbance. And not at all when it came to personnel.

Heads had toppled here and there, a few doctors had discovered vocations in gynaecology, a handful of nurses had been redeployed on *univermag* checkouts. But the old guard was, for the most part, still the old guard. Who, they asked, had the experience to replace them? Who knew the ropes as well as they? Or the straps, the straitjackets, the chemical restraints?

Belov, a mainstay of the Komitet in the old days, a doyen of political medicine, still ran his wards with the same untrammelled clinical freedom he had formerly exercised. And, from time to time, more circumspectly but not less efficiently, he continued to carry out favours on behalf of those of his old friends who still walked the corridors of the security apparatus. Old habits die hard. Some do not die at all.

'He says Gould has had as many drugs as his system will tolerate. If you repeat the thiopentone sodium, you run a serious risk of cardiorespiratory failure.'

'I haven't finished with him.'

'No matter. He's no use to you dead.'

The woman fell silent. The little room which they had chosen for their meeting had been used for the storage of drugs. Its shelves and cupboards were virtually empty. What had not been used had been stolen to be sold on the black market. They were in a place of echoes. Along white corridors of crumbling tiles, tired footsteps and creaking trolleys moved in an unending procession. Doors opened and doors closed, keys turned in heavy locks, the high voices of inmates sang or gibbered or subsided into sobs. Echoes. And faceless, nameless ghosts.

The heavy man's name was Pavlychko. A Ukrainian, he had advanced rapidly through the ranks of the KGB. In Kharkov, as a young recruit, he had shown himself ingenious in the identification and reorientation of potential informants within the burgeoning dissident movement. That had been in the early sixties. Following the successful wave of arrests in 1965, many of which had originated in information wormed by him out of poets and musicians, he had been promoted, sent to Kiev, and put in charge of an anti-dissident programme there. When Andropov created a Fifth Directorate within the KGB for the express purpose of suppressing dissent, Pavlychko had been chosen to head its Kiev branch. A second wave of arrests had followed in 1972.

Lucky, clever, smooth-faced Ostap Pavlychko had progressed to a job in Moscow. When the Fifth Directorate was wound up and made the Directorate for the Protection of the Soviet Constitution, he had been transferred to the notorious Second Chief Directorate, the domestic security service, with the rank of major in Department 17.

Now, like a wingless phoenix, he had risen out of other people's ashes to occupy a key position in postcommunist Russia's own internal security apparatus. He was a dream. No, perhaps not that. A thing of nightmare permitted entry to other men's dreams. And a full and busy time he had of it there. The new world in which he moved was not so very different from the old. Better than most, he knew that his new masters were not in charge, that their dream was rushing to a terrible awakening, and that he, never having shut his eyes, would be ready when the time came for another change.

For all that, he was subtly and vitally afraid of the woman with whom he spoke. Irina Kossenkova had never officially served in any branch of the security apparatus, nor was she now employed officially by the state. This technical independence of officialdom had invested her with an air of mystery that was itself her greatest source of strength and the key to innumerable locked doors. Not knowing quite who she was nor exactly how much power she wielded or did not wield, others were wary of her, and were inclined to bestow on her greater influence than she might otherwise have possessed. Pavlychko knew only too well how dangerous it could be to cross her.

'I'm not so sure,' she said. 'If the people in whom I am interested could be made to believe that he died in the explosion, it could serve my purposes very well. They would not suspect that I or anyone else had spoken with him.'

'That would be very difficult. There have already been reports . . .'

'I want him dead in any case. He knows too much. Too much and too little, a very bad combination. We cannot release him, that is out of the question. And keeping some-one out of circulation is no longer as simple as it was. There are too many risks attached. I don't want him popping out of nowhere in ten years' time, telling some reporter all he knows.'

192

'Would anyone believe him?'

'I think it possible, yes. It's too much of a risk to assume otherwise.'

'It could be made to seem as if he committed suicide. Put him in the river now, he won't reappear until spring. I take it you would like him to be still recognizable?'

'Yes, that's important. Will Belov oblige?'

Pavlychko shook his head. There were so many ghosts in this place, he thought. Sometimes he had been unable to get the sounds of its wards and corridors out of his head for days. His visits here had been the least pleasant of his duties. There was only one place he liked less: the special hospital in Siberia to which he had been taken several times by Kossenkova.

'Too risky. It was hard enough bringing Gould to the hospital. If he dies here, they'll demand a post mortem, depend upon it. These new brooms sweep very hard. And a post mortem could raise issues we'd prefer not to have raised. His body is still full of drugs.'

'Well then, have him taken wherever you think appropriate and do it there. Get Belov's advice on the drugs. Make it look like suicide, but don't put him in the river. I want him found within the next few days, the sooner the better. If they think he's on the loose somewhere, they'll only start looking for him. Understand?'

He nodded.

'See to it, then. And, Pavlychko . . . I'd like Belov out of the way as well. People have got into the habit of talking nowadays.' She paused, looking at him without blinking. 'You do understand me, don't you?'

He did, he did indeed. His entire life had been devoted to such understandings. They were his only anchor in a universe grown unstable and treacherous.

They came for him in the early morning as before, when the corridors were silent. No one walked at this time except the ghosts of the sane. The insane lay in their quiet rooms, some asleep, others watching for dawn. Often dawn did not come. Or if it did, it did not bring with it the light of a new day.

Where photographs of Lenin had once looked down on them now there were icons put there by newly pious nurses, the faces of imagined saints and martyrs, bluish-green in the steady glow of nightlights. Here and there an orderly sat, reading or playing solitary draughts. And the ghosts sat with them, or paced up and down corridors paved with small, cracked tiles, their heads shaved, their bodies bent almost double, their pink tongues on fire.

He was wakened by someone unfastening the straps that held him to the bed. Opening his eyes and turning his head, he saw two men. One he recognized as Pavlychko, though he did not know his name. The other man was the doctor, Belov.

'What's happening?'

'Time to go, Dr Gould. You're finished here.'

'Finished?'

'Time to go home.'

'I have no home. Nowhere to go.'

For a moment, Pavlychko seemed nonplussed.

'Here,' he said, holding a bundle of clothes out to Jack. 'Put these on.'

Belov finished unbuckling the last strap, and helped Jack swing his legs over the edge of the bed. The doctor smiled, as though he and Jack were complicit in some little act of treachery. For some reason, the smile filled Jack with dread.

'Where are you taking me?' he asked. 'Why am I being moved again?'

'You've told us all we need to know,' said Pavlychko. 'We're taking you home. Take that nightshirt off and put these on.'

Jack complied. The clothes Pavlychko had brought for him were, he realized, his own, the ones that had been taken from him at *militsia* headquarters. In a way, that was reassuring. The Ukrainian had seen to it that Jack's wallet and papers were all there, in his pockets. They would be needed to guarantee identification of his corpse. When the Italian consul returned, he would have work to do.

Jack dressed slowly, his fingers fumbling with zips and buttons. His powers of co-ordination had atrophied since being taken into custody. Belov helped him fasten his shirt-buttons.

'You will need these as well. It is very cold outside.' Pavlychko handed him an overcoat and a felt hat with earflaps.

They had brought a wheelchair for him, an old model with solid tyres and a sagging seat. Pavlychko walked ahead. They went down dimly-lit corridors filled with the odours of cabbage and carbolic, past barred windows, past locked doors, on floors streaked with old, dark stains, walking with hushed steps. In one room an old inmate heard their stifled passing and shivered, remembering the hours before dawn on so many cold mornings of his past.

Outside, a car was waiting. Since Jack's confinement, snow had come to Moscow, not softly as at his arrival, but in mad, drifting storms. It was as though a white hand, immovable, frosted, and immensely strong, had been laid across the entire city.

Taken from the comparative warmth of the hospital, Jack gasped in the sudden, numbing cold. The freezing air leapt at him, seizing his breath, searing his lungs. Pavlychko led them across a heavy swathe of trampled snow to where the car was standing waiting on the road-way. Snowploughs had been through that evening, clearing a rough track down the centre of the road, leaving a way for drivers, provided their cars could take the strain. Belov opened the rear door and helped Jack inside. Pav-lychko folded the wheelchair and manhandled it into the boot, then took the driver's seat.

The streets through which they drove had a wasted, abandoned air, as though a witch's curse had turned the world to salt. Few lights were lit anywhere, they passed no other moving cars, no one was walking. Moscow was like a city come to punishment. On either side they saw mounds that were cars buried in snow. They crossed silent junctions, beneath nets of frozen trolley-bus wires.

'Where are you taking me?' Jack asked. He had never felt himself so utterly lost. He was with strangers in a world that meant nothing to him. In the freezing cold he was coming awake rapidly, every moment more aware of the predicament he was in.

'It's not far now, doctor. We're going to put you up in a hotel until tomorrow. You can sleep until later this morning, then we'll help you pack and take you to the airport. Everything's been arranged. The tickets, everything.'

Suddenly, the street in front of them opened up and Jack could make out the towers of the Kremlin, rising behind the flat expanse of Red Square. He recognized the Arsenal tower, with the dome of the Senate building to its left, and realized that they had been travelling from the north-east.

A few minutes later they drew up outside a huge building diagonally opposite the State History Museum. A sign outside declared it to be the Moskva Hotel. Jack had heard of it on his first visit, when Iosif had warned him against staying there. The Moskva had never really been a place for foreigners, being reserved almost exclusively for Party officials visiting the city. It had a grim and sullen look, as though determined to cling to its privileges against the tide of liberalization.

Pavlychko and Belov together helped Jack out and back into the wheelchair. A path had been thoughtfully cleared as far as the entrance. An old man was on duty behind the glass doors, bent over on a stool. When Pavlychko knocked, he glanced up. He did not seem surprised by such late arrivals. Rising painfully, he came to the door and unlocked it. Pavlychko said nothing as they entered.

They passed a Spanish restaurant on the ground floor and went up a flight of stone stairs to the next level. There was no one at the reception desk, no one in the porter's lodge. The vast lobby was deserted. Belov wheeled Jack to a bank of six lifts and pressed a button. The lift took a long time to arrive. The lobby was cold, silent, lit only by ten-watt bulbs. Jack wondered why they had bothered to bring him here for what they had to do. It was so elaborate, he thought, when a pillow in his hospital room would have served them as well.

The lift arrived. Pavlychko pressed the button for the fifteenth floor. He had toyed with the thought of arranging a fall from there, but dismissed it. Kossenkova wanted there to be no doubt about Jack's identity. Pavlychko's original plan was still the best. The lift rose slowly, but he was in no hurry. He placed a hand on Jack's shoulder and smiled.

The door opened on to a lonely corridor. The further end was invisible from where they stood. Just before it was a vestibule decorated with framed posters of the city. Behind her desk, the *dezhurnaya* was enjoying a well-earned nap. She was a middle-aged woman. Sometimes, waking in the early hours like this, in the silence, she would think that she had spent her whole life here, at the head of this corridor, watching these doors open and close again. She had never met the women from the other floors.

Waking at the sound of the arriving lift, she looked up. Pavlychko flashed an identification card at her. The initials KGB still commanded respect and compliance. The woman handed Pavlychko a key, then leaned back in her chair and closed her eyes again. Whatever was happening, she did not want to know.

It was a short walk to room 1520. Pavlychko opened the door and stood aside while Belov pushed Jack inside.

The room was decorated in the heavy Stalinist style of the 1950s. Overstuffed armchairs, long, dust-filled curtains stretching from the ceiling to the floor, gilded light fittings, a radio that looked as though it would still blare out speeches by Malenkov or Bulganin. On one side stood an enormous bed draped in a heavy blood-red quilt.

Belov helped Jack out of his outer clothes and jacket.

'I want you to lie down,' he said. 'This won't take very long. You don't have to be afraid.'

They lifted him from the wheelchair and manhandled him on to the bed. It was the hardest bed he had ever lain on. He wanted to get up and run, but his legs had no strength, and together his captors were more than a match for him.

'Why is this so important to you?' he asked.

Belov shrugged. To him, all that was important was doing what he was told.

From a briefcase, Pavlychko took a large bottle of tablets. They were long and white. Jack guessed that the bottle held about two hundred. The Russian label read 'Sodium Amytal 200 mg'. Belov came from the bathroom holding a glass of water aloft like a trophy. He set it on the bedside table, alongside the tablets.

'Let's sit up,' he said, helping Jack lean against the wooden headboard.

Pavlychko unscrewed the bottle and tipped about a dozen tablets on to his palm.

'Dr Belov would like you to take some tablets,' he said. 'Just a couple at a time. There's no need to hurry. We don't want you to be sick and throw them back up again.'

'Why don't you just give me an injection and be done with it?'

Belov shook his head.

'It's better this way. Trust me.'

He handed the glass to Jack. Pavlychko held out two tablets.

'If I refuse?'

Pavlychko took an object from his pocket. It was a razor blade.

'Please take the tablets. It will be more pleasant for you.'

Jack hesitated, then took the proffered tablets. The drugs he had already been given had taken away his willpower. He had no fight left in him. What was the point in fighting the inevitable? He placed the tablets in his mouth and swallowed them down with a sip of water. Pavlychko held out two more. Then another two. Jack wondered how long it would take.

CHAPTER TWENTY-SEVEN

They did not hear the door open, did not hear it close. The first Pavlychko knew that something had gone wrong was when he saw Belov jerk and fall forward across the bed. He reached forward and, as he did so, saw the gunshot wound in the back of the doctor's head.

He spun round. A man was standing about six paces away from him. He wore a fur hat and overcoat, and in one hand he held a gun fitted with a long suppressor. The gun was pointed at Pavlychko's head. The man held it steady, like an extension of his hand.

'I don't want to have to use this a second time,' the stranger said. His accent was Slavic, but not Russian. He was in his thirties, blond, very calm. He left no room to doubt who was now in charge. 'Stand up,' he ordered. 'Slowly.'

Pavlychko obeyed.

'Now, take your gun from your pocket using your left hand.'

Breathing heavily, Pavlychko brought out a Tokarev TT-33.

'Throw it on the bed.'

Pavlychko tossed the gun down. This could not be happening, he thought. Not to him. Not here.

'Do you know who I am?' he asked.

'I know exactly who you are,' the man said. What the hell was he, wondered Pavlychko. Belorussian? Czech? Polish? 'I wouldn't place much weight on it any longer, if I were you. Now, get Dr Gould to his feet, please, and help him to the bathroom.'

'Dr Gould is in no condition to . . .'

'I will not ask a second time. Please believe me.'

Pavlychko lifted Jack and dragged him to the bathroom. The man retrieved the pistol from the bed and followed at a safe distance.

'Dr Gould, are you still awake?'

Jack nodded. He was beginning to feel light-headed.

'Help him to the washbasin. Now, put your fingers down his throat until he throws up. And hurry.'

Holding Jack round the waist with one arm, Pavlychko shoved two fingers into his mouth and pressed down. Jack started to retch, and then threw up what little there was in his stomach.

'Outside now. Help him into the wheelchair.'

Pavlychko got one arm round his shoulder and helped Jack stagger to the chair. With every step he took, Jack felt a little strength returning to his legs.

'Now, on the bed.'

Pavlychko lay down, protesting. The stranger moved beside the bed.

'Sit up.'

Taking the glass, he handed it to Pavlychko.

'You can't make me . . .'

The stranger emptied half a dozen tablets on to his hand and passed them to Pavlychko.

His hand shaking, Pavlychko began to down the tablets in nervous gulps, choking and swallowing, choking and swallowing.

'That's enough.'

The man took the glass and set it back on the table. Jack noticed that he was wearing thin gloves.

'Open your mouth,' the stranger ordered.

'I can pay you,' said Pavlychko. 'Whatever you want, I can arrange for it. Believe me. I'm a rich man. I have powerful friends.'

'At the moment you only have powerful enemies.'

The stranger leaned across and slipped the suppressor

into Pavlychko's open mouth. Pavlychko's eyes opened wide in terror. The gunman shook his head once. And fired. The pillow on which Pavlychko's head had been resting filled with blood. Pavlychko's eyes stayed open.

The stranger unscrewed the titanium suppressor from the vented muzzle of his pistol. The weapon was a Heckler & Koch P9S, chambered for subsonic .45ACP cartridges. The slow speed of the projectiles was essential to eliminate the crack a high-velocity round would have made leaving the muzzle.

Pocketing the suppressor, the man slipped the pistol into Pavlychko's lifeless hand, wrapping his fingers loosely round the grip. He picked up the Tokarev from the bed, checked the magazine, and put it into his other pocket. Let the *militsia* worry about how a man like Pavlychko had come into possession of an H&K pistol. And let them work out why he had shot Belov and killed himself after two attempts. None of it would stand up to a skilful forensic enquiry. But he wasn't really worried about that.

'Come,' he said. 'We've got a long way to go.'

It was only then, as he smiled down at him, that Jack realized where he had seen the man before. It was Henryk, Stefan Rosewicz's guard-dog from the woods of Summerlawn.

PART FOUR

CHAPTER TWENTY-EIGHT

Eastern Siberia

Very little ever broke the routine. Black Nurse, White Nurse, Grey Nurse. The orderlies with their trolleys. The cleaners once a week. Dr Voroshilov with his medications. Dawn, noon, sunset. Spring, summer, autumn, winter. But mostly winter. Winter and bitter cold, frost on the windows, icicles hanging from the ceiling when the season was at its height.

In the early days there had been a day room. The orderlies had taken them there every morning. There had been less pleasant trips down the green-tiled corridor that led to the doctors' office. They remembered questions, injections, beatings. Just like the Jerries, but with a different accent. Even the beatings had had a different rhythm. They remembered a garden without flowers where they had been permitted to walk in pairs during the brief summer. Loneliness. Overwhelming loneliness.

The questioning had stopped in time, and with it the beatings. And the walks, and the visits to the day room. They were too old now, so they lay in bed remembering. Good old Blighty. Good old Vera Lynn. They told ITMA jokes and sang their snatches of half-remembered songs. In the early years, the religious ones had prayed. Now, there were no more believers.

Even now, no one really understood what had happened. They would never forget those farcical war crimes trials. All of them had been charged with various offences against the German *Volk*, found guilty, and sentenced to differing periods of imprisonment or, in a few cases, to death. But one day a year or so after that, there had been sounds of fighting in the prison. The next thing any of them had known, their cell doors had been opened and they had all been liberated by Soviet troops. Their jubilation had been shortlived. By the next day, they were back in their cells.

Weeks of questioning had followed. Their new interrogators had been thorough. It was apparent that they wanted to reconstruct what had been divulged to the Germans and, more importantly, how much of it had been true. But by that time truth and fiction had grown so entangled for them that giving straight answers to even the simplest of questions was no longer possible, if it had ever been.

In the second month of interrogation, they were suddenly told that they were to be moved out. That same day everyone had been taken out of Friedrichshain into the sunlight and then locked up in the backs of heavy lorries. A long, disorienting journey had followed, some of it by road, most by train. At its end they had been set down here in the early hours of a freezing spring morning. Cuthbertson, who spoke a little Russian, had told them they were in Siberia.

The door at what was popularly known as Land's End opened quite abruptly. Two doctors in white coats appeared, one male – Voroshilov – one female – Voznesenskaya. Behind them came a tall woman in an ankle-length fur coat. She had a pale, thin face, large spectacles, and an aristocratic manner that seemed out of place in the world they inhabited.

Watched by all their glimmering eyes, she walked slowly down the centre aisle, like a visiting queen or – had they known of such a thing – prime minister come in the wake of some terrible disaster. Forty-seven years too late. Light fell through the tall windows in her wake. She paused at the foot of Ramsey's bed, conferring in hushed tones with the woman doctor. An orderly came behind, wheeling a battered trolley which had been piled high with buff files. Old, familiar files. Catching sight of them, their old ears could hear the crack of bones in the still air.

The woman in the fur coat snapped a finger and the orderly brought the trolley to her. Without haste, she leafed through the files until she found the one she wanted. Holding it in front of her like a shield, she stepped towards the man in the bed.

'Mr Ramsey?'

Ramsey peered dully up at her. Most of his teeth had gone. What was left of his hair had turned yellow. His hands rested on top of the starched bedclothes like stiff claws.

'Yes,' he said. 'That's me. You know it's me. I've never gone away.'

He chuckled drily at his little joke.

'Well, Mr Ramsey.' She looked at him for what seemed a very long time. 'How would you like to go home?'

'I beg your pardon. My hearing's not too good.'

'I asked if you would like to go home. To England. To Wolverhampton. To your wife and child.'

A most terrible fear took hold of Ramsey then. He had not thought that the angel of death would come as a woman in a fur coat, though by now nothing would have surprised him. He looked at her, speechless. She was opening the file. It must be a record of his life, he thought. A bloody queer record it would be too. He coughed.

Kossenkova held up a photograph. It was a colour photograph of an elderly woman in a cardigan. She showed it to him. He had never seen a colour photograph before.

'That's your wife, Mr Ramsey. She's changed a lot, I know, but that's Ethel. Don't you recognize her?'

Enormous tears formed in Ramsey's eyes. It wasn't fair, a voice inside him protested. To kill him so cruelly. After all he'd been through.

'And this is your son. Eric. You never saw him, did you?'

A man of about fifty, balding, with a ginger moustache.

'And these are your grandchildren. Mark and Rachel. You'll be a great-grandfather soon, I expect.'

'What ... do you want?' He choked the words out unevenly. 'I've done nothing to you. What are you doing this for?'

'Please don't be upset, Mr Ramsey. I've come to help you. If all goes well, you can go back home. But first I'd like you to look at some more photographs. And then I'd like to ask you a few questions.'

She held out a fresh batch of photographs. Not domestic snapshots, not family photographs. These had been taken from German intelligence files dating back to the war. They showed men and women who had worked in various capacities for the British secret service.

'Now, Mr Ramsey,' Irina Kossenkova said. 'Let's see if you recognize anyone here. And then I want you to tell me all about October.'

She held out the first photograph. He looked down, still bewildered. In his head, he could hear them all singing.

We'll meet again, don't know where, don't know
    when ...

CHAPTER TWENTY-NINE

Paris was wrapped in fog. Outgoing flights were grounded, air traffic control was sending incomers to the south. Their plane had been diverted to Lyons and then made to wait another half hour while it circled beneath a slack sky, waiting for permission to land. Jack came awake a few minutes before they started the descent. Beside him, Henryk gave a thumbs-up sign. He was doing his best to be a likeable fellow, the sort of man you wouldn't think twice about sharing a jar with in McDaid's at the back end of a grey Saturday. But Jack had seen him kill two men without turning a hair and, hard as he tried, he could not dissolve the blood from his mind, nor the care with which it had been spilled. Not even gratitude could wipe out the jagged stain it had left.

They had wasted as little time as possible in Moscow. Just long enough for Jack to be checked thoroughly by a competent doctor, then out through the back door. In the good old days, they wouldn't have got as far as Krasnogorsk or Lyubertsy. An iron ring would have come down round the city. But Henryk had played all his cards right. Furnished with his magic ID card, Pavlychko had guaranteed himself immunity from the unwanted attentions of chambermaids and *dezhurnayas*. The bodies lay undisturbed for several hours.

A British passport, visa, tickets, and other papers had been waiting for Jack in the small apartment Henryk had rented through a property agency known as the Vremya Co-operative. Once Jack was fit enough, they had travelled by rail to St Petersburg, en route to Finland. They went hard class, on tough plastic seats, through a frozen landscape that never varied. A car would have attracted too much attention. No rightminded foreigner would have attempted those roads in such weather. Flying out would have meant running the gauntlet at Sheremetevo I or II. Henryk did not know how far Irina Kossenkova's writ ran nowadays, but he thought it best to err on the side of generosity.

Though Henryk did not know it, they had made their getaway barely in time. Pavlychko's as-yet-unexplained disappearance had set alarm bells clanging in Kossenkova's naturally suspicious head. She ordered a search at the Moskva, and the bodies were found.

Jack and Henryk had left Moscow's St Petersburg station on the afternoon Aurora service. Three hours later, photographs of Jack were being circulated in the station's main concourse. Henryk's instinct to change in St Petersburg, rather than take a direct service to Helsinki, had been sound. All Moscow—Helsinki trains were suddenly subject to unusual delays at the Luzhayka border crossing. But buses were still going through at Brusnichnoe. By the time the guards there had copies of the photograph, Jack and Henryk were stepping off the coach to stretch their legs in Kotka.

And now France. Down there, Stefan Rosewicz was waiting for him. Jack did not know why, could not really guess why. Except that Rosewicz knew more than even he did about the Jesus scroll, and that the scroll was at the centre of everything. What most disturbed Jack was the possibility – he thought it a near certainty – that Rosewicz had been behind the explosion that had killed the Sharanskiis. Thinking back, he now considered it very likely after all that the Pole had had a hand in the murders of Denis Boylan and Moira Kennedy, though he was still very far from having a motive to explain their deaths.

But he was certain of one thing. If Rosewicz had indeed

been responsible for the deaths of Iosif, Leah and Sima, it would be his duty to kill him. Almost, he thought, his pleasure. Looking at the formidable Henryk by his side, he wondered how that might be possible.

The landing was bumpy, but everyone cheered anyway. Jack's British passport received no more than a cursory glance at the control desk. Henryk had to go through a different channel. Jack wondered what his nationality really was.

Irina Kossenkova had not notified any foreign authorities of the fugitive she was seeking back in Russia. She had thought of doing so, but dismissed the idea as one that carried needless personal risks. Too many questions in the wrong quarters might have proved awkward. Not for the first time, she regretted the passing of the old order.

She had another reason for not telling the British, especially not British intelligence. With Jack Gould or the scroll in her hands, she would have a powerful bargaining chip. If they, on the other hand, were to get hold of the Irishman, the tables would be turned. They would try to find the scroll before her. And that would leave her with nothing.

A car with a uniformed driver was waiting for them at the airport. They arrived in Paris after seven o'clock, pulling up outside a large house in a wealthy right-bank district not very far from the Arc de Triomphe. It was a typical *haute bourgeoisie* house of the Second Empire, five storeys high, with a hipped mansard roof and wrought-iron railings across the balconies on each floor. The front door was set behind an elaborate black and gold gate, also in wrought iron.

The door was opened by Mrs Nagle. She smiled and took Jack's hand.

'It's grand to see you again, Dr Gould. Who would have thought when we last met that we'd be seeing one another again in Paris?'

'I'm pleased to see you, Noreen. You look well.'

'You're not so bad yourself. A bit tired-looking.'

'Yes,' he said. 'I am tired.'

A look of genuine concern crossed the housekeeper's face.

'We'll look after you here. You've no need to worry about that. But here I am chatting away, and all the time Mr Rosewicz is expecting you. I'll get a terrible ticking off if I keep you here any longer.'

Rosewicz was in his study, waiting for them.

He had not changed. The old sometimes age rapidly, but the Pole looked, if anything, more youthful. He surprised Jack by embracing him warmly the moment he stepped through the door, as though they had parted on the best of terms.

'My dear Jack, how glad I am to see you. After so much time. So much wasted time. You look well.'

'I'm very tired,' was all Jack could think to say.

'No matter. You will be looked after here. My own doctor will visit you this evening. He is a good man, you can depend on him. I have arranged for a nurse to be in attendance for as long as is necessary. We must get you well. Indeed, we must.'

'Why . . . Why did you bring me here? How did you know I was in Russia? How did . . . ?'

Rosewicz raised a hand, laughing.

'Please! So many questions. I can see your interrogators taught you well. You have to rest, then you can ask. Ask all you want, I will answer what I can. But now, Henryk will see you to your room. I think you can trust him now, can you not? I think you and he got off to a bad start the first time you met.'

Jack did not feel like arguing. But he would not be sent to bed meekly, like a child.

'There is one question I have to ask,' he said. 'Before I go anywhere, before I try to rest. Not later. Now.'

212

Rosewicz stiffened slightly.

'Very well. I will try to answer.'

'I want to know if you were responsible for killing Iosif Sharanskii and his family.'

Rosewicz's mouth opened. He seemed genuinely shocked. Clearly, whatever question he might have been expecting, this had not been it.

'Good heavens, Jack! I am surprised you can ask such a thing. What puts such a thought into your head? Kill him? Of course not. I did not know him, but I knew of him, and I knew his work. From all accounts, he was a good man, an honest scholar. I was grieved when I heard how he died. And his wife and child with him. You are right to feel angry.'

Rosewicz paused.

'We can talk about this again, if you like. But now you are tired and in need of sleep. Good, refreshing sleep without drugs.'

He walked with Jack as far as the bottom of the stairs. As he began to climb, Jack hesitated and turned back.

'What about Summerlawn?' he asked. 'I went there recently. It had been burned down.'

Rosewicz's face clouded.

'We will not talk of that,' he said. He turned to his assistant. 'Henryk, see that Dr Gould has everything he needs.'

Jack did not know how long he slept. The room in which he had been put had no clock. He would sleep for long periods, assaulted by strange dreams, then wake briefly before returning to an even deeper sleep and even stranger dreams. Sometimes on waking he would find the room perfectly dark, so that even his own hand was invisible to him. At such times, he was seized by a wild apprehension that he was in custody again, in a cell in Russia, and he would lie awake listening for footsteps until sleep smothered him. And it was then the footsteps came, down long corridors of stone, and with them voices whispering in a language he did not understand.

At other times, dim light had entered the room round the sides of heavy curtains, and he knew he was no longer in a cell; though where he was he could remember only occasionally. His room had a bathroom attached, which he used from time to time. He found light food and fruit juice on a table. Once he looked for a telephone, but could find none.

Early one morning he woke to find Rosewicz leaning over the bed with a look of concern on his face.

'Good morning, Jack. I hope you have slept well. How are you feeling?'

'I . . . I'm not sure. Not very good. My head hurts.'

'Yes. Dr Ganachaud said it might. He is due again shortly. I hope he has been looking after you well.'

A clouded memory of brief medical examinations and the ingestion of pills fluttered through Jack's head. He remembered Belov suddenly.

'How long have I been here?' he asked.

'You came here three nights ago. You slept for almost twenty-four hours, but yesterday only for a few hours at a time. Today you will stay awake.'

'Where am I?' he asked.

'In my house in Paris. We are in the seventeenth arrondissement. I think you know the city.'

Very well, thought Jack. Almost too well. Caitlin had given him Paris once, it had been her first gift to him. After her death, he had vowed never to return there.

'I know parts of it,' he said. 'But not this area.'

'No matter. We are not far from the Champs Elysées. Near the Parc Monceau.'

'I know where you mean.'

'Well, perhaps when you are feeling better we can go out together. I will show you the sights. But for the present you must rest. You have been ill. You have been through a great deal, and it has taken its toll. But you are still young and healthy. You will recover. Dr Ganachaud is very hopeful. He says you may get up this afternoon. Your regime is to be changed. Less sleep now, a little exercise. There is a diet sheet which you are to follow religiously. It is for detoxification. You have had poisons pumped into your system, but Ganachaud will get them out. He has given you homoeopathic medicines. I hope you have no objection. It is quite normal here in France. So many of the doctors here receive a homoeopathic training. But perhaps it is not to your Irish taste.'

Jack shook his head. He was hardly in a position to argue about what was done to him.

By the second day, Jack was feeling as though he wanted to live again. Ganachaud visited him every morning, examined him, and gave him a mixture of pills and powders manufactured by a pharmaceutical company called Boiron. The special diet worked wonders. Jack was given a massage twice a day by Henryk, and had gently-paced workouts with him in a small, expensively-fitted gym. Rosewicz came in from time to time in order to ask how he was. He seemed anxious about something, and impatient.

On the third day, Henryk brought Jack to Rosewicz's study on the ground floor. For a moment, as he entered the room, Jack had a sense of *déjà vu*, as though he had been transported back to Summerlawn. Rosewicz was behind the desk. He wore a green silk dressing-gown and thin gold spectacles.

'You look so much better, Jack. I am truly amazed. My confidence in Ganachaud and his little sugar pills has been much reinforced.'

'Why did you bring me here?'

The old man gestured towards an armchair.

'Please, Jack, you should take a seat. Do not try to do too much all at once.'

'You haven't answered my question.'

'I saved your life. Isn't that enough?'

'I want to know why. What you had Henryk do wasn't easy, it wasn't cheap, and it didn't concern you. I want to know how you knew I was in Moscow, how you knew where I was being kept.'

'Very well. Sit down and I will tell you what I can. I have asked Mrs Nagle to bring us some tea and cakes. Ganachaud says you may have a little ordinary food.'

At that moment, there was a knock on the door and Mrs Nagle entered, carrying a silver tray.

'Mrs Nagle,' Rosewicz said, standing to take the tray. 'You remember Dr Gould, don't you?'

'Of course I do. And I'm very pleased to see you looking better, sir. I didn't say so then, but I didn't think you looked at all well when you got here.'

'I'm fine now, Noreen, thank you.'

She seemed uneasy. Smiling, she turned to Rosewicz.

'Will that be all, sir?'

'Yes. I'll ring when I want the tray collected.'

When they were alone again, Rosewicz poured two cups of Gui Hua and passed one to Jack.

'Have a *financier*,' he murmured, pointing to a plate of small canoe-shaped almond cakes. 'My good Mrs Nagle goes to Lenôtre on the Avenue de Wagram every morning for them.'

'I don't feel hungry.'

'Nevertheless, I insist. You will be surprised by how good they are.'

'I need to know why I am here.'

'Yes, of course. You have a right.'

Rosewicz bit a tiny piece from his *financier* and sipped the gold-coloured tea. Then, from a cardboard box on top of the desk, he took out a metal cylinder. Jack felt his pulse quicken. Rosewicz opened the cylinder and took out a parchment scroll. He passed it across the desk to Jack.

'Do you recognize this?' Rosewicz asked.

Jack felt giddy, as though the room was spinning round

him. He had to hold the arms of his chair to stop himself swaying.

'You don't seem well, Jack. What's wrong?'

'Where . . . ? Where did you get this?'

'I will tell you in a moment. First, I would like you to look at it and tell me whether or not it is the scroll that was stolen from Iosif Sharanskii's apartment shortly before his death.'

Jack pulled himself together. He unrolled the top end of the scroll and scanned the first lines.

'Yes,' he said. 'This is it. There's no doubt about it.'

Rosewicz reached a hand across the desk and retrieved the scroll. He slipped it carefully back inside the cylinder.

'Jack, how would you describe this scroll?'

'Describe it?'

'Yes. What does it consist of?'

Jack paused.

'Surely you've read it yourself.'

'Yes, but you are the expert. My skills are very limited beside yours.'

'It is a letter. First century, I think. It contains what I think may be a reference to the mass suicides at Gamala. That would date it after the year 67. The author was an Essene, as was the recipient. That's all I know at the moment.'

Rosewicz looked at Jack without saying anything. He tapped the cylinder and replaced it in the cardboard box.

'This scroll. Where did Sharanskii find it?'

'In the State Library. It's part of a large collection. Look, I did agree not to reveal any details. I'd like to keep that agreement.'

'Of course. But you are certain that this is the scroll that was stolen.'

'Yes. Did you steal it?'

They both knew what the question implied. Rosewicz slowly shook his head.

'No. Henryk purloined it from the people who were

holding you captive. I think you know Irina Kossenkova, the woman who questioned you. What I do not understand is why she and her associates should go to the trouble of stealing it. Why anyone should take such trouble, not just to steal it, but to kill Sharanskii and Volnukhin in order to conceal the theft.'

Jack sat up straight.

'Did you say Volnukhin?'

Rosewicz nodded.

'He was found shot in his apartment some days after Sharanskii was killed. I imagine you were to have been the third victim. Now, why should this letter be that important?'

Jack said nothing.

'Could it be,' Rosewicz went on, 'that it was this that they were really after?'

From a stiff brown envelope he took a large photostat. It was the same one that he had shown Jack during his stay at Summerlawn. He passed it across the desk. Jack glanced at it. He had been wrong. It was not a reproduction of another copy. It was a photograph of the very manuscript he had last set eyes on in Moscow, in Iosif Sharanskii's flat. Not the decoy letter which Iosif and he had placed in the cylinder and for which they had obtained so many permits, the parchment scroll on the table in front of them, but the Jesus scroll itself.

CHAPTER THIRTY

'I'm not sure,' whispered Jack, desperately trying to stay in control of a situation fast running away from him. 'I . . . I seem to remember that you showed me this photostat once before, while I was staying at Summerlawn.'

Rosewicz smiled.

'That is correct. But you have also seen the original. And very recently. In the Russian State Library, to be precise.'

Jack shrugged.

'That's possible, I suppose. But there were so many scrolls, there was no time to look at any one of them for very long.'

'Nevertheless, you did see this scroll. And I do not doubt that you spent more than a few minutes looking over it.' Rosewicz sighed. 'Jack, please – there is no point in keeping up this pretence. I am trying to help you. I know all about this scroll. If you want revenge for Iosif Sharanskii and his family, if you want to keep the scroll from being stolen, perhaps destroyed, then you must help me.'

'I can't see how you can know about something like this,' said Jack. 'If, as you say, the original is in the State Library in Moscow. Unless, of course, you have just been there yourself.'

'That was not necessary. I have corresponded with a man called Grigorevitch. I think you know him. He was head of the department in which Iosif Sharanskii worked.'

Jack shook his head.

'I have heard his name, that's all. Iosif mentioned him once or twice.'

'And did he mention that he told Grigorevitch about his discovery of this scroll? Sharanskii was the only person with access to that locked room who could have known what the scroll really was, what it represented. That is why he asked you to come to Moscow. And, I believe, that is why you were planning to fly out again so quickly. As you say, you'd hardly had time to scratch the surface of the collection. I think Sharanskii wanted you to take the scroll out of Russia, probably to Israel. I can guess his motives. But the scroll that was stolen from your flight bag is not the one he gave you. The much less important scroll we have just seen was substituted for it, either by you or by Sharanskii. I am sure you know where the real scroll is. All I want you to do is to help me find it again.'

'And then?'

Rosewicz frowned.

'Good heavens, why do you ask? Then we do what you and Sharanskii planned all along. We have it authenticated, we see it placed in the safest and most reliable academic library, and we make it available to the world of scholarship. Perhaps we even set up a separate institute for its study. An institute under your personal direction.'

For a few moments, Jack believed him. Then he glanced at the hand with which Rosewicz held the fine porcelain cup and noticed the little finger. The top joint was missing. Jack remembered what Iosif had said to him that afternoon, not long before his death: . . . *it is as I thought. He is the same Rosewicz. Jack, there is something you must to know about this man. It is most important.* And now that Jack thought of it, he wondered how either Rosewicz or Henryk had known that the stolen cylinder had been in his flight bag. Either they had excellent knowledge of Irina Kossenkova and her doings, or they had arranged the explosion themselves.

'I'm sorry,' Jack said. 'But I can't help you. If two scrolls were swapped, Iosif must have been responsible. I can't think why. But he told me nothing about such a substitution.'

Rosewicz was growing visibly frustrated. Clearly, the interview was not proceeding as he had anticipated.

'This is really very stupid of you, Jack. I thought I knew you better than this. I admire your loyalty, or whatever you choose to call it; but I do not admire your lack of good sense. You know perfectly well what I am talking about. You know that I have helped you, that I have saved your life. And yet, knowing the contents of that scroll, knowing its implications, you will do nothing to ensure that it passes into safe hands. You must be aware that it is not just an extremely valuable document, but also a singularly dangerous one. In the wrong hands, it could be the cause of unimaginable harm. Conversely, if it were to fall into the possession of an innocent party, they would be exposed to very great danger. Either way, you have a responsibility to pass on whatever information you possess.'

Jack looked round him, at the walls packed with priceless books, at the long, cold window giving on to a shaded Parisian garden, at the two oil paintings, one on either side of the deep, mahogany-panelled room. Everything here spelled power rather than scholarship, affluence rather than altruism. What sort of man was Rosewicz? What had Iosif Sharanskii thought him to be? His own daughter had feared him, had warned him against him. *Please watch out for my father. Don't trust him. I don't think he means you harm, but you could be harmed in spite of that.* What had she meant? Had she known something that Iosif Sharanskii had also known, something in Rosewicz's past that would make him a dangerous man to know? In spite of everything – in spite of the deaths of the priest O'Mara, of Denis Boylan and Moira Kennedy, of the Sharanskii family – Jack knew no actual evil of the man. Only rumour, only speculation.

'If this scroll was in a locked room in the State Library as you say,' Jack said, 'how is it that you had a photostat

221

in your possession years ago? An old photostat. Thirty or forty years old, perhaps.'

'Forty-nine years old to be precise,' said Rosewicz. 'You know yourself that the documents you were shown had not been in the State Library for very long. Only since the end of the last war. Before that, they were in the hands of the SS, and before that in Jewish libraries and *genizot*. So, what should you conclude? I will tell you. Photostats were made of many of these documents by SS archivists during the occupation of Poland. After the war, only the original documents were taken to Russia. The Soviets had no interest in copies, only originals. And the photostats had been stored in a separate location, in order to preserve something of the collections they represented, in the event of a bombardment or some other disaster. There were so many tragedies then, preservation was in everyone's mind. It was my good fortune to obtain some of these photostats while I was still living in Poland. And I was fortunate enough to be able to read and identify the document we are now discussing.'

'I don't understand,' Jack protested. 'If you knew it was in the Lenin Library all along, why did you bother asking me at Summerlawn if I had seen it? You know nobody was ever admitted to those rooms until this year.'

Rosewicz smiled and shook his head.

'My poor young friend, the ill treatment meted out to you by the Russians seems to have addled your brain. I did not know where any of those documents had actually been sent, nor what the Soviets intended to do with them. Indeed, I had no way of knowing what had survived and what perished in the terrible days towards the end of the war.

'Sometimes an unprovenanced papyrus would come on the market – the underground market, that is – and some of us would surmise that it had, perhaps, come from the Soviet Union. We could never be sure, of course, but it was always a favoured possibility. They had astonishing treasures, we knew that; and they were always hungry for hard currency. It is hard to believe even now that they did not try to turn their booty into cash. But it seems that nothing or very little surfaced until earlier this year.'

'Perhaps the scroll you want is still there,' Jack suggested. 'I don't think Iosif would have taken it without permission. That would not have been in his character. And we only had permission to take the scroll you have in that box.'

'It is not in the library,' said Rosewicz. 'Volnukhin's death gave Professor Grigorevitch free entry to the collection. He had a colleague with him, an expert in Syriac literature, a man called Nabiev, a Tajik. Perhaps you have heard of him.'

'Syriac is not the same as Aramaic.'

'Nevertheless, it's close enough for the purpose they had in mind. Grigorevitch himself knows Aramaic better than Sharanskii thought. I gave him a copy of this photostat. He and Nabiev knew exactly what they were looking for. It took them two days to sift through everything. The scroll was definitely not there.'

Jack got to his feet.

'I'm sorry,' he said. 'You'll have to excuse me. I'm feeling tired, and I think I should lie down. Dr Ganachaud was emphatic that I should not overtax myself.'

Rosewicz did not move a muscle.

'Jack,' he said, his voice low and coaxing, like a parent negotiating gently with a recalcitrant child he does not yet wish to smack. 'When we last met, I was a trifle harsh with you, perhaps even unjust. I had discovered that you had fallen in love with my daughter. So I sent you away. That was patriarchal of me, the act of a man locked in the moral patterns of a dead generation. I apologize. I am not a modern man, I do not possess modern values, if that is what they are. I freely admit that I should not have interfered in a private matter between two adults. If it is any consolation to you, I know that Maria reciprocated your feelings. That is why I asked her to leave Summerlawn that morning. For her to have become your lover or your wife would have involved –' he paused '– would have involved complications.'

'You said she was already engaged to someone else.'

'Yes. And soon after that she married him.'

In spite of all that had since happened, Jack felt the statement like a hard blow in the pit of his stomach.

'However,' Rosewicz went on, 'the marriage has not been successful. Maria and her husband still live together outwardly as man and wife, but it is no more than a formality. They do not sleep together. She tells me they have not done so for some time. He is a wealthy man, a powerful man. And, like Maria and myself, he is a devout Catholic. Nevertheless, I feel certain that an annulment could be arranged. In fact, I could guarantee it.'

Jack felt himself go cold. He had never been in such a marketplace before.

'What exactly are you suggesting, Mr Rosewicz?'

'Better I do not have to spell it out. That would be clumsy, and I seek above all else to be a man of refinement. However, let me say that I believe we can be of mutual assistance. You are a lonely man. You have suffered several tragic losses in a matter of only a few years. Is it not time you considered a second marriage? With a woman whom you love deeply? It would be so easy . . .'

That was all he was able to say. Jack did not even bother shutting the door behind him.

CHAPTER THIRTY-ONE

For the next few days nothing more was said about the scroll. Though he was angry about Rosewicz's attempt to suborn him through the least subtle of temptations, Jack's resistance had been deeply undermined by the knowledge that Maria might not, after all, be lost to him. He had not forgotten her, not for a moment. And now, when he was at his weakest and most in need of her, she had been brought out for his inspection, like a stolen treasure, the more precious because lost.

He needed her desperately, now more than ever. The losses of Iosif, Leah and little Sima had intensified his grief for Caitlin and Siobhan to such an extent, he feared he would go mad with it. He had no home, no sense of place or time, he had no one to whom he was of any real importance. What Stefan Rosewicz was offering him was nothing less than a second chance at life itself.

To have that chance, he knew that all he had to do was guide Rosewicz to the Jesus scroll. If three people whom he loved had not died on its account, he would have given it to him there and then. He thought that, after all, it was his to give. But he would not give it to a pimp.

And yet he was tempted from more than one direction. What could he do with the scroll on his own? He could hardly keep it to himself. Rosewicz was a private collector, but Jack knew from the experience of working in his library, that he was scrupulous. No doubt he would expect to share in the credit for the discovery. Jack suspected that he wanted to fund the institute he spoke of himself. It would be the Stefan Rosewicz Institute, and it would make its founder famous, it would secure for him a sort of immortality. What harm was there in that, provided bona fide scholars could study there, provided the scroll and any ancillary materials were freely available to the world of learning?

There was another concern, one Jack had not voiced to Rosewicz. He could not remember what he had said under the influence of the drug Belov had administered to him. He vaguely remembered talking about the scroll and identifying its author. But had he also told her what had been done with it? If so, another life was in imminent danger and could only be saved if Jack told Rosewicz what he knew. Even then it might be too late.

The day following his interview with Rosewicz, he was allowed outside for the first time. Henryk took him for a short walk in the Parc Monceau. The weather was crisp, there was a promise of Christmas in the air, evident in the bright faces of the children being walked there by their nannies. The park exuded exclusivity. The houses whose windows faced on to it were many-storeyed like Rosewicz's, and decorated with exquisite balconies. Even the trees and bushes and winter flowers seemed to have acquired an air of cultivated superiority. Everything was trim, nothing was left to chance, not even the carefully manufactured Roman ruins.

Jack watched the faces of the children. They were such quiet, well-behaved specimens, he could not imagine them running or pulling one another's hair. They walked and spoke like small adults. Jack knew they would grow up and live in apartments filled with glass, surrounded by family photographs framed in silver, elegant and untouchable. Each year they would discuss the latest winner of the Prix Goncourt, three times a year they would visit the Opéra on gala occasions, once a month they would dine at Le Véfour in small, exclusive parties. He did not envy them their tightly-ordered lives. At the heart of each of

226

them would lie one unhappiness or another. Unhappiness glossed over by the sterility of manners.

More than once, he thought of Sima at the zoo, spinning like a coloured top through the seconds and minutes of her last hours. And he thought at other times of Siobhan, running to her death.

Henryk kept a close eye on him. Jack guessed he had instructions to see that Jack did not try to make a break for it. He knew there was no point. Even if he found a gendarme, what would that achieve? Jack had no doubt that Dr Ganachaud would explain with great finesse that his patient was in a delicate mental state.

That evening Jack came down to dinner to find that Rosewicz was not alone. He found him seated in the little anteroom where he liked to take an aperitif before his evening meal, side by side with a man dressed in clerical garb, with the distinctive scarlet trimmings of a cardinal.

'Jack, do come in. Let me introduce you to an old and dear friend of mine, Cardinal Leon Ciechanowski. Of course, Leon was not a cardinal when I first met him. Were you, Leon?'

The cardinal smiled. It was obviously a joke the two had shared for a long time.

'Not even a priest.'

'Leon, this is Jack Gould. You must treat him gently; he has been very ill.'

Ciechanowski stepped forward, extending his hand. He was a small, plumpish man, not at all the sort of figure Jack associated with the cardinalate. Jack thought him an unlikely friend for Rosewicz, if external appearances were anything to go by.

'I have heard a lot about you, Dr Gould. But I'm sorry to hear that you have been ill.'

'I'm much better now, thank you. Mr Rosewicz has been looking after me very well.'

'Excellent. You could not be in better hands. But you must be careful. Your host is a dangerous man.'

'I think I know that already,' said Jack. He wondered what sort of fencing match he had been invited to.

'No, I am sure you do not. Stefan is a rogue. He has countless vices, and others that I am sure I know nothing of. Fate deals cruel blows. Some sort of substitution took place all those years ago, when we were young men. He was destined to be the cardinal, I the scholar. Stefan would have been dignified in scarlet, don't you think? Whereas I . . .' he patted his belly '. . . have never graced my office as it deserves.'

Rosewicz put a hand on his friend's shoulder.

'You do yourself a grave injustice, Leon.' He looked at Jack. 'Leon spent many years in Communist prisons. He was one of those who kept the church alive in Poland when the country was under the heel of tyrants.'

The cardinal smiled. Jack thought he looked uncomfortable.

'Well, Stefan, I think you exaggerate a little. Things were not so bad. And they are not much better now. Freedom is not always a blessing for the church. Sometimes faith thrives better when it is oppressed.'

'But you have at least the opportunity to worship openly.'

'Those who wish to, yes. But the power of the church in Poland is not as great today as it was when the Communists were in power. We were in opposition then. Now we are part of the establishment, and we are starting to lose ground again.'

Mrs Nagle arrived at that moment, to say dinner was ready. The conversation continued over the meal. Jack warmed to the cardinal. He was a lively, sincere and humble man who took his vows seriously. That he had suffered much was evident from one or two remarks he let slip, but he did not dwell on the past, nor did he adopt a martyr's pose. He laughed a lot and had a store of jokes, many of them wickedly funny.

The meal was outstandingly good. Mrs Nagle, a fine enough cook given the ingredients available to her on a daily basis at Baltimore, had blossomed in Paris. With half a dozen words of basic French at her disposal, and a nose for raw materials, she had been let loose on the shops and markets of the arrondissement with an elastic budget. The results were little miracles that would have graced the tables of the finest Parisian restaurants. No wonder Rosewicz kept the woman to himself.

Aided by the food, a range of unusual wines from Philip Thustrup's little shop in the rue Laugier − a rare bottle of Romanée-Conti, a 1928 Latour, and finally a Château d'Yquem from 1937 − and the cardinal's wit, the evening could not have been anything but cordial. Jack ate sparingly but well, and permitted himself a single glass of the Romanée-Conti. There was port afterwards for the old men. The date on the bottle was 1871, and it was with great reluctance that Jack turned down the offer of a sample.

Taking their glasses and the bottle, Rosewicz and Ciechanowski led Jack to the study. Firelight and lamplight created a soft, impenetrable world. Outside, a wind had risen. It came in irregular gusts against the windows, rattling them sharply for a moment, then tearing off again in search of something less solid. There were three leather armchairs, well worn but highly polished. When they had settled, Ciechanowski rested his glass on a little table by his side and turned to Jack.

'I have enjoyed meeting you, Dr Gould. Or perhaps it is time I called you Jack. We have had a fine evening together, have we not? I hope it will not be our last. People say that so often at dinner parties, it has almost ceased to have meaning. But I mean it. When do you return to Israel?'

Jack glanced at Rosewicz, but no help was forthcoming.

'I don't know. As soon as Ganachaud pronounces me fit, I suppose. Stefan will have a better idea than I.'

'You look fit enough to me already. Don't let these French doctors mollycoddle you, Jack. What with their *homéopathie* and *phytothérapie*, their *crises de foie*, their *modificateurs du terrain*, it is like a little jungle here. They are such strict people. They take their lives and their livers so very seriously. You should go as soon as you feel ready in yourself. Do you not agree, Stefan?'

'Entirely. Paris is not healthy in the winter. If I were Dr Gould, I would head for Israel and the sun. A few weeks on the beach at Eilat would do more good than Ganachaud and all his pills and tinctures.'

The cardinal took a sip from his generously-filled glass.

'This is delicious, Stefan. I have not tasted a port like this since . . . Well, since I last visited you.'

'I keep my best bottles for these occasions, Leon. That is the last of the 1871s.'

'Don't worry. I know where you can find more. I will have a word with the nuncio in the morning.'

Ciechanowski turned and fixed his gaze on Jack. Jack noticed that he had suddenly grown serious. When he spoke, his voice had lost its former levity.

'Jack, I am worried about something. I hope you do not think I am interfering, but Stefan has told me about the tragedy that occurred in Moscow, and how near you came to dying yourself. It grieves me to hear of such things. When the Cold War ended, I had hoped we might have come to peaceful times at last. But now there are wars in Europe again, and in all likelihood more to follow.'

He paused. Jack guessed what was coming next.

'Stefan has also told me about the scroll. Or should I say, the scrolls? I will be very frank with you. I know you will not object. Part of me wishes you had never found the scroll that Stefan is trying so hard to locate. The letter in Our Lord's hand. Far better for all of us if it had remained buried somewhere, somewhere no one would ever have stumbled across it. But it seems it was not God's plan that it stay hidden.

'And I must confess that another part of me is racked with excitement. That is the expression, is it not? When I think that you have touched with your bare hands a parchment that was handled by Jesus Christ; when I think that we now possess our Saviour's words, written in his own hand, I am speechless.

'And yet I have to say that I am afraid. Afraid for several different reasons. My greatest fear is that this scroll is, after all, nothing but a forgery, a despicable attempt to embarrass the church, something created in the time of Stalin. Before anything else, I need your reassurance on this matter. You have seen the scroll. You have read it. I do not doubt that, before you set eyes on it, Iosif Sharanskii had already carried out tests in an attempt to authenticate it. So, please — I want you to tell me what you think. I need to know. Is it a fake?'

Jack took a deep breath. He was very tired. The food and pleasant company had lowered his defences. Ciechanowski had won his confidence. He could not keep up the effort of lying any longer.

'No,' he said, very quietly. No one else said anything. He repeated the word, more loudly this time. 'No. It is quite genuine. Iosif and I were agreed on that. We may have been mistaken, of course. Time will tell. But I am willing to swear that it is genuine.'

The cardinal closed his eyes, as though praying. From the corner of his eye, Jack saw Rosewicz smile softly to himself. He had been vindicated. Well, thought Jack, so what?

The silence continued for a long time. Ciechanowski remained deep in thought or prayer, it was not clear which. When he opened his eyes again they had an unfocused look. Though he addressed Jack, he spoke almost as though he were alone, as though the room were empty of anyone but himself.

'I am a believer, Dr Gould, though at times even I am not sure what it is I believe in. Does that make sense to you? You are an unbeliever, perhaps it does not make sense. When I was a young man, I believed in God – a conventional enough belief, even banal, but sufficient at a certain age to sustain a life of self-denial, which was what I really wanted. I do not know why. Young men are such strange creatures, even to their older selves.

'But with time such a life grows harder. It is not so much that the flesh is weak, but more that the spirit is complex, and the mind is prone to wander. So it is that we come to other beliefs, other visions. An absent Godhead is not enough. Hume's pendulum swings very heavily. I believed in so many things then: in my country, in peace, in purification through war, in justice, in punishment, in something I called mankind. Some of these I even believed in at the same time, if you can credit that.

'Because I was a Christian, I knew that one day I would have to believe in Jesus. Not taste or sample him, not sip him in the Mass, not give mental assent to the abstractions of Paul, not crucify myself alongside him in some juvenile denial of my human needs. No, I had to devour him, I wanted to swallow him whole. I knew there was more, but it was so hard to find what it was. I believed in whatever came to hand. The saints, the sacraments, the Virgin, life everlasting: anything to put off the day. Anything but come close to that beating heart. Do I frighten you?'

Jack said nothing. The fire burned in the grate. Outside, the wind swept the gardens and the roofs clean.

'I got there in the end; I don't know how, I could never guide you there, I have no map for such a journey. Perhaps no one has, perhaps everyone has to find his way there alone. But he was there, as I had known he would be, he was waiting for me. All alone. That was the awful thing to me in my arrival, how alone he was. Nothing can fill the wilderness he lives in. Not the church, not prayers prayed, not hymns sung – nothing. Each one has to appear

232

before him just as I did, the alone meeting the alone.'

He paused. Even in his unbelief, Jack was tormented by the thought of that cosmic loneliness. It touched something in him. It tore at rough edges he had thought smoothed by time.

'And now,' Ciechanowski continued, 'you bring me this. As though you brought me Jesus himself. I cannot tell you how hard it is for me, how the thought of it stings me.'

He looked at Jack.

'You know that you will hurt many, many people if you publish this letter?'

Jack nodded.

'Willingly?'

Jack shook his head.

'Then why would you choose to do so?'

'Because it is the truth,' Jack said haltingly. 'If it is what it seems to be, then no one has the right to bury it again, no one has the right to censor him. It would be another crucifixion. The church will just have to let people make of it what they will. No doubt it will destroy the faith of many. But you of all people should know that faith is not that easily driven underground. What sort of faith is challenged by the true face of what it believes in?'

Ciechanowski did not answer at once. Jack could not guess what he was thinking, what arguments he was revolving in his mind. For all his humour, he was a serious man at heart.

The cardinal nodded. Jack noticed that a rosary had appeared in his hand as though from nowhere, and that he was twisting its beads slowly between his small, awkward fingers.

'Yes,' he said, 'you are right. What sort of faith is that? This has been a hard century for the church, but I do not believe that the obscurantism of the past is a solution for our problems. We have no more right to suppress the words of Our Lord than we have to withhold his body from those who seek it.

'You were right to be careful. There are evil men who would make the scroll the focus for their own greed, or who would use it as a tool for political ends. Some of them have already made their play. There will be others. It is imperative that the scroll be rescued and placed in safe hands. I give you my personal guarantee that, if it is passed to me, I will use all my power to safeguard it. I will place no restrictions on scholarly access to it, nor on publication of details in the press. There will be no cover-up. And, when the time is ripe, I guarantee that it will be published under my auspices.'

Smiling suddenly, he added, 'With the help of Stefan's money, of course.'

He stopped speaking and looked at Jack. His fingers were still, the rosary motionless. Outside, the wind fell quiet.

'Well, Jack — it's your decision. What do you say?'

The tiredness and the misery were like a heavy weight on Jack's back. Here in front of him was someone who offered to lift it from him, to give him peace again.

'We swapped it,' he said. 'I was to take an ordinary scroll with me, the one Stefan has in that box on his desk. The Jesus scroll went to Israel the day before with a friend of Iosif's. A man called Isaak Berchik. He will keep it safe until I get in touch with him.'

CHAPTER THIRTY-TWO

Strangely enough, it had not occurred to Jack that he might be a prisoner in Rosewicz's house. The circumstances of his rescue in Moscow, his subsequent illness, and the comparative familiarity of his surroundings had all lulled him into thinking of himself as the guest Rosewicz insisted on calling him. He had, of course, expected a little soft resistance should he try to leave while the whereabouts of the scroll remained a mystery. But once he reached his decision to tell Cardinal Ciechanowski about Berchik, he felt no further apprehension on that score.

He was, therefore, all the more shocked the following morning when, after breakfast, he decided to go for a stroll on his own, only to find the way barred by a surly and unresponsive Henryk. He had, in truth, not considered himself a prisoner requiring liberation or flight. Now, however, sent back to his room until Henryk was free to chaperone him outside once more, he realized that a prisoner was exactly what he was.

A quick search of the room itself confirmed this suspicion. The narrow windows were securely fastened, the glass wired to alarms. Behind a large gilt mirror, he found a camera recessed in the wall, connected no doubt to a monitor somewhere below stairs. He realized that he had never attempted to open the door of the room himself: he had all he needed in the small guest suite, after all, and had always been escorted in or out by either Henryk or Mrs Nagle. Now, trying the handle, he found that the door was firmly locked.

His suspicions regarding Rosewicz, rendered quiescent the night before by good food and bonhomie, were abruptly resurrected. Loath as he was to extend those suspicions to Ciechanowski, he was none the less assailed by a terrible dread that he had somehow betrayed the innocent Berchik into unscrupulous, perhaps even bloodstained, hands.

That evening at dinner, having exhausted every indirect avenue of escape as fruitless, he tackled Rosewicz himself.

'Why am I a prisoner in this house?'

Rosewicz, who was at that moment lifting a tiny forkful of fresh truffle to his lips, raised his eyebrows. Removing the delicacy lightly with his lips, he ate it slowly, savouring it.

'Prisoner?' he exclaimed, as though the word interfered with his appreciation of the truffle. 'A prisoner here? Whatever makes you think such a thing?'

'I was prevented from going out alone this morning. Henryk stopped me. When I got back to my room, I found that the door had been locked and the windows shut fast. There is a camera through which it is possible to monitor my every movement. For all I know, there is another in the bathroom. I think you owe me an explanation.'

Rosewicz lifted another tiny helping of truffle to his mouth. Again he took his time before answering. The truffles had been bought from La Maison de la Truffe that morning. They had arrived from Périgord overnight.

'I understand your concern, Jack. You have been through a harrowing experience. Ganachaud tells me he does not expect you to recover from its effects for some time. Physically, you are almost back to normal, but there are mental scars that will take a long time to heal. In one form or another, they will be with you for the rest of your life. But I think you know that. You would not expect otherwise. Nor will I patronize you about them, since I think you know more of such things than I, even at my age.

'However, Ganachaud warned me that your period of confinement in *militsia* headquarters, followed by the interrogation in the Matrosskaya asylum, may have been more traumatic than even you are aware. Hostages, especially when they have been subjected to humiliating treatment or torture, generally undergo some form of counselling on their release. Regrettably, the rather special circumstances of your imprisonment and escape make that a little difficult to arrange. Ganachaud has done what he can and, whatever my friend Leon Ciechanowski may say in jest of French physicians, I think you will find that his treatment will have real value. Do not dismiss Ganachaud lightly. He learned his homoeopathy under Rousson and Zissu. He lectures on the subject at the Sorbonne medical school.

'But to return to the subject of your supposed confinement here. I am sorry about the locked door. That should not have happened. You are free to go anywhere in this house. If Henryk ever seems over-officious or rude, speak to me at once. He will not do it again, I promise you. Your door was kept locked while you were ill as a security precaution. That is why the camera is there, why the windows are alarmed and the glass toughened. None of this is intended to keep you in. It is to keep others out.'

Jack leaned across the table.

'Who, for God's sake? This is Paris, not Moscow.'

'Nevertheless. You will remember that I had high security at Summerlawn. This house is no less protected. There is, first of all, my collection. You will be relieved to learn that it was not damaged when the house was burned down. Then, there are other treasures that would repay a burglar's time and effort.

'But it is you, my dear Jack, that are the special problem. You must not think that, just because you have escaped to Paris, you are now safe. I think you should be told a little about the woman who had you taken to the

Matrosskaya. Her name, as I said, is Irina Kossenkova. She was once one of the most powerful women in the Soviet Union, as considerable in her own way as Aleksandra Kollontai was in hers. But Kossenkova's name is not one you will ever see in any official record. Until a few years ago she headed a small security organization virtually independent of the state apparatus. She was answerable only to the Presidium of the Supreme Soviet, or, to be precise, to the President in person.

'Her function was to provide the head of state with a personal intelligence system independent from the KGB or GRU. The Komitet knew of her existence, of course, and knew that she was one of the few people in the Soviet Union who stood outside their power. On the contrary, they knew very well that a mere word from Kossenkova was enough to have the most high-ranking KGB officer dismissed. Or worse.'

'How do you know all this?'

Rosewicz shrugged. He had finished his truffles. Jack had not even touched his. Their pungent, autumn-filled aroma hung over the table like incense.

'You must have guessed that a man in my position, a Pole with a great deal of money and close connections in the world of finance, must from time to time have had occasion to do business with more than one of the world's intelligence services. I have performed many favours for Western agencies, and they in turn have helped me with information and expertise. Let us leave it at that.'

He paused and glanced at Jack's plate.

'Do you not care for truffles?'

Jack shook his head. He was not really hungry, and he had never had the money or the opportunity to acquire a taste for such delicacies.

'If you will permit me, then. They are available for such a short time.'

He placed Jack's untouched plate on top of his own.

They were dining this evening off plain white porcelain, against which the truffles stood out hard and black. Lifting a small piece to his mouth, Rosewicz ate in silence, then turned his attention back to Jack.

'Kossenkova has survived the transition remarkably well. She saw it coming before all but the sharpest minds in the KGB. Some say she helped engineer it when she saw what way things were going, what would happen if radical changes were not made. They say she was close to Gorbachev, and there are even rumours that she was one of the figures behind last year's coup, acting on his behalf in an attempt to get rid of the hardliners.

'Whatever the truth of that, the fact is that she survived and survived well. Not only that, but she was able to preserve most of her old organization. Intelligence agents have immunity to change, you know. That is something history should have taught you. New regimes cannot afford to dispense entirely with the skills and the knowledge of the old hands. Some have to go to the wall, of course. There are criminals among them, murderers, torturers, men whose public exposure serves as a symbol of change. Or, rather, as a veil, yes? A means of covering the truth. Which is, of course, that things have not changed at all. Not in their essence.

'As for the others, the background men, the grey, thinking men who concentrated on the accumulation of knowledge, the amassing of files on internal opponents and external enemies — these never get thrown out, they are never put to the wall. They are too valuable. Irina Kossenkova was too valuable. Is too valuable still.'

He paused. All round, portraits of sharp-featured men and languid women watched them at the table, an old man eating, a younger man struggling to regain control over his life.

'She is more powerful than ever now,' continued Rosewicz. 'Her only enemies are ghosts: Dzerzhinskii, Yezhov, Beria, OGPU, the GPU, the KGB. All gone now, all lost.

She is all there is left. Without her, Jack, I assure you there would be chaos in Russia. Anarchy, perhaps civil war. I do not exaggerate. She and her organization are all that stands between the Russians and disaster.'

He paused to finish the truffle. Each time he ate one now, he wondered how many more there would be. There were so few in any year, and so few years before death.

'But it is possible that that is not enough. Irina Kossenkova is powerful, but only in the context of a state that may be terminally ill. Whatever strength she has is undermined by the weaknesses of the system she serves. But there is no other system. If it falls, she will fall with it.

'She is desperate for influence, no matter where, no matter with whom. Inside Russia, she can do as she pleases; but that is of little use if all she has to play with are broken toys. To give her the strength she needs, she must have an infusion from outside. And now she thinks she has found it. And that you and I have stolen it from her.'

'The scroll? How could that possibly help her?'

'Oh, you are very naïve, my Jack. It would be everything to such a woman. If she possessed it, had absolute control of it, think what power that possession alone would give her over the church in Russia. The church to which so many are beginning to turn again. And what might she not do with it in order to gain influence elsewhere: with the Vatican, perhaps, or with the leaders of American Protestantism? Their great Moral Majority. I can only guess what plans she might have, how she might think to use your scroll for financial or political ends. All I am certain of is that she knows it will give her the edge she so desperately needs. Nothing simpler. Nothing more.'

'But . . . I still don't see . . .'

'Why she should come for you? My dear boy, she knows by now that I stole the scroll from her and that I helped you escape. I am, therefore, her chief target, am I not? But she dare not strike me as long as the whereabouts of the scroll are unknown to her. She must suspect that I have it, but she knows I would not be such a fool as to keep it here. On the other hand, I am sure she knows nothing yet of the substitution. Unless . . .'

Rosewicz looked at Jack.

'. . . unless you told her under the influence of the drugs Belov gave you.'

'I'm sorry. I can't help you. I honestly can't remember what I said.'

'No matter.'

'But if she has the scroll . . .'

'In that case, I shall have to take it from her. Either way, your own life is in danger. If she does not already know about the substitution, but has reason to suspect it, she needs you to tell her where it can be found. Once she has that information, you are more than just an embarrassment to her. You know too much. That is why Pavlychko was ordered to get rid of you. The scroll is of no use to her if the whole world already knows its contents. Do you see? She will leak a passage here, a sentence there. Sow doubt, breed confusion, bring church leaders to her, men who will be prepared to do anything to see the scroll, or suppress it, or destroy it.

'That is why we need Ciechanowski. And why you must be kept safe, here in this house. Believe me, if you set foot out of here alone, your life won't be worth a centime. For Irina Kossenkova, you are a threat to be eliminated. For me, you are a precious asset. You can help authenticate the scroll, you can present it to the world. There will be an institute, Jack, just as I promised. And you will be its director. You have my word. Once matters have reached that stage, the game will be worth nothing to Kossenkova. She will back off. She will no longer have anything to gain by pursuing the scroll or you. It will be time for her to look elsewhere for her salvation.

'So you see, Jack, that staying here under my protection

and collaborating fully in my scheme is the only hope you have to live a long and fruitful life.'

The old man smiled and laid his fork down quietly on the white plate.

CHAPTER THIRTY-THREE

He went for a walk most days. Henryk stayed close to him, never letting him out of his sight. Jack knew he was armed, and suspected he was not alone. Rosewicz would not skimp on something as important to him as Jack's survival. Without the eminent Dr Gould and his proven links to Iosif Sharanskii, it would be difficult to explain how Rosewicz had come to be in possession of the Jesus scroll.

Jack guessed what Rosewicz was planning. Once it was announced that the scroll had resurfaced, the Russians were bound to make an official protest. By then, Rosewicz and Ciechanowski would have their institute ready, if only in embryonic form: a building, perhaps, and a skeleton staff. There would be a room in which to hold press conferences, a public relations director, a computer to prepare briefings. Jack was willing to bet steep odds that it would be located in Poland. Rosewicz would have rigged up some sort of provenance for the parchment, without tying it down to any one town or library. The scroll would be Polish in origin, Jewish only in the vaguest way (in order to gain some credibility and sympathy by association with the Holocaust), but certainly never German or Russian in a legal sense. The Polish government angle would be dealt with by the Vatican, probably in the form of some sort of joint ownership, with the Church the active partner. It helped that there was a Polish Pope.

And Jack was reasonably sure that Ciechanowski would by now be employed in opening negotiations with Volnukhin's successor at the Russian State Library. They would want everything. To give the scroll a context, to create an unassailable core for the institute, to avoid the risk that there might be other fragments, perhaps whole documents, of equal or similar value. Other letters by the same hand, letters from others addressed to Jesus, pieces by his brother James – who could tell?

But what if the Russians, led by Kossenkova, had got to Berchik first? Rosewicz had said nothing further about Iosif's friend and courier. Jack was not sure he would tell him the truth anyway, especially if things went wrong. He wondered what Rosewicz would do if Kossenkova beat him to it. Just how powerful was he anyway? He had taken the Russians once by surprise. He could not expect to do that again, not if they were taking extra precautions. But there had been Rosewicz's unguarded comment: *In that case, I shall have to take it from her.* Jack felt certain that Rosewicz was not a man to make idle threats.

Before long, Jack started feeling at a loss for things to do. He needed something to occupy his mind. Ganachaud's treatment had worked wonders, but as he himself told Jack, there are things only time can heal properly. 'Time,' he had said, 'and occupation. You must not have too much leisure in which to dwell on things. I advise you to get back to work as soon as possible.'

Jack put the idea to Rosewicz, who sympathized but said he would prefer Jack to stay with him until the institute was up and running.

'Does that mean you've found Berchik?'

Rosewicz shook his head.

'Not yet.'

'But I gave you clear details. The address he was to go to in Tel Aviv, the department of the Jewish Agency that was handling his immigration.'

'He cannot be found. But I am confident that neither he nor the scroll can have left the country.'

Jack felt worried. For all his evident instability, Berchik had understood the importance of the mission he had undertaken, even if he had not known the identity of the document he carried with him. Jack was surer than ever that something had happened to the writer.

'Please do what you can. He was just a courier, nothing more. He knows nothing about the scroll or anything else, I assure you.'

'You have my word. We shall do all we can.'

'But in the meantime, I can't just sit round here waiting, reading crummy thrillers and watching television.'

'You don't like French television?'

'I hardly speak French. Listen, Stefan, I need to do something serious. Ganachaud said as much. You still have your library. There must be plenty of work to be done in there.'

Rosewicz seemed to reflect for a moment.

'Yes,' he said. 'Ganachaud has spoken to me as well. He says you are much improved. Well, you are right. The library is still here. But I think it will be a waste of time for you to do cataloguing or anything similar. I think you should start work on the authentication of the scroll. Yes? There is a great deal that can be done in the absence of the original. I have the complete set of photostats prepared by the Germans. You have your transcription. I can supply you with a complete set of the Huntington Library photographs of the Qumran material, Tov's microfiche edition of the scrolls, facsimiles of any other documents you need – Oxyrhynchus fragments, the Bodmer and Rylands material, Nag Hammadi codices, Cairo Geniza texts. I've got concordances, dictionaries, Bibles, apocryphal texts. There's a copy of Kiraz's concordance to the Syriac New Testament – I doubt if you've even seen it yet – it only appeared a few months ago. If there's anything else you need, you know you only have to ask for it.

'I also have files on the SS acquisition of Jewish manuscripts. You will be able to make conjectures about where the scroll came from, how it got to Poland, and – just possibly – where it may have been kept there. What do you say? Do you feel up to all that?'

Jack nodded. Rosewicz was using him again, precisely as he must have intended to do from the start, from perhaps as far back as that summer at his house in Ireland. But what did that matter if it gave Jack the chance to do what he wanted to do anyway, under circumstances that could scarcely have been improved on?

He started work after lunch. The walks in the Parc Monceau continued, morning and afternoon, on Ganachaud's advice. Jack and his keeper became familiar sights on their regular route, to the left down past the lake and the Roman colonnade, round by the pyramid and the tombs, across to the children's playground, out past the rotunda at the Boulevard de Courcelles gate, and back home.

He got to know the regulars, the old dowagers in their fur coats, the pram-pushing nannies who did their shopping at Maxipuces and managed to look as chic as anyone human had a right to, the joggers going round and round the perimeter, the children taking a short-cut from the Lycée Carnot. He liked to get there just before three o'clock, to watch the younger children from the private schools nearby, brought to the park for their recreation period at the end of the day. They ran and shouted and chased one another like madmen up and down the paths, while their teachers chatted together, oblivious of the racket they made. He noticed that blue jeans and black padded anoraks were in style. Some of the little girls were pretty. Once, watching them play, he found himself in tears.

The rest of his time was spent in the library, reading, filing, sorting. The text of the scroll became the centre of his life. Each day he felt himself grow closer to the Jesus of history, the real Jesus, the forgotten, mythologized, emasculated firebrand, whose face would not fit in any modern church, or, for that matter, most modern synagogues. As he read other texts, cross-referencing, establishing analogues, integrating each of the concrete

246

references in the letter to the shifting contexts of the synoptic gospels, then with extra-biblical material like the Gospels of Thomas and Peter, he felt as though he had started to breathe the actual air of first-century Palestine. It smelled of dust, and Temple incense, and Roman leather, of God, and prophecy, and the end of the world coming. But above all, it smelled of blood. The blood of sacrifices, of pigeons with their throats cut falling like rain on to the high altar. The blood of slaves, whipped into submission by a brutal overlord. The blood of rebels on high, wind-swept crosses.

In the afternoons, he devoted himself to the study of Rosewicz's collection of German material. It slowly dawned on him just how extraordinary was the range of materials the old man had assembled.

During the second week, Rosewicz was away from Paris for three days. He would not say where. Security was tightened in his absence. A bodyguard was placed on each floor of the house, five in all. Henryk posted himself at the door of the library during the hours when Jack was working there.

Snow fell. Rosewicz came back and locked himself away in his study for several hours. That evening, two men in suits arrived after dinner and were shown in to Rosewicz at once. They remained closeted with him until well after midnight. The following morning, returning from his walk, Jack noticed a stretch Volvo 760 by the kerb outside Rosewicz's door. Inside were three men, including one of the visitors from the previous night. Two wore expensive civilian suits, the third a high-ranking military uniform of unclear nationality. They were all Europeans, or so it appeared to Jack. Rosewicz did not appear for lunch.

Something was wrong with the German documents. Jack understood libraries and filing systems. Someone had gone through these papers systematically, removing all files with a specific alphabetical prefix within an otherwise clear sequence. He could not be certain, but it seemed to be one of a number of possible variations: CN, DN, CO, or DO. Also he noticed that, although there should have been records relating to all the main towns in eastern Europe which had SS headquarters, there were no files for anywhere in Croatia.

'Time for our walk, doctor.'

Henryk had appeared at Jack's desk out of nowhere.

'What are you doing here, Henryk?'

The guard was normally excluded rigidly from the library. It was usually Rosewicz who reminded Jack that it was time for his constitutional.

'Mr Rosewicz told me to take care of you today. He is very busy. He has many visitors.' Henryk looked at his watch. 'I think we should go, otherwise it will be dark before we are finished.'

It was a strict rule laid down by Henryk and endorsed by Rosewicz that they neither went outside nor lingered there when it grew dark. The entire system of security Henryk had devised revolved around lines of sight, watchers, stringers, and something called CVC – the Constant Visual Contact which either he or one of his men had to maintain with the object of their protection.

It was in Rosewicz's nature to prefer to operate a system like this in the plush heart of Paris, rather than pull out into the countryside, where he and Jack might go to earth together until the crisis abated. For the same reason – his nature – Rosewicz had lived grandly at Summerlawn, and in Paris taken a house in one of the best districts. To have done otherwise would never have occurred to him. What was the point of wealth if you could not conspicuously consume it? What was the sense in power, if to hold on to it you had to skulk in the shadows, fearing your enemy at every moment? In Henryk he had the best available: absolute loyalty coupled with absolute efficiency.

Jack glanced at his watch. The day was drawing on. For a moment, he was minded to call the walk off. But he had grown accustomed to the routine of it, and today he felt the need of exercise, for he was cramped and uncomfortable after too long and intense a session at his desk.

'I'll just fetch my coat,' he said. Rosewicz had given him a heavy overcoat, long and stone-coloured, designed by Zegna. 'We can walk quickly and be done by the usual time. Do you feel up to a jog?'

'You're coming on well, doctor. I'd not have thought it, that day in the hotel. To be honest, I thought then he'd done for you.'

'He came very close.'

'He has explained to you about the woman? Mr Rosewicz, he has explained about Kossenkova?'

Jack nodded.

'Good. She does not leave things unfinished. Do not forget that. Stay close to me in the park.'

Jack put on his coat, scarf and gloves, and they set out. The park was a wonderland of frost. The trees glistened with tiny icicles. The paths had been swept, but the lawns and flowerbeds were deep under snow. Jack felt the sharp air in his lungs, wiping away both the sour dust of Palestine and the gas-tainted atmosphere of Nazi-occupied Poland. He broke into a gentle trot, with Henryk beside him, effortlessly alert.

A woman was sitting on a bench about a hundred yards ahead of them. She was wearing a long black coat with wide, fur-trimmed lapels, and a low-crowned sable hat. As they approached, Jack tensed, sensing that there was something familiar about her. The distance between them lessened rapidly. Jack slowed down, more than ever certain that he did know her, and that she was waiting there for him to pass.

'Henryk,' he whispered, his voice coming in staggered gasps as he forced the thin air in and out of his lungs, 'who is that woman? Do you recognize her?'

He heard the click of a gun as Henryk drew back the bolt on his automatic with one hand.

'Stop here,' Henryk ordered. He had taken the gun from

his pocket. There was an echoing movement to their right, behind a cover of trees.

At that moment, she stood, turning to face them. Jack felt the blood drain from his face. Breathless as he was, he felt himself grow suddenly faint. It was as though he were falling from a great height; from a clifftop or the sky itself. Maria's face had caught him unawares. As pilots fall for a trick of light and crash, so he had been blinded and was tumbling rapidly to earth.

CHAPTER THIRTY-FOUR

'It's all right, Henryk,' he said. 'You can put your gun away.' He went on walking.

She waited until they were only a few feet away.

'How are you, Jack? Henryk?'

Of some women, it might simply have been said, 'she was just as beautiful', or 'she had not aged', or 'it seemed as if she had been gone only moments, not years'. All that is cliché, and nothing about Maria Rosewicz could have been clichéd.

That she was still beautiful, that her beauty at once delighted and stung him, that the woman standing on the path in front of him was in every aspect the same woman whose image he had carried about with him for four years, Jack did not for a moment deny. But it was not her resilience that struck him first or hardest. It was the unanticipated change that he saw stamped on her every feature, an alteration so marked he almost thought he had been mistaken after all. She was sad, and more than merely sad. The shine had gone out of her, the entire thing, the high, shaking, lightning-quick, luminous thing.

He stood wooden in front of her, his hands and his feet cold, his breath warm for less than a moment in the frozen air. She did not smile. She held her hands in her pockets, pulling the coat tight across her front, in a weak gesture of self-defence. Her breath streamed out in a cloud that lost itself above her head. She was the first to disrupt the silence.

'Henryk, I want to speak with Jack. Karl's over there,

walking with Paul.' She pointed across the path to where, tiny in the distance, a man in a tan coat led a small boy by the hand.

'Why didn't you come to the house, Mrs von Freudiger?' Henryk asked. The unexpected, expected name found its way into Jack's chest, huddling down there as if thinking of ways in which it might hurt him.

'We've only just arrived. I already knew Jack was staying here, and my father said I'd find him here with you. Paul wanted to play on the roundabout.'

Henryk looked nonplussed. Clearly, Maria's arrival had disturbed his sense of routine.

'I really think this isn't the place. There's a security consideration.'

'For God's sake, Henryk, I'm not going to run off with him. I just want to talk. In private.'

Henryk shuffled uneasily.

'Very well,' he said. 'But we have to be back before dark.'

'Don't worry. We'll walk ahead. Just stay behind us, we won't go far. We'll head for the house.'

Moodily, Henryk did as he was told. Jack noticed him speaking into his handset, no doubt to give reassurance and instructions to his fellow watchers. They set off, Henryk ten or twelve paces behind.

'How are you, Jack? You still haven't answered me.'

'How do you expect me to be? I can't . . .' He tried to control his emotions. 'Your turning up like that was a hell of a shock. I . . . I never thought . . .'

'You'd see me again? No,' she sighed. 'There was a time when I thought that too. And here we are having another one of our walks together. Not so sunny today, though. Funny old world.'

'Not very funny at all.' He halted, turning to her. 'Maria, I . . .'

'Please don't, Jack. No recriminations. Look, I must introduce you to my husband and child. Just a moment.'

She called loudly, her voice carrying through the crisp air. The man with the child turned and waved. Maria shouted again, and they started in her direction. Jack watched them come, powerless to stop their advance, like a man dreaming and struggling vainly to awake.

The little boy left his father and ran towards Maria. He was about three years old, a perfect reproduction of his mother. Maria had dressed him in a smart red coat with large black buttons, red leather boots, and a Scandinavian skiing hat with a sort of pom-pom on top. She took the child in her arms and swung him round several times, kissing him. He laughed as the skiing hat fell off into the snow. Maria set him down, laughing with him, and put the hat back on his head.

The boy's father reached them. Maria grew serious at once and turned to Jack.

'Jack, this is Karl, my husband. Karl von Freudiger. Karl, Dr Jack Gould.'

Jack stretched out a hand automatically, returning von Freudiger's smile. The clothes, the shoes, the haircut, the way he wore them, all suggested a man who has never known anything but a life of wealth. He was taller than Jack, aged somewhere in his mid-fifties, and athletic-looking.

'I'm very pleased to meet you, Dr Gould. My wife has told me a lot about you. What good friends you have been in the past.' The accent was German, but very polished, no more than a touch of colour in his speech.

'We haven't seen one another for years.'

'So I understand. It must be remedied. When my father-in-law has finished with you, you must come and stay with us at our house in Essen. I am told you have been ill.'

'I'm much better now, thanks.'

'Nevertheless, you are in need of a rest, and I can guess that Stefan does not give you one. Maria will make the arrangements.'

'And this is my son, Paul.'

She pronounced the name in the German fashion, to rhyme with 'owl'.

'*Komm, Herzchen, sag* "hello, how do you do?"'

The little boy held back awkwardly.

'He's a little shy, especially when I ask him to speak in English. Aren't you, my love?'

Suddenly, the boy's father bent down and snapped at him in German.

'*Also, Paul, tue was deine Mutter dir gesagt hat! Antworte den Herren sofort!*'

The boy flinched and stammered a greeting. Jack glanced at Maria. She was visibly upset by the unnecessary scolding. Jack held out his hand and took the little boy's.

'I'm very pleased to meet you, Paul. I hope we can be friends.'

The boy smiled bravely, but his father's harshness had brought him close to tears. Jack expected Maria to say or do something to comfort him, but she remained passive, watching. Jack could see this was not the first time she had seen her child rebuked.

'Karl,' she said, 'why don't you take Paul to play on the roundabout? I want to chat to Jack. We've a lot to catch up on.'

Von Freudiger seemed to hesitate, then nodded.

'It has been good to meet you, doctor. I look forward to seeing you again. Be sure to tell Stefan that you are invited to Essen and that he is not to keep you a day longer than necessary.'

Then, taking his son by the hand, he went off towards the lake. There was a little roundabout on the other side, with a stagecoach, a tank, a fire engine, and other vehicles. But the little boy did not seem eager to ride on any of them. He kept looking round at his mother, as though in distress that she was not accompanying them. Maria smiled and waved at him, then, when they had gone a little way, turned to Henryk.

'Henryk, will you please stop breathing down my neck? Dr Gould and I are old friends. I want to be able to talk to him without thinking I've got a bloody chaperon two paces away. Just get on with your job of protecting him.'

Henryk complied without much grace.

'He's a lovely child,' said Jack.

'Paul? I would go mad without my little Paulchen.' She smiled at him, and he could see that she was not joking. 'When I look at him, I sometimes think of you, how you lost your daughter. I never understood before, but now . . .' She shivered. 'If I lost Paul, if he was ever taken from me, I really could not bear to live.'

'Why should anything happen to him? He looks fit and healthy. I'm sure you look after him well.'

'I try to, but his father . . .'

'I noticed. I'm sorry.'

'No, it is I who should be sorry. Karl can be such a pig. He embarrassed you, speaking to Paul like that. Sometimes he . . .'

She paused.

'Here I am, talking about my family troubles already. You were always a wonderful confidant.'

'More than that, I thought.'

She reddened and walked on for a bit without answering.

'Why did you leave?' he asked. 'You didn't even contact me.'

'I tried, but Father intercepted my letters.'

'You could have telephoned.'

'I didn't want that. To talk. It was too late by then, anyway. I was already married. The wedding took place two weeks after I left Summerlawn. My father insisted.'

'Your father insisted? What about you? What did you want?'

Flustered, she looked away from him.

'Jack, you have to understand. I had no choice. I had to marry Karl.'

'Had to? Were you pregnant?'

She looked at him, shocked.

'I'm sorry,' he stammered. 'I had no right to ask that.'

'The answer is no. Paul is only three. I had no choice because Father had already arranged the marriage. When I was twelve.'

'Twelve? Good God, Ireland isn't Saudi Arabia.'

She nodded. He noticed that her eyes were moist. All about them, a light snow had started to fall.

'What if I had asked you not to marry him? What if I'd asked you to marry me instead?'

'Please,' she said, 'don't ask me that. There was nothing I could do. Karl was – is – extremely powerful. Not even my father would have dared to cross him. It was . . . a marriage of convenience. For political reasons. Not financial, that did not enter into it. Both my husband and my father are very rich men, neither has need of the other's wealth.'

'Who is he?'

'Karl? He's a German industrialist. West German, at the time we were married. He is the fourth generation of a family of glass manufacturers from Essen. They produce glass for much of the Ruhr pharmaceutical industry. Also more specialized items for scientific laboratories in Germany and abroad. They've a factory in Dortmund producing optical glass – lenses for cameras, binoculars, microscopes, gunsights. Karl is one of the wealthiest men in the Ruhr. In 1980, the state awarded him the *Grosses Bundesverdienstkreuz*. A very great honour for an industrialist. Since then he has become wealthier and more powerful every year.'

Jack stopped and turned to face her, forcing her to stand still.

'What do you want, Maria? You leave without a word, then you reappear without warning. What's wrong?'

'Nothing's wrong. Let's keep walking, Jack.'

She pulled his arm sharply and made him continue.

'You don't look happy,' he said. 'Are you happy?'

'Jack, I haven't come here to talk about myself. About being happy or unhappy. This is important. I've come to get you out.'

'Out?'

'Out of Paris, out of my father's clutches. For God's sake, just shut up and listen to me carefully.'

'I don't understand. Why . . .'

She cut in again.

'Let me do the talking, Jack. You can ask all the questions you like afterwards. Just don't interrupt me now. For your sake and mine, just listen. In about a minute, we're going to reach the way out on to the rue Rembrandt. It's a one-way street, with the traffic coming towards the park. One block down, it runs into the rue Murillo. That's another one-way, but this time the traffic runs to your right, down into the rue de Courcelles and on into the Avenue Hoch. On the right-hand corner of the rue Murillo, parked against the kerb, there's a dark blue Citroën BX.

'As we get near the gates, I want you to start walking a little more quickly. Just enough to get some more distance between us and Henryk. I'll set the pace. At the gates, run. Take the right-hand gate: the others are padlocked at this time of day. Once you're at the corner of Murillo, head for the car. You'll see a coloured man at the wheel. He'll have the engine running. Open the door, grab him, and pull him out. Don't worry, he's expecting it; but make it look realistic. Push him to the ground, jump in, and drive off.'

'What about you?'

'Me? Don't worry, I'll be all right. You'll probably hear me shouting behind you, but just ignore that.'

'Where do I go? I've never driven in Paris. I can't find my way round the place to save my life.'

'That's exactly what you will have to do. Once you pull

off, switch on the cassette player. There's already a tape inside. Keep your speed to about thirty or forty miles an hour where you can. The tape will give you instructions. Just follow them and you'll be all right.'

'But what are you going to do?'

'That's the gate coming up now. Just a bit more pep in the stride, not too much. If he shouts or starts running, make a break for it.'

Jack did not even try to understand what was happening. All he knew was that he was about to take a leap in the dark that could as easily end in his death as in his freedom. They were almost abreast of the gate when a crazy thought leaped into his mind, that Maria might, even in all innocence, be working for Irina Kossenkova.

'Mrs von Freudiger! Slow down!' Henryk's voice barked behind them.

'Maria, I have to know . . .'

'Jack, you have to trust me. Please. You've got to go through with this all the way. Once you go through that gate, there won't be any turning back. Is that clear? If my father's people don't kill you, there are others who will.'

'But . . .'

'Hold on,' she hissed, her attention all on the gate. She was still picking up speed.

They were there. He glanced through the gate. The street beyond it was empty of traffic. He could see the intersection lower down. Henryk was coming up quickly behind them. He had seconds in which to make up his mind.

'Go now,' Maria whispered. 'Hurry, my love!'

He turned and broke away, sprinting for the gate. Behind him, a loud cry split the air, Henryk's voice at full volume. Then a second from somewhere in front of where he had been. And Maria's voice, calling his name.

The street rushed past on either side. He had to swerve to miss pedestrians. Behind him footsteps rang out on the snow-covered pavement. Reaching the corner, he stumbled and fell, then picked himself up, narrowly missing a woman and child as he staggered to his feet.

The car was waiting as Maria had said it would be. He stepped off the pavement and rushed up to it. The driver turned his head and grinned at him. He had already wound the window down.

'Just make it look natural, Dr Gould,' he said in English, with an accent that might have been Senegalese or Mauritanian. 'Hurry up, man, pull the door open.'

Jack acted automatically. He was not thinking now. There were more shouts. He pulled the door open.

'Haul me out. Be quick about it.'

Jack grabbed him by the edge of his coat and pulled him bodily from the car, then pushed him away. The driver played up, skidding on the wet snow and falling to the road. Jack leapt in, threw the gear into first, and put his foot down hard.

The car swung into action, sending a spray of snow and ice up from its wheels as it swerved out into the road, missing a passing cyclist by inches. The door was still open as he slammed into second gear and roared off.

He picked up speed quickly. The engine had been finely tuned. As he did so, the door slammed shut. Instinctively, he glanced into the driving mirror, which had already been positioned at the correct angle for him. Henryk was standing in the middle of the road, shouting helplessly into a handset. Another man sprinted up to him. Moments later, they were gone.

On the pavement, a tired old woman in rags, burdened with plastic bags, stranded among affluence, looked up, startled and shivering.

He switched on the cassette.

Good afternoon, Dr Gould. You are heading west on the rue Murillo. I'd like you to slow down. Any moment now, you'll be coming to the rue de Courcelles. Take your time at the junction,

*and turn right. Remember, you're in Paris, not Dublin. Stay on
the right-hand side . . .*

The voice was English, urbane, and without emotion.
He hardly heard it. He could focus on only one thing:
Maria's final words to him: 'Hurry, my love!'

CHAPTER THIRTY-FIVE

The recording guided him skilfully through the late-afternoon streets, warning him in advance of intersections, advising him of necessary or useful lane changes, exhorting him to drive carefully, at an even pace. He did not know whether the police were on the lookout for him or not. The driver whose car had been 'stolen' would be obliged to make a fuss and ask for a gendarme, unless he had been able to slip away in the confusion. Perhaps a passer-by had already telephoned the police: it was a law-abiding area. But Jack thought Henryk would not be too happy about that. He would not want Jack to fall into the hands of the gendarmerie, if he could help it.

As he drove, he wondered for the first time why it had been necessary to go through the charade. Why not a car with a driver who knew Paris, waiting for Jack to jump into the passenger seat, just like a getaway car in a movie? Why all the bother with a fake driver, a cassette, a scheme that could so easily go wrong?

In a few moments, you'll be coming into the Place de la République de l'Equateur. You'll see a Crédit Lyonnais on the left corner and a branch of Weston shoes on the other side. Cross the junction and make a left turn at the shoe-shop into the Boulevard de Courcelles.

Of course, Maria would not want the getaway to look contrived. A planned escape would have thrown suspicion on her. By making it look spontaneous, she could pass herself off as an innocent bystander as readily as Karl or Henryk or any of Henryk's back-up team.

He still could not begin to guess her motive. And, listening to the cassette, it really hit him for the first time that she was not in this alone. The arrangements had been elaborate, and he had only started. Which meant that Maria was working with or for someone or, more probably, some organization opposed to her father or to whatever organization he himself was working on behalf of. The possibility of Kossenkova struck him again, but this time he dismissed it out of hand. Whatever she was up to, he was sure Maria was not in league with the Russians.

You're coming into the Place des Ternes. There's a large flower-stall right in the middle of the square. You'll see a bar called the Lorraine on your left and a CIC bank on your right. Make a right turn . . . Follow the traffic sign on your left saying 'Porte d'Asnières, Périphérique' . . .

His journey took little more than fifteen minutes. His final instructions were to turn in to a street in the Clichy district. There he would find a red garage door. He was to sound his horn, the door would open, and he was to drive in.

The moment he did so, lights went on, the car door was opened from outside, and he was hurried out by a group of men whose only distinctive feature was that they all wore short leather jackets. There was no time to see anything more.

Within seconds he was bundled into the rear seat of a second car, a door was lifted at the rear of the garage, and they were heading out into the night. This time, there were clearly no instructions about holding to an even speed. The driver put his foot down and kept it there.

It was dark by now. The man in the back seat beside Jack said nothing. The city passed by jubilantly, as though it were the scenery for a dream, and Jack not quite placed in it, and yet somehow, in his passing, belonging there. On each side, the coloured lights of shops and cafés were messages from a world he could reach out to but never touch. And the traffic in a constant stream, and the road riverlike with snow and ice and reflected lights. On a tall Christmas tree made festive with red and yellow lanterns, a toy angel turned tin wings to the wind.

The driver wore a small leather cap and a tiny ear-ring in his right ear. Sometimes, as he drove, he sang in a soft voice the lyrics of songs that Jack could not identify.

> Quand je m'trimbale
> Une p'tit' poupée dans mon tape-cul
> C'est comme si je lui faisais
> Panpan culcul . . .

From time to time, Jack caught sight of his face in the driving mirror. Alert, mobile eyes, a mouth set hard to correspond to the mood of deep concentration in which he drove. He knew the streets the way other men know the way to the pub or the office. In a city of reckless drivers, he handled his car with precision and skill, darting through the impossibilities of the late-afternoon traffic, turning with inches to spare into narrow side openings, skimming lights, cutting through back streets, doubling back − all to ensure that they were not being followed.

It was not until they found themselves on the open road after Gennevilliers that the man in the back started to relax. He leaned back in his seat and took a short pipe from an inside pocket.

'Do you mind?' he asked. English, a public-school accent. Jack could not see him very well, but he guessed him to be a middle-aged man of medium height.

'Go ahead.'

'It's just that people nowadays . . .'

'Be my guest.'

The man lit up, making a great ritual of tamping and lighting and puffing. Before long the car had begun to fill with poisonous fumes.

'Sorry about all the dramatics,' the man said, once he

was satisfied that his pipe would stay lit. 'We don't usually carry on like this. But when needs must . . .'

'We've not been introduced,' said Jack.

'Sorry. Stupid of me. I have the advantage of you there, of course. Name's Felix. Or at least, that's what you're to call me.'

'You're not really Felix, then?'

The man laughed.

'Good God, no. Nobody in this wretched business is really anything. Sometimes I wonder if we're really human. You did well back there. We had to spring it on you, I'm afraid. It was all down to some rather tricky timing. We wanted you out ASAP, but we couldn't just send in the cavalry. It had to be someone you knew, someone you'd trust. Your friend Mrs von Freudiger — we can use her real name, you know it already — agreed to set it all up. But she's not exactly a free agent. She had to get her husband and the boy to Paris as well, otherwise he wouldn't have let her go. Took a bit of organizing this near Christmas. It only came together yesterday. You'll have guessed by now that we had to go through all that rigmarole about stealing the car in order to make it look like a snap decision on your part. She'd have blown her cover otherwise.'

'Blown . . . ? I don't get you. What the hell is going on?'

'What is going on, Dr Gould, is that you have just been rescued by a branch of British intelligence. Maria von Freudiger is one of our agents, working for us on a very delicate operation in which you have quite inadvertently become involved.'

'I take it,' Jack said slowly, 'that this has something to do with a scroll that went missing in Russia.'

Felix nodded. Jack caught a glimpse of his face in the light of a street lamp, momentarily. He was a very ordinary-looking man, with a sandy moustache and glasses. Outside, a large sign read 'Cergy-Pontoise'.

'Yes,' he said. 'You've hit the nail on the head.' He paused and reached down for something. 'By the way, I should have asked – would you like a shot of something? I've got whisky, quite a good one, I think; or brandy. That's pretty decent too.'

Jack hesitated. He realized that he was still shaking. It couldn't be half an hour since his getaway.

'Do you good,' Felix said.

'Yes, all right. Some brandy, please.'

Felix switched on a little light and busied himself with bottles.

'Straight? Soda?'

'Straight.'

'No ice, I'm afraid. You'd need a Roller for that.'

'Plain is fine. I'll have it just as it is.'

'Good man. They said you wouldn't make a fuss. Not the fussy sort.'

'They?'

'Oh, just some people. You'll meet one of them later.'

He passed a large tumbler to Jack.

'Sorry, no brandy glasses.'

'I'll make do.'

Jack took a large sip. The liquid took him in the throat at once, making him cough, then calming him.

'Where are we heading?' he asked.

'Don't know exactly. Ask Elvis there in the front. We're taking you out by small boat. Too many risks at the airports or the big ferry ports. Rosewicz will have men all over them by now. Some his own, some police he controls.'

'I asked where we were headed, not how we're getting there.'

'England, of course. London. Where else?'

'Well, it might not be my choice. Have you thought of that?'

'Yes, of course. Look, please put up with us for a while at least. We can't easily get you out of here to Dublin or Israel, or wherever else you might fancy. We've got tickets

265

for London, and there's nothing either of us can do till we get there. After that, it's up to you.'

'Really?'

'Please don't sound so distrustful. I know you've been through a lot, but it's not a good idea to wind up distrusting everybody. Turn you paranoid. You're not our prisoner. Once we're in London, you're free to go where you please. If you want to leave, it will be your decision. We won't try to stop you.'

They had turned off at Chennevières on to the N1, heading north for Beauvais. There was open countryside around them now. It had grown dark. The road ahead was stark and empty. In white fields, trees stood gamely in a rising wind.

'You didn't go to all this trouble just for me to walk away at the end of it,' Jack said.

Felix knocked his pipe out into a crystal ashtray. He began to fill it again, scooping loose tobacco from a soft leather pouch.

'No, you're perfectly right about that. We'd be disappointed if you left. Disappointed and worried.'

'Worried? Why's that?'

'Because your life would be in danger, and we would not be in a position to take steps for its protection.'

'Danger? Danger from whom?'

Felix put his pouch back into his pocket and proceeded to pack the tobacco down firmly into the bowl.

'Surely you know by now. Or guess. From Stefan Rosewicz, of course. From Irina Kossenkova. And from some people you don't know about. Friends of Rosewicz. You really have got yourself mixed up with some dreadfully unsavoury people.'

'I see.'

'I've no wish to sound melodramatic, but we really are your only hope. Sorry to be so blunt about it. But a man in your position . . .'

'What about Maria? Is she in any danger?'

266

'No more than usual. That is, of course, another consideration. Something for you to mull over.'

'What is?'

'That if you stick around and help us out with a few questions, you'll get to see her again. I gather you're rather fond of her.'

'You seem to know a lot about me. For someone I've never set eyes on before.'

'Part of the job. In our trade ignorance is not bliss.'

'Did she tell you that about my feelings for her?'

Felix struck a match and held it to his pipe, sucking furiously. It took him two more matches to get it going properly.

'Mm, yes,' he said, picking a sliver of wet tobacco from his tongue. 'Matter of fact, she did. Thought it would help us set up the escape effort. Reckoned you'd be likely to trust her, put yourself in her hands. Quite essential that. You mightn't have run otherwise, might have been a disaster. And there was the husband thing. Shock of seeing him, she thought that would ginger you up. But don't get me wrong.' He puffed clouds of foul-smelling smoke into Jack's face. 'She's awfully fond of you. Scout's honour, she really is.'

PART FIVE

CHAPTER THIRTY-SIX

*The Office of the Sacred Congregation for the Doctrine of the Faith
Vatican City*

The room was smaller than he had expected, the trappings less
sumptuous than imagination had foreshadowed. But then he
ought to have known that every effort would be made to keep
things reasonably informal. The Sacred Congregation liked to
avoid all associations with the Middle Ages, or with the days
when it had been known as the Inquisition.

'Father Labrouste, please be seated.'

The speaker was Bottecchiari, the Cardinal Prefect of the Sacred
Congregation, the man Labrouste considered his most dangerous
enemy here. The rest were French-speaking cardinals and bishops
chosen from among those serving on the Congregation, together with
one or two from outside. Less than a dozen in all. No bigger than the
average university selection board. But considerably more formidable, especially when you had been brought before them on what
amounted to a charge of heresy. The term had not been used yet, of
course. It was for the Congregation to determine whether there was
heresy afoot at all. But Labrouste knew why he had been summoned.

'Father, we are delighted that you have given up some of your
valuable time to come here today from Louvain. We will try not
to detain you long. This meeting is merely a colloquium, a
conversation designed to help us understand one another better.
Whatever conclusions we reach today will be sent to the cardinals
of the Congregation on Wednesday, and their decision forwarded
to the Holy Father on Friday. Unless, of course, we think it
necessary to impose yet a further delay.

'However, I have no doubt that will not prove necessary and that we will receive all the clarification we need this afternoon. I trust you are comfortable. We have no wish to appear intimidating.'

'Not at all.'

Labrouste's hands were sticky with sweat. The men in this room could destroy him. Nowadays, of course, they did not take you out to be burned at the stake. The auto da fé was hardly the style of the modern church. But they had other racks to stretch a man on, and other stakes at which to burn him.

'Father,' Bottecchiari went on, 'we are here to discuss some of the contents of a book you published last year, a work entitled La Foi et la Loi Judaïque à l'époque du Temple Hérodien. I take it we are correct in ascribing authorship of this book to you?'

Labrouste nodded. His mouth was dry. All round the table, eyes were fixed on him.

'Very well,' said Bottecchiari. 'The book, as you know, puts forward several novel theories concerning the life of Our Lord, theories which have given rise in certain quarters to no little disquiet. I am sure your views have been misunderstood by some of your readers. That is why we have asked you here today, to clear up any of those misunderstandings. Perhaps you would like to begin by providing us with a brief summary of your main thesis, in your own words. So we know where we are.'

He had known this day would come from the moment he first put pen to paper. But he had felt himself compelled to write what his investigations told him was, if not the truth, at least an approximation to it. He still believed in God, still loved the Church. But he knew, as certainly as he had ever known anything, that the Church was lifting its arm and that, before today's sun set, it would have begun to crush him.

He cleared his throat and began to speak.

CHAPTER THIRTY-SEVEN

There had been a boat waiting at Ambleteuse, a small port just north of Boulogne. Felix had sent Jack down below to sleep in the cabin. He had stretched out on the narrow bunk, exhausted yet mentally restless, half sleeping, half waking, tormented by his doubts about Maria. 'Hurry, my love.' Had that been affection or premeditated encouragement?

They had passed at intervals through patches of hailstones that clattered like tiny meteoroids against the portholes of the little boat. It was a night of cold, a night of storm, and they were tossed on crumpled waves like a paper boat in a child's pond. Jack had lain in the bunk, listening to the sea fling itself against the flimsy hull. He was reminded of the slow crashing of Atlantic waves on the rocks below Summerlawn, all that vanished summer.

Jack had only the haziest picture of London, though he had visited the city often. Most of his visits had been on business of one kind or another, and had generally involved sessions at the British Library, the School of Oriental and African Studies, or the Jews' College. Travelling for the most part by tube, he had formed for himself a distorted map whose landmarks were a blur of stations on the Piccadilly Line, the lifts at Russell Square, the bookshops in and around Great Russell Street. He knew parts of Bloomsbury quite well, and Covent Garden, which he had visited with Caitlin, and Charing Cross Road, where there were more bookshops, and Cromwell Road, near the old air terminal, where he had once stayed in a cheap hotel. The fringes he knew not at all.

Driving into the city in the early hours of the morning, he was tired and disoriented. The roads and buildings here were all entirely unknown to him. They could have been taking him anywhere, he would not have known. He had not been brought to London to browse in bookshops or attend a seminar, though he still could not guess the real reason for his rescue. He saw signs for Sevenoaks and Westerham, then Orpington and Bromley, but they were only names to him. The city grew thick about them. It was well after midnight, but there was still some traffic about – lorries, a few taxis, a late-night bus taking cleaners home from the City.

They drew up outside a semi-detached house in a quiet street that had stunted trees all down one side. There were no lights in any of the houses. A street light gave illumination every hundred feet or so. The house in front of which they had stopped was protected from the road by a tall laurel hedge. Built in the 1930s, it boasted a porch and a door in which was set a panel of mass-produced stained glass. A light was burning in the porch, the only one in the street. A name by the door proclaimed the house's name to be 'The Laurels'. Behind the hedge, a pocket-handkerchief-sized garden lay stripped and bare in the porch light, waiting without much hope for spring and whatever came after.

Felix rang the doorbell. Moments later, a light went on in the hall and footsteps approached the door. There was a pause as someone fumbled with a chain.

The door was opened by an emaciated man in open-necked shirt and trousers. His thin neck and hollow cheeks suggested illness, but his manner had the effusiveness of a schoolboy on an outing. He wore gold-rimmed spectacles tight against his face.

'Felix, as I live and breathe. The Dunkirk spirit is alive and well. We must hold a reunion in forty years' time.'

274

He glanced at Jack.

'And you must be Dr Gould.'

Jack nodded.

The thin man stretched out a hand.

'Parker. I've heard a lot about you. But you must be freezing out there, come on in.'

He stood aside to let them into the tiny hall. Someone had tried very hard for ordinariness. The milkman calling for his weekly payment would have seen nothing to excite comment. Horse brasses on one wall, an anonymous landscape probably picked up on a Sunday afternoon in the Bayswater Road, plastic flowers in a brass vase, Wilton stair-carpet with a sickly floral pattern. The English home on its best behaviour.

Parker led him into a kitchen at the back of the house, done out in much the same taste as the hall. He could not decide whether it was the real thing, rented or bought intact for whatever purpose the house served, or a facsimile, lovingly put together by an interior designer specializing in the mannerisms of the lower bourgeois lifestyle.

'This is what we call a ''safe house'',' said Parker, perceiving his interest. 'You may have heard the expression.'

'From time to time, yes. Is it?'

Parker cast him a puzzled look, then caught his meaning.

'Yes. Yes, in fact it is. Very.'

'It doesn't look very safe to me.'

Parker shrugged.

'No, it wouldn't. Me neither, if the truth be told. But there are those who know about such matters, and I find them to be invariably correct. We are not so much impregnable as invisible. Only the Holy Ghost could find us here.'

'I was assured that there was to be no pressure on me. That I would be free to go where I liked.'

Parker nodded. He looked like an ageing man, but Jack

realized with a shock that he was probably no older than his forties.

'You are free. But I take it that Felix has explained the possible consequences of your departure.'

'After a fashion, yes.'

'I would recommend that you stay at least for tonight. There is no compulsion, but I would suggest that you are hardly in a position to find alternative accommodation at this time or in this area. And I think you have other problems. You have no money, no identification, no one whom you can readily contact.'

'I have friends in London. At the university and the British Library.'

'I can assure you that their phones are already tapped. Not by us, I hasten to add. There will be a check on your bank account, so drawing funds will alert someone to your approximate whereabouts.'

'Why am I so important?'

'In yourself, you are not. But you have access to information. You would do well to spend the night here. If you agree to speak to us, co-operate in what we are trying to do, we will make you comfortable.'

'And in return?'

'In return, we will be beholden to you. On your own, you will be a sitting target for those wishing to eliminate you. You are a stranger to these matters, but let me assure you that they are not. On your own, I guarantee that your body will be washed up on a bank of the Thames within a week. We, on the other hand, can provide you with a measure of protection. Given the chance, we can eliminate the threat entirely. Sleep on it. Do nothing rashly. Mrs von Freudiger took an enormous personal risk to get you here. You owe her something.'

'I'd like to see her.'

'That will not be possible.'

'I would still like to see her.'

Parker hesitated.

'It is very difficult. Perhaps even dangerous. We cannot let you put her at jeopardy. Nevertheless, I'll see what can be done.'

'Tomorrow?'

Parker shook his head.

'No, that's out of the question. I don't think you appreciate her position. Every step she takes has to be thought out well in advance. A single false move on her part and she would join you in the Thames. Or, more probably, the Ruhr. She is due in London between Christmas and the New Year. I will see if something can be arranged. You will just have to be patient.'

'Very well. I'll stay for tonight.'

'Excellent. Why don't you join us in a cup of cocoa?'

CHAPTER THIRTY-EIGHT

After breakfast the next morning, Felix took him to the dining-room at the back of the house. Parker was there already, fiddling about with an old-fashioned cine projector. Next to it stood a more modern slide projector fitted with a carousel.

'Morning,' he said when Jack walked in. 'Something nice for breakfast?'

'Bacon and eggs.'

'Thought so. Mrs Bidwell believes in a fry-up. None of that low-cholesterol rubbish for her or her boys. You'll see. You'll leave this place two stone heavier than you came in.'

'I didn't think I was staying that long.'

'You haven't seen Mrs Bidwell's fry-ups.' He threaded a piece of film through a sprocket. 'It's the devil's own job this, getting it through. You'd think we were more advanced these days. Still, it's an old film. Super-8 or something. I'm not technically-minded myself.' He glanced at the window. 'It's a foul day outside.'

Jack followed his gaze to a small, bedraggled back garden. Pruned rosebushes in their winter nakedness, wet grass, weeds, a creosoted fence, a potting shed.

'Who owns this place?' he asked.

'I haven't the faintest idea. I was taught not to ask questions like that. I suppose it belongs to some nameless government department somewhere. There'll be a fictitious owner's name on the deeds, I expect. God knows. Why? Are you thinking of buying it?'

Felix was lighting up again. Jack wondered how many pipes he got through in a day.

'Have you had news of Maria?' he asked. 'Is she all right?'

'Right as rain,' Felix said. 'We've got people watching the house in Paris. She went for a ride with von Freudiger this morning, over at the St Germain forest. She and her husband keep horses over there in stables. One each, for when they visit.'

'You're sure she's safe?'

Felix shrugged.

'Can't say, old boy. Expect so. The place is still in a bit of a tizz, mind you. The von Freudigers are off back to Essen this evening. Can't say I blame them.'

'There,' Parker exclaimed, standing back from the projector. 'Don't blame me if it goes up in flames.'

A screen had already been set up on the wall opposite.

'Dr Gould,' Parker asked, 'would you be good enough to sit down in that chair there, please? Thank you. Please don't ask any questions until we're done. Then you can fire away.'

He turned to his colleague.

'Be a good chap, Felix, and close the curtains.'

Felix ambled over to the window and drew a pair of chintz curtains across it. They were surprisingly heavy. When they were shut, not a glimmer of light came through.

A cone of white light, hard-edged, broke the darkness in half. On the tiny screen, numbers counted down rapidly. There was a flicker. Then music. And, with the music, the stark emblem of a vanished tyranny.

When the film was over, Parker let the reel run through. There was a forlorn flapping sound as the take-up reel spun with the loose end of film. The white beam still sliced the darkness, raddled with specks of dust. Felix's voice came out of the far corner.

'A fake, of course, and a very clever one. Took a long time to make. Almost too late by the time it was finished. But it served its purpose.'

'What was that?' asked Jack.

'Questions later.' Felix turned his head to Parker. 'Next, please.'

The projector went dead. A second beam shot out in place of the first. There was a soft click, the carousel turned a fraction, and a slide slid deftly into place. A face appeared on the screen.

'SS-Standartenführer Wilhelm Klietmann,' recited Felix. 'Whereabouts currently unknown. Aged twenty-nine at the time this photograph was taken. He had been newly appointed commandant of the Friedrichshain prison in Berlin. The prison was part of a large complex similar in dimensions to the bunker in which Hitler and his aides hid out at the end of the war. It was situated in what was until recently East Berlin. The prison had been in the Russian zone for about a month when Klietmann was made commandant.'

'But . . . that's impossible,' Jack blurted out.

'Fantastic, yes. Impossible, no. The complex was very deep and much better hidden than the Hitler bunker. I doubt very much if even the Führer knew of its existence. It is still there, incidentally; but only a small handful of people know of its existence.'

Another click, another slide. An elderly man in the circular hat and robes of a German judge.

'Judge Erwin Oberhauser, President of the War Crimes Tribunals held in Friedrichshain Prison between the twenty-fourth of June and the seventeenth of August 1945. In the dock were seventy-two British intelligence agents arrested at various points during the war. Among them were members of a clandestine unit known as October. The trials were held in the presence of senior Reich officials, members of the German General Staff, and representatives of the judiciary. Needless to say, the whole thing was a sham. All the real Reich officials, the Wehrmacht and SS officers, the judges and lawyers were dead, in hiding, or under arrest.'

Another click. A picture of the inside front page of *The Times* came on to the screen. At one time this had been the first news page. The headline read: *German War Crimes Court Sits in Berlin. Death Sentences Expected for Agents of British Aggression.*

'That is an announcement of the first session of the war crimes trial at Friedrichshain. Like the trials, it is a fake. Both the film you saw and this newspaper, along with numerous other forged documents, were essential factors in an elaborate scheme to extract confessions from the seventy-two agents held at Friedrichshain.'

Click. A courtroom hung with NSDAP insignia and presided over by a forty-foot eagle. A shaven-headed man stood in the dock, his head bowed. A panel of five judges faced him from a high podium.

'The first session of the trials. The prisoners were brought before the court separately. Each trial lasted less than a day. Once basic guilt had been established under the cover of false legality, the convicted men were brought before a judicial commission set up to determine the scale of their crimes and to extract information relating to Allied war crimes as a whole. That was a sham as well, of course.'

More trial photographs. A single slide of a man hanging on a wooden gallows.

'Some were hanged. The ones they thought would be less useful to them. *Pour encourager les autres.* You see, what they were trying to do was quite simple. They wanted information. But the men they had arrested were all trained and dedicated agents. Not quite men of steel, there is no need for hyperbole. But men who were nevertheless determined not to divulge anything beyond their name, rank and number.

'The fake newsreels, the newspapers, all the forged documents, and above all the trials, were designed for one purpose only: to destroy the morale and willpower of the men still in their power, and to provide grounds for long-term interrogation. We know that many of the Nazi war criminals at Nuremberg, or Eichmann in Jerusalem, were prepared to divulge facts about themselves and their activities, even about their colleagues, which they might have held back had they been arrested while the war was still in progress. The same principle applied here.'

Click. A tall gateway with an inscription over it in an unfamiliar language. Heavy wooden gates partly open. Guards on either side. Barbed wire.

'This is a concentration camp in the Croatian town of Klanjec. It was an Ustashi internment centre for Serbs during the last world war. One hundred and twenty thousand people died there between 1941 and 1945.'

Jack felt bewildered. He could not understand the relevance of any of this to the matters in which he had been involved. Nor could he see how mock trials of Allied prisoners in Berlin could be connected to a Croatian concentration camp.

Click. A young man in an old-fashioned military uniform. Something about him seemed familiar to Jack.

'This man was commandant of Klanjec from September 1941 to October 1942. During that period he was responsible for several thousand deaths. Anything about him strike you as familiar?'

'He's familiar, but I can't say why.'

Click.

'This is a close-up from the last photograph.'

The slide now on the screen showed the commandant's right hand. It was lifted towards the camera. Between his first and middle fingers he held a lighted cigarette. Jack looked closely. The tip of the little finger was missing.

Click. The commandant's face in close-up.

'Stefan Rosewicz,' Jack said. 'It's a photograph of Stefan Rosewicz.'

CHAPTER THIRTY-NINE

'His real name is Andrija Omrcanin.' Felix spelled the name. 'I'm told that's the pronunciation. He's a Croat by birth, but his mother came from Kraków, so he speaks Polish fluently, and he's never had any difficulty passing himself off as a Pole. During the Second World War he served as an officer with the Ustashi. You have heard of them, I take it?'

'Only vaguely.'

'They were a fascist terrorist organization led by a man called Ante Pavelic. They came to power in Croatia in 1941, breaking away from Yugoslavia. Pavelic was proclaimed dictator. The country came under Italian, then German rule, but the Nazis gave Pavelic more or less a free hand. In the next four years, the Ustashi massacred half a million people. Political opponents. Serbs, Gypsies, Jews. Anyone they had reason to dislike. They more or less invented ethnic cleansing. Much of the time they didn't shoot or gas their enemies. Nothing so sophisticated. They preferred to cut throats or gouge out eyes or tear off limbs. It was the most barbaric regime of a barbaric age.

'During the war, the Ustashi organized a campaign to convert the Orthodox Serbs to Roman Catholicism. Rose-wicz played a leading role in the crusade. Like his leader Pavelic, he was a staunch Catholic. Jews and Orthodox Christians offended him. So he determined to slaughter the first and convert the second. Any who refused to convert — and there were plenty of those — were sent to join the Jews. Thousands were put to death or ended up in Ustashi-run concentration camps, which amounted to the same thing. You might think about that the next time you hear a news report about Serbian atrocities. Things are never as simple as the "News at Ten" makes them appear.

'After leaving Klanjec, Rosewicz was put in charge of the Ustashi Office of National Reconciliation. A euphemism for the forced conversions. When the war ended, Tito's people put him high on their wanted list.

'You might think that would have made him a pariah, that he would have been hounded from place to place until the forces of justice or even personal revenge caught up with him. That would be naïve. There is very little justice in the world.'

Another click. Rosewicz's face was replaced by that of a thin, bearded man. He was standing behind a desk, and on the wall behind him hung a framed photograph of Adolf Hitler.

'Ante Pavelic, the Croat leader. His official title was Poglavnik. This photograph was taken in his office in Zagreb around 1944. Note the armband.'

On Pavelic's upper right arm was a black armband bearing a swastika.

Click. A shot of Pavelic meeting Hitler. Smiles all round. *Click*. A shot of him standing in front of a table on which stood two candles, a crucifix, and a crossed gun and dagger.

'This was taken before the war, when the Ustashi were still partisans out in the woods. They held elaborate initiation ceremonies.'

Click. Pavelic in military uniform greeting a man in white clerical robes. Jack felt a tremor of surprise.

'This photograph was taken in April 1941. The other man is, of course, Pope Pius XII. Believe me when I tell you that this is not a fake. The British Foreign Office issued a protest on the occasion. A very strongly-worded protest, even in the language of diplomatic protocol. The official Vatican response was that the Poglavnik had been granted a private audience in his capacity as an eminent Catholic, not as the Croat Head of State. I make no comment on that, it is outside my sphere of competence.'

Click. Two more men, also in clerical dress, but this time black.

'The date is 1953, the place the church of St John Lateran in Rome. The two priests are celebrating mass on the 500th anniversary of a Roman ecclesiastical institute, the Istituto di San Girolamo. It's still there today, on the Via Tomacelli. Number 132.

'The plumpish man to your right is Monsignor Juraj Magjerec, at that time the institute's President and Rector. His companion is Father Krunoslav Draganovic, its Secretary. Both men are Croats. Indeed, the Istituto di San Girolamo was the official centre for the Croatian priesthood in Rome.'

Click. A photograph of a dignified building in bright sunlight. A young woman was passing by, smiling at the camera. On the steps, a priest looked in the other direction.

'The institute as it looks today. If you don't mind, I'd like Parker to read a description of it as it appeared in 1947. Two years after the end of the war. The description is that of a spy who had been infiltrated into San Girolamo by Robert Mudd, an agent working for the US Counter-Intelligence Corps.'

Behind them, Parker cleared his throat.

' "In order to enter this monastery one must submit to a personal search for weapons and identification documents, must answer questions as to where he is from, who he is, whom he knows, what the purpose is in the visit, and how he heard about the fact that there were Croats in the monastery. All doors from one room to another are locked and those that are not have an armed guard in front of them and a password is necessary to go from one room to another. The whole area is guarded by armed Ustashi youths in civilian clothes and the Ustashi salute is exchanged continually." '

Felix continued.

'About the same time, an Italian secret police agent described San Girolamo as "a den of Croatian nationalists and Ustashi". It was said the walls of the college were covered in pictures of Pavelic.'

Felix paused. In the background the projector hummed gently to itself.

'I hope you are not growing confused, Jack,' Felix said. 'This is very important. The fact is that San Girolamo was the centre of one of the largest and most successful Nazi-smuggling rings in Europe. One of the infamous Vatican ratlines. Draganovic helped more Nazis flee to South America than ODESSA or Die Spinne combined. And not just Croats. Germans, Austrians, Poles, Czechs – anyone in need of assistance.

'You can ask me any questions you want afterwards. There's plenty of time. I can show you papers, photographs, published materials, anything you want. I have evidence for everything I'm telling you.'

'How do I know they're not all fakes too? How do I know you didn't make all this up yourselves?'

'You don't, Jack. At least, not as long as you're here with us. Once you leave, you're free to check for yourself. Go to any major library. The Public Records Office. The US National Archives in Maryland. The Wiener Library. Yad Vashem. They'll show you all you want to see, answer any questions you may have. I can give you the names of independent researchers. University professors. Believe me, this is genuine.'

Gradually, the force of what Felix had said sank in. Not even British Intelligence could manipulate the archives in places like the Wiener Library or Yad Vashem.

'Very well. I'll take your word for it. For the moment. But you're right, I am getting confused.'

'I don't blame you. And at the moment we're only touching the surface. Let me try to make things clearer. Before the last war, the Catholic Church was heavily involved with right-wing politics in central and eastern

Europe. The great threats for the Church were atheistic communism and liberalism. They were like twin plagues that were poised to destroy Christian civilization. Church leaders regarded any measures they might be forced to take against them much in the light that doctors or nurses look on sanitation or immunization. The Vatican saw itself as the nerve centre in a showdown between God and the Devil. The world was changing, and not, as they thought, for the better.

'There were plans to establish a Catholic Federation in eastern Europe. The aim was to combat Soviet propaganda. Some prelates wanted to restore the Habsburg monarchy. Pius XII and his advisers wanted to divide Europe into two blocs – one in the West as a bulwark against America, the other in the East as a fortress against the Reds. Politicians set up Christian Fronts in several countries. They were generally nationalist and violently anti-communist. In many cases, they were the main recruiting-ground for the new fascist parties.

'One of the most important was an alliance of militant Catholic lay associations with a long-term aim of uniting all the nations from the Baltic to the Aegean in a single Catholic Federation. The Federation was also to be known as Intermarium, "the Region between the Seas". It was to be a new Holy Roman Empire.'

Jack shifted uncomfortably in his seat. On the screen, the image of the Istituto di San Girolamo hung naked in the darkness, bright sunshine concealing darker shadows. What was the priest turning away from? The girl or the camera?

'I still don't see . . .'

'Please, Jack, be patient. I'm trying to avoid unnecessary detail, but some is essential if you're to follow me. Shall I go on?'

'Yes, of course. It's just that . . . No, it's all right. Go on.'

'Andrija Omrcanin – let's go on calling him Stefan Rose-wicz – was an active member of Intermarium. He belonged to an old Catholic family from Zagreb. One of his ancestors was a big shot of some kind in the wars against the Turks. He was killed at the Battle of Mohács in the sixteenth century. Stefan's brother Dragutin was a priest. They made him a bishop in 1936. Through him, Stefan and several of his friends came in contact with a French cardinal, a man called Tisserant. Tisserant was secretary of the Vatican unit responsible for co-ordinating the Church's anti-communist Crusade in the East, the Congregatio pro Ecclesia Orientali. The Congregation had already been training hundreds of Uniate missionaries in Rome and sending them into the Soviet Union. Tisserant was looking for ways of spreading his influence.

'In 1938, Rosewicz and his brother had a meeting in Rome with a group of Catholics selected from different parts of central and eastern Europe. They included priests and laity. By the end of the meeting, they had set up what I can only describe as a cabal within a cabal. This was a secret council whose primary function was to run the affairs of Intermarium on behalf of the Congregation. The larger organization would serve well enough as a public front for the Vatican's general political programme in the region. Meanwhile, the self-elected Council would make the real policy decisions, reach deals with politicians, and infiltrate the higher echelons of society. They called themselves Crux Orientalis. In English, the League of the Eastern Cross.'

There was a click and another photograph appeared on the screen. Another gateway with the same unintelligible inscription.

'Another Ustashi concentration camp, this time at Karlovac.'

Click. A pile of bodies, naked, awaiting burial. Legs, arms, gaping mouths. The familiar unfamiliarity of mass death. Jack's heritage. Everyone's heritage.

'Seventy thousand Serbs and Gypsies are known to have been put to death here. It may be a low estimate.'

Click. The head and shoulders of a thin-cheeked man with staring eyes. He wore a clerical collar.

'Father Ljubo Vrancic, camp commandant. A friend of Stefan Rosewicz. A wanted war criminal, still at large. He and Rosewicz escaped to the West together. Vrancic was one of the founding members of Crux Orientalis.'

'A priest?'

'He celebrated mass every morning in the camp chapel. Believe me, Jack, you are entering places I would rather not take you.'

Jack stared at the face on the screen. He had known men like him. They had taught him at school, he had confessed his childish sins to more than one of them, received absolution, returned to a state of grace.

Click. A man in SS uniform. Very erect, with alert, nervous eyes, a look of intense concentration.

'SS-Oberführer Andreas Buchheim. The commander of Einzatsgruppe A, based in Lithuania. A founding member of Crux Orientalis.'

Click. Click. Click. Photograph after photograph, all members of the League. Czechs, Poles, Balts, Croats, Germans. SS and SD officers, Nazi party officials, two Gauleiters, a Reichsstatthalter, several SS und Polizeiführer, a cardinal, a bishop, several priests, two abbots.

Click. An old man in spectacles, his temples fringed with wispy grey hair.

'Professor Lucjan Gierek. Head of the Department of Biblical Studies at Kraków University before the war. A fanatical member of the League.'

Felix paused. Jack sensed that he was preparing to bring his threads together. And then? Would he weave them into a pattern or shear through them with a single cut?

'In 1942, Professor Gierek was made responsible for the codification of a collection of Jewish manuscripts looted from synagogues and libraries in the Lódz region. He and a band of assistants followed the Einsatzkommandos into the ghettos. The troops would clear out the people, then

Gierek and his people would take what they left behind.

'One day early in 1943 – this will not come as a surprise to you – Gierek realized that they had stumbled quite by accident across a document of unparalleled importance. He told none of his colleagues. But he did tell his superiors in the League. One of those superiors was Bishop Dragutin Omrcanin. The brother of Stefan Rosewicz.'

CHAPTER FORTY

'Rosewicz already had an amateur interest in biblical matters. His brother sent him to Poland, where he checked the scroll with Gierek. When he accepted it was genuine, the bishop spoke with friends in the Vatican. You can imagine how excited they were. But it wasn't long before someone pointed out that a discovery like this could cut both ways. They needed time, and they needed control of the document, so they instructed Rosewicz's brother to make sure Gierek kept his mouth shut, and to bring the scroll to Rome straight away.

'There were two complicating factors, however. The first was that the scroll formed part of an important collection listed in SS records, so getting it out would involve some sleight of hand. A more serious problem was that, by the time the Vatican knew what was going on, the Italian government had surrendered to the Allies. That was in September 1943. After that date, getting anything safely into Italy was an uphill job. More importantly, there was the risk that, if the Allies managed to push north according to plan, Rome would fall into their hands. The bishop was no fool, nor were his friends at the Vatican. They knew there was a more than even chance that the Germans would be pushed out. The scroll was safer for the time being in Poland.

'We're not quite sure what happened next. The scroll was stored somewhere in Poland, in SS hands, as far as we can tell. Rosewicz returned to Croatia, where he was promoted to Pavelic's inner circle.

'At the end of the war, two things happened more or less simultaneously. Both have a direct bearing on current events. The first was that Stalin took any Nazi booty he could lay his hands on and had it shipped out of central Europe to Russia. I think you know about that already. The original plan was to turn the Jewish material over to anti-Semitic researchers in Moscow and Leningrad. The shit hit the fan in the Vatican when they heard about it. Some bright lad realized that the Soviets might publish the scroll and use it as part of their anti-religious propaganda. So Tisserant put in one of his Uniate agents and had the entire collection transferred to the Lenin Library. The plan was to take everything out later on and smuggle it into Italy, but the entire Vatican intelligence network in Russia was blown sky high a couple of years afterwards. End of story. Until now.

'The second thing was the survival of Crux Orientalis. The film you saw at the beginning of this session was, as I said, the basis for a series of spurious war crimes trials held in East Berlin. The organization responsible for holding those trials was, in fact, not the SS, but the League. Not all of those involved in the deception knew that, of course. The soldiers on guard were ordinary Waffen-SS troops. They thought the whole thing was a rearguard action of some sort. But the leadership, men like Klietmann, were all long-established members of Crux Orientalis.'

'The POWs,' Jack interrupted. 'The ones you say were put through these mock trials – what happened to them?'

Felix did not answer at once. Jack sensed that he had not expected the question.

'Happened? Why, I'm not absolutely sure. As I said, some of them were executed. As for the rest – I imagine they were released eventually. Or perhaps they all died in Friedrichshain.'

Jack suspected he was lying, though he could not guess why. Felix went on.

'The information the League obtained by means of those interrogations gave them considerable leverage in post-war Europe. They couldn't regroup openly, of course. Too many of their members were wanted by CROWCASS and other war crimes agencies. But they had a hell of a lot of highly classified information and plenty of ways of turning it to their own advantage. The basis was already being laid for the League's influence in the post-war period.

'Most of the League's central committee succeeded in escaping, thanks to Draganovic and his ratlines. There were numerous ways of getting to Rome once the war was over, and once anyone got there he could be sure of a warm welcome at San Girolamo. As with most of the other ratlines, the secret lay in using the confusion that existed with regard to DPs – displaced persons. Draganovic was running the official Croatian Committee of the Commissione Pontificia d'Assistenza, the Pontifical Welfare Commission. That gave him access to genuine and forged papers, things like Red Cross passports.

'He got Pavelic out to Argentina, where he set up an Ustashi élite squad to assist General Perón. And he slipped Rosewicz through the nets as well, through Rome and on to Genoa, where he was put on a boat for Ireland. When he resurfaced, Andrija Omrcanin had become Stefan Rosewicz, with papers to prove he was Polish.

'But it wasn't just papers he took with him. The Ustashi didn't abandon Croatia without taking a few souvenirs. Pavelic managed to move over four hundred kilos of gold and God knows how much foreign currency into Austria. Other Ustashi leaders drove truckloads of treasure in the same direction, and some of this made its way to Italy. By this time, Rosewicz's brother had settled himself in at San Girolamo, and he was in a position to see that a goodly proportion of this booty made its way into the family coffers.'

The light of the projector flickered suddenly and went out. They were plunged in darkness.

'Damn,' Parker exclaimed. 'The bloody bulb's gone again.'

Moments later, the main light went on.

'It doesn't matter,' said Felix. 'We'd more or less come to the end of the slide show anyway.'

He stepped away from the wall and took a chair facing Jack. Parker remained standing by the projector.

'By the 1960s,' Felix went on, 'Rosewicz and his colleagues had established branches of Crux Orientalis in about a dozen countries. Argentina, Uruguay, Paraguay, Brazil in Latin America. France, Germany, Austria, Italy, Poland, Czechoslovakia, Hungary, Yugoslavia in Europe. They continued to put money away in bank accounts round the world, looking forward to the day when they could start having a direct influence on political events again. There's a central group in the Vatican. You'd be surprised if I told you just how high up it goes. And you'd be surprised if I told you the names of some of the Catholic politicians who are active members.

'The collapse of Communism has been the signal the League's been waiting for. This is their chance to start the ball rolling again, to establish that new Holy Roman Empire I told you about. All it needs is the Vatican's backing, and they can put their own people into power almost anywhere they please. I don't have to tell you how important religion has become as a factor in modern politics. But the League knows they don't have for ever. A lot of the impetus behind the religious revival in places like Poland was nothing more than anti-government feeling. Under the new capitalist systems, there's a danger people will just go down the secularist road like the rest of Europe and America.

'That's why they're so desperate to have the Jesus scroll. They know that, if they play it properly, it could be the trump card they've been looking for. It would give them leverage within the Vatican, as far up as the Pope himself. The Polish origin of the collection makes that even more attractive.

'And if they can turn the scroll into some sort of super-relic, it could spark off a religious revival right across central and eastern Europe. It's exactly what they need.'

Jack shook his head.

'It won't wash. As soon as the scroll is translated and published, it will have the opposite effect. It will prove just how far removed the Church has always been from the real Jesus. That scroll was written by a pious Jewish rabbi, not the Son of God.'

Felix nodded.

'You may be right. But in the end that won't really matter. I think Rosewicz may have an even better plan.'

'A better one?'

'To reveal the scroll as part of a Jewish conspiracy against the Church. The mood in Europe is ripe for that. They've already started ethnic cleansing in Yugoslavia. The neo-Nazis are attacking Gypsies and other foreigners in Germany. Anti-Semitism is back in fashion in France, if it ever went out. Crux Orientalis means business. Bad business. We need you to help us stop them.'

CHAPTER FORTY-ONE

The next three days were spent in a sort of debriefing, a dialogue that went on for hour after hour, the questions and the answers running into one another until they became blurs in Jack's wilting consciousness. He had agreed to help. What choice did he have, morally speaking? His parentage in part bent him to it. So too his love for Maria, in spite of her parentage, and whatever might come from that love. Felix and Parker had delineated a great evil. Unwitting though his own involvement in its meshes had been, it was intricate and complete. To disengage himself was neither really possible nor proper.

The very process of enlightenment had bound him hand and foot to his enlighteners. He was beholden. To Maria for freedom, to Felix and Parker for what he knew of the truth. He did not for a moment suppose they had told him all they knew, or even a fraction of it; nor did he suppose they had any intention of doing so. And he guessed that Felix had lied to him more than once, above all with regard to the prisoners-of-war about whose fate Jack had asked. He presumed that was the way of their world. They had regaled him with shocking facts, not because they felt any obligation towards his enlightenment, but for the psychological impact they were certain the film and photographs would have.

They were, for all that, not merely proper to him but, after their fashion, kind, and he was then more in need of kindness than at any other time in his life, with the exception, perhaps, of the months following the deaths of Caitlin and Siobhan. His dreams had become dark again. He knew, of course, that they were using him, that he and the things he knew were mere assets to them. But he did not feel threatened by their questions, whether physically or morally. They did not want confessions; they just wanted help and they thought he could give it.

They worked together, spelling one another through the long hours: Felix, who was slow-spoken and thorough, and Parker, who could be witty when he chose, and who was always perceptive. They sat with him in a front parlour with a piano and an old gas fire, in antimacassared armchairs, like old friends playing at riddles.

The informality, the ordinariness of the setting helped somehow. He was set at ease. They treated him as an honoured guest. It was fortunate for his peace of mind that he was not possessed of X-ray vision. Had he been able to see through the living-room wall into the living-room of the house next door, number 37, his perception of things would have been profoundly altered.

There, he would have seen two more men, younger men in slacks and sweaters, crouched at a battery of audio-visual recording equipment. The mirror over the fireplace in number 35 – Jack's house – concealed a large hole through which a video camera filmed everything he said and did. The apparently casual arrangement of chairs in the living-room concealed their deliberate placement, designed to give the camera a good angle.

Each day at six on the dot, a motorcyclist rushed the video- and audio-tapes to technical labs in Baker Street. There they were copied and distributed to a select committee on a 'need to know' basis, after which they were subjected to careful scrutiny by supposed experts in the nuances of voice and face. Did he show signs of stress when he mentioned this, did he avert his eyes when he spoke of that?

The curious thing was that it never occurred to Jack to question the credentials of his interrogators. Had it been the mere fact of their Englishness, the pedigree of their accents, the reassuring tweediness of their dress that had at once convinced him that they were bona fide? Or had Maria's blessing gone with them, covering them in probity as a dying man's confession mantles everything it touches with conviction?

Felix came at things tangentially, like a harpoon-bearing skin-diver sneaking up on a shoal of unsuspecting fish. He looked like a schoolmaster, and something in his manner suggested that, or a social worker. His earnestness was offset by a wry humour that surfaced at the most unlikely moments. He ate bars of sickly milk chocolate, and offered them to Jack as though they would assist him in remembering.

There was an air of singularity about the man that had struck Jack the first time he saw him. He had the mannerisms of someone who has been single all his life. A little fussy in his clothes, neat in his habits, particular in saying 'please' or 'thank you', as though not entirely grown away from childhood.

He was not a homosexual, who simply has no interest in women, nor a self-willed celibate, afraid of sex, nor even a grown-up child with, as another generation might have expressed it, 'no passionate parts'. He just seemed a lonely man who had, at a certain moment in his life, on the morning of his fortieth birthday or his forty-first, come to understand that life could hold no companionship for him. That was how Jack saw him during the first day and for much of the next.

So it was surprising to hear him remark late on the second day, apropos of some quip of Jack's, that his wife would have found the comment funny. Jack could not square this marriedness of Felix with his seeming aloneness, and realized he must now seek for the causes of that false air of singleness in something else. In lack of love for his wife, perhaps, or in her neglect or despising of him.

But the more he reflected on those and other possibilities, the more Jack thought he would have to seek a very different reason.

Parker had a spare and wounded look, a gaunt face punctuated by dark, eagerly mournful eyes. He seemed ascetic; by choice, thought Jack, rather than nature. He tortured himself, or had been tortured; but that was not the word Jack used. He preferred to say 'wounded' to himself when he thought of it, for that expressed the thing better. And what took him by surprise on the first day – like the surprise of learning that Felix was married – was the discovery, not simply that this wounded man could smile, but that in doing so his entire person would be transformed. These smiles were, admittedly, rare, but when they came they would take Jack by surprise again and win him wholeheartedly to Parker's side, whatever side that might be.

He asked Jack question after question about his father, and, though he could not perceive their relevance to anything, Jack answered all of them happily. There were, in particular, questions about his father's life in the camp. Which camp had it been, how long had he spent there, what had happened to him afterwards, how long had he spent as a refugee? And then questions about his father's family. How many of them had died in the camps or the ghetto, how many had survived, where were the survivors living? And, at almost every stage of this catechism, how did Jack himself feel about this, how had he reacted as a child to that?

And then, more bewildering to Jack, the questioning moved on from his father to Caitlin. How exactly had they met? Could he remember having seen her on campus before that, even vaguely? Had she ever introduced him to other members of her family? What had she told him about her parents, about their lives or their deaths?

The sessions were never long, and in the breaks they would sit in silence drinking tea or coffee and munching on biscuits. Sometimes, while Parker did the questioning, Felix would sit apart at a table playing patience with small laminated cards. His games never seemed to come out, but he never grew impatient, never tired. The soft sound of shuffling became a regular accompaniment to the other game Jack was playing with Parker.

There was a housekeeper called Mrs Bidwell, a narrow-hipped widow in her mid-fifties who brought their beverages on a tin tray and recharged their plates with HobNobs and McVities Digestive. She would cook their breakfasts and prepare their 'proper meals' at lunch and dinner, serving them in the dining-room at the rear of the house. Sometimes, during the sessions, they could hear the muffled sound of her television drifting through the walls. The sound appeared on the audio-tapes and had at first required an explanation for the uninitiated.

Jack listened to all the questions politely and in silence, Parker followed by Felix, Felix followed by Parker in regular succession, until he hardly knew them apart or why he was there, why any of them were there. He told them all he could, faked nothing, held nothing back, and all because of a trust that was building with no other mortar to hold its walls than Parker's occasional smiles.

'There are two kinds of patience,' Felix told him during one of the breaks on the first day, when he taught him the best games. 'Some depend solely on the shuffle, they will come out or not come out purely by chance. You have to wait, you have to try again and again. Others are part shuffle, part skill. Make the wrong moves and you will block yourself.'

He played a game called Beleaguered Castle twice, showing Jack the problems, and each time it came out beautifully; and then a king was dealt to the top of a row, and all the twos were underneath, and the game blocked and would not even allow a first move.

*   *   *

'What was in Rosewicz's papers, the ones he had from Germany? Did they include reports from Einzatsgruppen?'

'What does Berchik look like? Is he a tall man, thin? Does he have a beard? How long had Sharanskii known him?'

'How many scrolls would you say there were altogether? How many fragments? Do you know the provenance of any of that material?'

'How many photostats altogether? Originals or second copies? Were they grainy?'

'What was the cardinal's name? Are you sure? What did he look like?'

'Did your father know the date of his mother's death? How many miles did they walk? Where is your uncle Josef now?'

'What was the name of the café where you say you met Caitlin? Did you speak to her first, or she to you? Are you sure? What did you do before you were lovers? How did she die? What did you feel? What do you feel now?'

Why were they asking so many questions? And why those questions, questions about things that could have no possible relationship to what was happening?

'Where's Maria?' he asked. 'I'd like to speak to her.'

'She'll be here, I promise you. In a few days. After Christmas.'

At night he slept in the front bedroom. A bodyguard stayed outside Jack's door all night, or so Jack assumed, for he was there when he went to bed and there again first thing in the morning when he came out to go to the bathroom. His name was Norman. Parker and Felix had other rooms, but they too stayed in the house.

In the mornings Jack would be wakened by the sound of a milkman doing his rounds. Later, if he looked through the curtains, he saw people getting into cars and driving off to work, a postman delivering mail, children on their way to school. There was an air of complete suburban normality about the street. But downstairs, Norman sat in a chair in the hallway with a submachine gun cradled in his arms like a sleeping child.

CHAPTER FORTY-TWO

They spent Christmas with him, as though by some quirk of genetics they had become family. As though, by disgorging what he knew, he had achieved parthenogenesis.

On Christmas Eve he was driven into town. Felix accompanied him. They drove through the streets for a while like tourists, taking in the decorations and the lighted shop windows full of Christmas goods. Oxford Street and Regent Street were crowded with people doing their last-minute shopping. Moscow and its drab queues seemed a million miles away. Children with bright faces hurried past, clinging to their parents' hands. Jack looked away hurriedly.

'Is there any shopping you want to do?' Felix asked.

'I'd like to get something for Maria,' he said. 'But I've got no money, and Parker said it might be dangerous to draw some from my account or to use my credit cards.'

'That's all right. We can advance you whatever you want. Have you thought what you'd like to get her?'

'I don't know. I hardly know what she likes.'

'What about perfume? You can hardly go wrong.'

They went to Harvey Nichols, where he bought her a large bottle of Shalimar. He remembered with great clarity that it was the perfume she had been wearing that last night in the observatory at Summerlawn. He had asked its name then, almost casually; but now it seemed almost a talisman.

The salesgirl tied ribbons round the box and wished him a happy Christmas. She was French and very beautiful. As he thanked her, Jack felt a wave of sexual desire pass through him. It was the first time in years that he had felt such strong need. The perfume, the feelings it recalled, the sales assistant's unexpected beauty, had all caught him unawares.

They went outside on to Sloane Street. In the shop windows, white angels lifted frosted wings. A band was playing 'Silent Night' nearby. As he walked to the car, he noticed with astonishment that his cheeks were wet with tears.

On Christmas Day there was turkey stuffed with chestnuts, plum pudding from Marks and Spencer, crackers from John Lewis. He was reminded of the imbalance there had been in his own upbringing, celebrating Christmas with his mother and her family, and Rosh ha-Shana with his father and friends. Neither one thing nor the other, neither fish nor fowl. Afterwards, and on Boxing Day and the day after, a Sunday, they watched television and rested. Felix taught him to play bridge imperfectly. Norman came in to make up a fourth hand. His friend, the man whose name had not been given to Jack, remained outside, 'to keep an eye on things'.

On the day after, Maria came. She brought him a card with a reindeer on the front, one that played 'Jingle Bells' when it was opened. He gave her the perfume, and she seemed overwhelmed by it. There was also a book for Paul, a copy of *Where the Wild Things Are*, which Felix had picked up at his request. She seemed more delighted with it than with the perfume. In return, she had bought him a grey silk Armani tie, exquisitely soft to touch.

'This is beautiful,' he said. 'But I don't know when I can wear it. I hardly think they'll let me out.'

'Don't let them bully you,' she said. 'They'll have to let you out if you insist. They're not your keepers.'

'Aren't they?'

She shook her head. Sunlight had entered the room, not golden, but bright enough to touch her dark hair with fire.

'Not in the sense you mean. They want to protect you.'

'Your father wanted to do that. That was the whole point of Henryk. He rescued me from Moscow. You must know about that. I don't see how this differs.'

'My father would have sold you to the highest bidder. As it happened, he was that bidder himself, and so, as long as you were with him, you were safe. But the slightest change in his strategy would have left you as helpless as a baby.'

'And Felix and Parker won't do that? Won't contemplate a change of strategy? What are they really after – do you know?'

'They want to destroy the League. It's important to them, and the scroll is a major element in the whole scheme. That makes you important. I don't think that will change.'

He told her about the questions concerning his father and Caitlin, and asked what they could mean. She said she could not guess, but there was something in her eyes that suggested she knew more than she was willing to tell him.

'What about you? How did you get here? They said your husband won't let you out of his sight.'

'That's not entirely true. Karl is jealous, but he is also proud. I have started to build a career for myself as a concert pianist. I play mostly here in London. Sometimes Karl comes with me, but quite often he is too busy. So I travel alone. I'm here for three days to give a recital in the Purcell Room.'

'I remember,' he said, 'that first day, when I rang your father. I heard you playing in the background.'

She laughed.

'I wasn't very good then.'

'Are you good now?'

She looked sadly at him.

'Yes,' she said. 'I am very good. But I'm far from the

best. There were much better students in my year at the conservatory. Some of them will have brilliant careers. Others won't. Talent isn't everything. It costs money to go on tour, it costs money to perform before you're well known. A lot of people don't have that money and can't get a patron, so, if they don't win a major competition, they end up playing in orchestras. Or, in some cases, working as session musicians in recording studios, or giving up music altogether. As a professional option anyway. So, you see, I'm one of the lucky ones. My father's rich. My husband's richer. So I play. Their rich friends come to my concerts and clap for all the wrong reasons. They'd think I was good if I played half the pieces in the wrong key or backwards.'

'Does that depress you?'

'Of course it does. You know it does. That's why I'm telling you, because you understand. But I want to play. I'm good enough for the concert stage, and I'm also rich enough to get through the first few years. It's my good fortune, and I shouldn't despise it. I'm not going to make any gestures, Jack. I can't afford gestures.'

'And Karl? What about him? Do you play for him?'

She shook her head.

'No,' she whispered. 'He's tone deaf. He goes to concerts, but he has no ear for music. My father once said he goes to hear the people.'

'I don't understand.'

'Not coughs or applause, I don't mean that. He listens for the other sounds, sounds only someone like him will ever hear. Money has a sound. Did you know that? And power, that has another sound. It's very similar, but an expert can tell the difference. Beauty. Sex appeal. Weakness. Susceptibility. Vulnerability. Greed. Ambition. To Karl, they all have their individual sounds; he has perfect hearing, he hears melodies where you and I would detect nothing but a shuffling of feet.'

She paused. They were in the living-room. Felix had made mulled wine. Each had a glass on a low table. Maria

306

glanced up from time to time at the mirror over the fireplace.

'I'm playing tonight,' she said. 'I'd like you to come.'

'Will Karl be there?'

She shook her head. He thought she blushed.

'I'm on my own tonight. He's in Dortmund this afternoon, meeting some financiers.'

'Then of course I'll come.'

'There'll be a ticket waiting for you at the box office.'

She stood to go. He stood as well, stepping close to her.

'Maria. I feel as if everything's still in mid-air. Where we left it that night in the observatory.'

She glanced at him timidly. Her tongue darted out to lick the corner of her mouth nervously. She looked round at the mirror, catching sight of her own face reflected in it. So many reflections, she thought, so many mirrors. And at times, she thought, you were not the watcher but the watched, not the mirror but the reflection. She took a step towards him. He was about to hold her again, but she held back.

'Not here,' she said, speaking softly. 'Later. Tonight, after the performance.'

'You're sad,' he said.

'Am I?'

In answer he reached for her hand. This time she did not draw it away. But still she made no further move towards him. She could feel the presence of the mirror behind her back, the brittleness of the glass. If it should crack, she thought, if it should break . . .

'I have to go,' she said. 'They're expecting me for a rehearsal. I'm already late.'

Norman went with him to the concert. Tickets were waiting for them, as Maria had promised. They arrived just minutes before the performance started. The hall was packed. As Maria had said, much of the audience consisted of men and women from the better-heeled end of society.

They chattered and laughed among themselves like birds in a cage. Jack remembered concerts he had attended with Caitlin in Dublin's National Concert Hall; and smaller recitals, like this one, in the Examination Hall at Trinity.

The lights dimmed. Voices fell silent. Someone coughed. Maria came on stage. She wore a long black dress set off the shoulder and ornamented only by a plain silver brooch. Jack could not take his eyes off her. For most of the performance he was too deep in the sight of her to be wholly conscious of what she played. The first half consisted of a Prelude and Fugue in D Minor by Bach, followed by Schubert's Sonata No. 10 in B flat. At the end of each piece, there was ecstatic applause. For the second half, she played four Chopin ballades, and for her encore she had chosen Chopin's Nocturne in C sharp minor. Slowly, unwillingly almost, Jack began to realize that she had not been telling him the truth, or, at least, not all of it.

She was not merely good, she was outstanding. It was not simply the bravura of her fingering, or the uncanny precision of her timing that arrested her listeners. It was that she brought to each piece she played, to each note, and to each pause a depth of feeling that seemed to Jack quite unsurpassed. Several of the pieces — notably the second movement of the sonata, and the nocturne — had evidently been chosen to convey a mood that was overwhelmingly gentle, wistful and sad.

The music was perfect for the season, for that bewildered interlude between Christmas and the New Year, a time of festivity past, when the death of another year was a matter of days away. A time to think of what had been done and of what had been left undone. Of sin and the impossibility of living. He thought of Caitlin and Siobhan, of his father dying alone, of Iosif and Leah and Sima. And every time he looked up, Maria was there.

She had left a message with his ticket, asking him to see her afterwards. He made his way backstage, accompanied by the silently watchful Norman. A small room had been set apart for her to dress in. It was packed with friends and admirers. Norman seemed uneasy at having to look out for Jack in a crush, so they hung back at first in the corridor outside, beneath a fire extinguisher that had been partly ripped from the wall. People came and went, offering congratulations, forming little parties for pubs and restaurants, kissing and embracing and smiling brittle smiles.

Jack listened to their high voices, their cries of acclamation, seeking for those other, less readily distinguishable sounds of money, lust and envy. He thought of leaving. He felt out of place here, out of his class. The coming and going of so many insiders only served to point up his unsuitability for a woman like Maria. Alone together that summer, cut off from either of their worlds, they had come close; but what had ever made him think that he was the sort of person who could share her life? Her existence was so much broader than his, her world so wholly different from any world he had ever known. He stood in the cold corridor, feeling his courage ebb with every passing minute.

Just as he had almost made up his mind to go there was a flurry at Maria's door, loud cries of 'goodbye, darling' and '*ciao!*', then a crowd of expensively-dressed concertgoers vanished through the swinging door that led back to the auditorium and the exit. When he looked round at her door again, she was there, watching him.

'I'm tired,' she said. 'My manager will drive me back. I'm staying at Brown's Hotel. Come in half an hour. Use the Albemarle Street entrance, but be careful: Karl has people watching me all the time. I'm in suite 516.'

Jack waited until the half-hour was up, anxious and perplexed. Norman drove him to the hotel. He knew what was going on. It was not for him to approve or disapprove, but he did not like anything that made his job more difficult.

'Just leave me here, Norman. I'll be all right.'

'You know I can't do that, Dr Gould. I have my orders.'

'Wait in the lounge, then. You can have tea or something.'

Norman seemed ready to protest again, but he understood that some sort of discretion was called for.

'All right,' he said. 'But if word gets back . . .'

'It won't. I promise.'

She was wearing the perfume he had given her. Just as she had worn it years before on a warm summer's night, watching the stars. When he took her in his arms it filled him. As though he had been suddenly filled with stars. He had been so empty, so perilously empty, that the mere inhalation of her perfume was enough to satiate all his senses. Touching her, it was as though he stretched out a hand from the emptiness in the hope that, somewhere among all the debris of things, they might connect.

Their first embrace was the longest either had known. He would not let go of her, not even to let her undress. It was enough to hold her, to fill himself with her inch by inch and moment by moment. Her silk dress rustled every time he moved against her, like grass or leaves under wind.

At intervals he would draw back a little in order to look at her face. She would hold his eyes with hers.

'I love you so much,' she whispered. 'So much.'

He ran a hand over her cheek. As though all her nakedness were there, and all his. Now that he was with her, he could not imagine not being there. Now that he wanted her, he could not imagine a cessation of desire.

'Your wife,' she said. 'Caitlin. Do you miss her?'

'Yes,' he said. 'All the time.'

'It will never heal?'

'No,' he said. 'Never.'

'And this?'

'This will never heal,' he said. As though she had wounded him. As though she had been a knife he had grasped with his hand open and bleeding.

She drew away further this time, and reached up to the

straps holding her dress, and untied them, quickly. The dress fell in a rush, like a wave touching the shore. He saw Caitlin's face and Caitlin's body, and they were wiped away as she came close to him again. And all the slowness left him, all the waiting and the needing to wait, all the patience, and this time, when he embraced her, he was on fire.

CHAPTER FORTY-THREE

They lay in bed after making love, and for a long time neither spoke. From time to time they could hear the muffled sound of cars. There was a clock in the room that ticked gently, and in the bathroom a tap dripped very slowly into a handbasin. Jack listened to Maria breathing beside him, and if he looked he could see the gentle rise and fall of her breasts. Their skin touched, leg to leg and hip against hip. They held hands across her stomach. Even now, he wanted her. Possession had not destroyed desire. She was inside him now, the sight, the touch, the perfume, and all he needed to do was close his eyes carefully, and he could see her vividly, her face and eyes, the marvellous contours of her limbs.

When a long time had passed, Maria broke the silence.

'Was it worth waiting for?' she asked.

'I'd given up waiting,' he replied. 'I thought there was nothing to wait for. I thought I'd never see you again.'

She was silent again for a while.

'I waited,' she said at last. 'I knew — that we'd meet again, that we'd be lovers like this.'

'And was it worth it?'

She looked at him. Her eyes were very serious. As though she were again at the keyboard and playing.

'Not if that were all it amounted to. Sex in a hotel bedroom. I waited for more than that. Much more. I waited for everything.'

'Everything?'

'To have a life with you.'

She sat on the edge of the bed, staring at her reflection in a mirror opposite. They were so very near, she thought, but the tiniest thing could destroy it all again. And this time for ever.

'Then you'll have it,' he said. 'A life together. You'll have a divorce. And we'll get married.'

'If it were only that simple. Karl's a devout Catholic. He won't give me a divorce.'

'Surely that's his problem. You can have a legal divorce.'

She hung her head.

'It's not that simple, Jack. I'm a believer. I attend mass regularly. And I have to think of Paul. He means everything to me, Jack. Even more than you. I can't just leave Karl. Not if it means living in sin.'

'What about this? What is this?'

She shrugged.

'This is different. This is once. Tomorrow I'll be back in Germany. It would be a different thing to make it regular. To live with you as though we were man and wife.'

'But you said that's what you wanted. Everything. That's what you said.'

'I know.' Her voice was very small, as though it had become the tiniest fraction of her.

'Do you love him? Is that what you're really trying to say?'

She shook her head. She would not look at him.

'No,' she whispered. 'Don't you understand? I don't love Karl. It's you I love, but it makes no difference.'

'No difference?'

'Did they explain to you? About my father? About the League?'

He nodded.

'Yes, a little. But it doesn't affect the way I feel about you. You're not your father.'

'Did they tell you why I came to them?'

He shook his head.

'No. I just assumed . . . Actually, I'm not sure what I assumed.'

'I always knew about the League. Not what you know, not what I know now. But as a child my father told me about it. The way some fathers tell their daughters they are Masons or members of a lay fraternity. Like belonging to the Legion of Mary or the Knights of Columbanus. That sort of thing. We weren't to talk about it outside the family, though. It was a sort of private affair, something Polish. There was no Irish branch. My sister and I were never taken to meetings or anything.

'Then, when I was first in Rome, I was approached by someone from British intelligence. I didn't know that's what he was at first, of course. They don't introduce themselves. You don't get somebody walking up to you and saying, "Hello, my name's Brown, I work for MI6."

'We seemed to meet by accident. He became a friend. I don't know how the subject of the League came up. It seemed accidental too, but I'm sure he engineered it. He told me things I had never heard before, about what the League did in the war. I refused to believe him at first, but he said he could put me in touch with someone who knew more, someone who could show me evidence. In the end, they convinced me, but I refused to work for them. They said they wanted inside information about my father, about his activities on behalf of the League. They told me he was one of the League's chief paymasters. I refused to believe that, that he could be so deeply involved in something so evil.'

She paused.

'And then I married Karl.'

For the first time he sensed something more than simple sadness in her voice. Something closer to true misery, even to despair.

'Shall I tell you about Karl, about what sort of man he is?'

'You told me he was rich and powerful.'

314

'That is not my husband, that is Herr Karl von Freudiger. That is what he is in the boardroom, at receptions, at trade fairs, when he meets with cabinet ministers. I married someone else, I live with someone else. He does not mistreat me, you must not think that. Beating me or insulting me or stopping my allowance, he would do none of that. It would be too bourgeois. He is a snob, he believes inflexibly in his class. It is almost mystical with him. His behaviour is moulded by it. Even the tiniest actions. The lower classes beat their wives, the middle classes are beasts to them, but his class knows how to behave. A beaten wife will not look good at a reception, a frightened wife will be clumsy at a dinner party or a ball. That is unthinkable. Appearances must be preserved at all costs. So he does not beat me and he does not fly into rages.

'Instead, he is cold. You cannot know how cold he is. He frightens me with his coldness. Like ice. He does not love me. He never has. I knew that from the beginning, when we were first married, but I hoped it might change in time. At first I tried to love him. I tried very hard. He was kind and thoughtful, and I thought that, if I worked hard enough, I might transform kindness into love. I was wrong. He had passed beyond that long ago. Beyond love. His failure had nothing to do with me, although he has often tried to make me feel that it had.

'But this is all a digression. The crucial thing is that I began to suspect that what I had been told about the League and about my father had been true. I discovered things by accident. Chiefly things concerning Karl's father, Reinhold.

'Karl owes everything he has to his father. Reinhold is still alive and well, although he is nearly ninety now. At his birthday last year, all the important people of the city were present. The chairman of the Chamber of Commerce, a representative from the Ministry of Trade in Bonn, even the Catholic bishop. During the last war, Reinhold was a *Wehrwirtschaftsführer*. I don't know exactly what that is in

English. A "Leader of the War Economy". What it means, of course, is that he helped keep the Nazi war effort going. His company manufactured sights for guns, windows of toughened glass for aeroplanes. He was awarded the Eagle Shield.'

She paused. He didn't want to talk to her about this. All he wanted to do was touch her, make love to her, lie with her until morning.

'In February 1933, less than a month after Hindenburg made Adolf Hitler chancellor, a man called Hjalmar Schacht invited twenty-five of Germany's top industrialists to a meeting in Hermann Goering's house in Berlin. Both Hitler and Goering were present. Schacht had just been made president of the Reichsbank. He was a close friend of my father-in-law. At that meeting, Reinhold and the rest pledged financial support for the Nazi Party. On that occasion Schacht collected three million marks. They guaranteed success for the Nazis in the years ahead.

'In fact, Reinhold was already a member of the Keppler Kreis, a circle of pro-Nazi industrialists formed two years earlier. They bankrolled Hitler until he got into power. A lot of money was paid into a special account, Sonderkonto S, at Kurt von Schröder's bank.

'After the war, Reinhold spent a little time in an internment camp. He was accused of various war crimes, mainly the use of slave labour in his factories, and sentenced to life. He was one of the war criminals held at Landsberg prison, along with the other convicted industrialists. They released him in 1951, along with Alfried Krupp. Like Krupp, they restored all his wealth. Karl has told me that his father was wealthier when he came out of prison than when he went in. His factories were still functioning: he had Karl to thank for that. And the fact that the Allies were so keen to get Germany back on its feet again.'

'Wouldn't his factories have been heavily bombed during the war?'

She shook her head.

'That's what everyone thinks. Allied bombing never destroyed more than twenty per cent of Germany's wartime capacity. The bulk of German industry wasn't even scratched. Von Freudiger Enterprises didn't lose so much as a day's output from the day the war started to the day it ended. After that, it was business as usual.'

There was a lull in the conversation. Maria had come to a point in her life where she no longer knew what her destination was, or even what direction she was travelling in. Tonight she was a mixture of love and guilt. She was sitting naked on a bed with the only man she had ever loved, trying to justify in his eyes her betrayal of a husband and a father, trying to find a way to tell him why they could not meet again. Partly because it was too dangerous, partly because she feared the guilt would destroy her.

And beyond that? Could she bring herself to tell him what she wanted most to tell, the secret of how they had come to meet?

'Is that why you hate Karl?' he asked. 'Because his father was a Nazi?'

'How could you think that? No more than I hate myself because my own father was an Ustashi killer or because my uncle gave SS troops his blessing before they went out killing Jews. The fact is that Reinhold was a dedicated member of Crux Orientalis. He gave it much of the funding it needed in the early days. Von Freudiger Enterprises still donates five million Deutschmarks annually. Reinhold holds high office in the inner circle. Karl is Keeper of the Keys of the German chapter. He was initiated when he was seventeen.

'Reinhold and my father were once very close. I'm not exactly sure why. Something happened during the war to bind them together. But that is how the marriage between Karl and myself came to be arranged. It's a sort of political union, to stave off a split between the German and Croatian branches of the League. Originally, Karl was to have married my sister Katerina. But . . .' She hesitated, looking away from him. Again that reflection, her face and body in the glass. And behind them? Deeper than glass?

'But she died, as you know. So I was chosen to take her place.'

'But . . . that's barbaric.'

'Is it? Is it more barbaric than two people meeting in a disco when they're drunk or stoned out of their heads? Or some crummy marriage bureau where they charge fifty pounds and let a third-rate computer choose your mate for life? You mistake their barbarity. I could forgive my father his marrying me to Karl. I could forgive Karl for taking me that way. There's nothing noble about it, but it's been going on for centuries.'

'I still think they are barbarians.'

She nodded slowly.

'Yes. But not for those reasons. That has always been the tragedy of the extreme right. They believe in civilization, in culture, in order, in social discipline. But in trying to achieve it they produce nothing but chaos, nothing but barbarism.'

'And you? What do you believe in?'

She looked at her body.

'In me,' she said. 'In my son, Paul. In my music.' She turned. 'And tonight I believe in you. Is that enough?'

'I don't know,' he said. Then, changing the subject, he took her hand. 'Maria, I want to be by myself for a while. Ever since the car bomb I haven't been alone. I was with Kossenkova, then your father, now I'm with Felix and Parker.'

'Now you're with me.'

'I know. And I want to be with you again. Tomorrow. The day after.'

She still could not bring herself to say it, that this would be their last meeting.

'I have to go back to Germany tomorrow. It's not something I can get out of.'

'Very well. But tonight, I want to ask you to turn a blind

eye. I just want to get away for a while, to think a little. I'm just worried that I'll get you into trouble with your bosses.'

She shook her head.

'It isn't like that,' she said. 'They don't pay me. I wouldn't accept money if they offered it. I supply them with information about the League, what little I can find. I choose to do it, for my own reasons. It's my way of telling them that I exist in my own right. When I was a child, my father betrayed me. He sent me to church and encouraged me to be religious. At one time I thought of becoming a nun.'

'I'm rather glad you didn't.'

She smiled.

'Nevertheless. And now I find that his religion was a sham. Or that it was sincere and yet deeply contradicted by his actions. So I betray him in turn. I have a duty to do it. My whole life has been comfortable. I've lived in luxury, I still do. I could buy this hotel if I wanted to. The whole street. Believe me, you don't have any idea how wealthy they are. I owe all my comfort to something thoroughly debased, something repellent. What would you do in my place?'

'Do you find me repellent now?'

'You? Why?'

'Because I've become part of it.'

This was the moment, she thought, the moment to tell him. But she could not, and the moment passed.

'No,' she said. 'You're not part of it. You're just a sideshow.'

They made love again, not desperately as before, but slowly, with great care. And in the mirror she watched his back and his head as he moved above her, as though he were embedded deep within the glass, as though the glass went on for ever, in its own dimension, as though she stood apart from skin and glass alike, a ghost watching, brought to orgasm by a body it had thought discarded.

*　　*　　*

She showed him how to leave without Norman noticing. Brown's has two entrances: one on Albemarle Street, the other on Dover Street. Norman was sitting in the lounge by the first entrance. Jack had only to slip past and take the other way out.

Maria waited for about an hour, to give him plenty of time to get clear of the area. She had given him money, enough to see him through several days; and she had told him that, if he wanted more, he would only have to go to the Deutsche Bank in Bishopsgate and there would be £10,000 waiting for him. More if he needed it, he had only to ask. She was giving him his freedom. But they both knew how little value it had.

It was after two o'clock when she went down to tell Norman Jack had gone. The lounge was empty. Most of it lay in darkness. A light had been left on in the corner where Norman had been seated, and someone had kept a fire going. It was almost out now. Norman seemed to be asleep. She crossed the room on tip-toe, to avoid waking him suddenly. He was very still, slumped forward slightly in his armchair, partly in shadow.

'Norman,' she whispered.

He did not move. She repeated his name, more loudly this time. She touched him gently on the arm.

He fell back, and as he did so Maria caught sight of the gash in his throat, the red line that ran from the left ear to the right. In the light, she saw that his front was wet with blood. And she knew that she must not scream, and that she must go back to her room quickly, without anyone seeing her, and close the door, and lock it. As she stood, she heard footsteps approaching in the passage outside.

CHAPTER FORTY-FOUR

On leaving Brown's, Jack had formed only the haziest idea of what he intended to do. He knew only that he had to be away from everyone – Felix, Parker, even Maria, in a sense – and that he had to try to sort out his thoughts. He walked quite aimlessly, through Mayfair down to Oxford Street, then west to the Edgware Road. From time to time a taxi passed him, but he made no attempt to hail one. Where would he ask the driver to go? If Parker was right, somebody would be keeping an eye on his friends' houses. It sounded far-fetched, but he could not afford to take the risk. He had no idea what any of these people could really do.

Once or twice he formed the impression that he was being followed. He thought he heard footsteps behind him, but whenever he looked there was never anyone there. In the end he put it down to nothing more than his own overstrained nerves and the tricks the dark and silence can play in city streets late at night.

He found himself by and by in a long street of cheap hotels. A few carried signs in their windows declaring 'Vacancies'. He felt tired and cold and lost. Maria seemed far away, like a morning dream remembered on the edge of sleep the next night. He went up the steps of a hotel on his left, an establishment named the Goya, and rang the bell. Through the glass door he could see into a half-dark hallway. He could make out a noticeboard to which maps and brochures had been pinned. A small shelf holding tourist board pamphlets and theatre flyers. A copper warming-pan against one wall. Nobody came. He rang again. The bell chimed somewhere at the end of the hall.

A light went on. Moments later, a woman wearing a red nightgown and a thick knitted cardigan came ambling down the hall. She was thin, with high cheekbones and straggling grey hair. She squinted at him through the door, pulling a face, then drew back a chain and released the catch on the lock.

'Weren't you given a key?'

'A key? No, you don't understand. I'm not one of your guests. I was hoping I could take a room, though.'

'Jesus. Have you any idea what time it is?'

'I'm sorry. I've lost my watch.'

'Past flipping two in the morning, mate. Nearer three.'

'I'm sorry. But your sign does say you have vacancies. I'll pay in advance.'

'Too bloody right you will. Come in for God's sake, it's freezing out there.'

She pushed him into a small room at the front.

'You Irish?' she asked as he bent to sign her book.

'Yes,' he said, sensing the wariness in her voice. 'Is that a problem?'

She shook her head; but he had a good idea what was passing through her mind. Stray Irishmen without suit-cases coming to the door of a London hotel in the early hours were apt to be looked on with a good measure of suspicion.

'There's an extra ten,' he said. 'For waking you up.'

She took it without thanks and stuffed it into the neck of her nightie.

'I'll put you in room seven. It'll be cold, mind you.'

'That's all right.'

'Breakfast's from seven to nine. Not a minute later. I'm never late, and I never wait: that's my motto. The room's yours till eleven. Any later than that and I'll charge you for another day.'

She gave him a key and showed him to the room. He

saw her scrutinize him as he closed the door. Fixing his face on her memory, that's what she was up to. Just in case someone came round asking questions. ' 'ortunately, he thought, it was possible someone woul ồ ị just that.

He slept in shirt and trousers at first, for warmth. In the middle of the night – he guessed it must have been four or five o'clock – he woke to find himself hot and sweating, so he stripped to his shorts. It was hard to get back to sleep after that. The nylon sheets were unpleasant to the touch. Outside his window, early-morning traffic had started to go past. An occasional lorry, several motorbikes. He thought of Maria. She had wanted to tell him they must not meet again. It had not been hard to guess. But he was glad she had lacked the courage. She could not refuse another meeting, if he decided to go back to her bosses. And he was determined to persuade her to drop the whole thing, to leave her husband and move to Israel with him.

Once he slept briefly, dreaming not of Maria but of Caitlin. When he woke, he could remember nothing of the dream but the sound of his own voice, calling Caitlin's name. Until that night she had been the only woman he had ever slept with. It made him afraid, for he thought he might lose her now, that his feelings for Maria might drive out Caitlin's memory. And with her, perhaps, much of what he remembered of Siobhan. He thought that would be unbearable.

He came down for breakfast at half past eight. The landlady lent him a grubby map of London, and he worked out that he was in Sussex Gardens, near Paddington Station. As he was about to refold the map, he noticed that Paddington Cemetery was not far away. All at once, his dream returned to him, and he knew what he wanted to do.

A taxi took him to Tennyson Road. He remembered arriving there with Caitlin years before, when she had taken him to see her parents' grave. It had been his only contact with her family. Last night he had dreamed that he was there again with her, but that, when he turned to speak to her, a gravedigger told him she was in the grave as well. Now, in an effort to set his mind at rest, he had decided to find out if she had had brothers and sisters, aunts or uncles. Felix's questions had unsettled him. If there were living relatives, Jack needed to ask them about the woman he had married.

In the cemetery, small ghosts of Christmas were everywhere visible. The living had come with holly wreaths and potted poinsettias for their dead. The graves wore a festive air, red berries and dark green leaves, a sprig of mistletoe for a lover's head. The air was crisp and clear, like glass. If he stood very still, if he held his breath, if he shut his eyes, he could feel the glass break, a sliver at a time, and him underneath, and Caitlin, holding hands. A sprig of mistletoe for her grave. He had not visited it for several Christmases now. And Easter was so many months away.

It took him almost an hour to find the grave. The inscription had not faded, had not been added to. James Patrick Nualan, born 30 May 1915, died 27 June 1975. His loving wife Mary, born 12 January 1917, died 17 October 1977. With Jesus. Beneath, a carving of the Sacred Heart. A fresh wreath lay propped against the headstone. No name attached. Someone had been here. Someone cared.

He found another taxi and was taken to the cemeteries office in Clifford Road.

'I want some details about a grave in Paddington Cemetery.'

The superintendent was a young man with a heavy cough.

'That could be difficult.'

'Why's that?'

The man shrugged and coughed.

'Well, we bought the cemetery back in '86. Off the City of Westminster, as it was then. This was before they sold the rest of their cemeteries off for a quid apiece. The thing is, the records for Paddington Cemetery is kept in two places — some here, some in a strongroom down the cemetery itself. There's no logic to it. Some here, some there: it's pot luck, really.'

Jack gave the details from the grave. A search revealed nothing.

'How long ago, did you say?'

'One in 1975, the other in 1977.'

'We'll go down to Paddington, then. We might be lucky.'

They were. The record was in the strongroom, the names of next of kin: Terence and Jean Nualan, 16 Eversholt Villas in Camden Town. Terence had paid for the headstone, supplied by Kelly's, a stonemason in Primrose Hill.

Another short taxi ride took him there. Eversholt Villas was a terrace of mean houses trying hard to fall on better times. Less upwardly mobile than slipping sideways. Individual owners had gone on regular Saturday-afternoon pilgrimages to MFI and B&Q, returning with louvred shutters and Georgian doors. One had a bay of Victorian windows complete with panes of bullseye glass. Mock styles jostled one another for prominence, sometimes on the same house: Tudor with Georgian, Victorian with ultra-modern. He rang the bell at number 16, a mixture of Le Corbusier and Nash.

A boy of about twelve opened the door, a regulation boy in faded jeans, old before his time, wearing trainers on his feet and an American baseball cap on his head.

'Yeah?'

'Is Mr Nualan at home?'

The boy stared at him, twisting his lip.

'Who wants to know?'

'I want to speak to him. He doesn't know me.'

'You from Social Services?'

'Do I look as though I am?'

'Yeah.'

'My name's Jack Gould. Is Terence Nualan your father?'

'Could be.'

'Look, I'm not here to make trouble. I want to ask him about your grandparents.'

'Which ones?'

'His parents.'

'They're dead.'

'Yes, I know.'

There was a shout from further down the hall.

'Kevin! Who is it?'

The boy turned and bellowed back.

'Man in a coat. Wants to ask you something.'

A man appeared from what Jack guessed to be the kitchen. He was holding a steaming mug of tea in one hand, a chip butty in the other. A large man, thick-necked, beer-bellied, greasy-haired. Not at all like his sister. Something began to die in Jack.

'Terence Nualan?'

The man nodded.

'That's my name. What d'you want?'

Jack could pick out the last traces of an Irish accent. Caitlin's had been stronger, but more refined.

'My name's Gould. Jack Gould. I'd just like to talk to you, that's all. About your sister. About Caitlin.'

The man stayed where he was. Tomato ketchup dripped from the butty on to his hand. He licked it off.

'Caitlin? Who the fuck's Caitlin?'

Jack felt as though a dagger were twisting in his stomach.

'You're the son of James and Mary Nualan, aren't you?'

Nualan nodded.

'The James and Mary Nualan buried in Paddington Cemetery?'

'Look, mister, what's this about? I've got things to do.'

'I'm sorry, but it is important. Did your parents die in 1975 and 1977, and are they buried in Paddington Cemetery?'

'I said they was. What about it? You the law?'

'No, nothing like that. It's personal. I . . . knew someone, someone called Caitlin Nualan. She showed me that grave, your parents' grave, years ago. Here in London, she brought me here. She said they were her parents.'

The man's eyes narrowed.

'You having me on or what?'

'Did you have any sisters? Maybe with a different name. Not Caitlin, something different perhaps.'

'I was an only child. There were no others. No brothers, no sisters. My mother couldn't have any other children. It broke her heart. What do you want, coming here with stupid stories about sisters? You trying something on? 'Cause if you are . . .'

Jack shook his head. The dagger was tearing him to shreds.

'I must have made a mistake,' he said. 'That's all. The wrong grave. I must have gone to the wrong grave. I'm sorry to have bothered you.'

He turned and walked back into the street. The boy closed the door behind him, swearing under his breath. Jack walked away. He knew with absolute certainty that it had not been the wrong grave. And as he walked away, he thought he understood why.

CHAPTER FORTY-FIVE

'I can't go back.'

Maria was sitting in a room at her agent's house in Kensington. Felix and Parker were with her, and a third man whose name she did not know. Her agent, Jacques la Charité, was a Canadian national who had been in the pay of at least three intelligence services since the mid-sixties. He had originally been recruited by Canadian intelligence in order to enable them to get some of their people backstage during a visit to Toronto by the Bolshoi. After moving to London in 1974, he had been passed on to the British for similar purposes, while his fluency in French had made him useful from time to time across the Channel. Felix had thought of him immediately when he realized they would need a cut-out between themselves and Maria. He also happened to run one of the best music agencies in the city, so there was no professional conflict.

'My dear, you have to. You have no choice.'

Felix had a temper, which he was doing his best to keep under control. As their conversation proceeded, he felt that control slip inch by inch. One of his best men had been brutally killed under circumstances that had called for crisis management of the most delicate kind – the imprecations of Brown's manager were still ringing in his ears. The most important pawn in his game had run off. And now the agent on whom he relied totally for what inside knowledge he had of the League's doings was telling him she could not return to Germany.

'Yes,' she replied patiently. 'I have all the choice I need.

You told me when this started that if I ever wanted out, all I had to do was tell you and it would be done.'

'It's not as simple as that. We've reached the most critical point in the entire operation. You can't just walk out on us now.'

'You said the service would provide me with a new identity, somewhere to go. I don't care where it is. Australia, New Zealand, it doesn't matter. Just as long as I can get out of this and take Paul with me. I've got money in a Swiss account. More than enough. I just need you to do the things you said you'd do. I can't do them for myself.'

'I'm disappointed in you, Maria, really I am.' It was Parker's turn to speak. They were playing her by turns, while the third man watched. 'I never thought you'd let us down so lightly.'

'Let you down? Jesus, it's my life we're talking about! If I go back there, I'm as good as dead. Don't you understand?'

'I don't think you can assume that.'

'You don't think so? Then who the hell killed Norman?'

'We don't know. But I'm willing to bet it wasn't Karl. It's too blatant. I'd put my money on one of Kossenkova's people.'

'But you don't know that. If you're wrong, you'll find me with my throat cut as well.'

'Maria.' It was the third man, the man whose name she did not know, not even his working name. He was well-dressed in an understated way. She could have named his tailor or his shirt-maker. He must be, she thought, not only senior, but the latest in a very long line of senior people. His father before him and his grandfather before that would have known how to command the same attention with a single word, with a man's name, or a dog's.

'I beg you to listen to me.' He spoke almost lazily, as though his thoughts were on something else entirely, and yet managed to convey an impression of tense seriousness. It was, she thought, because his manner implied that what he said mattered very much, not to the one who said it, but to the person to whom it was said. Not to him, but to her.

'I do not have to tell you how important this business is. You know almost as much as we do. The League is close to reaching a position it has not enjoyed since the last war. For all we know, it may have reached that position already. In a very short time, they may be impregnable. I do not say that lightly. But I wonder if you understand properly what I mean by it.'

She said nothing. It was not merely his manner, she realized, but his eyes as well. They were not piercing, not cold, not feverish. Just sad. It was a little like looking in a mirror.

'They will have their people where they want them. A few at first, then others, when we are not looking. We may never know who they are. We know only the centre, not the periphery. That is both our strength and our weakness. If we can destroy the head, the octopus will die of its own accord. If we cannot, it will continue to grow without our really knowing where or how until it is too late.'

He paused. Felix watched him admiringly.

'They are already in key positions in the Vatican, we are reasonably sure of that. They have industrialists like your husband in several countries. They have local mayors and MPs in their pockets. Need I go on?

'The scroll is in some sense the key to their success. Whether they choose to publish it or suppress it, it makes little difference. As long as they can control it in some way. We have to know whether or not they have it in their possession.' He paused and looked at Felix.

'Tell her,' he said.

Felix straightened his tie, a nervous gesture he had had since his schooldays.

'Berchik is dead,' he said. 'Israeli intelligence found his body yesterday. He had been hidden in a cave near Qumran. Perhaps it seemed like some sort of poetic statement, we don't know. But the scroll is gone. His flat in Tel Aviv has been thoroughly searched. His relatives in Israel have been discreetly questioned. Finding the body only confirms our fear. Either Kossenkova or your father has the scroll. We are sure there is no one else in the game. But we have to know which of them has it, before they have time to act on its recovery.'

The third man spoke again.

'You will be placed under round-the-clock protection. Everything you say or do will be monitored. At the first sign of possible violence, a team will go in to take you out. Neither your husband nor your father will act against you while you are with your child. Stay with him as much as possible.'

'And you expect me to find this scroll under those conditions? I don't even know what it looks like. I wouldn't know it from any of the others in my father's collection.'

'We don't expect you to find it,' said Felix. 'Just gauge the atmosphere. You can be sure that your father and Karl will be jubilant if they've got it. If not, they're likely to be tense and nervous, wondering what Kossenkova's up to.'

'That's hardly a cast-iron way of finding out.'

'No, but it's all we've got.'

'Maria.' The third man's voice again, still soft. 'If you don't go back they're certain to suspect. They'll take Paul away, make sure you never see him again. What they'll do to Jack, I leave it to you to guess. It's your responsibility. It's for you to decide. But we can help you. Think about it.'

'Is this a threat?'

'Of course not. How could it be? Why would we threaten you?'

'Why wouldn't you?'

'That's not how we work, Maria. You know it isn't.' Parker sounded indignant, as though personally insulted.

'Do I? What do I know about how you work?'

'You're right.' The thin man was still trying to steer his

course between Felix and Parker. 'You know nothing of us. But you do know a great deal about your father and Karl and their associates. You know a little about what they're capable of. You know I'm right about Paul. He's your husband's heir. The heir to the von Freudiger empire. Just how far do you think you'd get with him without our help? Or perhaps you intended to leave him behind?'

Maria did not answer. Even a short time away from Paul was a torture to her. And, she knew, to him. She slumped in the chair, feeling the will to struggle leave her.

'A twenty-four-hour watch, you said?'

'We'll give you a hidden microphone. Like the ones in the movies, except that this will be smaller and will work. That way, our people can monitor everything that goes on. We want you to insist on spending New Year at your father's house in Paris. If they have the scroll, Karl may want to go there anyhow.'

'What about Jack?'

'That's rather more difficult. Thanks to you, we've no idea where he is.'

She hesitated. It seemed that, in order to save Jack's life, she might have to betray him.

'We have an arrangement,' she said. 'A letter-drop. He'll be there tonight to pick up any note I leave. Or to leave one himself.'

The thin man smiled. None of this was proving as difficult as he had feared it might.

CHAPTER FORTY-SIX

The Serpentine was empty. No model boats, no small yachts, no anglers. Just a few couples strolling side-by-side along the path that leads from the Dell to Kensington Gardens. A cold wind blew across the water. Pieces of paper lifted and fell. In the distance, London rose out of the trees quietly.

She was waiting for him beside the lake, her reflection in the water broken by ripples. Although she heard his footsteps approach, she did not turn until he was right beside her. She felt his hand slip into hers.

'I thought you were supposed to be in Germany,' he said.

She shook her head.

'I leave this afternoon. I had to see you first. Let's start walking.'

With her hand still in his, she set off along the path that skirted the lake.

'You can't stay on the run, Jack. You need papers, money. I can give you money, but without papers you won't be able to draw it from the bank. And I've no way of providing you with identification.'

'I've taken care of it myself,' he said.

She looked at him, surprised.

'I went to the Irish embassy,' he explained. 'Told them I'd lost my passport. They made me get a certificate from the police: that was the riskiest bit. Dublin are faxing over my file. I should have the passport in a week or so. It cost me £49.'

'You still have to pick it up,' she said. His manner was awkward. As though he was distracted by something. 'That could be risky.'

'You said yourself there's no simple way for me to get papers.'

They continued walking. Like lovers. Adulterers in a public place, people with nowhere to go. Nowhere safe, nowhere warm. Not even a bed in an empty room.

'Have you had long enough?' she asked.

'Long enough?'

'To sort things out. What you want to do.'

'No,' he said. 'There are too many things to think about.'

'What sort of things?'

He stopped walking and turned to face her.

'Among others, why you lied to me about your sister. Why your father lied. You both knew all along.'

She stared at him, stunned into silence. He watched her, knowing that he had at last touched on the truth.

'I . . . I had no choice,' she stammered. 'My father . . .'

'No choice? You go on about having no choice. No choice in who you marry, no choice in how you spend your life. But you do have choices, everybody has choices.'

She bowed her head.

'Keep walking,' she said. 'It's cold here.'

They walked a little further. A man passed them, walking his dog. In the distance, a group of children played.

'How did you find out?' she asked.

He told her about his visit to the cemetery, his meeting with Terence Nualan.

'Why didn't you tell me, Maria? When we were at Summerlawn. You could have told me then.'

'Would it have helped?'

He shrugged.

'I don't know. It might have.'

'I knew what my father was. I wanted to spare you that.'

'Why did Caitlin change her name? Why all the

mystery? And, incidentally, which was she: Caitlin or Katerina?'

'Caitlin. That was her real name. She hated her father. Our father. I think she'd discovered a little about his past. She never told me. I wish now that she had done, but there was a gap of several years between us, and she must have thought I was too young to be told things like that.

'She left home at eighteen to study at Trinity. I think she chose Semitic languages deliberately, as a kind of challenge to father. He was an amateur orientalist, she would become the real thing. He'd always despised her, I don't know why. She was intelligent – I don't have to tell you that. But he disliked intelligence in women. He can cope with something like musical talent, that fits his preconceptions well enough. But academic ability, a talent for hard mental work, he always regarded that as a male prerogative. The better Caitlin did at school, the higher her grades, the more praise her teachers heaped on her, the more he hated it.

'Her decision to study Hebrew and Aramaic was the last straw. He practically threw her out of the house. I think it was almost a relief to her. She had money of her own, from our mother. And she met you. I knew about it. She confided in me at first, we used to meet secretly. But then he found out and I was forbidden to see her again. Otherwise you and I would have met a long time ago.'

She paused and looked at him. For all that she knew things were hopeless anyway, she could not bear the thought of losing him. It was something after all to be loved.

'He never spoke to her after she wrote to say you were getting married. She was cut off as though she was dead. He never mentioned her name again in the house, forbade me to refer to her. Of course, he knew all about you. He'd had men check you out. I think he came very near to having you killed.'

Jack remembered the break-in in Paris.

'Killed? Why? For marrying Caitlin?'

'No, because you're Jewish. Half Jewish.'

'But he invited me to Summerlawn himself.'

'By that time Caitlin was dead and he'd discovered that you could be valuable to him. He knew a lot about you, even thought he could trust you. I think it was a sort of revenge for what she'd done to him. He, the amateur, could take control, could employ the professional to work for him. You would be his skivvy, never knowing who he really was. And I think . . .'

She halted. Wind hit the water by her side, sending small waves to the shore. A plane flew overhead, high, without a sound.

'Yes?'

'I think he knew what would happen. That you would fall in love with me. The only flaw in his calculations was me. I don't think it even crossed his mind that I might fall in love with you. He never saw me as anything more than a woman, you see. And in his view women can never initiate. To men like him, we're always passive. Objects for men's feelings, never capable of forming feelings of our own, or of acting on them.'

They continued walking. Through the tunnel and into Kensington Gardens.

'Norman is dead,' she told him.

'Norman?'

There was a bench nearby. They sat down while she explained.

'They want me to go back,' she said when she had finished. 'To Karl.'

She explained a little more.

'It's too much of a risk,' he said.

'I have to. For Paul's sake.'

'You won't be much use to him if you're dead.'

Without warning, she bent forward and kissed him hard on the lips. A moment later, she pulled away. As she did so, her lips brushed his cheek, and she whispered rapidly in his ear. The next moment, he saw a man approaching from the right. Felix. He looked round. Parker was coming towards him from the left.

'Please go with them, Jack,' she said. 'It's for the best. And remember that I love you. As much as Caitlin ever did.'

CHAPTER FORTY-SEVEN

Essen, Germany
29 December 1992

She finished reading and laid down the book. It was sad, she thought, that she could not tell him who it was from. Not yet. Perhaps never: she did not expect to see Jack again. Paul looked so pale tonight, she wondered if he could be catching cold. He had been distant with her since her arrival.

'Are you feeling all right, Paulchen?'

'I'm all right.'

She reached out a hand to feel his forehead, but he pulled away.

'What's wrong, *Liebchen*? You aren't normally like this with me. We're supposed to be friends, remember?'

'I don't like it when you go away,' he said.

'I know. And I don't like it either. I'd bring you with me if I could, but you know your father doesn't like me to. I'll talk to him. Maybe you can come next time. There's a lot to see in London.'

'*Mein Vater . . .*' Paul began, slipping into German at the thought of his father, then catching himself. 'Daddy says I have work to do here. That I must stay to help him.'

'Yes, of course you must help him. But you'll have to go to school before you can start work.'

'Daddy says I shall have a school of my own. That he will teach me himself.'

Maria looked at him, puzzled.

'He hasn't said anything about that to me. It doesn't sound a very good idea. There's a lovely school right here in Essen that you'll be going to next year. And I'm sure Daddy will help with your homework.'

Paul shook his head.

'No,' he said. 'That's not it. He says I have work to do, work for the Reich.'

Maria felt her heart sicken.

'"The Reich"? Is that what he said?'

The boy nodded.

'Do you know what that means?'

'No,' Paul said. 'Daddy said he would teach me. Only I don't like him to.'

'Why not?'

'Because he shouts at me. And when you're not here, he won't let me use my nightlight in bed. He says I have to learn to be a man. He makes me frightened.'

She saw how agitated he was growing.

'Lie down,' she said, 'and let me tuck you in. Have you said your prayers?'

He shook his head.

'We'll say them together, then,' she said. But her heart was elsewhere, still sickening.

Karl was downstairs in the library. She had not seen him for more than a few moments since her return.

'I hear the concert went well,' he said.

Maria nodded. He seemed to be in one of his rare expansive moods. There were drinks on the table. She poured herself a stiff gin before answering.

'Jacques says it was a real success. The tickets were sold out. But, best of all, we got some reviews. Excellent reviews. I've brought them for you.'

His face seemed to light up.

'Reviews? How delightful. *The Times*?'

She shook her head, laughing. She found it so hard to laugh here.

'No, I'm not in that league yet. But the *Ham and High*. And a nice little piece in the *Standard*.'

The light went out.

'Well, we must ensure that *The Times* writes a proper review next time. And the *Telegraph*. I shall speak with Dietrich about it.'

Her face fell.

'Oh, no, Karl, I'd much rather you didn't. I've told you before, I want to do this on my own. I want it to be my success, not something you or Daddy made happen for me.'

'Yes, yes,' he said, impatient. 'So you have told me many times. But I have also had to remind you that success does not just drop from the sky, that it is manufactured as much as glass. Do not believe everything you read about unknown artists struggling to the top by talent alone. Believe me, they will have made many friends along the way. If they are women, you can be sure they will have slept with a dozen men. But since you are not going to sleep with anyone but me, we must compensate.'

'And what's going to compensate me for your not sleeping with me?'

She had the answer, of course, but she could hardly tell him what – or who – it was.

Karl refused to rise to the bait. A gentleman does not let his wife manoeuvre him on to such topics. Especially not in a room the servants might enter at any moment.

'Your father has invited us to Paris for the New Year,' he said. 'I told him I would ask you as soon as you got back. We will leave tomorrow, if you feel up to it.'

She smiled. Now she would not have to persuade Karl herself.

'Yes, of course,' she said. 'I should like that. Paris is always lively at the New Year.'

'Unlike Essen?'

She nodded.

'Yes, very unlike Essen.'

'You have never liked it much here, have you? You find it dull. Industrial.'

'It isn't that. It was dull enough at Summerlawn. I know how to amuse myself. But it's so stuffy here. And, anyway, Paris is special. Even Hitler thought so.'

'Really?' His answer was quite cool. It was not normal practice in the von Freudiger household to mention the late Führer.

She bit her tongue. It had been a stupid slip. Or was she just growing unnecessarily anxious, fearful that her least remark might be misinterpreted?

'Well, no matter,' said Karl. 'Your father will be pleased. We'll take Paul. If you want, we can go to the Opéra one evening.'

'I'd like that.'

'It's settled, then. I'll tell Magda to start packing this evening.'

At that moment, the doorbell rang.

'Did I tell you my father will be with us for dinner this evening?'

'No. Is there any special reason?'

'Oh, I think he wanted to congratulate you on your concert.'

Reinhold von Freudiger seldom left home in the evenings. He lived alone with servants in a small house about a mile from theirs. For some time now, Karl had been pressing him to come to live with Maria and himself, but the old man refused. A move, he said, would be a sign of his dependence. As long as he remained in good shape, he would stay where he was. And he was, indeed, in above average physical and mental shape for his age.

A maid appeared to announce 'Herr von Freudiger'. Reinhold followed. He crossed the room to where Maria was standing and kissed her effusively on both cheeks. She relaxed. It looked as though he was in a good mood.

*　　*　　*

341

The meal seemed to take place on two levels. On the one hand, there was the usual discussion of family matters – it was a strict rule that business never be raised at table – and the relation of amusing anecdotes. Reinhold wanted to hear all about the concert: what she had played, why she had chosen this piece rather than that, whether or not there had been a significance in the fact that she had chosen two posthumous pieces, how she had been received. Unlike Karl, Reinhold was a genuine music lover, if somewhat limited in his tastes, and he felt genuine pride in having an accomplished pianist for his daughter-in-law. As far as that went, dinner proceeded smoothly.

On the other hand, Karl and his father seemed to be exchanging confidences throughout the meal, almost as though they were speaking code. There were guarded references to it being 'time for a change', to there being 'something in the air', to a long wait being almost at an end. All these things were said without reference to her, as though she were not there.

But it was after dinner that things began to grow distinctly unpleasant.

CHAPTER FORTY-EIGHT

They retired to the drawing-room for schnapps. Maria came too. She was acutely conscious of the tiny pick-up taped to her waist. More than ever, she was grateful that Karl no longer slept with her.

'We have decided to spend New Year in Paris with Stefan,' said Karl to his father. 'Why don't you come with us? You know how much he'd like to see you.'

'I'm too old to travel at this time of year.'

'Nonsense. Anyway . . .' Karl hesitated. 'I think he has something to show you.'

Reinhold looked hard at his son. A slow smile lit up his face.

'A . . . New Year surprise?'

Maria was sure he had been about to say something else. Karl nodded.

'Well, perhaps I shall go with you after all. I like to be in Paris at this time of year. There is a magic about the city.'

Karl glanced at Maria.

'Then you find yourself in agreement with Maria. She has been telling me how she prefers Paris to Essen.'

'Of course she does,' said Reinhold. 'Who could prefer Essen to Paris? Or New York to Paris? There is no comparison.'

'She has also been telling me how much the Führer admired Paris.'

'Yes, that is quite true. Paris he loved, but not the French. He considered it the most beautiful city in the world. The

Champs Elysées was the model for the great avenue he wanted to build through his new Berlin. The Führer was a man of taste. A lover of art and music. A visionary. If his plans had not been brought to nothing by the war, we would now have beautiful buildings everywhere in this country, and not the ugly monstrosities these so-called modern architects have been inflicting on us.'

'Forgive me,' interrupted Maria. She knew it was foolish, but something impelled her. 'I had always understood the opposite. That he was a man of quite limited taste. And limited intellect.' She was determined not to let herself be cowed by an old Nazi or his reminiscences of some golden age.

'Quite wrong!' Reinhold's cheeks had reddened, but he remained wholly in control of himself. Maria had never seen him lose his temper, even when pushed to his limits. 'The Führer was greatly maligned. The stupid British used to make fun of him, pretending he was nothing but a house-painter called Schickelgrüber. Such idiocy. He was a fine artist. I saw many of his paintings, he showed them to me himself, when I told him of my collection. I bought a couple.'

'Surely you can't have thought they had real merit?'

'Merit? What the hell is merit? You mean he was not a great artist? Well, I don't know. I am just an amateur. A businessman, not an art critic. But you, are you an art critic?'

'Of course not, but . . .'

'Then we are alike. I am a businessman, you are a musician. I don't say the Führer was a great artist, a Van Dyck or a Rubens. He was competent. But that is not my point. I mean that he had an artist's vision. A real vision, not diseased. Modern art has become diseased, you can't pretend otherwise. Picasso, Pollock, Dali, they saw the world like madmen. Where is the beauty in that? Where is the purity? But the Führer had a genuine vision, a sane vision, even if his technique was not always adequate. And you might say that his real vision was Germany. Or Europe. Or the world.'

Maria shuddered.

'The world isn't just a canvas for someone to paint on. You . . .'

Without a word, the old man stood and stepped across the room to a small lacquered cabinet. He took a tiny key from his pocket and used it to open the doors. Behind them were rows of small drawers. From one of these he drew out a silver frame. Crossing to Maria, he tossed it into her lap.

The frame held a black-and-white photograph showing two men shaking hands warmly. One was Adolf Hitler. She did not have to guess who the other was.

'For fifty years,' said Reinhold, 'I and dozens of other men like me have been forced to bury photographs like that in drawers or safes. Can you imagine what that means, to deny all you once were? To betray the best part of yourself? No, of course you can't. You can't imagine such loyalty, what it means, how it would destroy you to betray it.'

He resumed his chair. His habitual tiredness seemed to have left him.

'Now it's time for you to listen to me,' he went on. 'I've been quiet for almost fifty years. We've all been quiet. Ashamed of ourselves, of our past. Judases to our own natures. But you weren't there, you didn't see, you don't know. Your generation has been brought up on lies. The Germans were such wicked people. Hitler was such an evil man. His associates were thugs, monsters, mass murderers. You know nothing of the truth, of what they did for mankind, what they strove for, what they achieved. And what they were so cruelly prevented from achieving. By the Jews. The Communists. The Freemasons.'

'But surely you can't believe such drivel. About Jewish conspiracies. Not any more, not after . . .'

Reinhold turned to his son.

'She is your wife. Tell her to watch her tongue. Make her show some respect.'

Karl snapped at her.

'Be quiet, Maria. Listen to my father.'

'I don't want to listen to crap. I . . .'

'You will keep your mouth clean and you will listen. Otherwise I promise that I will drag you off that chair by the hair of your head and horsewhip you until you obey. Until you behave like a woman of your class. Do I make myself clear? Do I?'

It was the first time he had ever threatened her with violence. She could see that he meant every word. She could think of nothing to say. He took her silence for compliance.

Reinhold continued.

'There was a vision back then,' he said. 'We all had a vision, until it was snatched away from us. A new Germany. A new Europe. Not a gimcrack Bundesrepublik built by the Americans. Not this monstrous EEC that rides roughshod over national sovereignty, that does not even allow a state to make its own laws and act on them. Real greatness – that was our Führer's dream. Real prosperity. It was not a vision of material wealth, like the American dream. There would be physical wellbeing, but we dreamed of more. Our vision was spiritual. We dreamed of a new race of men. We were children of the half-light, but we knew the dawn would come. And when it did, the world would be populated by a pure race, a race of men and women dedicated to virtue. To true Christian virtue and racial wholeness. Do you despise such things, Maria, like the rest of your generation? Do you look down on all that, on the notion of physical purity joined to inner strength?'

He looked hard at her. She did not answer.

'Well, it no longer matters. Your generation has had its chance. Germany's a cesspool. Europe's a cesspool. America's a cesspool. But we're going to clean them out.

Haven't you seen what's happening? How people are making their voices heard again? Young people are demanding a new way, a new system, a new order. Communism has failed them. Socialism is nothing more than a slogan. People look back now and wonder how they could have been such fools, how they could have thrown away the world we built then. Peace. Stability. Justice.'

He watched her. She was trembling, unable to take in the enormity of what he was saying. What had been mere words in a file was taking on flesh, becoming horrid reality. He began speaking again.

'You liberals always think of yourselves as the salt of the earth, as though your filthy opinions were natural, God-given laws for steering the ship of state. Well, I assure you they are not. I assure you that good, pure-minded, God-fearing people will hiss and boo as they kick you out. Ordinary people, honest people, simple people who despise the things you make so much of. They want capital punishment and hard sentences for criminals. They want the soft treatment to end. They want the police to be given the powers to crack down on drug abusers and sex offenders. They're sick of leniency. They're sick of perverts and strident feminists and social security scroungers and illegal immigrants and the whole tribe of leeches sucking our societies dry. Believe me, girl, they'll rise up against you in their millions. They'll tear you apart. All you bleeding hearts will go to the wall, mark my words. We'll take back what was ours, you'll see, even if we have to claw it back from you an inch at a time. But we'll have it, that's for sure. Then the niggers and the Turks and the Jews and the perverts and the transvestites and the drug addicts and all the other rubbish will go where they belong. We've got God on our side, that's the important thing, that's the real issue.'

She listened to him with mounting horror, knowing that, dreadful as all he said was, he was right. They were rising up to sweep away everything they did not understand. She thought of the Irish, with their perennial obsessions with parochialism and bigotry, their antiquated laws on abortion and contraception and divorce, their deep hatred of women. The English, with their obsessive secrecy, their institutionalized racism, their political culture of greed and self-interest, their deep groundswell of intolerance, of populist cant, of naked, tabloid-driven, aggressive man-in-the-streetness. She thought of the French, with their long-standing anti-Semitism, their racism that was like a tumour that has never been excised, Le Pen and his followers polling vote after vote in every new election, swastikas on Jewish graves and over the doors of North African homes. The Germans, with their undying hatred for outsiders, for Turks or Romanians or Jews, burning hostels, beating up Gypsies. The whole pack of them, baying at the moon, howling for blood, tearing their continent to pieces again and again and again. A lump came into her throat as she realized how short-sighted she had been, how Reinhold and his prophecies of a right-wing ascendancy were indeed in keeping with the new mood of the times.

For some people, such a state of affairs was a cue for apocalyptic dreams, for wonders, for millenarian promises, for messiahs everywhere shouting 'I am here, I am here!', self-interest masquerading as piety, sackcloth and ashes, burnings at the stake, the burning of books, the burning of history, desperate, overblown religiosity. She began to understand why they needed the scroll, to grasp the part it would play in their schemes, how it would be their banner, their oriflamme, the emblem they would carry before them into battle.

She got to her feet. There was no spirit left in her for a fight.

'If you will both excuse me,' she said, 'I'd like to go to bed. I'm very tired.'

Karl nodded brusquely.

'Of course, my dear. It is already long past your bedtime.'

'Reinhold,' she went on, sick to her stomach, 'thank you so much for coming to dinner. It's always a pleasure to have your company.'

The old man stood, pulling himself rigidly to attention as he had been trained to do whenever a lady was on her feet. Karl had already risen.

'Goodnight, my dear,' he said. 'You must forgive me if I got a little carried away. But I'm an old man now, and I have very little time left. I need to say what I think. Perhaps you'll give a little thought to it.'

Smiling, she went to the door. Once it closed behind her, she burst into tears.

CHAPTER FORTY-NINE

Upstairs, she dashed to her bathroom, where she stayed until her tears had subsided. As she calmed down, she thought about Paul. He would be asleep by now. At least, she hoped so. Just to sit beside him now would help bring her back to normal. Whatever normal was.

She made her way to his nursery, at the far end of the corridor from her own room. Making as little sound as possible, she opened the door. The nightlight beside the bed was still on. She remembered the numbing arguments about buying it. Paul had always been afraid of the dark. Not a little, but deeply. Sleeping in the dark gave him bad dreams, very often nightmares. Karl had insisted that it would unman his son to indulge what he regarded as no more than a childish fear. Maria had argued otherwise and been rebuffed with harsh words. In the end she had resorted to the family doctor, who had agreed with her that a nightlight would be in the boy's best interest. He, in turn, had spoken with Karl. No more had been said. She had bought the nightlight herself in a department store in Essen. The nightmares had subsided and had lately shown signs of vanishing altogether. Yet Karl had never once admitted that his wife had been in the right. It would have choked him to do so. Now, it seemed, the nightlight was banned when she was away from home.

She tip-toed to the side of the bed. Her eyes adjusted to the dim light. She looked down. Something was wrong. Paul was not there. She ran to the door and found the main light switch. Bright light flooded the room. Crazily, she looked everywhere. The bed was made, as though no one had been sleeping in it. And Paul was nowhere to be seen.

Karl and his father were still in the drawing-room, drinking schnapps and talking. Sometimes they would stay up until very late. Late hours, Karl had told her very early in their marriage, were for men. Women could not look beautiful if they did not get adequate sleep. In time, she had come to learn that his late nights were a way of avoiding sex. Or, at least, sex with her. Sometimes he stayed out all night long, and she suspected that he then saw other women. Whores or mistresses, it made no difference to her.

'Where is Paul?' she demanded. She left the door open. What the servants heard was, she thought, no longer her business.

Karl barely looked round.

'Close the door, Maria.'

'I asked you where is Paul? He's not in his nursery. Magda isn't in her room.' Magda was Paul's nurse, chosen by Maria herself when her son was born.

Karl got to his feet. He barely looked at Maria as he went to the door and shut it. That done, he turned to her.

'Paul is being well looked after. You need have no worries on that account.'

'I want to see him.'

Karl glanced at his watch.

'By now he will be about one hundred and fifty kilometres from Essen. I have sent him to friends who will look after him properly.'

'Friends? What the hell are you talking about? He's my son. Why wasn't I consulted? What's going on?'

'I have been very patient with you, Maria. I have given you numerous chances. Above all, I have been patient with the way in which you have chosen to bring up my son. But now I have decided that enough is enough. The longer he would remain in your company, the longer he would be under your influence, the softer he would become. I shall not see my son grow into a homosexual or a limp-wristed effeminate. Do you understand? Your time with him is at an end. You may see him next year at Christmas, and each year after that. But that is all.'

She stared at him, open-mouthed, unable to take in what he was saying. Surely he couldn't do this, couldn't just take her son away from her.

'I don't believe this!' She knew her voice was growing shrill, but she could not control it. It was all she could do to stop herself leaping on him. 'You can't just take him away!'

'Maria, I think you are growing hysterical. It would be better for you to go back to your room.'

'Damn you! You have no right to do this. You're a stinking Nazi. You can't take my son from me. You stinking Nazi!'

'Go to your room, Maria! At once!'

'I'm going nowhere. I want you to bring him back. Do you hear me!?'

He struck her hard across the cheek. Quite expertly. Quite clinically. It was all he did. It was the first time he had ever done so, and it would be the last.

Fighting back the tears, she looked directly at him.

'My father shall hear of this,' she said.

Karl shook his head.

'There is no need. He knows already. And he agrees with me. You are an unhealthy influence on the boy. The matter is closed. I warned you earlier that I would horsewhip you. Believe me that I shall do just that. I shall bring the servants to this room, I shall have you stripped naked, and I shall flay the skin from your back. Is that clear?'

Above the mantelpiece, a gilded clock ticked, but to Maria it was as though time was standing very still. She could hear her breath entering and leaving her lungs, she could hear her heart stammering behind her breasts, she could hear the seconds striking the air, but deep inside her nothing moved.

'Is that clear?'

She was suddenly aware that her mouth was full of saliva. It tasted vile. She took a deep breath through her nose and spat full in his face. Without another word, she strode to the door and into the passage. She slammed the door behind her, very loudly.

It must have been very late when she heard the door to her room opening. She had lost all sense of time passing. A soft light was burning near the bed. She had not been sleeping, not really. From time to time she had drifted into a half-sleep, only to come out of it again, aching as she had never ached in her life. She wanted to die. A hand touched her cheek. The skin still stung from the slap Karl had dealt her.

'You will find it is for the best.'

Karl's voice was low and deliberately gentle. She twisted away from him.

'I'm sorry I hit you. But you provoked me. You know I cannot bear to be provoked.'

She said nothing.

'Have you been asleep?' he asked.

Still she said nothing.

'In your clothes? You cannot be comfortable.'

'He is my son,' she said, whispering the words into the pillow. But he understood.

'Yes, I know that. But you have not been a good mother to him. You have loved him, I know. But you have bent him, too. In time he would grow up bent like that. Soft, like his mother. It is something in a woman, to be soft like that. But not in a man. And not in this man. He has a destiny. He is no ordinary child. His life cannot be exposed to influences such as yours. I cannot explain, not now. But perhaps in time.'

She remembered her son's words to her earlier: *He says I have work to do, work for the Reich.*

He had brought his hand back to her cheek, caressing

it. The same hand that had struck it not so long before.

'You will understand in time,' he said. 'You may even thank me.' His voice was surprisingly gentle. She had not heard such gentleness in it for years. The same voice that had threatened her with a whipping not so very long ago.

His hand did not cease caressing. When she looked up, his eyes were there. He bent forward to kiss her. She could not remember when he had last kissed her. She felt herself curl up inside. She did not think she could bear it if he wanted more. She tried to duck away, but he brought a hand behind her head and kissed her on the lips, not brutally, but with such insistence that she found it hard to breathe.

'You have not undressed,' he said. She could feel his breath against her cheek, she could smell the spirits. But she knew he was not drunk.

'I would like to stay with you tonight,' he said. 'I would like to make amends.'

She shook her head, trying to pull away.

'Maria, we are still man and wife. In the eyes of God, we are one flesh. There is no sense in our always sleeping apart.'

No sense? After what he had just done? What had sense to do with it? She thought of Jack. Of his caresses. Of his entry into her with a mixture of trepidation and joy. A wave of nausea was building up inside her. He turned her on her back and began to unbutton her dress. As he did so, his lips touched her skin, moving from her neck towards her breasts.

That was when she remembered the live microphone taped to her waist.

PART SIX

CHAPTER FIFTY

London
Thursday, 31 December 1992

The cold wind that had been blowing through London for the past five days was turning vindictive. Not content with thinning the blood or chapping the skin, it seemed to bring contamination in its wake, like a comet. People were coming down with heavy coughs and a peculiar strain of influenza that laid its victims in bed for weeks at a time or killed them outright. Christmas had not brought an end to the recession, not even a tiny upswing. Every street had its quota of unsellable houses. Every shop had boxes of unsold Christmas stock. The faces of people encountered on the street or the underground were uniformly strained. No one looked to the New Year with much hope of change. Promises of the first shoots of spring were as risible as ever. The government was clinging on by a thread. There was talk of another election. The wind seemed to be everywhere, all the time.

Following Norman's murder, the safe houses in Battersea had been abandoned. They were to be put on the market at bargain prices. Repairs had already been made by night. The hole in the wall between the two houses had been expertly filled, the plaster smoothed over, the wallpaper made as good as new. In the garden of number 35, the wind moved slowly across the tops of the weeds.

They had moved Jack to a small hotel near King's Cross,

the sort of place a passer-by would avoid unless he was looking for a prostitute ready to turn a fast trick. It sported a permanent 'No Vacancies' sign in a dusty window. There did not appear to be any other guests. Inside, it was cleaner than its external appearance promised, and the central heating worked as faultlessly as any in the land.

Jack was treated well, but his little expedition to Paddington Cemetery had not endeared him to his watchers. A perceptible gap had opened between him and them. In spite of their protestations, he knew them to be disingenuous in proclaiming him a free man. 'Free as the wind,' Felix would say, or 'free as a bird'. Such phrases had grown cryptic to him, and he had started to visualize walls of stone and metal cages in his exegesis of them.

He was beginning to learn how, within the world of his new keepers, words may be stretched, sometimes a little, sometimes to preposterous lengths. He was given a television to watch, and plenty of books. Most days, either Felix or Parker would drop in for a chat. There were no more debriefings. It was like living in a waiting-room. At night, indeed, he could hear the sound of trains shunting at King's Cross or St Pancras.

There was another house. This one was in Chelsea, at World's End, not many doors from where the Koestler Foundation delved into the mysteries of chance and synchronicity. Here, Felix and Parker had set up a small operations centre which served as the focus for Operation Papyrus. It was an absurd name, they both knew that perfectly well, but it had served them well enough and, in the course of time, had acquired a certain patina, almost a mystique. Officially, of course, neither Operation Papyrus nor its nerve-centre existed. Had anyone inquisitive wanted to know, both Parker and Felix were on secondment elsewhere – Kuwait or Saudi Arabia or Bahrain, it was popularly assumed. There were good reasons for keeping the entire business tucked away in odd places, in little suburban houses and Chelsea backwaters, far from prying eyes.

In the mornings at World's End, they played Bach. In the afternoons, Telemann, in recordings by Maurice André. And in the evenings, Schubert. Parker, perversely for a man of his class and age, had a fondness for the music of Ravi Shankar, to which he had been fortuitously introduced at university by a girlfriend of more exotic tastes. The girl had gone in search of gurus, but he had retained his fondness for the strains of the sitar. He played snatches of the maestro's recordings in a separate room, where he worked alone. *Sindhu Bhairavi* was his favourite raga, and one that he played incessantly. Although a morning raga by strict interpretation, he paid no heed to such quibbles and played it at all times of the day. It was the only concession in his ordered, conservative life to the cult of the cosmopolitan.

The table had been set for a meeting. There were glasses, small bottles of Highland Spring water, notepads, sharpened pencils. Parker was already seated at the table. He seemed nervous, constantly tapping a pencil against the table-top. Felix was on his feet, looking through the window on to the King's Road. 'The endless procession', he was thinking. Why would a God create any of this? What was the point?

It was not that he was given to habitual meditation on the fleetingness of life or the inferiority of matter. He was not, at heart, a spiritual man. It was just that he felt all movement should be directed, that it should be a pilgrimage, whereas the comings and goings of most of us were, on due consideration, events of no greater moment than the daily reiteration of the tides.

'What if she doesn't come?' Parker asked, snapping the lead on his pencil.

'She'll come.' Felix did not move from his vantage point by the window.

Parker found a sharpener and began to forge a new point.

'She's taking a risk.'

'Only a small one, I assure you.'

Silence. Parker resumed tapping.

'What about Maria? Is there anything?'

'We had tapes this morning. Things aren't too pleasant at Essen. Karl has sent the boy away.'

Parker sat up straighter. The pencil became motionless.

'Really? You should have told me earlier. Why has he done that?'

Felix explained.

'And you believe him? You're sure that's his motive?'

Felix nodded.

'Quite sure. She nearly came a cropper, though.'

'How's that?'

'He wanted to make love to her. Quite out of the blue. She was wearing the mike. He'd got as far as unbuttoning her dress half-way, as far as we can find out.'

'Jesus.'

'She pretended to be sick. Then she really was sick. He went on back to his room. But if it happens again . . .'

'Do you think he suspects?'

'No reason to. He'd gone for her a bit. Slapped her. I think it turned him on. He's that type.'

'Isn't there a safer place for the mike?'

Felix shook his head.

'We considered a surgical implant, but she'd have to be hospitalized. It simply isn't feasible.'

He glanced out the window. A car had drawn up nearby.

'Here she comes now,' Felix said.

'Do you think this could be a mistake?'

'Too late to think of that now. Let's see it through.'

It was only a matter of minutes before the door opened and Irina Kossenkova entered the room. She was alone.

'Madame Kossenkova.' Felix had taken upon himself the role of host. 'It's an honour to meet you in person after all this time. I'm Jeremy Latham. Please let me introduce my colleague. This is Simon Worsely.'

Parker was already on his feet. They all shook hands. Parker took Kossenkova's coat and hung it on a hook behind the door. The richness of the sable looked out of place.

'Would you like some tea or coffee?' Felix asked.

'No, thank you. I ate aboard the plane. Mr Latham, my time here is extremely limited. If you don't mind, I'd like to get down to business right away.'

'Of course, I quite understand. Please, this is your chair.'

Once seated, Kossenkova glanced sharply round the room.

'I have your assurance that this room is sterile?'

'Absolutely. You must understand that it is as much in our interest as it is in yours for this meeting to go unnoticed. Everything that happens here today is off the record.'

'I am not sure our interests are that similar. However, I see no reason to make a fuss. I have put myself in your hands. What is your expression?'

'As soon hang for a sheep as a lamb?'

'Precisely.'

Felix and Parker sat together at one end of the table, facing their guest. Felix had arranged it so that she played the role of supplicant or interviewee. For all that, her presence dominated the room. She was not a woman to be cowed by the pettiness of someone else's stage management.

Felix started the proceedings.

'Madame Kossenkova. Thank you for responding so promptly and unselfishly to my invitation. By coming here today, I believe you may help avert the crisis that faces us.'

'It is your crisis, Mr Latham.'

Felix shook his head as though reluctantly.

'Well,' he said, 'I'm not entirely sure about that. But we'll come back to it later. First of all, I think I should tell you that there has been confirmation that Rosewicz is now in possession of the scroll.'

Kossenkova lifted her eyebrows a fraction, but said nothing.

'Our confirmation is so far only provisional,' Felix went on. 'But we are expecting something more final in the next day or two.'

'May I ask how you know this?'

Felix shook his head.

'That will have to remain secret. Let me only say that the life of one of our agents would be forfeit if anything leaked out.'

'Do you plan to take any action?'

'First, we have to know definitely that Rosewicz has the scroll. Then, we have to establish where he is keeping it. After that, it gets more difficult. I think you know why.'

She nodded.

'Because of the hold he has over you.'

'Primarily, yes. Which is why I have asked you here.'

'I can offer you only limited assistance.'

'What are you offering?'

'I have twenty-nine British agents. I have fresh dossiers on each of them, showing varying degrees of collaboration. I know the whereabouts of surviving family for seventeen of them, and I am confident of obtaining more. The security around the special unit has been trebled. If necessary, they can be moved at an hour's notice.

'I have also had a most detailed dossier prepared, in which it is made abundantly clear that post-war British intelligence used its former heroes as pawns in a most unpleasant game. As you well know, publication of such a dossier in the West would cause an outcry in parliament. There is already pressure from the Left to make the intelligence services accountable. This would almost certainly prove the final nail in your coffin. Now, I think you should tell me what you have for me.'

Felix looked at her carefully. Had she been responsible

for Norman's murder? Was she playing more than one game herself? He knew it was only too possible. But a trooper like Norman was expendable. A small price to pay in a game where the odds were so high.

'First,' he said, 'I need to know what guarantees you can offer me. This is, after all, a form of blackmail.'

'We are in this together, Mr Latham; please don't forget that. You will be permitted to send a small team of inspectors. All existing files will be opened. Once identities and so forth have been established, and provided we have an agreement, the rest is simple. The original files, together with my new dossiers, will be passed to you or, if you prefer, destroyed in your presence. The men in question will be removed from the unit. You will not see them again, you have my word for that. The unit will be shut down. That will be the end of the matter.'

Felix made a note on the pad in front of him. Putting down his pen, he folded his arms.

'Very well,' he said. 'I think we understand one another. Mr Worsely will go through our offer. If it is acceptable to you, I think I can say that we have a deal.'

CHAPTER FIFTY-ONE

Paris
Thursday, 31 December

'And you are sure it is not a forgery?'

Karl von Freudiger was enjoying a celebratory glass of champagne in his father-in-law's library in Paris. He and Reinhold had just been allowed to set eyes on the Jesus scroll for the first time.

Rosewicz shook his head decisively.

'Most certainly not. Our young friend Gould did some very good work for me, tracing its provenance. Once other experts get to work, there will be no reason to doubt its authenticity.'

'But you will need Gould to back you up. Provided he is willing to co-operate.'

'I don't think so. British intelligence have him under wraps again. And even if we could get him back, I doubt very much if he would lend his testimony. I'd prefer it if he were out of the way for good.'

'Is there any chance of that?'

Rosewicz nodded.

'I have men working on it at the moment. We can't go public until he's been dealt with, it would be too risky. Ciechanowski has everything ready in Warsaw, but I've told him to await my go-ahead. In the meantime, the scroll will be taken to Poland under the tightest security. We have secured the services of several Catholic scholars, all of whom are sworn to absolute secrecy. I do not anticipate any leaks. But I expect things to move fast once we make our announcement.'

Reinhold took a final sip from his glass and set it down.

'An excellent champagne,' he said.

'It's a Dom Pérignon de luxe that I bought in 1943. It had been taken out of France and sold to a handful of buyers able to appreciate it. You may have been offered a bottle or two yourself.'

'Yes, we had a lot of French wine in those days.'

'This was my last bottle. I took it out of Croatia with me and swore I would only open it when the scroll was restored and the League on its feet again. I'm pleased you enjoyed it.'

'Immensely. I feel very privileged. To be quite honest, I never thought I'd live to see this day.'

'Nor I. But we have. And now I feel as though my life is beginning all over.'

Reinhold laughed.

'You have been born again, is that it?'

Rosewicz nodded, but he did not appear to join in the joke.

'Yes,' he said. 'It is precisely that. This is a most serious business. We have all been reborn. Soon, we shall celebrate the rebirth of a united Catholic Europe. By the time our grandson is of age, there will be a Holy Empire for him to rule.'

'Provided he has the Holy Father's blessing.'

'I am confident we shall have that.'

'Stefan . . .' Reinhold hesitated. He was too old, there was too much between them. And yet . . .

Rosewicz looked at him. He could sense that his old friend had something painful to tell him.

'Yes, what is it, Reinhold?'

'It's about Maria.'

'What about her?' He turned to Karl. 'I thought you told me you had her under control.'

Karl nodded.

'It's not that,' Reinhold said. 'It's more serious.'

Rosewicz felt his heart turn cold. Surely it could not be true? Ever since Jack's escape, a thin shadow of suspicion had hovered over his daughter. But the escape had seemed so spontaneous, it had been impossible to prove collusion of any kind.

'Stefan, we have to decide what to do.'

'Not Maria . . .'

Von Freudiger nodded. What he was doing hurt him more than anything had hurt him in his long life. He knew how much Rosewicz loved his daughter. But he had no choice.

'It is not a question of maybe or perhaps any longer, Stefan. If she is allowed to stay free, she will lead them directly to the League.'

'She knows nothing.'

'She knows everything. I had her followed in London. She met Gould there. He was accompanied by a British agent. My people had to kill him in order to stay on Gould's trail. Last night Maria broke into Karl's study. We think she made microfilm copies of files. There is enough in there to destroy us.'

'Then take them from her.'

'It is not that simple.'

'Why not?'

Karl interrupted.

'Perhaps I can explain,' he said.

CHAPTER FIFTY-TWO

Outside, the city smelt of darkness. Long boulevards, lights, the descent of night. In Stefan Rosewicz's house, a servant was lighting lights. From the street, the entire façade began to glow. Then, one by one the curtains were closed.

One street away, a large Mercedes van stood parked outside an apartment house. It had been there since the previous day, and so far it had not received a ticket. There were no windows to the rear. Inside, four men sat at banks of controls. Each wore a set of headphones. Three were monitoring the situation inside Rosewicz's house, one through Maria's microphone, the others through various bugs she had been able to plant in strategic places since her arrival.

The fourth man, Ronald Harris, was the group leader and the co-ordinator for the team of armed men who were keeping a discreet watch on the house from outside. The team had been briefed to go in to take Maria out if there was reason to believe she was in imminent danger. The van was equipped with a direct satellite link to London.

One of the men at the console monitoring the house slipped off his headphones and switched his audio input to a central speaker. A light in front of each of the other listeners warned them to disconnect in order to listen to what was coming through. Harris spoke rapidly into his microphone.

'All units stand by. Switching to main audio channel.'

He slipped off his headphones and swivelled in his seat in order to listen to the direct pick-up. The man who had switched on the speaker was explaining the set-up.

'This is input from mike five. That's in the library. Mother put it there last night, when she had drinks with her old man. The quality's not too great.'

It is not a question of . . . . or perhaps any longer, Stefan. If she is allowed to stay free, ... directly to the League.

She knows nothing.

She knows everything. Last night she . . . . Karl's study. We think she made microfilm copies of files. There is . . . . to destroy us.

Then . . . . from her.

It is not that simple.

Why not?

The operator looked round.

'Jesus, they're on to her.'

Karl's voice went on crackling from the speaker.

She's working for someone else. In all likelihood, the British. They must have recruited her in Rome.

I don't believe . . . .

I'm afraid it's true, Stef . . . . The house is under surveillance. I've already told Henryk to . . . .

The operator turned to Harris.

'Tell your men to get her out of there now! And tell them to take care. The targets know they're being watched.'

Harris pulled his headphones back on and flipped a red switch on his console.

'All units! All units! Full alert. Please confirm your positions.'

He released the button on his handset. Loud crackling filled his headphones.

'Come in surveillance units. We have a red alert.'

No voice answered. The crackling in his headphones was loud and painful. At the other end of the van, someone had switched off the main speaker. One man continued to monitor the conversation in the library.

'Unit one. Do you receive me?'

The van filled with silence.

'Unit two. Do you receive me?'

Silence. One by one, the other men had turned to watch Harris.

'Unit three. Come in unit three.'

The operator monitoring the library microphone interrupted.

'Mike five's just gone dead.'

Harris got to his feet.

'Lewis, take a look outside. See what's going on. Take a gun with you.'

Lewis, who had been monitoring Maria, took a pistol from a box on the wall above his console.

'What about the woman?'

'I'll monitor her. I just want some feedback.'

He raised his handset and spoke into it.

'Unit one, please answer. Come in, unit one.'

Lewis went to the door and pulled the handle. It was jammed. He tried again, much harder.

'The door's locked.'

'What?'

The next moment, there was the sound of an engine roaring into life, then the two men standing were flung forward as the van lurched into motion.

'What the hell?!'

Harris picked himself up and hurried to the door separating them from the driver's compartment. The van was moving fast now, cornering at speed.

'Hey! Open up. We're still in the back!'

'Who is it? Chris? It's the sort of stunt he'd pull.'

'This is no stunt. Peter, keep trying the team. Mack, I

369

want you to patch us through to London. And be quick about it.'

Mack, at the main console, started pushing buttons. Harris went on pounding at the door.

'Lewis,' he called, 'get the rest of the guns out. We may need them.'

They turned another corner, then drew away fast.

'The satellite signal's dead.'

'It can't be.'

'I'm telling you it is.'

'Still nothing from the team.'

'Keep trying.'

There was a squeal of tyres. They rounded another corner. Harris banged on the door again. Lewis passed round the pistols.

'See if the rear doors are open,' ordered Harris. Lewis tried one, then the other. They were shut fast.

They did not stop for over half an hour. By the time the van came to a halt, they guessed they were well out of the city. The engine went dead. It was absolutely silent outside. Two men crouched facing the inner doors, two facing the back entrance. Several minutes passed, during which nothing happened.

Something clattered against the side of the van. A few moments later, they could hear footsteps on the roof. About a minute passed, then there was the sound of a small motor whirring. A heavy-duty electric drill. There was a high-pitched whine as the bit connected with metal. Moments later, a large hole was punched in the roof. Something heavy was clamped over the aperture. A narrow cylinder came through the hole, then collapsed into two horizontal nozzles.

'What the hell's that?'

There was a hissing sound, and the nozzles started to turn.

'It's gas!'

Harris tore his sweater over his head, grabbed the nearest

370

chair, and leapt up to block the nozzles. It was impossible. They were spinning much too fast. Gas had already started to fill the inside of the van.

CHAPTER FIFTY-THREE

In London the meeting with Irina Kossenkova was drawing to a close. A deal had been struck, a deal whose immediate result was to be the deaths of twenty-nine old men. No matter. Old men die every day, and others grow old to take their place. More importantly, to those in that little room at World's End, difficult secrets would die with them. There would not, they hoped, be new ones to take their place.

'I do hope, Madame Kossenkova, that this will be the first of many meetings. We've all buried our differences now. Once these small outstanding matters have been cleared up, I think we shall have a lot to talk about together. The world isn't quite an easy place yet.'

'No, you are quite right. Though it is still a little easier for you in the West than for the rest of us.'

'That's not quite what I meant.'

'No, but it is what counts. You still have problems of perspective. Once your great recession is over, you think all will be well. The world will be a happy place again. An easy place. You forget how hard life can be for other people. For most people. That forgetfulness will destroy you in the end.'

'I must say I expected better of you than that. That's the sort of thing your old hardliners used to trot out. You can't believe that rubbish any longer, can you? We're still in business. It's your lot who've gone bankrupt.' Felix was in fine form. It looked as if things were going to work out after all.

'I think you choose to misunderstand. The Communists were not really wrong, not about that anyway. Their problem, like yours, was hypocrisy. But they were not wrong about the suffering or the injustice. What we are doing here is an injustice . . . One injustice to mask another. The West is bankrupt in the ways that really matter. You're greedy, you're selfish, you care for nothing but power and money, and you have politicians to pander to your wants. All the beauty of your civilization is in the past. What have you now? Pop stars and hamburgers and soft drinks. More people visit Disneyworld than the Louvre. And now you have no enemy to prop you up. Wait and see. Rosewicz is not the last of the barbarians. There are others. They are waiting.'

In Paris, Stefan Rosewicz was waiting alone for his daughter. He was troubled and dismayed. The champagne was flat in his stomach, as flat as the years it had waited to be opened. He loved Maria, had always loved her, could not bear to be without her, least of all now, as old age began to press so heavily on him. Reinhold had insisted — reluctantly, but forcefully all the same — that she could not be allowed to live. Rosewicz had resisted him with as much force, maintaining that it was in their power to keep her alive yet incommunicado. She would have no further contact with anyone outside the family. Ever. There had been a fierce argument, which Rosewicz had won. For the moment.

There was a knock on the library door.

'Come in,' he called out, struggling for mastery of his voice.

The door opened, and Maria entered.

Back in World's End, there was a perfunctory knock on the door, followed half a second later by a junior from the listening room downstairs.

'Sir, Mr Hudson says you're to get downstairs right away, sir. Something's up.'

Felix was already on his feet.

'What do you mean? Whereabouts?'

'Paris, sir. Something's gone wrong. I'm not sure what, but Mr Hudson's in a terrible state.'

Suddenly, Hudson himself was at the door.

'You'd better come down quickly, sir. It's Paris. I think they've been blown. We had a mayday from Frog One' — Frog One was the van — 'but it was just a squawk. No message. The signal's dead. I think they've been taken out.'

Felix lost no time. He spoke to Parker, using his real name.

'Roger, get over to King's Cross. Get Gould out of there at once. Ring ahead, tell Bill to haul him out. Meet on the station concourse. Take the first train to Glasgow, then go to ground at Balquhidder.'

If the operation in Paris had indeed been blown, Rosewicz could have more men in London. Parker lost no time. He had a car waiting for him in the King's Road.

'Sit down, my dear, I'd like to talk.'

'What's wrong, Father? You look upset. Has Karl said something to you?'

On the table behind him, his life's work rested in a box. In front of him, the only truly beautiful, truly loved person in that life sat waiting for him to speak, but he hardly knew what to say to her. He had sacrificed her once already by marrying her to von Freudiger. Now he had to go through it again, but this time it would be more painful.

'It's over, Maria. We know. The game's over. Time to relax now, my darling. Time to tell me what's been going on. I don't want to know why. That would only hurt me. I will believe that you have been deceived. But it's finished now. All the deception. All the fear.'

In the safe house, Felix was trying to reassure Irina Kossenkova.

'They're bringing a car round to the back. You needn't worry, this house is completely secure.'

'As secure as your team in Paris?'

'We don't know they've been blown. This is purely a precaution.'

'I know a panic when I see one. If you've lost communications with your team in Paris, you can be sure Rosewicz has taken them out. He has the best people in the business.'

'I agree. But this house is safe. Not even London Central knows about it. I've got tight security all round.' He took her arm. 'This way. We'll use the back stairs.'

It was three flights to the bottom. Kossenkova had not had time to put her coat on.

'I'll just check that your car's there,' said Felix. He tried the door. It would not open.

There was a sound of feet on the stairs. Not hurrying feet. Slow, deliberate feet.

'Hudson, is that you? This ruddy door's jammed.'

No answer.

'Hudson?'

But it was not Hudson. It was not anyone he knew. The man did not wear a mask. He did not have to: there were not going to be any survivors to recognize him.

She had not denied anything. Without a word, she had just sat listening to his accusation. He had tried to get her to admit her guilt, to own up to what she had been doing, but she had stayed stubbornly silent. It was worse than an admission of guilt, that silence. It burned into him, it left marks on his flesh, like stigmata. That his own daughter, the daughter he had loved so much, had become a Judas, sickened him to his heart. Finally, he too fell silent. Once, he had thought she might become a nun and make him proud. How much better that would have been than music and treachery.

On reflection, he thought that perhaps that would be the best solution. An enclosed order, strict seclusion. It

375

would make his last years easier. She might find absolution in a life of prayer.

'Is that all, Father?'

He looked up. He had been lost in thought, staring into the open fire. Wearily, he got to his feet.

'Is that all you have to say?' he asked.

She hung her head. There was no fight in her. Silence was all she could muster. Death would be the cleanest solution, but she did not know how to face it. Not while Paul was alive, not while he needed her.

Her father came close. She saw him lift his hand, ready to strike. Her cheek still stung from the blow Karl had struck her, the skin was still swollen, like rotten fruit.

He looked down at her, knowing that, if he struck her, he would not be able to stop. There had been a child, a Jewish child in Klanjec, who had looked at him as though he held salvation in his hands. He had struck her, not one blow but many, so many he had lost count. It had all happened in a state of forgetfulness, so that the blows were all he could remember in the end. Not the child, not her eyes, not the look of appeal in them. Just the blows. His hand dropped slowly, trembling slightly.

'Father, I should like to go to confession. There is confession at St Charles this afternoon.'

Confession? Yes, why not? he thought. It would be a beginning. A step in the right direction. He would make enquiries about the convent this evening. Ciechanowski would arrange matters.

'Very well,' he said. 'Henryk will take you. He'll wait outside. You understand that he will have to do that. But he will not listen, you have my word. Confession is sacrosanct.'

She got up and went to the door.

'Maria . . . Please, my child, don't try to escape. They would rather you were dead, Karl and Reinhold. They don't love you as I do. Don't give them an opportunity.'

'I wish I were dead.'

'You mustn't say that. It's a sin to say that.'

'A sin? You would know about that, wouldn't you?'

He nearly rose to her bait. But he could not bear to learn how she hated him. Better that she should spend her life praying for him. It would be a bond between them, it would suffice for the years he had left.

'And don't try to get in touch with your friends out there,' he said. 'They've been taken care of. No one's coming to get you out. You must resign yourself to that.' He paused. 'When you confess, be sure there is nothing you leave unsaid.'

For he knew, even in his hope of a life of prayer and contemplation for her, that her life was worth nothing now, and that the League, should it overrule him, would snuff it out as a thumb and a finger together lift the flame from a candle's wick.

Parker screeched to a halt outside the hotel. It was a dead part of the day, there was scarcely anyone about. Serrat had come with him. These days he never went anywhere without Serrat. Parker could look after himself, but Serrat could look after him better still. Serrat was better built than anyone had a right to be, but he still would not have looked out of place on a dance-floor. He had forfeited neither grace nor style to the exigencies of acquiring and maintaining a powerful physique. His power resided in something other than mere muscle. His build was that of a dancer who can lift weights, not a steroid-handicapped victim of muscular overkill. And his physical grace was complemented by mental agility and a tranquil personality. Just having him around made Parker feel good.

They pulled in several doors from the hotel. Parker looked up and down. A hushed and ordinary street. A pimp on one corner, an Asian family with a pram, black students leaving a down-at-heel hostel. A black cab passed on its way to the station. No one got on or off round here. At the hotel, everything looked quiet.

'Stay here,' said Parker. 'Keep an eye on the front. Bill said he'd have everything ready. I should be out in half a minute.'

Serrat shook his head. He had the bodyguard's manner. Polite but firm.

'If there's trouble, I'm better equipped to handle it. Objectively. And I don't want you there to distract me, half my mind on you. You watch the hotel. Buzz me if there's any movement on the street.' He had curly hair. A wide grin.

Parker watched him stride slowly along the pavement, alert, inconspicuous, strong. He was the sort of man a pimp would instinctively shy away from. He made no particular effort to look dangerous, he never postured, but the taut readiness of his limbs communicated a warning to those who might best need it. Parker kept a careful eye on both sides of the street. No suspicious movements. He could see Serrat check the hotel façade. An economy of movement. Grace joined to maximum efficiency. His own eye followed Serrat's to the windows on the upper floors. No movement. Nothing out of the ordinary.

Parker watched as Serrat climbed the steps to the front door, watched him press the bell, watched him wait. He counted off the seconds, wondering why no one came. Serrat rang again. Parker got out of the car. Something was wrong. The front door was partly open. If Serrat went inside he'd need back-up. In spite of his assurance. He saw Serrat push the door.

The first flash reached Parker before the sound of the blast. A wave of hot air threw him back against the car, his arms raised to ward off the blow. And then, in rapid succession, he heard the thump, thump, thump, as fresh explosions ripped through each of the other floors, tearing the hotel to pieces.

CHAPTER FIFTY-FOUR

In the darkness, there was light, and in the light a promise of salvation, as tiny and remote as a star on the edges of the galaxy. *In the beginning was the Word.* They had made their Word flesh and hung it high above their heads on wood for an object of worship. Maria trembled at the thought of that. The arrogance of it. The hatred that had sprung from it. They had made an innocent race killers of God, and killed and banished them until their God had died a million and six million deaths.

Since childhood, she had been coming to perfumed darknesses like this. Her earliest memories were of her father holding her hand in his, of his murmured prayers in a language she did not understand, his genuflections, his moments apart from her, deep in the mystery he craved so eagerly. She thought of the blood that had been on his hands, those same hands, those same, gentle fingers. The blood of Jewish women and children, of Serbs whose only crime had been to worship the same God in different clothes. Did he confess those sins when he came here? Did he acknowledge that he had done wrong? Or was it still his dirty little secret, a winking, nudging, under-the-counter affair between him and his Croat-loving, fascist-protecting divinity?

On the pew beside her an old woman and a child were waiting in line for the confessional. The child would knit sins out of the gossamer of her life, and feel contrite, and say a Hail Mary as she might a lesson in school, rapidly and without real thought. She would grow wiser in time, and hide her sins until she learned to hide them from herself. And her visits here would grow less frequent until they finally ceased, and life would go on until a crisis dragged her back for absolution. By then, thought Maria, it would be too late. The damage would have been done, the wound gone deep, the poison leached into the blood.

The old woman got up and went inside the wooden booth. Maria heard the door close, caught the indistinct murmur of confession beginning. The hearts of the old are a mass of scars, she thought. Like her father's heart. Nothing could make it soft again, or supple. Not prayer. Not confession. Not daily attendance at the mass. And her own heart? What would take its scars away?

Henryk was standing a little distance apart, watching her like a hawk. She would not be able to slip away from him as Jack had done that time in the park. He was alert for anything now. She knew he had men posted outside, one on every exit. Unless she could grow wings, there would be no escape for her.

The old woman came out and the little girl took her place. Maria could not hear her, did not want to. She kept thinking of Jack, she could not help it. Even here in church, he was with her, the memory of his body, the touch and tremble of him. He was in the candles, fluttering, in the faces of the statues, watching her undress, in the red light of the altar, making her alive.

The little girl came out, glancing shyly round her as she stepped through the door. Maria got to her feet. She was the last in the queue. Out of the corner of her eye, she saw Henryk shift in order to get a good view of the confessional.

'*Bénissez-moi, mon Père, parce-que j'ai péché. Je ne me suis pas confessée depuis six semaines.*'

It was so hard to make a start. To stop everything pouring out. Not only her own sins, but all their sins. They were her justification.

'I feel confused, father. Frightened.'

380

'It's all right. There's nothing to be frightened of. This is God's house.'

It was not the usual priest, Father Seurel. Judging by his voice, this was a much younger man.

'Is Father Seurel not here today?'

'No, he's sick. I've taken his place. My name is Father de Galais. Please go on.'

She braced herself. Why was it so hard? When she had been small, she had taken a certain pleasure in confession.

'I'm guilty of betrayal, father. My husband. My father. I've betrayed them all.'

But she knew she must not talk about this, about her great betrayal. What she had done had been for the best, for the sake of something good. The sin was theirs. Let them confess.

'Go on.'

'I am guilty of fornication, father. I . . . I slept with a man who is not my husband.'

'I see. Was this on one occasion or several?'

'Once, father. Only once.'

She could not keep the regret out of her voice.

'I see. Were you seduced?'

'No, I . . . It's very difficult. Hard to explain. We knew one another a few years ago. Then I . . . My father arranged for me to be married to an older man. Father Seurel knows about that. We've talked before.'

'Go on.'

'I never loved my husband. Nor he me. I felt in need of love. And . . . this man, this other man, loved me. That's all.'

'And is he married too? This other man?'

'No. He had a wife, but she died. She was my sister.'

'I see. Your brother-in-law.'

'That's not the point. He didn't know. It's . . . hard to explain.'

'Have you resolved not to see this man again? Or, at least not to give in to him.'

381

'I didn't give in. There was no pressure. It was mutual. We wanted each other. You wouldn't understand.'

'No. But I have to try. And I can understand temptation. Even that sort of temptation. Believe me.'

'Is temptation such a bad thing?'

'If it ends in sin, yes.'

'Is that a sin? To love someone? To show you love them?'

'I don't suppose it is a sin to love. But to sleep with someone who is not your husband, yes, that is a sin. Perhaps not in the eyes of society, but in the eyes of the church. You know I don't have to explain this to you.'

'And was it a sin for the church to marry me to a man I didn't love?'

'You could have said no. During the ceremony . . .'

'Do you really think that I'd have gone that far of my own free will?'

'No, I suppose not. I'm sorry. But I can only speak as a priest. If you were married in church, you will remain married until one or the other of you dies.'

'Can't my marriage be annulled? Please say it can.'

'It's not for me to say.'

'Then just give me absolution. That's all I came for.'

'Very well. Do you heartily repent of this and all your sins?'

She hesitated.

'No,' she said. 'I can't say that. I'm not sorry for what happened.'

'Then why come here?'

'I don't know. I'm sorry. I've been wasting your time. I wanted someone to talk to.'

She stood and made to open the door.

'Maria.'

When she turned, she saw the priest's face full against the grille.

'Maria, please sit down again. I have to speak with you.'

'How do you know my name?'

'I can't explain. Not now. Listen to me carefully. You mustn't be too long or Henryk will get suspicious. I want to help you. Some people in the Vatican know what's going on. We are doing what we can to destroy the influence of your father's League. But we need your help. Has anyone told you that you are in danger? That the British team sent to protect you has been wiped out?'

'Yes. My father told me less than an hour ago. I think my husband wants me dead. He sent our son away. Paul.'

'Yes, I know about that. We want to help you get him back. Did your father say what they plan to do with you?'

'No, not yet. Do you know where Paul is?'

'Yes. My people say he's in a house at Arnstorf near Munich. But don't worry, he's quite safe. He's being well looked after. Our first priority is to get you out. There is also the matter of your friend Dr Gould. Do you have any idea where he is?'

'In London. But that's all I can tell you. The British are taking care of him.'

'In that case, he's in very great danger.'

'I don't understand.'

'There isn't time to explain properly. Just trust me. I'll see what we can do. You should go home now. Don't make a fuss. Keep calm. As soon as you know what they're planning, tell Mrs Nagle. She knows me. And she's devoted to you. She'll bring me any message you give her. Trust her. Once we're ready to make a move, I'll pass instructions to you through her. Now, I want you to say ten Hail Marys and perform an act of contrition. I absolve you in the Name of the Father, the Son, and the Holy Ghost. *Allez en paix, mon enfant.*'

She saw his hand move in the sign of the cross, then the shutter closed. When she came out, Henryk was still waiting.

CHAPTER FIFTY-FIVE

'Get in the car. Quickly!'

Parker looked round. Jack Gould was standing behind him, his hand on the passenger door. There was no time for questions. Parker turned and climbed back into the driving seat. Jack got in beside him.

'I thought you were dead,' said Parker.

'So did I. Let's get the hell out of here.'

Parker thumped the accelerator. As they roared away, they could hear the sound of a siren somewhere in the distance. Parker could see the headlines already. He wondered who was going to have the job of explaining what had happened, and who would be given the blame. Some poor mug of a policeman as usual, he imagined. And the IRA as scapegoats.

'How did you get out?' he asked.

'Bill Blair. He had your warning about three minutes before the attack. Didn't lose any time. Came to my room and hauled me out like this.' Jack was dressed in only a shirt and trousers. 'Next thing I knew I was half-way down a fire-escape. Then there was some shooting and Bill went back inside. He told me to get round to the front and find somewhere to hide until you came along. That's what I did. What the hell's going on?'

'I wish I knew. My guess is that the League is flexing its muscles. I've just tried calling my base at World's End; the line's gone dead. They've taken out our team in Paris. I've got orders to take you up to Scotland.'

'What about Maria? Is she all right? Where is she?'

'She's in Paris. I don't know how she is. Once I can re-establish contact with Felix . . .'

'What do you mean, you don't know? You sent people to protect her. You sent her back on that understanding. Is that the team that's been wiped out?'

'I'm sorry. We can't foresee everything. Nobody expected this.'

'The hell they didn't. Can you get me to Paris?'

'Paris? I told you, I've got orders to take you north. Once we get there, I can re-establish communications.'

'Pull over,' ordered Jack.

'What?'

'You heard me.'

They were in heavy traffic, heading for the A1. Parker found a gap and drew in to the side of the road. Jack made to open the door.

'Please, Dr Gould. Stay where you are.'

'You bastards let her go back to her husband. And now you tell me you can't even protect her.'

'Jack, this is a war. Things that are happening now are a continuation of events that occurred in the 1940s. You hardly understand what's going on.'

'I understand that Maria is in danger. I have to go there.'

'Don't be a bloody fool. How do you expect to get to Paris? You've got no money. No papers. Not even a coat. I promise you, this isn't over yet. Maria will be quite safe.'

'You said that before.'

Jack opened the door and started to get out. There was a click behind him. He glanced round to see Parker holding a pistol.

'I told you not to be a fool. You have a part to play in all this. And you still owe us a favour.'

Jack looked at him steadily for a couple of moments.

'Go fuck yourself,' he said. He got out of the car and slammed the door behind him.

CHAPTER FIFTY-SIX

'Maria, this is Sister Zofia. She has travelled all the way from Czestochowa overnight in order to be with you today. I'm afraid she speaks only Polish. You'll have to do your best. When you were little, your Polish was very good. It won't matter once you get to Poland. You'll be asked to take a vow of silence.'

The nun stood to one side. Her long, old-fashioned habit seemed out of place in the beautifully-furnished room, with its rich fabrics and priceless ornaments. She had the wasted look of someone who has turned her back on life. Clearly, her surroundings did not matter to her.

'Does she know that I don't want to go?'

'She is not interested in what you want. All she knows, all she wants to know, is that a cardinal of the church, a cardinal who happens to be the special patron of her order, has asked her to accompany you on your journey from Paris back to Czestochowa. I shall send one of my men with you to ensure that you are both safe. And that you do not make any foolish attempt to escape. Once you reach the convent, you will become the responsibility of the Mother Superior. Her name is Mother Alice. It's a house founded in 1644 by Matilda of Radomsko. The order is known as the Sisters of Penitence.'

'Father, don't you see? What you're doing is grotesque. It makes a mockery of a true religious vocation.'

'What you have done makes a mockery of all I hold sacred.'

'Sacred? Is there anything you hold sacred except yourself?'

'Maria, please don't fight me. This is the only path I have open. Karl will kill you. Do you understand that? He knows about your liaison with Jack Gould. He wants you dead. You should think yourself lucky that I've got the backing of Ciechanowski. He's managed to persuade Karl and his father that this will be for the best.'

'And exactly how long am I expected to spend in this place?'

Her father looked at her. Looked at her with a wild, unguarded stare that revealed more than he had intended.

'How long?' His voice was hollow, without affect. 'Do you really not understand yet? You will never come out of there. It is to be your prison. They will bury you there.'

Her eyes opened wide in disbelief. They were in a little morning-room at the back of the house. The walls were hung with mirrors in gilt frames. Everywhere Maria looked, she saw her own reflection staring back at her.

'I want you to pray for me, my love. Night and day. Whether I am alive or dead. You . . .'

He caught her as she fainted. There were tears in his eyes. His hands trembled as he took her in his arms and kissed her.

She woke in the night, covered in sweat. Cold sweat that had already been on her skin a long time and grown stale. Ganachaud had given her strong tranquillizers, and she had slept unpleasantly under their influence.

When she looked round, she saw that someone was sitting beside the bed, reading by a soft light. It was Mrs Nagle.

'Noreen. What are you doing here?'

'Your father asked me to keep an eye on you, miss. He's very worried about you.'

Maria found it hard to speak.

'Can you help me sit up, Noreen? I feel stiff all over.'

'You poor thing. You've been out of it for hours. Your father says you've to be ready to travel in the morning. There'll be a car downstairs at eight o'clock.'

Mrs Nagle lifted Maria's head and propped her back with pillows, then helped her up on to them.

'Does that feel better?'

Maria nodded.

'I feel terrible.'

'Well, I have to say, you don't look too good, miss.'

'Has my father told you what's happening?'

'Not really, miss. Just that you're going to Poland and won't be back in Paris for some time.'

'He's sending me to a convent, Noreen. For the rest of my life.'

There was a shocked silence, then a snort of disapproval.

'He can't do that, miss. They'd never let him.'

'It's been done. The arrangements have been made. Please, Noreen, can you take a message to Father de Galais?'

'To be sure I can. I'll get you a pen and paper.'

CHAPTER FIFTY-SEVEN

Paris
Monday, 4 January 1993

Jack had been watching the house for two days now, but still nothing had happened. Several people had gone in and out, but no one he knew, apart from Henryk. He was growing impatient and afraid, and was terrified that he might start making mistakes. There was no room for mistakes in what he was doing.

Getting out of London had not been unduly difficult. Suffering badly from the cold, he had walked all the way from Kentish Town, where he had left Parker, to the Irish embassy in Grosvenor Place. It was a long walk, and he was exhausted at the end of it.

At the embassy, he picked up the passport he had ordered previously. The clerk recognized him and made no difficulties about handing it over. Jack thanked him and prepared to go.

'You can't go out like that,' the clerk said.

'I'll be all right once I get some money for a coat. I can get money from the bank with the passport.'

'Sure, you'll freeze to death. You've no clothes on you at all. Wait here.'

Within minutes, the man was back with an overcoat Jack's size.

'It'll fit you fine. You can bring it back when you get your own.'

Jack was speechless at the unprompted generosity of the

gesture. It was almost impossible for him to believe that somebody could be offering him something without wanting something in return.

'Have you money on you at all?'

Jack shook his head. He was still too exhausted to argue.

'Sure, you'll only end up crippling yourself. How far have you got to go?'

Jack mentioned the Bank of Ireland branch in Queen Street, though he had no intention of going there. Coming to the embassy had been risk enough.

'Well, here's ten pounds for a taxi. You can pay me back when you bring the coat.'

'I don't know how to thank you.'

The man looked intently at him.

'You can thank me by taking yourself and your problems out of England. I don't know what's going on, and I don't want to know. But I do know that there are people looking for you, Dr Gould. Not nice people. Do you understand me? Be off with you, now. I'll be in serious need of that coat before I leave here tonight.'

Jack headed straight for the Deutsche Bank on Bishopsgate. Forty minutes later, having satisfied the assistant manager that he was who he said he was, he was standing on the pavement outside ten thousand pounds richer than he had gone in.

From Bishopsgate, he went to Dickins and Jones in Regent Street, where he bought himself a change of clothes, a quilted anorak, a money-belt, and a rucksack. A courier rushed the coat, money and a note of thanks to his friend at the embassy, while Jack took the first available train to the south coast.

A fellow-student at Trinity had once told him how easy it could be to hitch a lift on a small boat crossing the Channel. At shallow anchorages along the English and French coasts, Customs control is minimal or non-existent. Responsibility for the declaration of arrival and departure is vested in the boat's skipper: forms are kept at harbour masters' offices, where they are duly completed by the conscientious and ignored by others. The smallest anchorages do not even have offices.

With ten thousand pounds, it was not difficult for Jack to find someone in Dymchurch willing and able to drop him unseen on the French coast, within walking distance of the railway station at Le Tréport. From there, it was a short trip to Paris.

He bought himself three second-hand medium-sized vans, all different makes and colours, each one from a different *voitures occasions* dealer. There was parking space for rent at a garage near the Gare St Lazare. He kept two vans there while he used the third, changing them every hour or two, and parking in a different place each time he went back to the rue Fortuny. It was clumsy, but it was the best he could do under the circumstances. He used Zeiss binoculars bought in town, training them on the front door of Rosewicz's house. He had no idea how good Henryk's security system was, but he guessed it would not take them long to spot one of the vans.

Rosewicz came out, escorted by Henryk and another man. They drove off in a black Citroën limousine and were gone for around two hours. During Rosewicz's absence, the surroundings of the house were quiet. No one went in, no one came out. One of Henryk's men stood by the door, speaking occasionally into a hand-held radio. Jack did not even know if Maria was still here, or if she was alive. Anxiety gnawed at him every moment he sat there, watching, unable to act. He ate and drank in the rear of the van, and used a portable toilet, so that his times away from the house might be kept to a minimum. He was waiting for Mrs Nagle to go shopping.

Rosewicz returned. A small grey figure, blurred in the lenses of Jack's binoculars. He went into the house without pausing. Jack wished he could gain access to a vantage-point directly opposite the house, get a glimpse through a window, see what was going on. But the only two buildings from which surveillance like that might have been possible were both private dwellings, and Jack was sure Henryk would have found a way to ensure that they could not be used by hostile parties. From his observations, Jack guessed that a family of five lived in one house, an elderly couple in the other.

Lunchtime passed. The streets became quiet for a while, as though everyone was at prayer. Jack ate a ham sandwich and washed it down with coffee from a flask. It would soon be time to drive off in order to change vans.

A car drew up alongside the house, a black Mercedes with tinted windows. Jack focused the binoculars carefully on its rear doors, but no one got out. He swept the lenses across the pavement and saw Henryk's man speaking into his handset. Still no one got out of the car. The house door opened and Henryk came out with two other men. While they kept watch in both directions, Henryk went to the car and opened the rear door. Jack refocused.

A single passenger stepped out on to the pavement, a man. His face was turned towards Henryk, away from Jack, and for a moment, it looked as though he would be swept inside before Jack had a chance for a good look at him. Then, just as he was about to go through the door, he looked round at a young woman in a fur coat. Jack caught only a fleeting glimpse, but it was enough. The next moment, the man known to Jack as Parker had disappeared inside with Henryk.

CHAPTER FIFTY-EIGHT

Mrs Nagle came out twenty minutes later, carrying a shopping basket. She was dressed as though it were market day in Baltimore, in a green tweed overcoat and purple headscarf. For a moment, Jack was uncertain what to do – follow her or wait for Parker to reappear. Realizing there was nothing he could do about Parker whether he came out again or not, Jack started his engine and drove slowly down the street, keeping several yards behind Mrs Nagle. She walked at an unhurried pace, imposing the rhythms of her native Cork on the streets of Paris.

She turned the corner into the rue de Prony. Jack saw a parking space and pulled into it. Pausing only to shut off the engine, he leapt out and hurried after her.

'Mrs Nagle.' He spoke her name softly, not wishing to startle her.

She turned calmly.

'Well, and you took your time getting here,' she said.

'Can I talk to you?'

'I'm sure you will, whether I want you to or not. You'll have to walk along with me, though. I've a five-course dinner to be getting ready for tonight, and I've scarcely time for the shopping as it is.'

He fell into step beside her. They had hardly gone a couple of paces before he blurted out what was at the front of his mind.

'Mrs Nagle, is Maria all right?'

'Fine, she's fine. No harm's come to her, you can set your mind at rest. Not as yet, anyway. She said I might expect you here asking questions, though she'd no idea when you'd turn up. I'm told you and herself are great friends these days.'

'What did she tell you?'

'Tell me? Oh, nothing much. It's not what she tells me, it's what she doesn't. I've known her all her life, and there's little enough she can hide from me. Now, I don't say I approve of what you're up to; she being a married woman and all. But then I can't say I'm over fond of that German husband of hers, either.'

'Is she still in Paris, or have they gone back to Essen?'

'Neither one nor the other.' Mrs Nagle explained about the convent at Czestochowa.

'Before she left, she gave me a note to hand to you.'

Stopping, the little housekeeper rummaged in a vast leather handbag that seemed to have no bottom, an ancient one Jack remembered from his days at Summer-lawn. The note was buried deeply; not hidden exactly, but well out of casual sight beneath a heap of pens and hair curlers and religious tracts.

Maria had wasted nothing on emotion. The message was short and to the point: 'Go to Father de Galais. Mrs Nagle will tell you where to find him.' It was her handwriting. That was all that mattered.

De Galais arranged to meet Jack at Les Cinq Étoiles, an old fashioned zinc bar on Guy Môquet, near the railway sidings. He was waiting when Jack entered, a pale-faced man in cheap spectacles, all elbows and knees, a gangling, spidery cleric with the detached gaze of someone whose chief knowledge of life has been through books and other people. He ordered two glasses of Armagnac. While Jack listened, he tried to explain what had happened to Maria.

'Can't we get her out?' asked Jack. 'Surely nobody can be kept in a religious house against their will. This isn't the Middle Ages.'

'You're quite right, of course,' said de Galais. 'I could

apply to the Vatican, to one of the under-secretaries of the Congregation for Religious and Secular Institutes. They have authority to act in such matters. I am sure the Prefect could order an investigation. But I fear that the moment Ciechanowski got wind of pressure from a quarter like that, Maria would conveniently disappear to another convent. The cardinal has plenty of them at his disposal, I can assure you. This time we would have no warning of where she was to be taken. We could lose her for good. Believe me, doctor, some of these places are like pits. Bottomless pits.'

'But we can't just leave her there!'

'No, of course not. I am not suggesting that. But if we are to secure her release, I'm afraid we shall have to go outside official channels. In the meantime, there are more pressing issues.'

'More pressing? Maria . . .'

'Maria will be safe for the present. Believe me. They have her where they want her, they think no one else knows. So let's leave her there until we're in a position to act.'

Jack examined the priest more closely. A close-shaven head, long, brittle fingers, hollow cheeks. What Jack had mistaken for detachment was something else: self-possession or awareness.

'How did you get involved in all this?' he asked.

In answer, the priest reached into his pocket and took out a thin wallet. From it he extracted a photograph, which he laid on the table facing Jack. It was a black-and-white portrait of a bearded Conventual friar, one that appeared to have been taken some time ago.

'His name was Kolbe. Maximilian Kolbe. He was a Polish Franciscan. A Polish friar who died at Auschwitz. He died voluntarily, in order to save the life of a Jewish inmate, a married man. He was canonized a few years ago.

'Dr Gould, you have heard terrible things about what some priests did during and after the war. I make no apology for those things. It is not in my power to do so. They happened. Given similar circumstances, I do not doubt that they could happen again: the same things, or ones very like them. Part of me is afraid that the time for such things may not be far off. The Church is not a communion of saints, doctor. We are all sinners. Priests are no better than ordinary men, though many of them like to behave as though they are.'

He sighed and closed his eyes. Jack could sense that he was tired.

'But I believe they should be better, at least a little bit. I believe Maximilian Kolbe was better than many of his fellow men. For what that is worth, I think his sacrifice makes up in a small measure for the things Krunoslav Draganovic and those others did. It does not make up the balance; I realize that. There would have to be a lot of Maximilian Kolbes to even the scales, and I'm afraid saints don't appear as often as we would like them to. But maybe you don't believe in saints.'

'I've never met one. Perhaps I've just been unlucky.'

De Galais paused, sipping from his little glass. The voices around him were loud and coarse. Amid them, the priest's voice was thin and edged with a slight tremor. And yet Jack found no difficulty in hearing him. For all its weakness, the voice carried in the racket of the bar.

'What do you know of liberation theology, doctor?'

Jack shrugged.

'Almost nothing. I'm a textual scholar, not a theologian.'

'Well, I don't intend to give you a lecture. The name comes from a book written by Leonardo Boff, a Peruvian priest. It's an attempt to adapt Marxist theory to Christian purposes. Except that the people who preach it aren't communists. All it amounts to is the belief that Christians should make what Boff called "an option for the poorest". Like Jesus, he said, we should put the poor before the rich. The weak before the strong. You wouldn't think that could cause such a fuss, but it did. In countries like Brazil or Argentina or Chile, it made the ruling classes very unhappy. The Church had traditionally been associated with the state and the military. If priests and bishops ever had anything to do with the masses, it was to preach obedience to them. And now here were priests going into the slums and asking for a little justice on behalf of the people forced to live in them.

'The present Pope had a lifelong hatred of Communism, so he thought liberation theology must be nothing more than an attempt to smuggle it into the Church through the back door. He condemned it, and he still condemns it. I cannot tell you how much that saddens me. In the Third World, the Church of Christ is still associated with the ruling juntas, not with the poor or the suffering. With the killers, not their victims. The result is that ordinary people are losing faith and turning their backs on the Church.'

He paused again, catching sight of his own reflection in the polished metal of the bar.

'Some of us think there has to be a better way. We believe that the future of the Church, perhaps its very survival, lies in the hands of the oppressed, not the oppressors. We want to ally ourselves with the common people and their struggles for freedom and justice. Christ would not be found in the palaces of dictators, he would be living in the *barriós*, with the poor.

'A few years ago, a group of priests at the Vatican, myself included, formed a loose association whose purpose was to monitor right-wing tendencies within the Curia. We produced situation reports on the activities of the various Congregations and Commissions, especially the Secretariat of State and the Congregation for the Doctrine of the Faith.

'There'd be a leak here, a revelation there, and sometimes we'd be able to pass on a timely warning to a clerical activist in Venezuela or a sympathetic bishop in the Philippines. We built up a network of friends around the world, and information began to travel in both directions.

Sometimes we'd get advance notice that the local hierarchy was moving in a dangerously conservative direction, and we'd be able to get word to one of the more liberal cardinals, someone who might be in a position to take private action or at least advise others against whatever they were planning.

'Then, in 1985, we started to get reports from Europe about an organization called Crux Orientalis. I assume you know what I'm talking about.'

Jack nodded, but said nothing.

'Bit by bit, our reports built up into a pattern. We now know there is a conspiracy at a high level within the Church to restore links with various fascist organizations throughout Europe. Conservative priests have been initiated into Crux Orientalis in large numbers. They have bishops, archbishops and cardinals who are ready to lend support to their aims. And we think the document known as the Jesus scroll is to play an important part in the revival of Catholic fascism.'

'I think Rosewicz has the scroll by now.'

'Yes. That is almost certain. And we shall have to act now if we are to take it from him in time.'

'We?'

'A few of us have formed a second circle, much smaller than the first. We call it the Maximilian Kolbe Society. He is the symbol of what we stand for. He gave his life for a Jew. In other words, he saw the Church as having a universal mission. Ciechanowski, Rosewicz and the rest merely want to use the Church as a scaffold for a sick sort of nationalism. They want a Polish Church, a Lithuanian Church, a Slavic Church, a Baltic Church, an Aryan Church. We reject all that. And we mean to defeat it. If we don't . . .'

He said no more for a while. On the television above the bar, a boxing match thumped and plodded its brutal way to exhaustion. Tired men let their eyes follow the slow punches, the weary weaving and dodging, without really watching or caring. Others stared into their emptying glasses or argued with friends. Jack caught snatches of their conversation.

Ce salopard de raton m'a roulé! J'ai casqué une fortune pour du toc.

Ils sont tous des salauds.

Qu'est tu veux? C'est un trou, ce quartier. Rien que des boug-noules. Rien que des moricauds.

Everywhere, conversations were peppered with words like *raton* and *noraf*, derogatory terms for North Africans. 'Coons', 'dirty Arabs', 'shitty little Algerians', 'hustlers' — the hatred and the contempt poured out like a stream of vomit, effortlessly. Here were the planks and nails and hammers that would in time erect scaffolds and the high, blind fences of internment camps.

'Father, I need you to explain something.'

Jack told de Galais about his sighting of Parker that afternoon.

'You're surprised?' The priest leaned back in his chair.

'Well, yes. Of course I am. He and Felix told me they were working against Rosewicz, that they were trying to stop the League. I thought you'd know that.'

There was a pause while de Galais got more drinks. He looked out of place in the smoke-filled atmosphere, but no one seemed to pay any attention to him. Whenever he came to Paris, this was his regular bar. He had been coming here since long before entering the priesthood, with his father. And once, he often remembered bitterly, with a woman.

'You must have realized by now, doctor, that no one in this business is to be wholly trusted. Not even the Church. I do not ask you to trust me; not, at least, until you know me much better. Nevertheless, I hope you will believe what I am about to tell you. If you do not, there are plenty of independent sources you can check. For the basic information at any rate.

'The fact is that, after the Second World War, Western

intelligence services came to depend heavily on networks that had originally been set up by the Nazis. They needed agents who could infiltrate the new communist apparatuses in the East. Men and women who could be relied on as committed anti-communists. Who better than ex-Nazis, former agents of German intelligence? Or others willing to be trained.

'One of the main channels through which the British recruited their agents in Eastern Europe was Crux Orientalis. In 1946, the East German secret police received a tip-off about an ex-Nazi operation in Berlin. Your English friends may have told you about it.'

'The Friedrichshain prison business? Yes, I know.'

'But they may not have told you what happened after that. British intelligence got wind that East German security were planning a raid. The English already had people in East Berlin, but they wanted more. Friedrichshain was the key to the entire Crux Orientalis network. The British couldn't do anything for the people arrested at the prison, but they could offer help to members of the network outside. There was no time to lose before the net closed in. A British intelligence colonel called Saunders had already set up an escape route through West Berlin. He made it known that it would be available for Crux members. They got over five hundred former Nazis out in a single month, one of the biggest operations of its kind. And six months later they started sending them back in. Only, this time they were working for the British.'

'What about the Allied prisoners they'd been holding in Friedrichshain? The POWs.'

'They went to Russia. That's the last anyone saw of them. The British made no effort to get them out, because they could have blown the entire intelligence operation centred on Crux Orientalis. There was a British network called October. Several of their chief agents were in Friedrichshain. October had been working in Yugoslavia, in conjunction with Tito's partisans. If they had been allowed to return to Britain, they could have made things difficult for Rosewicz and his friends. So it was decided to let them go.

'We recently learned that they were kept in a special hospital in Siberia, where they were interrogated. In time, the Russians realized their value. They were used as blackmail, to act as a check on Western intelligence work.

'Your friend Felix hoped to resolve the situation with the help of Irina Kossenkova. But it appears that Rosewicz got in first. That makes the British extremely vulnerable. If the prisoners are released, there could be a scandal of immense proportions. Not only would connections between the Secret Intelligence Service and Crux Orientalis be brought into the open. People would learn that their own authorities had connived at the continued imprisonment of British war heroes.

'I think that's why your Mr Parker is here today. He wants Rosewicz to get him out of his mess. And in return he will offer a new deal with Crux Orientalis. A deal to take them into the twenty-first century.'

All round them, the voices of the new century were already whispering. Fires would burn, and books, and the bodies of men and women and children. And the voices would grow louder, until their bellowing would be heard all round the world. A man's skin would set the price on his life, his foreskin determine his fate.

'Is it too late to stop them?' Jack asked.

De Galais shrugged.

'Perhaps. We are not very powerful. We can only do so much. But I want to try. I want to start tonight.'

'Tonight?'

'I'm going to try to get into Rosewicz's house. To steal the scroll. You know the way. And you know what the scroll looks like. Will you help me?'

CHAPTER FIFTY-NINE

Czestochowa, Poland

' "To pray for those who have no time for prayer; to believe for those who can no longer believe; to give praise for those who are lost in pain; to accept death that they may live." '

The Abbess set the Community Book aside on her uncluttered wooden desk and looked into Maria's eyes. The book's black leather cover was worn by years of pious handling; it seemed to be made of accumulated ages and guilt.

'That is why we are here,' Mother Alice said. 'Why you are here. Our existence serves no other purpose. It is easy to say, but very hard to live. We have none of us been chosen, we are not God's elect. But in our fashion we strive for a state of grace in which our prayers may take effect.

'You have been brought to this house under unusual circumstances, circumstances of which I do not intend to speak. Nor will I allow you to speak of them. What matters is that you are here and that you will stay here. You are older than most postulants, more accustomed to life in the world. That will cause problems, but we shall overcome them. Over the coming years, you will learn to bend to our rules. If you do not, you will be broken. Do you understand me? You will be broken on a wheel of penitence. That is our way.'

Maria said nothing. Everything that had happened to her in the past few days had rushed past as if in a dream.

Before leaving Paris, Karl had spoken with her briefly and without emotion, warning her that if she attempted to leave the convent she could expect no mercy. He did not say it in so many words, but she knew very well what he meant: that she would be hunted down, brought back to Essen and killed.

'You may as well resign yourself to what's ahead of you,' he had said. 'Kicking against it won't help. Arguing won't make the slightest difference. You'll just make things more miserable for yourself. They want obedience, and they know how to get it, believe me. These sisters have had centuries of practice. You can fight all you like, but in the end they'll wear you down. If I were you, I'd make up my mind to get on with it from the first day. You've made a mess of being a wife and a mother. I'd hate to see you fail at this too.'

She was in a white-painted room bare of ornament, save for some old and discoloured lithographs of saints and a large crucifix on one wall. The furniture was plain and uncomfortable-looking. Straight-backed chairs, a tidy desk, a locked cabinet. The well-scrubbed wooden floor was cold against her naked feet. Only the aged and infirm were allowed to wear shoes. On her arrival, she had been stripped, bathed, and dressed in a postulant's habit of heavy black serge. The two nuns who had assisted her had remained silent throughout. Maria had tried to engage them in conversation, but they had resisted her with stony stares, and in the end she too had fallen silent.

'This is a contemplative order,' continued the Abbess, 'and here you will be taught to contemplate and to pray. We have no other function. Our rule is perpetual silence, a silence that may only be broken in the confessional, or when summoned to my presence, or in the direst emergency. That silence extends to music. There is no music here, save what our own voices sing in the choir. You must cease all thought of any other music. I do not want to hear you hum or sing. And when you are alone in your cell, you must concentrate your mind on prayer to the Virgin, not the recapitulation of musical pieces.'

The Abbess spoke good German with a southern Polish accent. She was elderly, but nothing about her suggested fragility. Her face was partly hidden behind an elaborate starched coif. The Sisters of Penitence had been utterly untouched by the recommendations of the Second Vatican Council; they retained their sixteenth-century habits without modification, along with the rules and conventions that went with them. The convent had no electricity, no telephone, no radio – no trace of the twentieth century. As though time had stood still, as if the house itself was a time machine, and all in it travellers swept back to a harsher, sterner past.

'You will rise each morning at five. When the bell sounds, leap from your bed and make yourself ready for mass. Imagine that your bedding is on fire. If you allow sleep to draw you back to its embrace, it will become your master. After mass, there will be breakfast of bread and hot water. We do not drink tea or coffee or other stimulants. Our food is not spiced. We eat to stay alive, and we live in order to pray. Remember that. Do not rush to eat, and do not waste a crumb. Waste is a sin that will be severely punished.

'After breakfast, you will proceed to the chapel for Divine Office. There will be two hours of Exposition, followed by a spiritual reading lasting one hour. Then lunch. Then Benediction.'

The Abbess's voice droned on, mostly unheard by Maria in her semi-trance. Hour after hour of Office, to bed at nine, up again at midnight for Night Office until two, a little sleep, up at five, only enough food to keep body and soul together, summer and winter alike, never varying, never ending. A pattern of days and months that would weave themselves at last into an unmarked grave.

'When you come to take your vows, you will see that the first of them is poverty. You have brought nothing into this house with you, you will bring nothing out. Whatever you need must be asked for. Soap and toothpaste are rationed. You are allowed two handkerchiefs a week and two sanitary towels each month should you have need: see you come to me for them. If you need medicines, you must let me know in advance and come to me whenever they are required. But only essential medicines are allowed within these walls. We are not here to pamper ourselves. You will not be given painkillers or sleeping pills or drugs of that sort.'

The room had no window. It was a world of walls. A cold, unwelcoming world without physical or spiritual warmth. She had arrived in Czestochowa that morning, crossing the frontier at Görlitz, then travelling down through Wróclaw. After a brief drive through open country, they had come to the outskirts of one of the ugliest towns Maria had ever seen. Everywhere, steelworks and textile factories belched toxic fumes into the grey air. A staggered ring of ugly housing developments like tired blockhouses slouched inwards to the centre, like a great *enceinte* of grey concrete to protect it from invasion. And in the centre, high on its hill, the famous monastery of Jasna Góra, where the Black Madonna waited for pilgrims. And high about it the monastery walls, built as fortifications to keep out tides of Swedes and Russians and Germans, rose on all sides like buttressed cliffs.

They had driven past the hill and the Staszica Park, then north on to Ulica Starucha, where the convent waited behind yet more forbidding walls. Here the bodyguard had taken leave of them. Maria and the silent, uncomplaining Sister Zofia had been let in through a narrow side entrance, and immediately separated. Maria was taken in hand by a severe-faced nun who was, she later learned, the Novice Mistress. The crash of the gate closing had sounded unbearably loud in her ears, like a judge's voice sentencing her to life imprisonment.

'You will be given a cell on the first floor. You are to keep it clean at all times. No other nun is to be invited into it, nor are you permitted to enter their cells. Particular friendships are not allowed. You are permitted only religious pictures, and those in moderation. You will find no mirrors anywhere in this house: you will have no need of one.'

Maria looked at her. There was no compassion in her eyes. Only the steel put there by a lifetime of rigorous self-control, by day after day of chastity and obedience, by unrelenting prayer and the suppression of every human emotion save that of self-hatred.

'I am not here of my own will,' said Maria.

'That is not my concern. If you have brought a will here with you, I assure you it will be broken. If you harbour thoughts of returning to the world, I advise you to put them from you. Before long, you will enter your novitiate. Four years after that, you will make your final profession. You will be a bride of Christ, you will wear his ring on your finger and his name on your heart.'

'I already have a husband.'

The Abbess shook her head.

'Steps are already being taken to have that marriage annulled. You may not be a virgin, but you will be taught the meaning of chastity like any unsullied postulant.'

A bell rang, lonely and strangely pitched in the silence.

'It is time for the Office. The Novice Mistress will instruct you after this. I pray you do not give her occasion to bring you before me. If you do, I warn you now that you will think hard before doing so again.'

It did not matter to Maria what punishments awaited her. One thought only passed through and through her head, that, in spite of everything, in spite of all their vigilance, in spite of their hunters on the streets, she had the upper hand. She had a means of escape, and, as soon as the right moment came, she meant to take it. And none of them would be able to follow her.

The Abbess led the way to the door. As her fingers touched the handle, she turned.

'My child,' she said, 'I would not wish you to think unkindly of me. I am hard because our lives here are hard. If they were not, our prayers would be so much noise. Behind these walls, we are not part of the world. For those of us who have been here all our lives, the world does not exist. We know nothing of what goes on there, we do not wish to know. I realize it will be hard for you here. I know that every day will be a torment. In my heart I pity you. And so I shall discipline you. For discipline is your only hope, mental and bodily discipline. Austerity and self-abnegation will make you strong in the end. I will help you all I can; the rest is up to you.'

She paused.

'Now, it is time for you to make ready. Time to begin your life of prayer.'

CHAPTER SIXTY

Jack checked his watch. It read 3.05 AM. Beside him in the darkness, Father de Galais shivered with cold. Or was it fear? Luck was with them. The moon was over ten days past full, and the sky was nervous with clouds. In black tracksuits and balaclavas, their faces blacked, Jack and the priest were almost invisible. Beside them, a third man watched the rear of the house through glasses. His name was Mélac.

Mrs Nagle had provided de Galais with a detailed description of the house's alarm system: where there were sensors, what type they were, where the control panels were situated, how many men stayed in the house at night. She had used a small camera to record details of the house's interior, as reinforcement for the descriptions Jack had been able to provide.

De Galais had then visited Antoine Mélac, a former parishioner from the days when he had served as a parish priest in the north-west of the city. Mélac, now aged almost sixty, had at that time already spent more years in gaol than de Galais had served as a priest. A burglar who could imagine no other way of earning a living, he had come regularly to the little church of St Joseph des Épinettes in the role of confessant, and in time he and de Galais had started meeting in the evenings at the Cinq Étoiles. Their lopsided friendship – interrupted by Mélac's spells in confinement at le Petit Nanterre and, later, de Galais' move to the Vatican – had worn well.

In spite of his trade, Antoine Mélac was an honest man.

He never entered an inhabited building if he could avoid it, never stole from domestic premises, never dealt with drugs or arms, never cheated on his mates, never carried a weapon, not even a knife, never put up a fight when caught. Even the police had a grudging respect for him.

He had readily agreed to de Galais' plea for help. No reward was offered, nor was one required: Mélac had been told that the job ahead of him was one that would assist the Church, that it involved property stolen from the Vatican, property that could not be restored through legal channels. That was all he needed to know; his piety took care of the rest. Mrs Nagle's descriptions, photographs and sketch map of the alarm system were converted by Mélac into a plan of attack.

The night-time arrangements at the Rosewicz household had been explained to them in detail by the ever-observant Mrs Nagle. For her, as for Mélac, the knowledge that she was aiding the Church was enough to still her conscience. De Galais had not been slow to tell her that she might also be helping Maria. That night, she had yet more work to do.

The routine, she said, did not vary substantially from one day to the next. Henryk, who introduced premeditated irregularity into all events occurring outside the house, had established internal patterns of severe exactitude, and no one – not even Rosewicz – was allowed to disturb them without giving notice. In this way, all unexpected occurrences, all deviations from the norm, could be instantly noted, investigated, and – should they prove to be threats – averted without trouble.

Rosewicz himself slept on the second floor, where he had a large bedroom suite entirely to himself. There were no guests. Much of the third floor was occupied by servants, including Mrs Nagle. On each of these floors one armed guard was stationed, sleeping, but connected by means of an intercom and alarm buzzer to the downstairs control room. Here, two men kept watch all night.

Henryk's own quarters were nearby, close to the library.

The control room was the nerve-centre of the house. Its chief feature was a bank of monitors, each of which was connected to a moveable camera. Each camera was fitted with an infra-red beam, allowing it to 'see' in the dark, and was set to cover a single doorway, staircase or passage within the house, as well as sections of the exterior. There were ten of them altogether. It was impossible for an intruder – assuming he should prove capable of disabling the sophisticated alarm system – to proceed any distance inside the building without being detected by the first camera he passed in front of.

If an alarm were triggered or an intruder sighted visually, one of the men on duty in the control room could seal off the area in question, provided doing so posed no threat to someone else in that section. That would allow the other guards to be roused and despatched to the scene of the intrusion, fully armed and ready to deal with the intrusion.

Mélac was confident they could make it, provided Mrs Nagle had done her bit inside. De Galais had procured for her a phial of salmonella bacteria that had been grown on rice; added to the evening meal of two of the security guards, the bacteria would cause severe food-poisoning, thereby eliminating some of the opposition without arousing undue suspicion.

Her second task had been more difficult. At intervals during the day, she had run risks to disable the passive infra-red detectors by spraying them with clear lacquer. The lacquer would prevent them detecting heat sources or responding to changes in temperature should a door or window be opened.

They had decided to go in through the rear door. Everything was still. The house was in darkness. Mélac led the way from the side, stopping them as they came within range of the security camera fixed on the wall above their heads. This was marked on their plan as 'camera one'.

As with all the others, everything camera one saw was

410

recorded on long-play tape. In the absence of incidents, the same tape would be recycled twice a day. Mrs Nagle had succeeded in swapping three of the tapes for blanks. The original tape had been given to de Galais that afternoon. It contained a Warhol-like sequence of the rear door at night. The mind-numbing stillness of the scene was the chief factor in their favour. Mélac had loaded the tape into a camcorder he carried in his bag.

A long cable running from the camcorder had been fitted at one end with a two-way patch-up lead. Mélac switched on the camcorder. He laid it on the ground and, holding the end of the cable in one hand, turned to de Galais.

'Help me up,' he said. 'Be careful not to let me slip in front of the lens.'

De Galais lifted him. In what seemed like a single movement, Mélac sliced through the camera cable with a sharp blade, stripped the wires that ran back into the building, and rammed the patch-up lead on to the end.

De Galais lowered him to the ground.

'They'll have seen the screen go blank for a few moments,' he said, 'then come on again with an identical picture. We clear out in case they send someone to check. Chances are they won't.'

Five minutes later, all was still quiet. The camcorder was turning slowly, feeding its false picture back to the control room. They returned to the door. Within three minutes, Mélac had picked both locks. He held his breath.

'If the alarm goes, run,' he whispered. Steeling himself, he pushed the door open.

Nothing happened.

A short flight of stairs led into a dark passage. They were near the kitchens here. Unless someone chanced on them on his way to raid the pantry, they were safe until they reached the end of the passage. There were no Passive Infra Reds in the central section of the house, in order to permit free movement of the security staff during the night.

A second camera faced into a well-lit corridor at right-angles to the one they were in. Henryk had not bothered to deploy a moving camera here, since the corridor was narrow enough to be covered by a fixed lens. Mélac bent down and took a small metal apparatus from his bag. De Galais lifted him up again behind the camera. Deftly, the burglar reached across and slipped something on to the top of the unit.

Held in place by a magnet, a bracket projected out well beyond the lens. From it hung a photograph in a rectangular metal frame. The distance had been calculated exactly. One of Mélac's friends had printed the photograph from a frame of video film. An observant watcher would have seen the picture on his screen wobble for a moment or two, but the chances were that his eyes were elsewhere when the switch occurred. Once the picture was in place, the image on the screen would be exactly as it had always been. Again, the boredom factor played its part. That and the fact that Henryk's most experienced surveillance operative was in hospital with indescribable stomach pains.

Mélac performed the same trick with the last camera, positioned to view the passage that led to the library. The control room was only two doors away, and absolute silence was essential if, having evaded so much electronic wizardry, they were not to be betrayed by the banality of human hearing. Mélac seemed nervous. It was not a job to his liking. Domestic premises, people in residence, too much security. He was not a superstitious man, but he had a bad feeling about this venture.

The library arrangement was similar to that at Summerlawn: an unlocked antechamber preceding a secure inner room where the manuscripts were kept. The silence penetrated everything. They held their breaths, as though hidden sensors might pick up even that. Inside the first room, they felt more secure. Mrs Nagle's searches had revealed no cameras and no passive alarms in this area.

Mélac set to work on the panel beside the inner door, while Jack held a small torch for him to see by. The burglar had explained that this was likely to prove the longest and tensest part of the entire operation. Jack and de Galais watched nervously as their companion fed random sequences of numbers to the panel.

It took twenty minutes. By then their nerves were raw and their hands sticky with sweat, even Mélac's. The silence felt heavy, like a physical substance pressing down on them from above, as though the house were made of silence and every sound, however tiny, was a crack that threatened to tear everything down. The door opened and they slipped inside.

Jack's hand went straight to the familiar switch, and a row of fluorescent tubes flickered into life overhead. The room was as he remembered it: narrow wooden drawers, each with its incised number, to hold flat manuscripts; cupboards for unrolled parchments and bulkier items; shelves arrayed with dictionaries, concordances and indexes, many of them purchased at Jack's request; racks of magnifying glasses, scalpels, tweezers, and other instruments; two desks with reading lamps and bookrests; and a low working table on which a couple of parchment fragments lay beneath sheets of glass.

Rosewicz had made no attempt to hide what they were looking for. On the contrary, it had been placed in full view, in the centre of the larger desk – a tall, cylindrical reliquary of Byzantine manufacture, decorated with icons and set with precious stones. While Jack and Mélac hung back, the priest, as though by a prompting of nature more than the grace of his vocation, advanced with slow steps to the desk. In his movements nothing could be seen of the tension that had held him until that moment. All his nervousness had gone in the presence of what he believed to be the only true relic of his dead saviour. De Galais had passed in a brief moment from burglar to priest, from thief to celebrant, as though he walked, not to a common desk, but to an altar decked with flowers and heavy with incense, on which his God dwelt.

The design of the reliquary was simple. Box-like, it represented a small shrine, originally intended, perhaps, for rags from a saint's cloak or the dried remains of a once-beating heart. Two doors at the front were evidently designed to permit access to the treasures inside. Depending on how Rosewicz had chosen to display the scroll, it might be possible to give themselves greater breathing space by substituting for it either another scroll of similar dimensions and appearance (Jack knew of several in the collection that would serve) or a metal cylinder like the one in which Jack knew the Jesus scroll had originally been transported.

De Galais reached out gingerly for the door. He pulled one wing open, then the other.

Jack heard the sharp intake of breath, even at a distance. Then de Galais was staggering backwards, holding his hands out in front of him as though to ward off a blow. Mélac caught the priest in his arms, steadying him.

'What's wrong?' Jack asked, but de Galais could not answer, could only flap his arms and gesture, with a look of horror, at the desk, at the thing on top of it. The doors shadowed the interior of the reliquary, concealing its contents. Jack left de Galais with Mélac and stepped to the desk.

Inside the little shrine, like a monstrous effigy of Babylon or Egypt, the tongue black, the eyes bulging, sat a human head. Mrs Nagle's head, cut off at the neck, drained of blood, staring in horror at the open room, her face like a face in a mirror of fear.

CHAPTER SIXTY-ONE

Rosewicz was waiting for them in the outer room, with Henryk and two other men. All but Rosewicz held guns.

'You've been wasting your time,' said Rosewicz.

Jack stepped forward, halting as one of the guards pointed a gun at him.

'Was it necessary to kill her?' he asked.

'Nagle? I was very fond of her,' Rosewicz replied. 'She'd been with me a long time. She loved my family, especially Maria. I suppose she loved her too much. One loyalty must have got the better of another. But however I try to explain it, it all comes down in the end to betrayal. It is a contagion. I know nothing better for contagion than hard measures. Infections must be cut off before they spread.'

'Is love an infection?' Jack asked.

'The wrong sort of love, yes. Misguided love, perverted love. Your generation would not understand. You think love higher than all other values; but you are wrong. There are greater things. Loyalty is one. To remain faithful, in spite of everything. Gratitude, honour, dignity, purity of heart, courage. All disparaged now. All forgotten.'

'I wonder you can talk to me about such things.' But Jack felt little rage. Only sadness. A biting, draining sadness. That an old man's life could end in such actions. That his end should be so like his beginning. Jack thought of all the people who had crossed Rosewicz's path and been destroyed. Denis Boylan, Moira Kennedy, Iosif and Leah and Sima Sharanskii in all probability, Isaak Berchik,

Noreen Nagle. How many had there been whom Jack had never met?

'I'm sorry, Jack. I never meant it to come to this. Our paths have been fated to cross at all turnings. Please believe me when I say how much I have admired you, even envied you. I'm sorry it turned out this way.'

He turned to the priest, who was still visibly shaken by his discovery.

'You are Father de Galais?'

'Yes.'

'You I feel no sorrow for. I am ashamed for you. A man of God, an ordained priest – that such a man could stoop to this. You came here to steal, you broke one of God's commandments. Well, you will have to pay the price. You know that don't you?'

De Galais said nothing in reply.

Rosewicz did not speak to Mélac, did not even look at him, as though he was not there at all.

'Very well,' he said finally. 'It has come to an end. I had hoped for something else. I have tasted bitterness all my life, I can still taste it. But I have sweetness in hand, sweetness before I die. I shall live to see the beginning of real godliness. In my day. I shall die like Simeon, comforted.'

'May God forgive you,' said de Galais in a quiet voice.

Rosewicz looked at him once, contemptuously, then away again, turning abruptly to Henryk.

'Take them away,' he said.

Outside, the darkness had not faded. Night still held the city with all its strength. And the cold was tight and mean. They took two cars. Three more guards had joined them in the garage. In the first car, Henryk and another man sat in the back with Jack and de Galais between; a third man drove. Behind them, the other men followed with Mélac. The burglar was distraught. They had watched him pleading, knowing it was useless, willing him to be quiet. Out of his depth, the little man's composure had utterly deserted him. Better than Jack or de Galais, he knew what sort of men his captors were. He had seen men like that in prison, had learned to steer well clear of them.

Nobody said a word, nobody even coughed. The silence was everything, the essence of the journey. Jack felt sick, horribly sick. Worst of all was the feeling of helplessness. He half turned to Henryk, impassive in the coming and going of light beside him.

'I know you don't like me, Henryk,' he said, 'and I don't expect anything from you. But this man here is a priest. It would be a mortal sin to have his blood on your hands. Let him go, Henryk. I should be enough.'

Henryk did not bother to look at him or speak. They were passing through streets empty of people, devoid of traffic. Streets without pity. Outside, frost clung to the edges of buildings. Henryk watched the city, his face reflected against its darkness. He was bored. He had been blessed by a cardinal, he had felt the firmness of his hand on his bowed head; one priest more or less did not matter to him. His understanding of God was perverse. In his tilted cosmogony, a cardinal stood closer to divinity than a priest, so a priest might be killed with impunity if a cardinal sanctioned it.

Jack felt his stomach churn. His hands were slippery with sweat. He was crushed in the back seat, his left hip against Henryk's. There was nothing he could do. Nothing anyone could do. The car moved on.

They drove down the Avenue Niel. Jack guessed where they were headed. His head was hurting, he wanted to throw up. Lights flashed in his face from time to time. On his right, de Galais sat motionless, praying.

At the Étoile, they turned on to Avenue Foch, driving straight down to the Bois de Boulogne, a vast green space of over two thousand acres on the city's western flank. A grey car slipped past them as they went through the Porte Dauphine entrance, vanishing into the darkness. The place was deserted. It was too late and too cold for the vice that normally kept the Bois alive well after midnight. The transvestites and the prostitutes were either at home or tucked up in someone else's bed for the night.

The emptiest section of the woods lies to the south, between the Longchamps and Auteuil racecourses. Once there, they drove along slowly until, abruptly, Henryk gave the order to stop. Behind them, the second car came to a halt.

The drivers switched off the engines and got out. Each held a torch. Henryk got out and ordered Jack and de Galais to follow him. As Jack stepped out of the car, he felt his knees buckle and almost give way. He found the most ridiculous thoughts going through his head: that it would be embarrassing to faint, or wet himself, or cry out – whatever it is men do in the moments before death. As if it mattered.

His life did not flash before him, he scarcely thought of people he had loved, of Caitlin, of Maria, of Siobhan, nor yet of himself. All those things, all those people were gone. His thoughts were of trivialities – of foods he had never tasted, films he had not seen, books he had not returned to the library. He felt a hand slip round his own. De Galais told him to stay calm.

They re-formed, keeping the prisoners bunched together in the centre, three guards in front, three behind, then set off along one of the *allées cavalières*, soft paths reserved for riders on horseback. On either side, winter trees stood as solemn witnesses. They proceeded only a little way. Henryk ordered them to move off the track, among the trees. Jack's thoughts were racing more and more out of control. There was so much to think about, so little time. If he could only have seen Maria one more time, even from a distance.

He thought of making a break for it, but knew he would not get more than two or three paces before being gunned down. De Galais held his hand more tightly. Jack was grateful for the warmth, the simple contact. Mélac came behind, stumbling, swearing under his breath. The ground beneath their feet was as hard as stone. Far off, at the Horse Guards barracks, a horse whinnied in the stillness.

'Here is good enough,' snapped Henryk. Freeing Jack from de Galais' clasp, he ordered him to kneel in front of a tree. Then de Galais beside him, Mélac next.

There were more thoughts now than Jack could cope with. More memories than he could process, none of them familiar – as though he remembered a stranger's life. He felt a gun barrel touch his neck, cold as ice. He heard de Galais beside him, praying in French, words Jack could not understand.

A shot rang out. Jack stiffened, wetting himself. He could not help it, he had lost control. A second shot. Jack's heart went crazy inside his chest, as though trying to tear free, to be anywhere but here. Three more shots followed in quick succession. A short silence, then another shot. And stillness. Great stillness.

A hand touched Jack's shoulder.

'It's all right, Dr Gould. You can get up now.'

De Galais' voice, unharmed. A terrible shuddering rippled through Jack's body. He had to struggle not to void his bowels. A knot of sour vomit pushed its way into his gullet and out through his mouth, scalding hot.

He felt hands helping him, then he was on his feet, in a circle of moving lights. At first he could make no sense of anything. Then, bit by bit, it all began to come together. On the ground, the bodies of Henryk and his men lay sprawled like dolls. The snow was spattered with blood. Henryk lay face upwards, his eyes wide open, one hand frozen in the act of clutching.

'Jack,' de Galais said, 'I am very sorry, but I couldn't tell you. We had to take precautions, but it would have been foolhardy to take you into our confidence. I hope you understand.'

Jack said nothing. Speech had left him.

'Jack, let me introduce you to the others. This is Father Gabriel McBride. He's from Dublin, like yourself.'

McBride nodded. He was a big man, bearded, with sad eyes. He had one arm round Mélac. The little burglar stood shivering, racked by dry sobbing. De Galais turned to the man beside McBride.

'That's Father Günter Erzberger. From Berlin. And Father Kazimierz Galcyzynski, from Wróclaw.'

The priests all held rifles fitted with night-sights. Each in turn nodded at Jack.

'I don't understand,' Jack said. 'How did you . . . ?'

'We were watching the house,' McBride answered. 'Augustin was wearing a micro-transmitter, so we had some idea what was happening. We just followed their cars at a distance.'

'But you're priests. Surely . . .'

'Jack, let's talk about all this later. We have to get away from here. Someone may have heard the shots. The barracks of the Garde Républicaine à Cheval isn't far from here.'

They left the bodies where they were lying, for an unlucky horseman or horsewoman to find after dawn. Back on the road, a grey car was waiting. They took it and one of Rosewicz's cars. As they left, it started to rain.

CHAPTER SIXTY-TWO

Rome
Monday, 11 January 1993

In the quiet back room of a little restaurant in Rome's Via Monterone, a select group of men was engaged in intense conversation. The restaurant, known as L'Eau Vive, is a curiosity in a city of curiosities. For one thing, it is run, not by an Italian *padrone*, but by a French religious order. For another, the tables are not served by *cameriere*, but by French and African nuns, white and black, all dressed in sober habits. Real nuns, not waitresses dressed to look the part.

Not surprisingly, ninety per cent of the restaurant's clientele is made up of better-off priests and high officials of the Church, many of them members of the Vatican Curia. The other ten per cent are mainly tourists who have gone there by accident or out of curiosity. There is a grotto in one corner, with a statue of the Virgin. And every evening at 10.30 prompt, the place comes to a standstill as the *Ave Maria* is sung. Whether one or the other sharpens the appetite or aids the digestion of diners is not on record.

The rear room is normally reserved for cardinals from the Vatican. But on this occasion the group who had taken exclusive possession of the little chamber for the evening consisted not merely of cardinals, but of a very particular circle from among their illustrious ranks. They numbered, to begin with, seven out of the eleven cardinals who headed the Sacred Congregation for the Doctrine of the

Faith, the ecclesiastical body responsible for the task of policing doctrinal orthodoxy and clerical morals. It had in former times been known as 'the Sacred Congregation of the Universal Inquisition', had changed its name briefly in 1908 to 'the Holy Office' (without any noticeable alteration in practice), and had finally been given its modern nomenclature in 1965, by Pope Paul VI, who had at the same time abolished the notorious Index of Forbidden Books.

Under Paul, the Congregation had been somewhat liberalized, but during the reign of John Paul II, that trend, like other liberal trends within the Church, had abruptly been reversed. The watchdog had grown new teeth, and more than one liberal theologian had lived to regret it. Under its new Prefect, Cardinal Vicenzo Bottecchiari, it had grown, if anything, more rigorous in its stance on doctrinal and moral divergence. Its shadow could be felt, dark and quietly alert, as far as the Philippines and Latin America.

It was Bottecchiari who had suggested this initial, informal – and strictly off-the-record – meeting between his own cardinals and several of their colleagues. Meetings held behind the walls of the Vatican itself never went unnoticed. There were prying eyes everywhere. But the sisters of L'Eau Vive, as well as preparing some of the best food in the Eternal City, were adept at providing their more eminent customers with a level of discretion available nowhere else.

Among those attending the meeting was Cardinal Zeffirino Della Gherardesca. He was the deputy head of the Pontifical Biblical Commission, a nominally separate body which shared offices with the Sacred Congregation on Holy Office Square. Established in 1903 by Leo XIII, the Commission was responsible for adjudication on matters of textual authority and the supervision of Catholic scriptural scholarship; its director was Bottecchiari.

Others included Cardinal Jacques-Bénigne Despréaux, the French chairman of the Pontifical Commission for

Sacred Archaeology, a graduate of the Saint Sulpice seminary, and a former director of the École Biblique in Jerusalem; Cardinal Francis Freedman, once a professor at Notre Dame, now head of the Pontifical Commission for Historical Sciences; Bishop Giangiacomo Amendola, secretary of the Congregation for the Evangelization of Peoples, the former Congregation de Propaganda Fide; Monsignor Tullio Mucchetti from the Commission for Oriental Churches; and two Polish cardinals from the Secretariat of State, Sienkiewicz and Kochanowski.

All these men knew one another and had at one time or another worked together, sometimes closely. In the Curial tradition, most served on the boards of other congregations, thus forming a closely-knit network of friendships and allegiances. Bottecchiari had chosen his little group with great care. The matter under discussion did not permit the smallest indiscretion.

'Does he actually say that there have been miracles?'

The speaker was Cardinal Pierluigi Sabbatucci, one of the longest-serving members of the board of the Sacred Congregation, a man noted for his inflexibility in matters of doctrine. His views had formed the undercurrent of the principal heresy debates of recent decades, including those surrounding the writings of Küng, Schillebeeckx and Boff. He was an ascetic man whose only known vice was the thin French cigarettes he smoked from morning to night. One was clenched in his right fist now, as he jabbed it towards Sienkiewicz, who faced him on the other side of the long table.

'As to that, I cannot be precise,' said Sienkiewicz. 'He alleges something of the sort, but he's not fool enough to come right out with a formal declaration. I've known Ciechanowski for many years now. The rest of you know him in varying degrees. I don't think anyone would suggest that he is a fool.'

'But he does speak of miracles?'

'He speaks of . . . events. *Avvenimenti*. Once, I think, he said *avvenimenti sacri*. A boy healed of a spinal tumour. A blind girl who can now see her mother's face. Psoriasis sloughed off like old skin.'

'*Sciocchezze!*' Sabbatucci gave one of his famous snorts and took a heavy pull on his half-smoked cigarette. Sienkiewicz took the opportunity to swig back the rest of his glass of *grappa* and to reach for the bottle for a refill.

'That's the stuff of all these quack medicine shows,' Sabbatucci went on. 'Maurice Cerullo can do as much and better. Any two-bit fundamentalist in the American south does it twice on Sunday. And you still say Ciechanowski's no fool?'

Sienkiewicz took a deep breath.

'He knows there can be no talk of miracles until there has been an official investigation and verification. At this point, he merely mentions incidents and leaves the rest to the Church. There is talk of a child seeing visions of Our Lady. Other children too, perhaps. A repetition of Fatima. Such things are not altogether unknown at Czestochowa. It is a major centre of pilgrimage after all. The Black Madonna there is highly venerated. It would not be surprising if Our Lady made a few appearances.'

'Centres of pilgrimage are notorious for fraud.'

'Nevertheless, Ciechanowski knows which cards to play and which to keep to his chest. Talk of miracles will spread whether the Vatican approves or not. There will be demands from the laity: the scroll must stay in Czestochowa, a shrine must be built to house it, the Holy Father must come to lay the foundation stone, and later to consecrate the finished building. And if I know the Holy Father, he will find it very difficult to refuse such a request. From Poland of all places.'

'It's clever,' said a man to Sienkiewicz's left, Amendola.

'I told you, Ciechanowski *is* clever. He knows his people. And, if I may speak without disrespect, he knows the Holy Father. They were sent to Rome together by Sapieha, and studied together at the Angelicum. He knows that Czestochowa is important to the Pope. It is the chief Polish shrine to Our Lady. That makes Ciechanowski's choice of location inspired.'

'Do you believe that?' Sabbatucci again, still manifestly irritated. 'That he has been inspired to bring his scroll there?'

Sienkiewicz shook his head.

'It would be premature to speak of any form of divine inspiration. I meant only that he has made a clever choice. If the Holy Father goes there, as Ciechanowski is bound to ask him to, he will consecrate the greatest shrine of Our Lord outside the Holy Land. Czestochowa will have both a Marian shrine and a reliquary for the most important object associated with Our Lord Himself.'

'He will have to be satisfied that the relic is genuine first. That will take a lot of doing,' said Cardinal Freedman.

Despréaux, chairman of the Commission for Sacred Archaeology, interrupted.

'I think we can confidently assume that it is a fake.'

Sabbatucci looked severely at him.

'Can we? You have already examined the document, I suppose? Unsubstantiated miracles I do not tolerate. Showmanship I deplore. But I also know Ciechanowski. Sienkiewicz is right. The man is clever, and I personally doubt very much that he would jeopardize his public reputation for the sake of a clumsy forgery. He says he has documentation to prove the scroll is genuine. What little of it I have seen has impressed me favourably. I think we should assume that the rest of his evidence will be of comparable quality. It will almost certainly withstand the scrutiny of whatever initial investigation you and your colleagues carry out. That means that, whether or not it is genuine, it is certain to provoke controversy. And if, after all, it does prove to be genuine or likely to be genuine, if the Church declares it to be in the hand of Our Lord, the controversy will not die down. On the contrary, it will become considerably more fierce. And that is why Cardinal Bottecchiari invited you all here this evening.'

He glanced towards the head of the table, where Bottecchiari himself was sitting, hands folded in front of him, listening carefully to the discussion. Bottecchiari nodded, but still did not say anything.

Cardinal Della Gherardesca of the Biblical Commission raised a tentative hand. Sabbatucci was his superior, and a man it did not pay to get on the wrong side of.

'Your Eminence, I fear I do not understand you fully. You say that the controversy will become fiercer should this scroll be declared genuine. I fail to see why that should be. Surely a declaration from the Papal See would be the end of the matter.'

Sabbatucci looked at Della Gherardesca with one of his more withering looks. The junior cardinal was himself a man of seventy and more, but Sabbatucci looked at him as though he were a schoolmaster and Della Gherardesca his idiot pupil.

'I should have thought that even a cursory glance at the translation of this document would have left no one in the slightest doubt as to its potential explosiveness. It will serve only to give succour to the Judaizers who seek to make sacred history a battleground for their sordid disputes. I refer, of course, to those scholars – and, I regret to say, there are not a few of them within the Church – who maintain that Our Saviour was nothing more than a Jewish teacher, a Galilean rabbi, a political extremist, an Essene – whatever strikes their fancy.

'All that rabble need is a piece of so-called hard evidence, and they will soon be hard at it, braying their crackpot theories in every theological college in Europe and America. You won't get air to breathe for the controversy it will generate. They'll chop down entire forests to print their books and monographs. Every second-rate journalist and half-baked biblical scholar will have a book published on the "Jesus Scroll Debate". They'll follow that with paperbacks on the "Jesus Scroll Scandal" and the "Jesus Scroll Cover-up". There'll be no end to it. It will be an industry.

'And, believe me, the Jews will make a laughing-stock of us. "After all this time," they'll cackle, "you're forced to admit that your precious Jesus Christ was one of us all along. Not the Son of God, not the Word made flesh, not the second person of the Trinity, but just a simple Jewish visionary and rebel whose only aim in life was to promulgate and preserve the Law of Moses."'

Sabbatucci stubbed out his cigarette viciously in the glass ashtray in front of him.

'If you think the Church can withstand a controversy like that, you're a bigger fool than even the Curia normally lets in. Take it from me, this scroll is a time bomb. It could tear the Church apart. Every line of it challenges the very foundations on which our Faith rests. It is my considered opinion that we must take steps to ensure that it is destroyed.'

CHAPTER SIXTY-THREE

There was a long silence, broken finally by Bottecchiari's acidly soft voice.

'Thank you, Pierluigi. As usual, you are not afraid to call a spade a spade. Everything you have said is correct. But I think you are mistaken to imply that only one option is open to us. This is an important matter. One to which we have to give the most careful consideration. And I think there are certain aspects we have to examine closely before reaching any decisions.'

He paused. Sabbatucci said nothing. Not even he had the nerve to interrupt the Prefect of the Sacred Congregation. Bottecchiari was a small man, but he managed to tower over everyone else. His skullcap rested precariously on a perfectly smooth bald head. He seemed like a man fashioned from wax. No hair grew on his face or hands. His lips had the tense softness of lips moulded from rubber.

The little cardinal sat easily in his chair. He wore an aura of absolute authority that vanished only when he was in the presence of the Pope. And even then, it was only dimmed a little, not extinguished. There were some – and by no means the least reliable – who said he would be John Paul's successor. Unless a far-ranging liberal backlash took place within the Church soon, that seemed a most likely outcome.

'Destruction of the scroll is certainly a possibility. It would not be difficult to substitute another papyrus for it, and in due course have the second scroll openly shown to be anything but a gospel in Our Lord's hand. Ciechanowski is unlikely to protest: he knows it would cause more harm than good if he were to do so. I think he is a loyal enough son of the Church to understand what his duty would be in such a matter.

'However, I think we would have others to contend with. Stefan Rosewicz for one. Karl von Freudiger for another. And there is the matter of this man Gould, the Irish scholar. Ciechanowski has papers in Gould's hand declaring the scroll to be absolutely genuine, in so far as concerns its age and provenance.'

He turned to Della Gherardesca.

'Zeffirino, you know about Gould. You've read his articles. Is he to be depended on?'

Della Gherardesca nodded.

'Jack Gould is eminent in the field. Not given to rash hypotheses. A secular humanist, but his work is very solid. People would listen to what he had to say. He would be believed.'

'And he is, of course, a Jew.'

'In part only. His mother was a Catholic.'

A look of distaste crossed Bottecchiari's face.

'No matter. The Jews will doubtless take his lead. We shall have to find a way of dealing with Mr Gould.

'But first I want to go through the other options in front of us. We can, of course, choose to play Ciechanowski's game. However, in return for the political and financial co-operation he seeks, we can insist that he move his institute to Rome. The Biblical Commission would then assume direct authority over the scroll and related materials. I understand that the Russians are proving very co-operative in the matter of the sale of the remainder of the collection from which the scroll originally came. I am told that Professor Grigorevitch has been very helpful.

'Once the scrolls are in Rome, we can appoint men of our own choosing to the institute – reliable Catholic scholars, men of proven loyalty, capable of defusing any possible debate by releasing excerpts from the scroll in small fragments and in an order determined by them. The institute would bury the implications of the text under a mountain of commentary and conjecture. Other materials could be made freely available to bona fide scholars round the world: their gratitude for favourable treatment from the institute will go a long way to offset any possible criticism there might be about the length of time it will take to publish the Jesus scroll in any form. However, I will say right away that this is not the solution I favour. There is too much that can go wrong.

'The approach I wish to recommend to you is more drastic, but more likely to meet with success. If it should meet with your approval, it is the one I shall put before His Holiness tomorrow morning. Put simply, it is this. Ciechanowski and his people want the assistance of the Holy See in order to achieve certain political goals. I propose that we meet them at least half-way; in return, they will place the scroll in the Holy Father's keeping. It will be placed in the Vatican archives, where it will be conveniently miscatalogued and, within a few years, utterly forgotten.'

Cardinal Freedman, the American, half rose to his feet.

'But . . . but that's outrageous. It's as bad as Sabbatucci's plan to destroy the scroll outright. Worse, because you're saying we should give Papal backing to a bunch of fascists.'

Bottecchiari barely looked at Freedman.

'Sit down, please, cardinal, and try to react to my suggestions with a little less emotion and a little more thought. I want all of you to think very clearly about what I am proposing.

'First of all, I prefer not to destroy the scroll, if only because a leak from Rosewicz's people or the Russians could cause the Church considerable embarrassment. Authentic or not, the public would quickly take the scroll at face value and condemn us for having deliberately destroyed the very words of Jesus Christ. The field would be open for endless speculation as to the true contents of the scroll. I do not have to tell you the sort of fuss that would cause.

'But the fact is that this scroll is only really dangerous to the Church in the context of current scholarship. Given another generation or more of properly guided studies by serious-minded Catholic academics, it may be that the letter could in the end prove a valuable weapon in the Church's armoury. At present, it's impossible to tell. I prefer not to pre-empt matters by getting rid of the scroll now. It may remain buried in the vaults for a century or five centuries, even a thousand years. That is quite unimportant. What matters is that its existence be kept secret now. Destroy it, and people will talk. Keep it, however deeply hidden, and some sort of accommodation can be reached. And, given time, all memory that the scroll ever existed will fade.'

The cardinal looked down the table. He knew he had their attention, but it was more than that he wanted. He also needed their absolute trust.

'The fact is, however, that I do not think the scroll will be the Holy Father's chief concern. He has much more serious issues on his mind. Gentlemen, I intend to say things which some of you may find disturbing. Ordinarily, I would not mention such matters, but now I feel I have no choice.'

He held his breath. Inwardly, he could sense a great chill crossing the fields of his life. He had been brought to this moment and this place, this room, by a destiny far beyond his control. A street boy from Naples snatched up and made a prince of the Church. Some men in this room came from long lines of aristocrats and church dignitaries, yet he had risen higher than any of them. For what? For this. He thought he could hear whispers in a great hall. And a door opening. A great door no human hand could push.

'Gentlemen, the Church is face to face with the gravest crisis in its history. The Holy Father's health is poor. He has aged greatly since his operation last year. When he visited Santo Domingo for the CELAM conference in October, only ten thousand people turned out for his public appearance. We had expected at least one hundred thousand. In other parts of Latin America, Protestant sects are stealing believers from the Church in growing numbers, something that has never happened on this scale before. In Africa, Islamic missionaries are winning souls while our churches are emptying. In Russia and parts of eastern Europe, the Orthodox and Uniate churches are gaining ground we lost decades ago. In Ireland, there is growing public support for contraception, abortion, and divorce – matters that were not even topics for discussion a short time ago. The *magisterium* of the Church is being challenged with startling frequency. Every year, as you know, thousands of priests and religious abandon their vocations. Pressure for the ordination of women is growing in many quarters. There are ever more strident demands to end the rule of celibacy. And I need not tell you of the moves afoot to treat sexual vice and perversion as normal, not only in the world, but in the holy Church as well.'

He paused. His words were sinking in. He had said nothing they did not know already, but for someone in his position to put these things together made the situation appear all the more grave.

'Our colleagues from the secretariat of state will know that their superior, Cardinal Di Rienzo, has prepared a document that is shortly to be presented to the Holy Father. I have been given sight of it, to ensure there are no errors of doctrine. It makes distressing reading. Di Rienzo's assessment is that the Church is facing challenges unprecedented since the Reformation. He believes that the twin threats of modernism and secular liberalism may yet prove too strong for us unless we can devise effective countermeasures, and I have to say that I am in full agreement with him. If we do not take rapid action, there is every possibility that the Church as we have known it will be dismantled by the next century. That is not the fantasy of an alarmist, but the considered opinion of one of the sharpest minds in the Vatican.'

In the restaurant outside the sounds of departing diners could be heard. But in the back room no one moved. It was as though they were in a trance.

'Gentlemen, it is just such a counter-measure that Cardinal Ciechanowski and his associates are offering us. If we refuse it, we may not have a second chance.'

He looked at Freedman.

'Francis, just now you used the word "fascist". Your misgivings are understandable and commendable, but they are, I think, misplaced. Fascism is a discredited political philosophy. It has had its day. The few groups of so-called neo-fascists in Germany and elsewhere are quite insignificant. The organizations with which we are being asked to ally ourselves are not fascists by that or any other definition, though they may accurately be described as conservative. I hope none of you will consider that a bad thing. I, for one, do not. Quite the contrary. I believe that it is only through close association with the political right in Europe that we stand any chance of extricating our beloved Faith from the abyss into which it is poised to fall.

'Crux Orientalis is a long-established lay brotherhood that exists for no other purpose than to serve the Catholic Church and to effect the restoration of a united Christian Europe. That does not seem a misguided dream to me. Without Europe, the Church is nothing. It is where the Christian faith first became powerful. However strong our presence in the Third World may be, it is, in the end, to Europe that we must look for salvation. It is the Church's fortress. If we have to retreat behind its walls for a period, it is best that we do so, and without delay.

'The Communists have gone, but if we do not hurry to step into the vacuum they've left behind, we will soon see believers leaving the Church like lemmings, even in countries like Poland. People turned to us as a focus for their opposition to an atheist state. Now they're starting to turn to the god of materialism instead. They think that if they can catch up with the West they'll be in paradise. We need a vision for them, a vision and a goal. Crux Orientalis can supply the people of Europe with both.'

Amendola, whose work brought him most closely in contact with non-Catholics and with the sensitivities any attempt to propagate the faith could arouse, cleared his throat.

'Your Eminence, I have to say something. I do not have to remind you of how much damage was done by groups like Intermarium or Action Française in the past. The fact that so many in the Church gave succour to war criminals has grown notorious. There are still those who say that Pius XII failed in his duty to save the Jews. These are unpleasant realities we have to live with. I would be extremely nervous about any possibility of returning to such alliances. As you say, the Church faces a major crisis. All the more reason to stay clear of people like these. They will tar us with their brush all over again. A charge of anti-Semitism would be like dynamite in the present political climate.'

Bottecchiari nodded sagely.

'I assure you, bishop, there will be no more Hitlers, no more Ante Pavelics. Just loyal followers of Christ working within the democratic system for much-needed reform. It is time for the Church to set the agenda again. The liberation theologians have had their way for two decades, and look where that has brought us.

'Given adequate financial backing and a steady supply of trained manpower, Stefan Rosewicz can guarantee seats for Catholic candidates in every local and general election that takes place in Poland, Germany, the Czech Republic, and the Baltic states over the next five years. With the Pope's blessing and open support from every pulpit, Crux Orientalis can transform the face of European politics. The past is past. What we need now is a policy of healing and unity. We must bring an end to the ethnic strife in Bosnia. We must ensure that the reunification of Germany does not end in bloodshed. The EEC is not a sufficient safeguard against the break-up of the continent.'

'What do you want us to do?' asked Sabbatucci.

'I want your support for the recommendations I intend to submit to the Holy Father. The superiors of my Congregation have already considered the matter of the scroll and are agreed that action must be taken to avoid scandal. With your blessing, I intend to recommend to the Holy Father that we reach a compromise with Cardinal Ciechanowski and set up a special commission to examine his proposals for extending the work of Crux Orientalis. Naturally, you will all have time for further comment. Do I take it that we are in substantial agreement?'

No one argued. The last drops of *grappa* were drained, chairs pushed back, and word passed that the cardinals were about to leave. Their private cars would be waiting nearby.

They left in small groups, some talking animatedly, others pensive. Sabbatucci and Bottecchiari remained behind.

'Well,' said Bottecchiari. 'It is done.'

'I pray you have made the right decision. If things should go wrong now . . .'

A nun entered, carrying a telephone, which she plugged into a socket in the wall.

'Will you need anything more, your Eminence?'

Bottecchiari smiled and shook his head.

'No, sister. I won't be long. You can start locking up.'

When she had gone, Bottecchiari picked up the receiver and dialled a Paris number. Stefan Rosewicz answered.

'Stefan? This is Bottecchiari. Are you alone?'

'Go ahead. Has your meeting finished?'

'A few minutes ago. Everything went as I expected.

But we may have a little trouble from Freedman and Amendola.'

'Don't worry. I'll see they are taken care of. Trust me. There will be no mistakes.'

PART SEVEN

CHAPTER SIXTY-FOUR

Paris, 13 January

Someone had left a rosary hanging on the wash-basin tap. Jack set it swinging, watched it come to a halt. He looked in the mirror as he shaved. Out of nowhere, or so it seemed, signs of advancing age had appeared on his cheeks and forehead. At this rate, he thought, he would be grey and wizened before he reached fifty. He drew the razor down his cheek one last time, washed off the cream, and dried himself. Father de Galais wanted to speak to them all. He looked at his watch. It was almost time.

The apartment consisted of five rooms above a small *épicerie* in the Marais. The windows looked out on to an old courtyard and the walls of the building behind. Freshly laundered underwear hung from an improvised line across the bath. The kitchen sink was filled to overflowing with unwashed dishes. There was a bowl containing cat-meat on the kitchen floor, but no cat. The three bedrooms were packed with bunk beds. There was no living-room. They ate and talked in the kitchen. It was more like a terrorist hideaway than a lodging for priests.

Jack had been with de Galais and his friends for nine days and was scarcely nearer understanding them now than he had been that first night in the Bois de Boulogne. At first they had seemed to him no more than killers: efficient, calculating, ruthless. The title 'Father' prefixed to each of their names had appeared no more than a witticism, as though they had been called 'Godfather'. He had felt profoundly grateful to them for saving his life, and he felt no sadness for the fates of Henryk and his men. But his gratitude had been laced with awe, with traces of fear; for they had been grim that night.

Over the succeeding days, however, they had revealed other sides of their personalities to him. McBride had taken particular trouble to befriend Jack, finding mutual acquaintances and familiar places to talk about. He was, Jack soon discovered, a decent, good-humoured football-player from County Clare, a product of Maynooth and the Irish College in Rome, a warm, placid man, and an infallible guide to the pubs of Dublin. He hated wine and despised French cafés, and his greatest longing was to be home in a place called Tobin's, half drinking hole, half undertakers. Tobin's had two doors: one opening into the bar, the other leading to the local funeral parlour.

The others Jack found more distant, yet placid like McBride, or, rather, self-possessed. He felt safe with them around. Erzberger said very little, in part because his English was weak; but once or twice Jack had caught expressions in his eyes that had said more than words. Determination, conviction, a sort of weary holiness that served well enough for the day-to-day business of making sense of things.

In spite of McBride's cheeriness, the dominant mood in the apartment was serious. The little group had a purpose, and Jack felt himself being drawn, against his will, into it.

'We are not killers by nature, Jack, nor by liking,' McBride had said to him on their first morning together, over a bowl of coffee. 'There was a time, and that not so long ago, that I'd have sooner cut off my hand than kill a man. I swear that's true. But I've seen things you'd scarcely credit, Jack, and I've been convinced. This is an evil thing, and it has to be stopped. In one form or another, directly or indirectly, the Church gave succour to evil men, and in places it continues to do so. I've seen the same thing in Ireland, I've had friends involved in gun-running and worse. I will not say where the guilt lies, Jack, or how high up the hierarchy it goes. I don't really know.

'But I do know that it has to end now. If we don't stop Crux Orientalis, millions will die again. So I'm willing to use force to stop them. I'd prefer not to, but if that's how it has to be . . .'

But it was not his arguments, however well rehearsed, that swayed Jack. It was the man's sincerity, his constant betrayal of himself, his inability to be false. At times, Jack thought he was talking to a child, but then he would look into those troubled eyes and see an adult, and an adult's pain, and something more than that.

'We still need your help, Jack,' de Galais had said. 'If we do find the scroll, we'll need you to confirm its authenticity. To tell us if we have the right one.'

So he stayed with them, waiting.

In the kitchen, de Galais and the others were waiting with a fifth man, a stranger.

'I'm sorry I'm late,' Jack apologized.

'You're not at all, Jack. Take a seat if you can find one. And let me introduce you to Father Masolino Buonamici. Father Buonamici has just arrived from Rome. He has something of importance to tell us.'

Buonamici was a tiny man, almost a doll. His skin contributed to this impression, having the smooth sheen of porcelain. Only his eyes disagreed with his outward appearance; they seemed old and painfully human.

'There is some news at last,' he said. 'Cardinal Bottecchiari had a private audience with the Holy Father yesterday. I have a transcript of their conversation, which you may study later. For the moment, I will summarize it. They were together for a long time, over two hours. A great many matters were discussed. The cardinal explained to the Holy Father the consequences of publishing the Jesus scroll. He had a copy of Dr Gould's translation, and he went through it almost paragraph by paragraph. By the time he finished, the Holy Father seemed convinced that publication was out of the question.

'That led Bottecchiari directly to his next topic, the need to formalize the relationship between Crux Orientalis and the Church. Bottecchiari's preferred solution to the difficulty was that the Pope should make the League a personal prelature, something like Opus Dei. That would give it a status resembling that of a diocese, because it would consist of priests and laity, men as well as women. But, unlike an ordinary diocese, it would have no territorial limitations. The Holy Father said he would give the proposal serious consideration.

'Bottecchiari went through the various alliances this would enable the Church to forge. By the time he left, the Holy Father had agreed to virtually everything.

'However, that is not the end of the matter. Once Bottecchiari was gone, the Pope summoned Sienkiewicz.'

De Galais raised his hand to interrupt Buonamici.

'Jack,' he said, 'Cardinal Sienkiewicz is one of the cardinals on our side. He has been a member of the Maximilian Kolbe Society for several years now, and is one of our principal sources of information inside the Vatican.'

Buonamici continued.

'The Holy Father was very frank. He explained his dilemma to Sienkiewicz. He said that, if the scroll could be taken from the League and destroyed or hidden, he would have no reason to grant them any favours. Apparently, he does not trust them. But if the scroll stays in their hands, he will have no choice. He will have to agree their terms. If necessary, he is willing to work with them. And he feels he owes them something in return for their stand against Communism.'

There was a tremendous silence in the room.

'How long do we have?' Erzberger asked.

Buonamici lifted his shoulders.

'A matter of days, I think. I don't really know. They'll hold on to the scroll until the whole thing's watertight.'

'I don't think so.' Augustin de Galais' voice was low but distinct. 'Bottecchiari's no fool. He'll bring the Holy Father and the Sacred Congregation round by an offer of the scroll; but he knows perfectly well that once the scroll goes out of the League's hands it's gone for good, and with it most of their influence at the Vatican. There'll always be time and opportunity for the Holy Father to think twice about Crux Orientalis and its policies. Or, if not this pope, the next.

'No, what they want is uninterrupted influence. That means they have to keep the scroll. I think the League will agree to its suppression, provided they get the power they're after and as long as the scroll stays in a vault somewhere under their direct control. It would be the ideal compromise.'

Buonamici nodded.

'I'd say you're right. Which means that, if we're to stop this, we have to get hold of the scroll within the next few days – if we're not too late already. Fortunately, I have some good news for you. I think I know where the scroll is being kept.'

CHAPTER SIXTY-FIVE

Wróclaw, Poland

The rally ended without violence. Afterwards, in the streets, there would be a few scuffles, but nothing serious, nothing that couldn't be taken care of: a couple of broken heads, a handful of smashed ribcages. All containable. The morning papers would report large crowds, little heckling, good behaviour. The clean image was due, more than anything, to the participation of Cardinal Ciechanowski and other church dignitaries. That the men with whom they shared the platform were notorious right-wingers was a fact played down by all concerned. 'New policies for a new Poland' was the slogan. The papers did not report that, here and there among the crowd, flags with swastikas had been displayed by the indiscreet.

Ciechanowski had spoken briefly and to great effect. He was a national hero, a leader of the opposition to Communism, an instrument of the old guard's overthrow. In his short speech, he applauded the gallantry of those who had fought the good fight in order to regain Poland's liberty, while alluding in only half-veiled terms to those traitors who would undermine the country's future by dragging the atheist, liberal philosophies of the decadent West into the still unstable fabric of Polish life and politics. The way was made easy for the speakers who came after him. One by one, they stood up and dropped their venom into the ears of their listeners. By the evening's close, a coherent right-wing agenda had been laid before the crowd. Little had been left to the imagination.

By then the cardinal was back in Czestochowa, meeting an emissary from Bottecchiari.

'Tell his Eminence,' Ciechanowski said, 'that I agree to what he proposes. But I cannot hand over the scroll. That really is out of the question.'

'I see. In that case, I am permitted to tell you that Cardinal Bottecchiari anticipated this. He has asked me to inform you of his willingness to reach a compromise. You are not to display the scroll, nor to erect a shrine to house it, nor to keep it in the company of other relics. You may not attribute miraculous powers to it, whether of healing or faith, nor may you acknowledge its existence or even hint at it. Where you decide to keep it is not his Eminence's concern, provided he has assurances from you that it is secure and that the secret of its existence will be restricted to the smallest number possible.

'In return, he guarantees the Holy Father's absolute co-operation in your political and religious programmes. Crux Orientalis will be granted the status of a personal prelature, and in eastern Europe it will be given priority in budgeting and manpower over Opus Dei. You must provide personal assurances that the politicians you select for your support and the work of the League will all be upright men, Catholics of a godly disposition. The Holy Father will not tolerate a repetition of the excesses committed by the League in its early days. There must be no return to intolerance.'

'That is fully understood. You have my unhesitating assurance. There will be no cause for scandal. Our candidates will be men of the highest virtue. You have my word on that.'

Ciechanowski smiled his famous smile, while he twisted his cardinal's ring slowly round and round one finger. In time, he thought, the present Pope would die. Perhaps very soon. And then not even this degree of subterfuge would be necessary.

CHAPTER SIXTY-SIX

Czestochowa, Poland
Thursday, 14 January

The old and the infirm were everywhere. Hotels and guest-houses were full, church hostels were turning even the sick away, there were signs at the gates of the city hospitals refusing admission to outsiders; and still they came, by bus and car, by train, on foot, on crutches, in wheelchairs pushed by grim-faced relatives. The lame, the palsied, the mutilated, the impotent, the heart-weary: they brought their wrecked bodies and ruined lives, their tumours and open sores, their cleft palates and club feet, their broken hearts, their emptinesses, their babblings, their tears. They wanted healing, they wanted reassurance, they wanted all the things they had never had: children, absolution, joy, a hand in the darkness, relief from pain; and whispers had reached them that they might find some of those things here, that the greatest of relics, hidden from them by the godless communists and now brought to light again, was performing miracles every day.

But now fresh rumours were going the rounds. That the Holy Father had ordered the relic destroyed; that it was to be returned to its former hiding-place; that it had been stolen; that a shrine was to be built around it. All that day, the queues at the little chapel in which the scroll was kept had been unending. The crowds that had once climbed the hill to Jasna Góra to adore the Black Madonna now went there to gaze from the distance on a document none of them could even read.

Even when the last pilgrims had been admitted at 9.00 PM, those left outside had stayed to sing hymns and light candles, holding vigil over the object on which they had pinned so many hopes. A notice outside the monastery gates announced that Cardinal Ciechanowski in person would celebrate mass there tomorrow. It was widely believed that he would make an announcement concerning the relic then.

In the monastery church, the air was thick with incense. The main lights had been switched off, but here and there a side-light or a candle burned among the shadows. The icon of the Madonna, virtually ignored for the first time in centuries, had been hidden behind the screen that protected it in the votive-encrusted Chapel of the Blessed Virgin. Footsteps echoed on marble floors. Hushed voices flickered in and out between high pillars.

In the side-chapel facing the one in which the scroll was kept, Gabriel McBride, Augustin de Galais, and Kazimierz Galcyzynski were keeping a vigil of their own. Behind them, Jack Gould waited nervously, hidden by shadows. They heard the great doors shut in the distance, then echoes shuffling through the empty spaces of the church until they disappeared. Heavy footsteps came from the entrance. Two guards arrived and took up positions on either side of the scroll chapel. They carried small Uzi sub-machine guns and wore military uniforms. Ciechanowski's influence stretched in many directions.

De Galais nodded. The three priests, dressed in clerical suits, stepped out of the side chapel into the choir. Casual, chatting, just three men going about their business. The guards glanced at them, then away again.

Galcyzynski detached himself from the group and strolled across to the guards.

'*Dobry wieczór*. Maybe one of you can tell me what's going on? My friends and I have been told to stay in the church tonight in case we're needed. Not that anybody's actually told us what we might be needed for. But we think it's got something to do with the relic you're looking after. Any ideas?'

The guard to whom he had addressed his remarks merely shrugged.

'I've got about as much idea as you, father. We've got orders to keep an eye on the place, see nobody tries to get in who shouldn't. You've seen the crowds that were in here earlier, no doubt. They'd tear the place to pieces if they got half a chance.'

The other guard leaned across.

'Father, I overheard someone say they're planning to move the relic later on tonight. Not very far – Wróclaw, Kraków, somewhere like that. So I'm told.'

'Any idea when? I'd like to know how long we're expected to stay here.'

The soldier shrugged, slipping the strap of his Uzi across his shoulder.

'Sorry. You'll just have to wait with the rest of us.'

Galcyzynski called de Galais and McBride over with a wave. They strolled across. No need to hurry, except that their hearts were beating twice as fast as they should and their palms were sticky with sweat. *Keep it slow, look as though you have every right to be here.* Nothing alarming about them, nothing threatening. No one is less out of place in a church than a priest. They were the insiders here, the soldiers intruders. The second guard let his Uzi hang down carelessly by his side.

'Our friend here says we'll be up all night,' Galcyzynski joked, still speaking in Polish. De Galais, who had not understood a word, smiled and stepped nearer the man on his right. The next moment, he nodded, and in a flash he and Galcyzynski had drawn guns and were pointing them at the heads of the two guards.

'We want the minimum fuss,' said Galcyzynski. 'No violence. We would prefer not to hurt you, least of all here in God's house; but if we have to shoot you, we will.'

The guards stood frozen while McBride reached over

and relieved them of their Uzis and their handguns. Then, with a wave, McBride gestured to the other chapel. Jack, also dressed as a priest, emerged from the shadows and joined them. McBride turned to him.

'Go ahead now and fetch the scroll, Jack. We'll hold this pair here till you've had time to check it over. But get a move on, for God's sake. There's no telling when someone else is going to turn up.'

Before entering the church, they had agreed that Jack should examine the scroll *in situ*. If it turned out to be a fake or a substitute – whether placed there originally or as a preliminary to moving the real thing – they would know their search was not over. There might still be time to get down to the vaults beneath the monastery – the most likely hiding-place for such a treasure – before an alarm was raised.

In order to avoid drawing attention by putting on the chapel lights, Jack carried a small flashlight. The narrow beam, travelling through the shadows, flickered over shining and mysterious things: fingers of gold, eyes of amethyst, the silver of saints' crowns, pearls on the edge of an angel's wing. And the incense was pronounced here, its effects more intoxicating.

With the others, he had stood disguised in the darkness, watching the long line of pilgrims shuffle and bend. He had seen the dying carried within sight of a last refuge, seen their thin hands lifted to a presence behind shadows, heard their weak voices raised in supplication, watched as their bearers set them down almost within touching distance of the scroll. In his heart, he did not, could not, believe, even though he knew so much better than they how genuine was the paper and how real the ink in which they invested so much faith, so much of their own hearts. But he had seen some stand up and walk away, he had seen a blind man cry out and dance in a moment of sudden vision, he had heard a dumb man sing. The song still lingered, like a lullaby after sleep. They had not been miracles, they had been intensifications of hope. But he had come to take even that away.

The light came to rest on a glass box set above an altar-cloth of embroidered silk. Inside the box, a papyrus scroll had been set up on one end. Jack's heart skipped like a stone on smooth water. He felt ripples pass through him. Even at this distance, he could not be mistaken. This time they had found what they had come for.

Jack already had a carrying case prepared for the scroll. Taking it from a bag slung over his shoulder, he set it down. The glass box had clearly been made for an art gallery or museum. Its lower rim was hemmed in bright metal, a stout lock held it fast to its base. The base in its turn was screwed down hard to the altar. He had not expected this. Forcing the lock or breaking the glass might very well trigger an alarm that would bring fresh guards running to the spot in seconds.

He knew he had only moments in which to make up his mind.

Breaking the glass was out of the question. The noise alone would draw attention. And there was a serious risk that the weight of the upper half of the box, collapsing on the scroll, might crush it into loose fragments and dust.

Quietly, he hurried back to the entrance to tell de Galais what was wrong. The Frenchman ran back in with him.

'Jack,' he said, 'you are wasting time. You have a screw-driver in your bag. All you have to do is unscrew the entire box. We can carry the whole thing with us.'

Jack shook his head.

'I'd already thought of that. We can't do it without damaging the scroll. It's extremely fragile. You can't imagine how fragile. Just shaking it about in there would probably be enough to break it into a thousand pieces. We have to pick the lock.'

'Mélac could have done it. But none of us knows how.'

They returned to the entrance. The guards denied having

450

a key or access to one. In the distance, footsteps sounded, coming their way.

'Inside the chapel! Quickly!' Galcyzynski hissed. They slipped into the darker shadows, taking the guards with them.

'What are we going to do?' pleaded Jack.

'I think I may have it,' said McBride. Passing his gun to de Galais, he pulled Jack with him further into the chapel.

'Give me that torch there, quick,' he exclaimed, almost snatching the flashlight from Jack's hand.

Moments later, he let out a cry of triumph. Jack saw him reach for a tiny reliquary that stood in a niche set in the side wall.

'Damn it, man, you can't break the glass,' cried Jack.

'Don't be so stupid. I've no intention of doing that. Here, would you hold this torch for me?'

While Jack shone the light on to the little casket, McBride brought a sturdy penknife from his pocket. The reliquary was encrusted with precious stones, all loosely embedded in silver collets set in wood. It was a matter of moments to find a diamond and ease it free of its mount.

They approached the glass box. Footsteps in the church, and the sound of voices. McBride ignored them. Jack felt cold with the fear of discovery. They would not get away a second time.

'Well,' said McBride, 'if you can remember your Hail Mary, this is the time to say it.'

He held the diamond to one face of the glass and pressed.

'Be careful . . . !' exclaimed Jack.

'Don't worry, I've thought of that.'

He continued pressing, running the diamond upwards in a straight line for about three inches. Making a second cut six inches to the right, and parallel with the first, he joined the two incisions with horizontal lines, forming a small rectangle. Using the edge of Jack's carrying case, he delivered a sharp blow to the rectangle, which promptly fell backwards into the box. No alarm sounded. Jack prayed the box had not been fitted with a silent one.

'Here,' said McBride, beckoning Jack nearer. 'This is the hard part. Catch a hold of that' – he indicated the upper edge of the rectangular space – 'while I cut out the rest.'

While Jack held the glass securely, the priest cut out a second, much larger rectangle. This time, when he knocked it out, Jack was ready to prevent the glass falling back and smashing into the scroll. Delicately, they eased the little pane out and set it on the floor.

Jack reached inside unhindered. An inch at a time, he slid the scroll out. For a moment he held it in his hands. McBride held the torch while Jack examined it. It took him only seconds to be sure. There was not the slightest doubt. The object in his hands was the real thing.

CHAPTER SIXTY-SEVEN

Convent of the Sisters of Penitence
Czestochowa

De Galais had obtained a form of ecclesiastical warrant from Cardinal Sienkiewicz, permitting him entry to the convent of the Sisters of Penitence. The warrant instructed the Abbess to bring her most recent postulant, Maria von Freudiger, to de Galais and, should the said postulant express a wish to depart the convent, to allow her to do so without let or hindrance. The terms of the warrant were clear and unequivocal.

Mother Alice was none the less put out. The warrant challenged her authority and her autonomy. Her special relationship with Cardinal Ciechanowski was being put in jeopardy.

'I am sorry,' she said, handing the paper back to de Galais, 'but it is impossible for me to comply with this. The cardinal has no jurisdiction here. Any such breach of custom would require the express approval of Cardinal Ciechanowski. I suggest you speak with him directly.'

'In that case, I think you should also look at this.' De Galais took a second paper from his pocket and passed it without comment to Mother Alice. She unfolded and scanned it; as she did so, her face paled visibly. Without a word, she folded it again and returned it to the priest. A heavily embossed papal crest could just be seen through the thick paper.

Only de Galais and Jack had come. The others, in charge

of the scroll, had taken refuge nearby in the home of a Society member. They knew they should have left Czesto-chowa and gone straight for the border as soon as they had what they had come for. But Jack had been insistent, and no one had felt morally able to deny him.

'I am sure,' de Galais said, 'that the Holy Father will show himself indulgent in the matter of reform in the religious life here. Assuming, of course, that he is aware of your willingness to co-operate in other matters.'

'You are wasting your time, father,' said Mother Alice. 'Maria von Freudiger is no longer here. Her husband came for her two days ago. You are welcome to search this house, but I assure you that you will find no trace of her. I regret what has happened. I regret it deeply. And I am very sorry for the young woman herself. But what is done is done. I hope there will be no repercussions for this convent.'

De Galais got to his feet. He looked at the old woman, not sure what he felt. Like so many, she had only been obeying orders. No doubt, in her heart of hearts, she had been acting from the best of motives. There was no guile there, he thought, no vindictiveness, no spite. And yet, in a sense he could not properly define, he felt himself in the presence of the essence of evil.

'No,' he said. 'No repercussions.' He paused, looking at her, trying to understand. 'Not in this life.'

CHAPTER SIXTY-EIGHT

Czestochowa
Friday, 15 January

Whichever way they went, getting to Rome would involve the crossing of at least three land borders – the Czech Republic, Austria and Italy in one direction, Germany, Austria and Italy in another, or Germany, Switzerland and Italy in a third. They did not even dream of trying to go through what had once been Yugoslavia. Air travel was both the simplest way out, and the most dangerous. They dared not entrust the scroll to anyone else, nor to the post or a courier service.

'It's ironic, isn't it?' asked de Galais. He and the others were holed up in a safe house in Kraków. Outside it was raining in a street of broken lights. 'Fifty-odd years ago, when Rosewicz and the rest had to make much the same journey, they seemed to have very little trouble making it to Rome. We could do with some ratlines of our own.'

'What you're forgetting,' said McBride, 'is that Europe was flooded with refugees back then. There was chaos everywhere. Exactly the right conditions for scum like that to slip through.'

'Plenty of refugees now,' commented Galcyzynski.

'Could we do that?' asked Erzberger. 'Pose as refugees of some sort, get ourselves as far as Germany or Austria?'

De Galais shook his head.

'We agreed that the best plan was to lie low here

in Poland till things calm down, then get out through Sweden.'

'I'm not so sure now,' said Erzberger. 'We hadn't counted on the scroll being the centre of so much attention here. They could mount a full-scale search for us. Door-to-door.'

De Galais disagreed.

'They won't do that,' he said. 'The last thing Ciechanowski wants is for word to get back to the Vatican that the scroll has gone missing. That would ruin everything for the League. Without the scroll they don't have the same leverage, certainly not with the Holy Father. They can't afford a hue and cry. The most they'll do is close the borders as well as they can, using some concocted story about church treasures being stolen. As long as we stay put, we're safe.'

'But not Maria,' said Jack. He was standing apart from the others, staring through the window into the rain-sodden street.

'Try not to worry, Jack. I've already asked our people in Germany to look into it. At the very least, we can find out what's happened to her. And if there's even a slim chance of rescuing her, I assure you we'll make the attempt.'

Jack said nothing. Watching the rain slide down the glass, he felt Maria slip away from him. And love. Youth, perhaps. Whatever of his past meant anything to him – Caitlin, Siobhan, his progress through the world of academia – had culminated in Maria and, in her, been torn from him. All that the scroll and its discovery were to him (and having it in his hands once more, seeing it, touching it, he could not imagine his life now without it) seemed no more than an encumbrance to be weighed against the continuation of Maria's life. Weighed and, if necessary, discarded.

Jack woke in a silence and a darkness that left him gasping for breath. He shared a room with Gabriel McBride. They slept side by side on thin mattresses, under inadequate blankets. There had been a dream, a dream in which Jack had watched a room filled with scrolls burning; burning and yet not consumed, like the fire on Sinai. The fire that spoke.

Now, in the darkness, the memory of fire hung above him like a memory of uncorrected lust. He thought of Christ. Not the pale Galilean of his mother's devotions, a blue-eyed miracle worker dreamed up in the dust of empire by cold Europeans; but a hook-nosed, dark-skinned Pharisee for whom fire and lust were equal parts of God's outrageous plan, a dreamer of dangerous dreams, Jack's father's brother.

Jack saw his Christ staggering through a broken-down ghetto like a drunk man, sidelocks swinging, skullcap slipping from his head, a Torah scroll tucked beneath his thin arm, spat on, stoned, kicked, surrounded by rings of ugly Aryan faces, surrounded by blue eyes and blond hair, running from a cross the size of the world. He saw him dressed in a striped jacket and trousers, with a number tattooed on his left forearm, staggering beneath the blows of a bull-whip. And in front of him, line after line of naked men and women with thorns on their heads, lash-marks on their backs, stumbling in silence through the gaping doors of gas chambers big enough to house the whole of mankind.

And he thought of trust and the betrayal of trust, of fire that burned and fire that did not burn. There was nothing between his heart and the moon, nothing but phantoms going round and round.

He got out of bed, shivering. It was excruciatingly cold. The house lacked proper heating. Jack was already dressed in trousers and a pullover. McBride was fast asleep. Jack could hear his breathing. It was regular, as though he slept without dreams. The priest was at peace with himself, not a man God would burn.

Jack found his shoes and slipped them on.

The scroll was where he had left it, after performing a careful examination earlier that day, in a locked cupboard at the top of the stairs. The key was still in his pocket. He opened the cupboard gingerly and lifted out the cylinder. It felt curiously heavy for a moment, as he first took it in his hands, as though filled with centuries, then it seemed to resume its proper weight.

As he turned, a light went on. Augustin de Galais was standing opposite him. He held a gun in one hand.

'Jack. I thought I heard a sound. What are you doing?'

He only seemed to notice the cylinder at that moment.

'Please don't try to stop me, Augustin.'

The priest eyed him sadly.

'Why would I want to stop you, Jack?'

Jack did not try to answer.

'He won't let her go, Jack. Not even for that.'

'I think you're wrong. I have to try.'

De Galais thought for a moment.

'Yes,' he said, 'you have to try. But not with the scroll. It's not yours to bargain with.'

Jack shook his head.

'It doesn't have an owner,' he said. 'Not me, not you, not the Pope. But if you keep it, you'll bury it. Or see it buried. That would be a crime. Worse than theft.'

'I want to see it published, Jack. As much as you.'

'No, that's not true. You have to give it to the Pope. Whatever happens, he has to know the original is safe, that there's no longer any opportunity for Crux Orientalis to get hold of it. You'll tell him it should be published, but he won't listen to you. They never listen to voices like yours or mine, their ears aren't properly tuned. He'll lock the scroll away. Or burn it.'

'But you would hand it over to von Freudiger. Or Rosewicz. You know what use they plan to make of it. What power it will give them. Are you prepared for that? Is your conscience prepared for that?'

'My conscience is my affair.'

'Yes, I would not say otherwise. I make no claims on it. But not the scroll. That is my affair.'

De Galais raised the gun.

Jack moved quickly, taking advantage of the priest's instinctive reluctance to fire. He swung his fist hard at de Galais' solar plexus, punching with all his strength. De Galais gasped, then choked on his own intake of breath. As he staggered back, his arm swung upwards, and Jack slipped in again, seizing the gun and tearing it from the priest's hand. He hated what he was doing, but more than that he hated to think of Maria frightened and dying in some sordid nightmare of Karl's making.

He hit the priest hard across the temple. De Galais fell wordless to the floor, a look of surprise and betrayal on his face.

CHAPTER SIXTY-NINE

Arnstorf, Germany

Paul could not remember when he had last been happy, could not conceive of ever being happy again. He was too young to contemplate suicide, even to know that such an option existed. But if he had known, he would have embraced the idea wholeheartedly, like a prisoner running for a gap in the wall. Save for one thing: the daily hope that, when he next awoke, it would be to see his mother's face again, bending over him.

He had started wetting the bed again, and every morning he was dragged from bed and beaten. Leni, the woman who looked after him, called him a baby and rubbed his face in the wet sheets, then shoved him under an ice-cold shower. At first he had cried when she beat him, but recently he had found the tears less ready to come. Something else was taking their place, something for which he had no words. All he knew was that it was a bad feeling and that it would not leave him.

There were no toys here, and no games to play, no other children to play them with. He had invented a little friend called Pieter, and at night in bed they had long conversations; but he still missed his mother more than he could bear. Mealtimes were solemn, adult affairs, with harsh instructions about finishing everything on the plate. A lot of time was spent outdoors, even when it was raining or icy. Leni said it was to 'toughen him'. He did not like the idea of being toughened. His father told him that it would 'make a man of him'. But if that was what being a man was about, he would sooner not become one. The shell that he had begun to build while in Essen, the shell only his mother had been able to penetrate, was growing harder and thicker every day. Sometimes he imagined it like a heavy slab of stone that blocked out all light and all sounds, keeping him safe from the strap and the sharp, unforgiving tones of Leni's voice.

The door of his room opened and Leni came in. She always came in without knocking, as though trying to catch him doing something wrong, or thinking wrong thoughts. Once she had caught him talking to Pieter and beaten him for 'daydreaming'. He did not like it when she came in without knocking.

'Stand up, Paul. You're to come downstairs at once. You have a visitor.'

For a moment his heart fluttered.

'Is it Mummy?'

Leni said nothing, and he knew that, if he asked a second time, he would be smacked. Leni was not particular about where she smacked him, or how hard. He had come to fear her more than any human being, with the exception of his father. And, of course, the Führer, whose unsmiling photograph looked down at him from every wall and whom he was being brought up to love and honour. He got off the bed and walked to the door, head held stiffly erect, like a little soldier, as he had been told.

Karl von Freudiger was waiting downstairs, in the library, into which Paul was only taken for punishments. When the boy saw his father there, he thought that must be why he had come: to punish him for some forgotten misdemeanour.

'Hallo, Paul. How are you?'

'Very well, Father. How are you?'

'Please sit down, Paul. I have some upsetting news for you.'

'Is it about Mummy?'

Von Freudiger hesitated.

'Your mother is dead, Paul. You will not see her again. Do you understand what I am saying to you?'

There was not a trace of emotion in Karl's voice. He did not bend to touch his son or to comfort him. The little boy looked at him without comprehension.

'Maybe she'll come next week,' he said.

Karl shook his head.

'No, Paul. Your mother is dead. When people die, they go away. For ever. You have only me now. Me and Jesus and the Führer.'

Something in Karl's voice or manner, something in the words that had been used, or in the gestures, however spare, that had accompanied them, got through to the child.

'No,' he cried. 'I don't want you. I don't want Jesus. I don't want the Führer. I want my mummy.'

Karl stood and crossed to the door.

'Leni,' he called. 'I think it is time for Paul's run.' He turned and looked down at the child.

'Remember, Paul, Jesus watches you all the time. He tells me when you do wrong. And the Führer watches us from heaven, where your mother is. I have to go now, Paul. I have important business in Essen. But I will be back soon.'

CHAPTER SEVENTY

Kraków, Poland

It took Jack over two hours to find the sort of place he was looking for: a good modern hotel. The Grand, on Ulica Slawkowska, had only opened a few months before and was still bright and shiny, in stark contrast to so many of the city's older buildings, eaten away by the acid rain that poured down on them daily from the steelworks of nearby Nowa Huta.

He still carried plenty of money on him, a great deal of it in high-denomination Deutschmarks. It could not be helped that his arrival at such an unusual hour, without luggage and carrying an Irish passport as his sole means of identification, was bound to be noticed. The chief risk he was running was that the police might already have his description and that they might have circulated it to hotels and guest houses. On reflection, however, he thought they would not have bothered. And he had no intention of hanging around here any longer than necessary.

Deutschmarks proved highly acceptable to the girl on the desk. For a moment, he thought she was going to say, 'That will do nicely, sir.' He could see her visibly swallowing her discomfort.

'A room, sir? Yes . . . yes, of course. For . . . how long?'

'Not long. Today. Until noon.'

'I . . . You will have to pay for the whole night, sir. The rate is two million zlotys.'

The staggering sum worked out at just over one hundred

pounds. He peeled off three hundred Deutschmarks.

'Will this be enough?'

She did a quick calculation, gave him some change in zlotys, and asked if there was anything else he wanted.

'Yes,' he said. 'Please leave instructions that I'm not to be disturbed.'

The international operator took only minutes to find the number and put Jack through to Karl von Freudiger. It took a little longer for Karl himself to come to the telephone. Jack had given his name. He supposed that the delay was, in part, to permit a trace to be started on the call.

'Here is von Freudiger. What can I do for you, Dr Gould?'

'You can bring your wife to the phone and let me speak to her.'

'My wife? Surely you are mistaken. I have no wife.'

'Please don't play games with me. You had a wife when I saw you last. Her name was Maria.'

'Yes, I know who you mean. That woman has entered a convent. She is a bride of Christ, or will soon become one.'

'I asked you not to play games. I already know that you took her out of the convent two days ago.'

'Dr Gould, just what is it you want?'

'I think you know. I think you know I have something you want back. It can be yours again on very simple conditions.'

A pause of three pulses, then von Freudiger's voice, changed.

'Which are?'

Jack could detect the eagerness in the reply. The German was no longer playing games.

'First, that you release Maria. Second, that, if she decides to go with me, we will not be interfered with or followed, now or at any time in the future. Third, that, if she asks for her son Paul, he is to be allowed to go with her.'

A long silence followed at the other end. Jack wondered if they had traced the call yet.

'I told you, Dr Gould. Maria has chosen to take the veil.'

'I can't believe that you're being so stupid. Let me put this more clearly. If Maria comes to any harm at your hands or anyone else's, I shall burn the scroll. That is a promise. You have no choice if you want to regain possession of the papyrus. You have to let her go.'

'How do I know you have this scroll?'

'You'll know when I hand it over.'

'What about your associates? I can't imagine they're co-operating in this.'

'You don't have to worry about them. They don't know where I am, or where I've put the scroll.'

Another silence followed, longer than the first. Jack thought von Freudiger must be talking with someone else. He thought he could hear whispers. When he spoke again, von Freudiger's voice was tense.

'What you are asking is outrageous. I cannot allow it. But I do wish to have the scroll. I am, therefore, willing to offer you one million Deutschmarks for it. Provided it is in good condition and . . .'

Jack slammed down the receiver. His hand was shaking. He remained sitting on the edge of the bed, trying to regain control of his breathing. To have been offered money, as though von Freudiger thought him capable of such an equivalence. But what if von Freudiger was just stalling? What if he really could not bring Maria to the telephone?

His hand still trembling, he lifted the receiver again.

This time von Freudiger answered in person. Jack cut in at once.

'Let's get one thing straight. This is not about money, and offers of money, however large, will cut no ice with me. I am doing this for Maria. Her freedom is all that matters to me. Now, please bring her to the telephone.'

'What if I told you she was dead? That I took her from the convent in order to have her killed?'

Jack felt sick.

'I would destroy the scroll,' he said, trying to stay in control. 'You would have lost everything.'

A pause. It seemed like centuries to Jack.

'She is not here. Not in this house. It will take time to fetch her.'

He felt relief wash over him like water.

'We don't have time. But provided she is alive, we can still reach a deal. Do I have your word that she has not been harmed?'

A longer pause. Jack could feel himself slipping. There was a crackling on the line. And a sound of someone breathing.

'You have my word,' von Freudiger said. 'She will be turned over to you. You will not be interfered with. But do not so much as mention my son's name again if you wish to come out of this alive. Now, when can you bring the scroll here?'

'No, that isn't how this is going to work. Listen to me very carefully. We are not equally matched. You have advantages I cannot compete with: money, manpower, weapons. That means that, if you want to do a deal, it has to be on my terms. If I feel threatened, I pull out. And the scroll goes with me. I tell you how it's done.'

There was a pause, then von Freudiger came back on.

'Very well. What do you want me to do?'

'First of all, I leave Poland unharmed. You do not try to stop me, and you do not have me followed. I may not be able to compete with you, but I'm not without resources. I will leave the scroll in Poland. It will be in the keeping of a third party with whom I have arranged to stay in contact on a four-hourly basis. If I fail to make contact over an eight-hour period, he has instructions to destroy the scroll. Is that understood?'

'Yes. What next?'

'You are to get Maria ready to meet me when and where I decide, within the next few days. If she does not arrive as instructed, I will order the scroll destroyed. Is that clear?'

'Perfectly. What will happen then?'

'That's all you need to know for the moment. I'll be in touch.'

Jack put the receiver down. It was not particularly warm in the room, but he was sweating. He wanted a bath and a chance to sleep, but he knew it would be a serious mistake. He had more important things to do.

Karl von Freudiger replaced the receiver, then lifted it and keyed in another number.

'Von Freudiger. Well?'

'The Grand Hotel in Kraków. Room 319.'

'Do what you can.'

He let the receiver drop back on to the rest and turned to a man seated near the desk.

'What do you think? Is he telling the truth?'

Parker shrugged.

'Perhaps. We learnt a lot about him while he was in London. He is basically honest. But there's a lot at stake for him in this.'

'Can you handle it?'

Parker nodded.

'I think so. What about you?'

CHAPTER SEVENTY-ONE

Dublin
Monday, 18 January

He entered Dublin in the early morning, trailing memories, sneaking glances to right and left like a criminal returning to the scene of a crime. Anybody's crime. All around him as he came through the madhouse of the airport, people were speaking in voices like his own, the intonations of Ballsbridge and Sandymount and Howth; yet he felt himself among them the most perfect of strangers. In the taxi he watched the city slide past like a strange city, someone else's town, a strumpet. A city famous for doors, whose reality was walls snaking within walls. A labyrinthine city, mazy, full of blind alleys and twisting corners. Somewhere in it his wife and daughter were buried. And with them all his past.

There was a room waiting for him in Buswell's, reserved by telephone before leaving Heathrow airport. His only luggage was the small suitcase in which the scroll was kept. To have left it in Kraków would have been foolish, even dangerous. He had no intention of letting it out of his sight. Locking his door, he slept until mid-afternoon.

It was a short walk to Grafton Street and Brown Thomas, where he bought himself two changes of clothes. He went into Bewley's for a coffee, watching all the while for a sign that he was being watched. The little suitcase stayed with him all the way.

He phoned von Freudiger from a booth near the Green,

to the company of a fiddle playing 'An Londubh is an Cheirseach'. The sun had set. In the fresh darkness, the music seemed more magical than human.

'Tomorrow morning,' he said. 'Ten o'clock, the front gate of Trinity College. Don't be late. You and Maria, no one else. Once Maria and I are safe, I'll tell you where the scroll is hidden.'

'How do I know you won't double-cross me?'

'We both have to take that risk. I've more to lose. So we do it my way.'

'I can't make it that quickly.'

'You can. I've checked the timetables. You can do it with time to spare.'

'Tell me where the scroll is now. Maria will be there in the morning, I promise.'

Jack put the phone down.

Without being seen, it is difficult to get a direct view of the front gate of Trinity College unless you go past in a car or bus. Jack went by three times on the upper decks of buses he boarded in Pearse Street. He saw them on his third pass.

Jack did not expect a double-cross before Karl was sure of the scroll. But he did not imagine the League would let him or Maria out of their sight until then. And once the scroll was in their hands again . . .

He got off the bus in Nassau Street and entered the college by the new side entrance; it had not been there in his day. In due course, he made his way round to Front Square. It was almost half-past ten.

Karl was scanning the crowds nervously. He wore a short green overcoat and carried an umbrella. Beside him, Maria stood as motionless as the statues of Burke and Goldsmith on either side. Jack watched her for a while, entranced, unnoticed in the gloomy vestibule beside the porter's lodge. He remembered her sister standing there so many years ago, in that same spot, in a summer dress, waiting for him after a lecture or at lunchtime, in the evening before they went together to the theatre. A wheel had come full circle. And in a moment he would know just what end it had spun him to.

He stepped out of the shadows. Maria saw him first. She did not cry out or run to him. He had not expected that. But he saw enough in her eyes to know he had done the right thing, whatever happened. She was pale, and her cheeks had grown gaunt in a matter of weeks. He stepped up to her and took her hand.

'You'll find the scroll in the Rubrics,' he said to Karl. 'Third door down. But you'll have to hurry before some sharp-sighted Fellow stumbles on it first and carts it off to join the Book of Kells.'

'Rubrics?' Karl stared at Jack, uncomprehending.

'Ask a porter,' said Jack, running through the gate, Maria's hand in his. If there was to be a bullet, this was the moment, he thought.

Parker saw them coming. He had men positioned on all the corners facing on College Green: one outside the Bank of Ireland, one on the corner of College Street, one diagonally opposite. He himself stood at the foot of Grattan's statue, immediately in front of the college gate. As he saw Jack and Maria start across the road, he spoke quickly into a handset.

Jack had hired a car from Boland's in Pearse Street. He was relying on the distraction caused by the scroll to give him and Maria time to get away. The car was parked on the street in front of the bank: a parking ticket had been Jack's smallest worry.

He saw them coming, even as he reached for the door. Four men in all, approaching fast. He recognized Parker immediately. There was a gun in his hand, concealed inside the fold of his coat.

'Please don't make a fuss, Jack. We don't want to alarm anyone. But if we have to, we'll do it here.'

Maria turned to him.

'Simon. What's going on? Where's Jeremy?'

'Jeremy is dead.'

Jack squeezed her hand.

'He's working for them now. I saw him visiting your father's house in Paris.'

Maria looked at Parker in alarm.

'Is that true, Simon?'

'Not for them,' Parker answered. 'With them. I'm sorry. But there's too much at stake. I'd like you and Jack to come with us quietly.'

'Simon, you don't have to do this. You've got what you want. Karl's picking it up now. All Jack and I want to do is get away from all of this. Please.'

'I'm sorry, Maria,' Parker said. 'It isn't that simple. I'd let you go if I could. But I don't have any choice. Karl wants you dead. He wants me to do it. He has to know he can trust me. Try not to make it hard for us.'

It was as far as he got. Without warning, two cars screeched to a halt beside them, almost causing a major pile-up. Masked men got out of each one. Parker and his men turned, reaching for guns inside their coats. But they never stood a chance. The masked men opened fire at once, dropping them with quick shots to the head.

'For God's sake, man, get in your car and clear out of here!' One of the gunmen had Jack by the arm. The voice was Irish.

The gunmen piled into their cars and were off before they had even had time to close their doors. All around, cars were stopping, pedestrians were running, some away from the incident, others towards it. The road was covered with blood. Jack saw Parker try to lift himself, then fall back. Maria knelt down, lifting Parker's head. But it was useless, life had left him.

On the pavement, a man detached himself from the bank railings and walked quickly towards Jack and Maria. Jack looked up. It was Gabriel McBride.

'Take her now, Jack. Get out of here while you still can.'

'How did you know we'd be here?'

'You were followed, Jack. We tapped von Freudiger's phone.'

'What the hell's going on?'

'You'll find out in your paper tonight. Now, clear out before the Gardaí come.'

The Rubrics is an early-eighteenth-century building of red brick, incongruous with the ubiquitous grey stone that grew up all round it. It bisects Trinity College crosswise at the rear of the main buildings. The cylinder was in a cardboard box at the bottom of the third staircase. Karl opened it and carefully extracted the contents: a papyrus scroll. The Irishman had kept his word. Karl almost felt sorry that it had been necessary to kill him. Smiling, he slipped the scroll back inside its container.

CHAPTER SEVENTY-TWO

Jack and Maria left Dublin on the first available flight. Lufthansa only operated direct flights to Munich on Mondays, Fridays and weekends, so they had to fly to London in order to connect with an early-afternoon flight to Munich. Somewhere around the Channel, Jack picked up a BBC radio news broadcast.

An extensive manhunt has been mounted in the Republic of Ireland to find the IRA gunmen responsible for the murder in Dublin this morning of four English businessmen. The shootings occurred outside the headquarters of the Bank of Ireland in the centre of Dublin just after ten o'clock, when a group of masked gunmen opened fire at close quarters. The victims, who have not yet been named, died instantly from gunshots to the head. In a statement issued by the INLA, the Irish National Liberation Army, it has been claimed that the four victims had been ranking members of British intelligence, sent to Dublin for purposes of political sabotage. There has as yet been no denial of this claim by the British authorities.

Jack explained to Maria about Gabriel McBride and his friends in violent places. And he told her what he could about Felix and Parker. There was, strangely enough, a further news item that chimed perfectly with what he had to say. The item had been tagged on to the bulletin more as a curiosity than anything.

An elderly man claiming to be Lieutenant Peter Ramsey, a British military intelligence officer during World War II, has turned up in London this morning. He arrived without papers on an Aeroflot flight from Moscow. According to a statement he

473

has now issued to the press, other missing British agents will soon be joining him.

Lieutenant Ramsey's wife, Ethel, a war widow living in Birkenhead, fainted on being told the news. Her husband was reported missing in action in 1944 and declared officially dead at the end of the war. Peter Ramsey – if that is who the man at London airport is – could be one of an estimated 30,000 Allied prisoners liberated by Soviet troops at the end of the Second World War and thought to have been subsequently removed to labour camps within the Soviet Union. Last summer, Russian President Boris Yeltsin admitted to the existence in that country of American POWs from Vietnam, Korea, and former Nazi-held territories. It is expected that Mrs Ramsey will meet the man claiming to be her husband sometime this evening.

'Kossenkova was killed in London along with Felix,' said Jack. 'Without her to control the situation back in Russia, somebody must have decided to lift the lid. Parker wanted to do a deal with your father. Some sort of damage limitation exercise. I think that's what he'd have called it.'

Maria said very little. She held Jack's hand and smiled at him from time to time, but her thoughts were not really with him. She knew that, if she did not get to Paul now, Karl might spirit the boy away somewhere she would never find him again. With the resources at his disposal, her husband had only to lift a finger to make Paul disappear without trace.

They remained in Munich for several hours in order to sort out some essential matters. Maria's bank accounts had not been frozen, as she had feared. She drew out a large sum, opened a separate account under another name, and gave instructions that whatever remained in her Essen account be transferred to it.

After that, they visited one of Munich's leading solicitors, a man called Hassler, who had offices on the Königsplatz. Hassler was a large, bearded man in opulent surroundings.

He had clearly made a handsome living out of other men's hardships, but seemed none the worse for it.

'*Grüss Gott,*' he said, standing as Maria and Jack were ushered in to his office.

'Thank you for seeing us at such short notice,' said Maria. She knew perfectly well that it had been her name and her money that had turned a three-week waiting-list into three minutes.

'My dear Frau von Freudiger, I am at your disposal. I only wish to know why you come all the way to Munich to find a solicitor. Please, sit down. And you, Herr . . . ?'

'Gould. Dr Gould.'

'*Es freut mich. Bitte nehmen Sie Platz.*'

Hassler listened with professional detachment while Maria outlined the circumstances of Paul's abduction. In return for a large payment (and the prospect of many more to come), the solicitor said he was willing to issue immediate instructions for legal action to be taken against Karl.

'However, until the case has gone to court,' he said, 'there is little more we can do. We will, of course, ask for an interim ruling to permit you access to the boy. Without such a ruling, unfortunately, there is nothing the authorities can do for you. I will have my secretary prepare a solicitor's letter, asking your husband to co-operate with any reasonable request you may make in the interim. In the letter I shall point out that any refusal to comply on his part may go against him when the case finally does come before a judge. Will that be enough?'

Maria shook her head.

'I just want to see Paul and make sure Karl doesn't try to take him elsewhere. Will your letter have enough legal force for that? My husband is a powerful man. Legal niceties aren't likely to be much of an obstacle to him.'

'You could always ask the police if they would be willing to send someone to accompany you. If the boy expresses himself willing to go with you, there is really not very much your husband can do to stop him leaving. But I'm not sure the local police will want to get involved in a domestic dispute. If you are willing to wait until the morning, I can contact a friend at police headquarters here in Munich.'

'That's very kind of you. But I want to see Paul today if possible. Just get your letter typed. It won't cut any ice with Karl, but it may be enough to persuade the people looking after Paul.'

Fifteen minutes later, the letter was ready. Hassler saw them to the door.

'Come back in the morning if you don't have any luck,' he said. 'We'll get your son back in your custody by this time tomorrow at the latest.'

Maria shook his hand and turned to go.

'Frau von Freudiger, I do not wish to seem presumptuous, but if there should be . . .' The lawyer paused. 'If there should be divorce proceedings, please bear in mind that I can guarantee you the maximum discretion. My clients are all from the best part of society. I understand the sort of problems a woman in your position may anticipate. Do please give the matter your most careful consideration.'

Maria thanked him and left.

Back in his office, Hassler sat for a long time behind his vast desk, contemplating the painting opposite, a Balthus he had acquired ten years earlier in Geneva. He had not attained his present position without getting to know a little about who was who in Germany, and what sort of power they wielded. He looked at the clock on his desk. Time to pack up for the day: he had a dinner engagement at eight.

He picked up the telephone and spoke briefly to his secretary.

'Miss Schneider, I'd like you to get a number for me. The name is von Freudiger. Herr Karl von Freudiger. He lives in Essen. If he's not there, find out where he is: he's bound to have a mobile number.'

*   *   *

De Galais had given Maria a rough address for the house at which Paul was being kept. He had told her that it was set in five acres of secluded garden on the outskirts of Arnstorf, on the narrow road between the two Simbachs, near the Austrian frontier.

They hired a car and headed straight there. It was dark by the time they left Hassler's. Jack drove as fast as he dared. At Arnstorf, Maria asked in the inn for Herr von Freudiger's house. Without hesitation, the woman behind the bar explained where she would find it. They drove out of the village and found themselves on a twisting country road.

Five minutes later Jack stopped outside heavy gates set among high hedges. At the end of a long drive, a large Bavarian villa with a sharply-angled roof could just be seen, nestling in a semicircle of tall trees. The windows were lit. Jack got out. To his surprise, the gates were unlocked. He pushed one back as far as it would go and returned to the car. There were cameras on both sides, watching.

They drew up outside the front door and got out. There was another car parked at the front of the house, a small Mercedes.

'That belongs to Karl,' whispered Maria. 'He keeps it in Munich to use when he flies in for business trips.'

Jack expected guards to appear, but all seemed quiet.

'I don't like it,' said Maria. 'It seems too quiet.'

The door was unlocked. Jack found the bell and rang. Once, twice. No one came. He pushed the door, and they stepped into a tall, oak-panelled hallway. Light was reflected from high windows above a wide wooden staircase. All round them the walls were decorated with various pieces of Nazi paraphernalia: flags, SS standards, portraits of Hitler. The house was silent.

'Something has happened, Jack. Something's wrong. Karl must have got here ahead of us.'

'I'll take a look round. You stay here.'

'No, I'm coming with you. If Karl's here, I have to speak to him. Try to persuade him to see sense.'

'Do you think he'll listen?'

'I'll tell him I've been to Hassler.'

Jack was sceptical about the impact that was likely to have on Karl, but he said nothing. They went into the first room on their left, a small sitting-room dominated by colour photographs of Hitler and Himmler. It was empty. Next door was a small gymnasium, fitted with wallbars, pommel and vaulting horses, rings, and parallel bars. It was a cold room. Where there were spaces on the wall, someone had hung photographs of lithe Germanic youths performing gymnastic exercises.

They crossed the hall and opened the door to the room on the right. It was a small library. Like the hall, it was decorated with memorabilia of the Third Reich; but here the pieces were more personal. There were several photographs on the walls of Reinhold von Freudiger in his honorary SS uniform, in the company of different Reich dignitaries; glass cases containing guns; several ceremonial daggers hanging from silk cords; a bayonet; an SS cap with death's-head crest.

In the centre of the room stood a large mahogany desk. On it were arranged stacks of files, all in uniform green covers. But it was not the files that drew Jack's attention. On top of the desk lay a metal cylinder. It was the container he had left in the Rubrics at Trinity College that morning. Beside it lay the fragments of a papyrus scroll, broken and scattered in all directions.

Jack stepped across to the desk and reached out a hand to pick up one of the fragments. As he did so, his eye was caught by something behind the desk. A vast pool of blood covered the carpet.

'Stay where you are,' he said.

'What's wrong?'

Jack walked round the desk. Face-down in the pool lay a man's body. There was no question that the man was dead: the back of his head had been sliced off. Beside the body lay the murder instrument, a long sabre, a weapon of the sort still used in some right-wing student fraternities for duelling purposes. It had probably been one of the ornaments hanging on the wall.

Jack knelt beside the body and gently turned it over. He heard Maria cry out behind him. The dead man was Karl von Freudiger.

CHAPTER SEVENTY-THREE

There was a sound in the doorway. Maria whirled round. A woman stood there, saying nothing, just staring into the room with a look of mingled fear and hatred on her face. She was perhaps forty years old, with short, greying hair, and she wore a long black dress. Her face and hands and clothing were covered in dried blood. In her right hand she held a gun pointed directly at Maria.

'He said you'd come. We thought you'd be here earlier. If you had been, you might have been in time to do something. Now it's too late.'

'Did you do this?' Maria asked. She felt nothing for Karl, his death left not even a ripple in her life. But inside she could feel the mounting terror, the dread that whoever had killed Karl had also attacked her son.

The woman's eyes opened wide.

'Do that? Kill him? What do you think I am? That's your father's work.'

Maria looked at her, refusing to believe what she had said. Jack left Karl's body and came behind her, putting his arm round her shoulder.

'I don't understand. What could my father have had to do with this? I don't know what you mean.'

'No? Well, I was here when it happened. If I'd had this gun on me then, I'd have shot him on the spot.'

'Where is Paul?' asked Maria. 'What have you done with him?'

'Done? I've done nothing. It's your father who's done everything.'

Maria was coming close to hysteria. She asked again, her voice breaking.

'I asked you where he is. You have to tell me. Is he all right?'

'Your father took him. Over an hour ago. That's all I know. If you hadn't interfered, this wouldn't have happened.' The woman kept the gun pointed at Maria's face.

'How did it happen?' asked Maria. 'What did my father do? Why did he take Paul?'

'Your father came here around noon. I let him in, of course; he wanted to see his grandson. Herr von Freudiger had left orders that he was always to be admitted. He spent some time with Paul, then waited in the library for your husband. He listened to the radio for a while. I gave him something to eat. He seemed on edge about something, very impatient; he kept looking at his watch.

'Herr von Freudiger arrived about two hours ago. I asked if he wanted anything to eat, but no, he had to come straight here to the library. "Wait outside, Leni," he said. "We shall want champagne to celebrate." Those were the last words he spoke to me. About a minute after he came in an argument started. I could hear them shouting from as far away as the kitchen, where I was getting the champagne from the refrigerator. They went on for a long time. Then there was a noise of something heavy falling, and everything went quiet.'

'Do you know what they were arguing about?' asked Jack. He was just about able to follow the conversation with his limited German.

'About that,' the woman said, pointing with her free hand at the remains of the papyrus on the desk.

'I think I understand,' Jack said.

'Understand what?' Maria did not take her eyes off the woman or the gun in her hand.

'Why your father was so angry. He realized he had been cheated. And that this time there would be no second chance.' He paused. 'The scroll Karl brought back from

Dublin wasn't the Jesus scroll, even if it looked a lot like it. I broke into the Chester Beatty the night before; it's surprisingly easy if you know your way round the alarm system: they hadn't changed it since I used to work there.

'I took a first-century scroll very similar in size and handwriting to the scroll Karl was expecting to receive. In the end, an empty cylinder would have done just as well, but I hadn't reckoned on Karl's back-up being so easily put out of the way.

'Your father must have gone out of his mind when he saw what I'd done. Karl would never have guessed the scrolls had been switched, but your father will have seen it right away. He knew the Jesus scroll backwards.'

Maria turned to the woman.

'Why did my father kill Karl? Just because he'd let Jack trick him?'

The housekeeper seemed reluctant to answer.

'Come on. You say they were shouting. You must have overheard.'

'Your father wanted to take your son away. He said it was all over, that they'd lost everything. Herr von Freudiger tried to reason with him. He said the scroll was unimportant, that we could win without it. Then your father killed him. The next thing I knew, he came storming out of the library and up the stairs. I rushed in here and found your husband like that. I didn't know what to do. I found this gun and went after him, but I didn't know what I was supposed to do. I had no orders, there was no one I could contact in time. I was frightened.

'I found your father coming down the stairs with Paul. He was . . .' She hesitated. 'He seemed out of his mind. Shouting, bellowing all the time. A madman. He had the boy in a tight grip, there was nothing I could do, not without the risk of shooting Paul.'

'Where did he take him?' Maria was frantic now, on the verge of collapsing from fear for her son.

The woman shook her head.

'I don't know. He just went out and put Paul in his car, then drove off. I don't know where they went.'

'Think, woman,' Jack pressed her. 'Did he say anything? Was he heading back to Paris? Poland? Where, for God's sake?'

'Ireland,' whispered the woman. 'I remember now. During the argument he said he was going to take Paul to Ireland. To some place called Summerfield. Is that right?'

'Summerlawn,' Jack exclaimed. 'He's taking him to Summerlawn. But why? I don't understand. The place was burnt down. There's nothing there now.'

Maria looked round, her eyes wide with fear.

'Oh, God, Jack. I think I know. Didn't you know what happened, how Summerlawn came to be burned down?'

Jack shook his head. He felt numb, everything was racing out of control.

'They tried to take the house away. There was to be a compulsory purchase. I'd gone by then, he was living in the house alone. He rang me that night, the night of the fire. He said he wouldn't let them get their hands on the place, that he'd sooner see it burned to the ground than have those grubby little civil servants turning it into a place for tourists to go tramping through. He burned it down himself, Jack. He got the best furniture out, his paintings, his books, his manuscripts. And then he took a can of petrol and put Summerlawn to the torch.'

She looked at him blankly. Her eyes had filled with tears.

'Don't you understand?' she said. 'I know him, Jack. I know him better than anyone. He's planning to do the same with Paul. He can't bear the thought of all his plans coming to nothing, of his grandson being shut out from his destiny. He'd sooner kill him than see that happen.'

CHAPTER SEVENTY-FOUR

'Give me the gun,' said Jack, holding out his hand. 'Please.'

She was clearly strung out, at the far edge of whatever it was held her together. Without a superior, someone from whom to take orders, she was nothing. But she was all the more dangerous. In their nothingness, the Lenis of this world strike out.

'I know who you are,' she said, taking a step further into the room and turning the revolver towards Jack. 'You're the Jew, the dirty kike who's been sleeping with Paul's mother.'

'Who told you that?'

'Herr von Freudiger, of course. He knew all along. You must have thought him stupid; but he knew. He knew everything.'

'It's not important now,' said Jack. 'Von Freudiger is dead. But there's still time to save Paul. You have to let us go. We can still stop Rosewicz.'

Leni shook her head.

'You can go, Mrs von Freudiger. You're nothing now. But not the Jew. He's responsible for all this. He has to pay.'

It would have been so easy, thought Jack, so easy to say, *No, I'm not a Jew, not a kike, not a yid. I'm a Catholic like you. Listen, I can recite my Hail Marys and Paternosters with the best of them. Do you want to hear me?*

But it was no longer that simple. He had come to a parting of ways. It was less what he felt himself to be than what the woman with the gun in front of him made him, what she herself stood for. She was just a wave in an ocean of hatred, but she could sweep him away for all that. He would not deny his Jewishness for her. It seemed to matter now.

'You go, Maria,' he said. 'Find your father. Get a chartered jet at Munich: there's still time.'

Maria shook her head. She reached out her left hand for his.

'He's dead, Leni,' she said. 'It's all over. He would understand.'

'No,' said Leni. 'I can't allow it. Someone has to pay.'

She began to lift the gun.

Jack scarcely saw what happened next. There was a blurred movement to his side. Maria took her right hand from her coat pocket, pointed a gun, and fired. She fired only once: a perfect shot that entered the forehead and exited in a jet of blood through the back of Leni's skull. Leni did not even have time to pull the trigger of her own gun.

When it was done, Jack took the gun from Maria and held her tightly. She sobbed briefly, then that too was done.

'We have to go,' she said. 'There's no time to lose.'

As they drove away, Jack turned to her.

'Where did you get the gun? I can't see where you can have found it.'

'I took it from Parker,' she said. 'Just after he was shot.'

'But how . . . ?'

Then Jack remembered her kneeling down, lifting the dead man's head. She must have pocketed the gun while he was preoccupied with McBride.

They drove a little further, down dark roads towards Munich.

'I still don't understand,' Jack said. 'How'd you get Parker's gun through airport security?'

'I had a little help,' she said. Opening her handbag, she took out a plastic card. 'Our friend Felix insisted I carry a gun whenever possible. If I was flying, I had a standard European security pass to get me through checks. I still had it hidden at home in Essen. When we left, I brought it with me. In case there was a chance to make a run for it. Getting out of Dublin was easy. They'd just been alerted that four British intelligence people had been shot in broad daylight in College Green. I was the last person they were going to stop.'

Jack covered the sixty-odd miles to the airport in well under an hour. They left the car near the rental office and ran into the main concourse.

'We need a private plane. A jet.'

Maria was the sort of woman who could walk up to an airport information desk and ask for something like that without seeming remotely ridiculous. The girl did not even blink. She directed them to a small office at the rear, beneath a sign that read 'Executive Charters'.

'There may not be anyone there,' said the girl as they left.

But there was.

He was a well-preserved fifty-year-old with the beginnings of a discreet paunch. He had that detached look of someone who spends more time in the air than on the ground.

'Ireland?' he exclaimed when Maria told him what she wanted. He spoke German with an eastern European accent which Maria could not quite place. 'What's going on? Tonight everybody wants to fly to Ireland.'

A man answering Rosewicz's description had left the airport an hour before on a chartered jet heading for Cork.

'Did he have a child with him, a little boy?'

The pilot nodded.

'That's right. The old man said he was his grandson. The kid said something about going back to his mother. The man had all the right papers. What could we do?'

'I'm the boy's mother,' said Maria. 'The man who chartered your plane is my father-in-law. The courts are

486

planning to give me custody of Paul, so my husband got his father to take him out of Germany. Here.'

She took Hassler's letter from her pocket and showed it to the man. He handed it back.

'I don't really need to know your business, lady. If you have the money, we'll fly you wherever you want to go.'

'Just get me to Cork.'

The pilot nodded.

'My name's Zamfirescu, by the way. Why don't you relax for a few minutes? Sit down. We've got a bit of paperwork to get through before I can get clearance.'

Every minute that passed until they were airborne seemed an age. Zamfirescu was infected by Maria's mood and did what he could to short-circuit the paperwork and obtain the necessary clearances in half the usual time. It still seemed to take an age.

The plane was a Hansa turbojet. Just before take-off, Zamfirescu came back to see they were strapped in properly.

'I've asked one of the radio operators here to make contact with my partner Schneider. He's piloting the plane in front, the one with your kid on board. They'll tell him to throttle back a little, try to delay their arrival in Cork. You may just be in luck.'

When they were in the air, Zamfirescu asked Jack to come forward. When Jack entered the cockpit, the pilot switched to English, which he spoke fluently.

'What's really going on?' he asked.

'What she told you.'

Zamfirescu shook his head.

'I may be dumb, but I'm not stupid. Just before we took off, there was a police alert. Some smart-ass lawyer in Munich told the cops one of his big industrialist clients had gone missing. A man called von Freudiger. Ever heard of him?'

Jack shook his head.

'The thing is,' Zamfirescu continued, 'that this von

Freudiger and a woman were found dead about an hour ago in a little place called Arnstorf. You wouldn't know anything about that, would you?'

Jack shifted uneasily. What did Zamfirescu suspect? And what would he want in return for silence?

'No,' said Jack. 'Why should I?'

'Well, perhaps your lady friend back there does. She's carrying papers in the name von Freudiger. Perhaps you hadn't noticed. I'd call that a big coincidence.'

'Yes, it is. Or are you suggesting that it's not?'

'I wouldn't know.'

There was a pause. In front of them, banks of dials sparkled.

'I take it you want more money,' said Jack finally.

Zamfirescu shook his head slowly. He kept his eyes on the instrument panel ahead of him.

'Luckily for you,' he said, 'I know a bit about this Herr von Freudiger. About what a big shot he is and so on. You hear a lot about people like him in this business. Also I know a bit about his politics. It's not much of a secret. His father was a Nazi, a friend of Hitler. Nice sort of person. He spent a couple of years in Landsberg prison, came out richer than ever. The son's a friend of anyone on the extreme right. I should say "was". Not much of a loss for anyone.'

'No,' said Jack quietly, 'I don't suppose so.'

'Not even his family, I'd imagine. Except maybe his father.'

Jack nodded.

'You could include his father-in-law,' he said.

'The one with Schneider?'

Jack nodded again. There was a brief silence.

'I'm a Romanian,' Zamfirescu said. 'I came to Germany four years ago with my younger brother Liviu. He brought his family, I came alone; I'm a widower. Last year Liviu was killed. He was out walking one night in Munich. Just going for a stroll. Some fascists knifed him in the street.

They're still looking for them, but they won't find them. And if they do . . .' He shrugged.

'Now, my sister-in-law and her children are forced to live in a hostel for refugees. Last month, a gang of fascists tried to burn them out. To hell with them, I say. To hell with von Freudiger.'

He looked at Jack.

'You'd better go back to your seat,' he said. 'There may be some turbulence. There's some rough weather ahead.'

Jack sat with Maria, doing what he could to reassure her without words. The plane droned on through deep night. If they looked through the window, there was only darkness. The world had been made from it. It was as if they had been cut off from everything. Jack told Maria of Zamfirescu's suspicions. She nodded, but said nothing.

Once, she looked at him for a long time.

'It hurts,' she whispered. 'So much.'

'He isn't dead,' he said. 'I'm sure your father would never hurt him.'

She said nothing at first, but he saw tears in her eyes. When she spoke, her voice was cracked.

'He would do more than that,' she said. 'His madness is very old and very deep.'

'Surely not as deep as that.'

She sighed. Absently, she wiped the tears from her cheeks. Fingers of darkness touched the plane.

'In the camp,' she said. 'The camp at Klanjec. It was his speciality.'

'I don't understand.' The tips of his fingers felt cold.

'The execution of children,' she said. 'And their torture.'

That was all she would say. They flew on into a gathering storm. He could think of nothing to say that might comfort her. Her hand in his was limp, like a rag, without strength.

The door to the cockpit opened. They were on auto-pilot. Zamfirescu appeared in the doorway.

'I thought you should know,' he said. 'Schneider's plane has just landed in Cork. We're forty minutes behind him.'

CHAPTER SEVENTY-FIVE

As they approached the Irish coast, the storm grew in strength. They were buffeted by strong winds and lashed by rain as they descended through steep banks of cloud. Suddenly the lights of Cork appeared beneath them, as though created out of rain and wind. They touched down in a heavy squall that threatened to twist them off the runway and hurl them into a field.

Zamfirescu joined them as soon as he had switched off his engines.

'I still have some things to do here,' he said. 'Will you both be all right?'

'I think so, yes,' said Jack. 'You've been very helpful.'

'Let me know the boy's safe. You'll find a car waiting for you: I radioed ahead. Schneider may know what way the man you're chasing took.'

'It's all right,' said Maria. 'We know where he's headed.'

Maria's card got them through customs without delay. They did not even check Jack's shoulder-bag, the one he had been carrying since leaving Dublin. Schneider was waiting at the other side. He said Rosewicz had taken a hire car, a Ford Granada, and that he had told Schneider he was 'driving home'. That was all the pilot knew.

They stepped out into a night of torrential rain. A car was waiting outside. Hearing it was for passengers from an executive jet, an enterprising garage had rustled up a Jaguar.

Maria drove. She was familiar with the road, and she

said that the act of driving would help keep her mind off other things. They drove south from the airport, away from Cork city, joining the N71 at Ballinhassig, then heading west through Bandon. At times the countryside was lit up by flashes of lightning.

'There's a risk of flooding on the Bandon river,' Maria said. 'We're finished if he gets through and we find the road closed behind him.'

'We'll worry about that if it happens.'

The car handled well, but the road was winding and treacherous. In places there were potholes that sent them bouncing over the wet tarmac. The rain sluiced from endless clouds, bathing the windscreen in a constant wash of running water. Theirs was almost the only car on the road. Anyone who could stay indoors was doing just that. They stopped once at a garage outside Clonakilty, where Jack bought two powerful flashlights. He thought it likely they would need them when they got to Summerlawn.

It was well after midnight when they reached Baltimore. Down here near the coast, the storm was, if anything, worse. The village was fast asleep. They sped through, passing on to the headland on which the ruins of Summerlawn stood.

'Why would he come here, Jack? On a night like this? It's madness. Maybe he went somewhere else. There's nothing here.'

'He told Schneider he was driving home. Unless you know of another house . . .'

Maria shook her head.

'No,' she said softly. 'No other house. There was only ever Summerlawn.'

The narrow road was awash with water. There seemed almost no difference between land and sky. They could not hear the sea. The only sound was the roaring of the storm.

Suddenly, broken gates appeared in the headlights. They lay wide open, half torn from their hinges. Maria braked and started to ease the Jaguar into the narrow opening. As they turned, a flash of lightning tore across the sky, lighting the headland. The jagged skeleton of Summerlawn leapt out of the darkness. A moment later it was gone.

Maria drove on carefully, keeping to the weed-choked drive. In a handful of years, nature had come to reclaim the walks and pathways that had encircled the old house. The headlights showed grass and bushes run wild, a tangled wilderness of untamed vegetation where there had once been trim gardens.

'Look!' said Jack, pointing ahead.

High up in the darkness there was a reddish light. As they watched it wavered and seemed to vanish, then returned brighter than before. Maria gasped. Surely her father would not set fire to the house again. But when she thought about it, she knew there had been nothing left to burn.

'The fire brigade managed to save a couple of rooms,' she said. 'Or at least stop them from being completely gutted. There are a few floors and ceilings left in the west wing. I saw them when I visited the house after the fire.'

'Could someone get up there?'

'Not safely. Large parts were burnt away. But, yes, it might be possible.'

She looked up anxiously at the trembling light, fighting back the tears, resisting the temptation to give way to the panic that was building inside her. And all the time she prayed to whatever wretched fragment of God stayed huddled there, that Paul might be safe, that he would come out of all this unharmed.

The Granada was parked at an angle across what had once been the main entrance. Jack took his shoulder-bag from the rear seat and stepped out of the car. Maria got out on the other side. At that moment, a second lightning flash lit up the front of the house. Thick ivy had already taken hold of much of the stone. The marks of fire could be seen around the tops of windows.

Within seconds, Jack and Maria were soaked to the skin. The rain was heavy and slashing, bitterly cold. A wind full of ice buffeted them, trying to throw them sideways across the drive. Jack grabbed Maria's arm.

'Take this torch,' he yelled.

They switched their lights on together. The beams cut through the rain and darkness, revealing the blackened façade of the house. Charred and splintered, the old door hung crookedly in its stone frame. It lay half open, revealing a dark, unwelcoming interior. They squeezed through the gap, their feet squelching in a bed of mud and thick, wet leaves.

The fire had started in the hallway. Summerlawn's once-grand staircase was nothing more than black and twisted sticks. The walls on which the portraits of Stefan Rose-wicz's ancestors had once hung were mildewed and stained. The floor was broken and filled with clumps of weed. High above them, holes had been punched through the roof; rain flooded into the hall without check.

They picked their way through heaps of debris to the rear, where a gaping doorway led into a transverse corridor. The rain was lighter here, interrupted by the rooms above. Jack and Maria ploughed through ashes and broken heaps of burned timbers. There was glass everywhere, and white plaster that had fallen from the walls and ceiling.

The only sounds were the falling of rain and the occasional crash of thunder. The storm seemed to be circling. Maria led the way. It seemed right to be here now, in the heart of a ruin her father had made.

A flight of stairs climbed to the first floor, broken but passable. The damage had been more restricted in this area. Wallpaper still hung to the walls in parts. The charred and soaked remains of heavy carpet still clung to the stairs in places. Water dripped everywhere. Lightning froze them as they climbed, bursting through an upper window somewhere.

They entered two rooms on the first floor. There was no

sign that anyone had been there. They were dark and sad, their treasures ripped away for ever. Someone had torn out a marble fireplace from one, leaving a raw wound. Not that it mattered.

The fire had done more damage to the stairs that led to the next floor. They climbed cautiously, a tread at a time, playing their torches over the section above to check for holes or other weaknesses. At one point, Maria bent down. She straightened, holding something.

'What is it?' whispered Jack.

She held it out to him. It was a page from a book, still dry. A page from *Where the Wild Things Are*.

They continued to the second floor. From a door on their right, a flickering light shone out. The floorboards were cracked and broken. At every step, Jack feared they would collapse, sending Maria and himself hurtling to certain death below. Keeping to the walls, he slid across to the door. Maria followed him.

It was Maria's old music-room. All the instruments were gone, the pictures of composers and harpsichord-makers taken from the walls. Smoke had blackened the rococo plasterwork, and rain had further ruined it. It had once been numbered as one of the finest pieces ever made by West.

Rosewicz had piled up pieces of broken wood in the fireplace and got a blaze going. He and Paul sat in front of it, trying to make themselves dry and warm. Paul was shivering, without even a coat or blanket. Rosewicz was sitting staring into the flames. They lit his face and threw his shadow out into the room like a banner of darkness. On his lap, he held a pistol. And from time to time his eyes would stray from the flames and rest on it, as though reading a message in the light reflected from its barrel.

CHAPTER SEVENTY-SIX

The beam of Jack's torch fell on Rosewicz, like a spotlight falling on an old actor come on stage to play his last role. Seeing the light, Paul lifted his head, staring round into the darkness. He did not recognize his mother, who was hidden in shadows behind the light of her own torch. Whether she was alive or dead, he did not know: his father had told him one thing, his grandfather another. He had been brought to this terrible place under the pretext of finding her, only to find himself tricked again.

'Paul!' called Maria, starting into a run. Jack darted out an arm to hold her back.

'Careful,' he said. 'He has a gun.'

Paul scrambled to his feet.

'*Mutti!*' he shouted. '*Mutti, ich bin hier.*'

Rosewicz glanced up angrily, startled by the intrusion. Seeing the lights, he leaped to his feet and grabbed the boy.

'Father! It's me, Maria. Please let Paul go. He's been through enough.'

'You have no right to come here!' yelled Rosewicz. 'The boy is mine now. You are dead. Both my daughters are dead. Because of you, the boy will have to die as well. When that is done, it will all be over.'

Maria tried to tear herself from Jack's grasp.

'No, Maria. Not while he has the gun. He means to use it. Leave him. Let me talk to him.'

'But he's got Paul. I have to stop him.'

'Not like that. You would never reach him. He'd shoot you, then kill Paul. Let me do it my way.'

He took several steps into the room. Maria followed, keeping her eyes on her son.

'You can have the scroll,' Jack said. 'I have it with me in this shoulder-bag. The real scroll, not a substitute. Take it. I don't care any longer what you do with it, as long as you let Paul go.'

'Dr Gould. Our paths seem fated to keep on crossing.' Rosewicz appeared to have taken rapid control of himself. 'You are very persistent. I had not thought it in you. Such a weak man, and yet so insistent. The Jew in you outweighed by the Celt. But persistence is not enough. You need brains as well. What fragments of intelligence you may have are not enough.'

'I know why you need the scroll. And I'm prepared to trade it. It seems a bargain to me.'

Rosewicz laughed. He was holding Paul round the neck, tightly.

'A bargain? A boy's life for a scrap of paper? Ink and papyrus? I've lived a life with scraps like that. They never brought me anything but grief. Do you think I would trade the boy for that?'

'I told you, this isn't a substitute. I have the Jesus scroll in this bag. You can examine it. I'll bring it to you.'

The old man laughed again, tightening his grip on the boy's neck.

'I don't want your scroll,' he said. 'I've done with all that. You've misunderstood completely. This has nothing to do with your precious scroll.'

Jack could not understand. Rosewicz seemed completely unhinged.

'Then what is it you want?'

'Want? I don't want anything. I've done with wanting. It's all over, don't you see? Finished.' He paused. In a quieter voice, he said, 'They let him out. Ramsey. They set him free.'

'I don't see . . .' Jack could make no sense of what Rosewicz was saying.

'Ramsey, Jack,' Maria broke in. 'On the plane from London, don't you remember? The English prisoner-of-war.'

'But how did . . . ?'

Then he remembered. Leni's voice, describing the events that had led up to Karl's murder. *He spent some time with Paul, then waited in the library for your husband. He listened to the radio for a while.*

'What's it about?' Paul asked. 'Why Ramsey? Why is he so important?'

'October,' answered Rosewicz. 'A British unit that worked with Tito's partisans towards the end of the war. They were sent into Croatia by the Special Operations Executive in October 1944, the month Belgrade fell to Stalin. The British had withdrawn all aid from Mihailovic's Cetniks earlier that year and put their full weight behind Tito and the communists. Ramsey was in charge of October. Their mission was to liaise between units in Croatia and the partisan groups in the rest of Yugoslavia.

'I was Ante Pavelic's head of security at that time. My position was subordinate to the Head of the Gestapo in Zagreb. In practice, however, I had considerable freedom of action. I was able to meet people who would have no truck with the Germans. Sometimes I made deals behind the backs of the Gestapo. We all knew the German Reich was finished, that it was only a matter of time before they had to pull their troops out and leave us to it. I knew that, if we were to survive, we had to make provision for the future. People were doing the same thing all over Europe.

'The League had already decided that, if we had a choice between the British and the Reds, there was no question which way we would go. So, when Ramsey contacted me saying he had a proposal to make, I didn't hesitate. I agreed to meet him in private. We spent an afternoon together in a small church outside Zagreb. It was early December.

His proposal was connected to a papyrus, an early Christian scroll in the possession of British Military Intelligence in Rome.'

Jack felt as though the ground were slipping beneath his feet. Outside, the rain battered down. A clap of thunder rolled across the sky.

'But that's impossible,' Jack began. 'The scroll was never . . .'

'You were misled,' Rosewicz interrupted. 'Felix did not tell you all the truth about the scroll. He said it never went to Rome, did he not?'

'How do you know?'

'Simon told me, of course. The man you know as Parker. Simon and I go back a long way.'

'He's dead,' said Jack. 'Parker's dead.'

'I'm sorry to hear that. Well, it scarcely matters now. Let me go on. We haven't got much time.

'Felix told you that we tried to send the scroll to the Vatican, but that conditions did not permit. That is not correct. The scroll was taken there and kept for a time at San Girolamo. But the Allies were in control of Italy by then. British intelligence got wind of something, and one of their contacts smuggled the scroll out of the Vatican. They knew about my brother, and they knew about me.

'Ramsey offered me a deal. He'd been told about the scroll before leaving Italy; his superiors knew it could be used as a lever with the League. You see, they were looking to the future too. Communism was on the march. They knew that, once the war with Germany was over, they'd have to turn their attention to the Soviet Union. Who better to help them against their new enemy than people who had already been fighting the Soviets? Our politics didn't matter to them, as long as we were anti-communist.'

A wash of lightning filled the room and was gone. Rosewicz did not once relax his hold on the boy.

'Ramsey's deal was simple,' he said. 'They would arrange ratlines for myself, my brother, and any members of the

League who wanted to go with me. There would be new identities waiting for us in western Europe. The scroll would be sent from Rome to Zagreb in my brother's keeping.

'In return, Ramsey wanted lists of names. Ustasi mostly, as well as some Gestapo and SS. Duty rosters, timetables, passwords. All sorts of details. Everything he needed to destroy Pavelic's regime. Well, I knew it was finished anyway. As I say, I was looking to the future. I gave him all he wanted. I held nothing back. Ramsey wasn't interested in money, but I gave him information about some of Zagreb's wealthiest citizens. Where do you think my own money came from? It was the endgame, you see. There were no more moves to be made. Or so I thought.'

He paused again. Behind him, the untended fire had sunk low. Soon, the room would be lit only by the torches.

'That January, there was a systematic culling of Ustasi members throughout the country. Ramsey and his men did their job well. In Zagreb, I waited for the scroll. It was to be the key. Not even Ramsey understood that. He thought it was just a fetish, a bargaining chip. But I knew that, once the war was over, we could use it to rebuild our power. My brother set out from Rome with it hidden among a large collection of similar documents, all of them taken from Jewish libraries in Poland.

'He was waylaid by communist partisans at Metlika. He and his driver were killed, and the documents found in the car were sent on to Belgrade, for the attention of the Russian military commander. He was responsible for bringing them to Moscow when he was recalled at the end of the war. And in due course the scroll disappeared into the Lenin Library. This is something we only learned recently.

'Iosif Sharanskii made two mistakes. The first was to stumble across the scroll. The second was to bring you in on his discovery. I knew you would be able to make the connection with the photographs of the scroll I'd shown you here. Sharanskii had heard rumours about me. And there were papers in the library that would have traced the scroll back to Yugoslavia and to me. I couldn't take that risk. But the bomb was meant for you and him alone. Not the woman or the child.'

Jack went stiff with rage and horror. Rosewicz had been responsible for the murder of Iosif and his family after all. The bomb must have been planted by Henryk. It was all Jack could do to stop himself making a dash for Rosewicz. But he held back, knowing that a false move could end in yet more tragedy.

'As for Ramsey and the October group, they were very unlucky. I had independence, but increasingly little power. The October ring was discovered by the Gestapo. Those who survived the initial ambush were arrested and taken to Zagreb. The Croats were executed, but they kept the British contingent alive. Orders were sent from Germany, telling Gestapo headquarters in Zagreb to ship them to Berlin. This was in the last days of the war, remember, when things were growing chaotic.

'I succeeded in arranging for them all to be taken to Friedrichshain. The decision to hold fake war crimes trials had already been taken by the German branch of the League. It was our intention to get whatever information we could out of the October group before hanging them and burying what they knew. Unfortunately, as you know, things did not work out that simply. Ramsey and his colleagues were taken to Siberia and locked away for nearly fifty years. I'm sorry for them. They were brave men; they deserved a better fate.'

Rosewicz paused. His fingers stroked his grandson's thin neck gently.

'And now Ramsey has come home. The conquering hero. Well, perhaps not. But his friends will follow, those that are left. It will be an embarrassing time for a lot of people, unless they put him under wraps. But for us it will be the end.

'The Ustasi contingent is a vital part of the League's

system of alliances. Once it becomes known that we made a deal with the British, they'll start to take reprisals. The League won't last six months. It's all over. Perhaps not in days, perhaps not even months. But it's over. Better to finish the whole thing now.'

He bent over Paul, stroking his hair.

'Paul was to have been our leader in due course. Now there is nothing for him to lead. I planned for the future, always the future. And now, there is no future.'

Jack saw the despair in the old man's eyes, heard the resignation in his voice.

'There can be a future for Paul,' said Maria, stepping forward. 'It's too late for you, but not for him. Let him go.'

For a moment, she thought her father struggled. The mad old man holding her son was also the loving father who had cradled her on his knee as a child, who had brought her presents and combed her hair. She took another step. Surely he would soften.

But it was too late. Rosewicz grabbed Paul's wrist and pulled the boy back to a door in the rear wall. The next moment, they had been swallowed up by darkness.

CHAPTER SEVENTY-SEVEN

Jack ran after them. He was within feet of the door when he stumbled on a heap of rubble and pitched forward on to his face. Maria picked her way to him and bent down.

'Are you all right?'

Jack picked himself up. He was only grazed.

'The door,' he gasped. 'Where does it lead to?'

'It's a back stair. It goes down to the garden at the rear.'

Maria helped Jack to his feet, and they ran to the door. The fire had taken hold here for a while. The walls were blackened, and whole sections of the stair had burned through. Rosewicz had somehow managed to drag Paul across a gaping hole on to the section of stair beyond. The wood was fragile, badly broken in places.

Jack reached the hole and prepared to climb down, holding a piece of banister that remained intact. As he did so, the rail and stair gave way, almost throwing him into the space below. Maria grabbed his arm, pulling him back. When they looked again, the gulf was too great. Rosewicz and Paul had vanished into the shadows.

'Quickly. Is there another way down?'

Maria nodded.

'The stairs we came up by. Then through the back of the house to the terrace, if we can get through.'

They ran, knowing that if Rosewicz got far enough away, he could easily give them the slip in the darkness. Slipping and sliding on the treacherous stairs, they arrived safely back on the ground floor and entered the corridor again.

The centre of the house had been most badly affected by

the fire. Fallen timbers lay everywhere, obstructing their passage. They climbed and twisted past in a frenzy. Even Maria, who had known the house since childhood, was bewildered and disoriented. The howling of the storm reached them from outside. The wind was fiercer than ever.

They reached the terrace at last and went down stone steps into the garden. In the open air, they were lashed by rain and wind. The booming of the gale made it almost impossible to hear one another.

'This way,' cried Maria, pointing to the west wing.

They ran to the door that led to the back staircase Rosewicz had taken. It was still and silent. Jack went inside, playing his torch up and down the stairs. He went up a little way, calling Paul's name. There was no answer. He went back to Maria.

'They must be down already,' he shouted. 'Which way would he go?'

'I don't know. He may be trying to get round to the front, to get back to his car.'

'I don't think so. I think he's past running.'

Suddenly, the wind changed direction, swooping round from the coast. A tremendous gust knocked them sideways. With it came a cry, a shout or a scream, suddenly cut off.

Jack did not have to be told where the cry came from. He had spent enough time at Summerlawn to know. There was nothing out there but the cliff. And beyond the cliff, the open sea.

They ran through the tangled garden, fighting the wind. There was a second cry, sharper this time. Maria shouted, but her voice was snatched by the wind and torn to shreds.

'Be careful,' she said. 'We're very near the edge.'

In the rain and darkness, it was difficult to make sense of the terrain. They could hear the waves now, crashing on the rocks below with an insane force.

'Paul! Where are you? Where are you, Paul?' Maria kept

on shouting, swinging the light of her torch back and forth in an attempt to find the boy and her father.

Suddenly, Jack's torch found them. Rosewicz had dragged Paul to the edge of the cliff. All it would take would be another shift of wind and a gust could carry them over.

Jack stopped, trembling. In his mind he could see another cliff. A red ball was bouncing through green grass to its edge. And a little girl was running, oblivious of danger, after it. Behind her, Sima came running.

'Take this,' he said, thrusting his torch into Maria's hand. 'Keep it apart from yours, so he thinks there are still two of us.'

Quickly, he moved to Maria's left, getting himself away from the wavering lines of light. The beams picked out Rosewicz and Paul, staggering together in the wind on the cliff's edge. Suddenly, a shot rang out, then another, as Rosewicz tried to knock out the lights. Jack dashed forward, getting as close to the edge as he dared. And all the time, as hard as he fought the wind, he had to fight himself, at the depth of fear the sight of the cliff had awakened in him. It was all his nightmares come true, all his fears become a single fear.

He was only feet away now, hidden from Rosewicz by the darkness. But what could he do? How could he get Paul away from the old man without alerting Rosewicz and making him jump with the boy still in his grasp? Jack got down on his hands and knees and started to creep forward. Once, he glanced over the edge and saw the white spray of waves breaking against the cliff wall. The sound of their crashing was much louder here, almost drowning out the noise of the wind. When he looked back, Rosewicz was backing nearer and nearer the edge. Only a couple of feet separated him and the boy from it. If Jack was going to act, it had to be now.

He stood and ran straight for Paul, snatching the boy round the waist and tearing him from Rosewicz's grip in a rugby tackle. They skidded forward across the muddy ground, then rolled to a halt about three yards away. Jack looked up to see Rosewicz tottering on the edge, fighting to regain his balance. The next moment there was only blackness. He thought Rosewicz cried out, though whether it was to pray or curse, Jack could never say. The next moment, his voice was swallowed up in wind and the roaring of the black sea.

CHAPTER SEVENTY-EIGHT

Qumran, Israel

They left Jerusalem shortly before noon, skirting the Mount of Olives as they drove down to Bethany. From there, they headed towards Jericho and then, turning south, wound down the long road that passes the Dead Sea on its way to Eilat and the Gulf of Aqaba. Far off to the east they could see Jordan and the Moab mountains, hidden behind an ochre haze. They passed heavy lorries, grinding their way north to Jerusalem, and a convoy of military vehicles bearing blue and white flags. A tour bus slowed down to let them overtake: pale, startled faces stared out at them from behind dirt-streaked windows. The road went on through dry country, the hills sharp and bleached, almost devoid of vegetation. Ahead of them, the great salt sea grew larger with every turn in the road.

They had come from a city of high places to the lowest spot on earth. From time to time, Jack would turn his head and glance at Maria, sometimes smiling, sometimes just looking. And she would return his gaze, or put her hand softly on his thigh, touching him briefly before taking her hand away again.

Paul was in Jerusalem with close friends, the Perlmans. The boy still woke violently at night, still cried out, still wet the bed. A child psychologist had assured them he would recover quickly, now he was reunited with his mother. But Maria wondered what scars would remain, how deep they would be. Paul did not ask about his father or grandfather, and Maria volunteered nothing.

Soon after reaching the northern edge of the sea, they came up on to a high marl terrace about a hundred feet above the road. They had reached Qumran. They parked on the plateau and got out of the car. Jack carried a small bag over one shoulder, and a camera. All around them were the scattered ruins of the long-vanished Essene community, the Jewish sect to which Christ had belonged, within which he had spent most of his short life. Here, not in modern Jerusalem, not in Bethlehem, were the stones on which his feet had trodden. While thousands of pilgrims walked each year on medieval pavements or bowed their heads in holy places 'discovered' by the Empress Helena three hundred years after Jesus was dead and gone, the contact they sought was here, in a handful of wretched ruins scorched by the desert sun.

A military patrol had parked near the tourist restaurant. Jack went across and asked to speak to the officer in charge. This was border country, and the army was constantly on the alert for infiltrators. To stray from the immediate area of the ruins would be to invite suspicion and even arrest. Jack showed his papers and explained why he had come. He carried a letter from the Department of Archaeology at the Hebrew University, stating that he had legitimate business in the cliffs near Qumran.

Leaving the plateau, he and Maria made their way down a steep gully, leading to the foot of the cliffs surrounding the site. He pointed out some of the caves, telling Maria which had held the most important finds. They walked in further, skirting the long fingers of rock sent out by the cliffs, finding more and yet more caves. The rocks were pitted with openings, some minuscule, others large enough to let a grown man inside without difficulty.

Her feet kicked up small flurries of dust from the gully floor, tiny pebbles rolled away from her, skittering aside without direction or aim. The ground was littered with them.

'Tell me what to believe,' she said.

He looked at her anxiously. The air was heavily laden with salt, with the sting of it. His breath was harsh. The light here modified everything. Sometimes it was not light, but the presence of something greater, heavier.

'I don't understand . . .'

'Is Jesus Christ . . .' She paused, uncertain how to proceed. 'Was he God? A man? What do I believe?'

'I can't answer that. You know I can't.'

'Why not? You've read the letter, his own account of himself. What did he think he was?'

'He didn't think he was God, I'm sure of that. Beyond that, I don't know. He had his own doubts, his own uncertainties. But none of that matters. Whatever the scroll says, the churches will make their own Jesus, a whole tribe of him to suit their own prejudices. They'll find ways of twisting everything he ever said to fit what they already believe. So you should go on believing whatever you believe now.'

'I don't know what that is any longer.'

He looked at her softly. The sun was in her eyes. She was beautiful beyond all expectation.

'We're alike, then,' he said.

The cave they chose was high up and hard to reach, one of dozens that had only been superficially explored. Inside, Maria shone a large torch while Jack took the scroll from the cylinder. He had brought with him a heavy earthenware pot, an artefact dating from about the same period as the scroll, of the type used to store written materials. It had been found about nine miles to the south, at 'Ayn al-Ghuwair. The scroll fitted it easily, with room to spare. Jack replaced the lid tightly and buried the jar beneath a heap of loose stones.

In a year or two, when it seemed that the time was ready, he would come back here with a full expedition.

They would explore all the caves in this section. For all Jack knew, they would make some real discoveries. But it was here, in this cave, beneath these rough stones, that they would stumble across the greatest discovery of all time.

He had considered returning the scroll to Augustin de Galais and his friends, but in the end decided against it. He knew that they would come under enormous pressure to bury or destroy it. Of their basic sincerity he had no doubt, but he found himself increasingly distanced from the values that they stood for. He had no doubt that Maximilian Kolbe had been a good man, a holy man; but he could not reconcile himself to the fact that the Church had chosen, out of the hundreds of thousands who had died at Auschwitz, to make a hero and a saint of one Christian. Six million Jews had died, and their names were all but forgotten. The Church had looked on, sometimes helping the victims, sometimes giving succour to their killers. There was a profound imbalance, a bend in the fabric of things that Jack could not tolerate. The scroll belonged to mankind, not the Church.

He took photographs of the cave from different angles, for future reference. To finish the reel, he sat Maria among the ruins. She smiled for him, like someone on holiday smiling for her lover. At her back, the sea lay flat and motionless. The afternoon sun was sinking towards the west, falling to Jerusalem and the sea beyond. The silence was intense. Jack could feel them all around him, his ghosts: Caitlin and Siobhan, Iosif, Leah, and little Sima, even Denis Boylan and Moira. Would any of them ever be at peace?

They did not know when or where the blow would fall. Perhaps never. The power of the League had been badly dented. Ciechanowski was in disgrace. Reinhold von Freudiger had committed suicide on hearing of his son's death. More POWs had been released from Russia, and some had already given press interviews. Jack and Maria took what precautions they could, but refused to turn their lives into the existences of hunted beasts. Maria had given her first Israeli concert, in the Wise Auditorium in the university. It had been an outstanding success. Paul had started kindergarten and was making rapid progress in Hebrew. They had sent him to a mixed school, where Jews, Christians and Muslims played together. He would fashion fragile bonds that might last until adulthood, that might break under unforeseen strains. He was the only real hope they had.

'It's time to go,' said Jack. 'Paul will be waiting.'

She stood and took his hand. If she listened hard enough, she could hear waves crashing on another shore.

Daniel Eastman's bestselling novels, available from HarperCollins*Paperbacks*

☐ THE LAST ASSASSIN	0 586 21163 2	£4.99
☐ THE SEVENTH SANCTUARY	0 586 07269 1	£5.99
☐ THE NINTH BUDDHA	0 586 07270 5	£4.99
☐ BROTHERHOOD OF THE TOMB	0 586 20433 4	£4.99
☐ NIGHT OF THE SEVENTH DARKNESS	0 586 20434 2	£4.99
☐ NAME OF THE BEAST	0 586 21088 1	£4.99

All these books are available from your local bookseller or can be ordered direct from the publishers.
To order direct just tick the titles you want and fill in the form below:

Name:

_____

Address:

_____

_____

Postcode:

_____

Send to: HarperCollins Mail Order, Dept 8, HarperCollins *Publishers*, Westerhill Road, Bishopbriggs, Glasgow G64 2QT.
Please enclose a cheque or postal order or authority to debit your Visa/Access account –

Credit card no:

_____

Expiry date:

_____

Signature:

_____

– to the value of the cover price plus:
UK & BFPO: Add £1.00 for the first and 25p for each additional book ordered.
Overseas orders including Eire, please add £2.95 service charge.
Books will be sent by surface mail but quotes for airmail despatches will be given on request.

24 HOUR TELEPHONE ORDERING SERVICE FOR ACCESS/VISA CARDHOLDERS –
TEL: GLASGOW 041-772 2281 or LONDON 081-307 4052